Miss
Appleby's
Academy

Miss Appleby's Academy

Elizabeth Gill

Quercus

First published in Great Britain in 2013 by

Quercus
55 Baker Street
7th Floor, South Block
London
W1U 8EW

A CIP catalogue record for this book is available
from the British Library

ISBN 978 1 78087 847 8
ISBN 978 1 78087 848 5 (EBOOK)

10 9 8 7 6 5 4 3 2

Typeset by Ellipsis Digital Ltd, Glasgow
Printed and bound in Great Britain by Clays Ltd, St Ives plc

AUTHOR'S NOTE

Last year, when I was thinking of writing a story about an American woman coming to the north-east of England to start up a school, I went to an exhibition by Tow Law History Society. Ron Storey, a member of the group, told me that in 1900 there was in Tow Law a school called Miss Appleby's Academy. My thanks to him for the inspiration for my story and to all the members of the society for their work over the years which has helped me such a lot. Besides which when I go and see them they make me feel as though there is a part of me which is always of the little pit town where we all grew up. So many of us have moved, but we have not gone far either geographically or emotionally. It is still home.

The Three Tuns in Durham City is a very pretty hotel and never did belong to Henry Atkinson as far as I know, but I remembered that my dad used to park his car at the County because the car park was bigger and walk through the County to get to the Three Tuns, and that seemed to me reason enough to include it in my story.

In memory of George, Jasper and Timmy,
who were the inspiration for Hector and Ulysses.

MID HAVEN, NEW ENGLAND, 1894

It snows a lot in New England. After the fall when the leaves have turned to lime and crimson and orange and given up the unequal fight and dropped from the trees like jewels the weather turns hard and great square flakes light the sky.

Emma Appleby, almost thirty, loved the winter best of all. Her father said that when she was his age she would long for the spring, but she delighted at making snowmen when she was small, skating on frozen ponds when she grew older, and she didn't think she would ever give up her regard for her favourite season nor cease to listen for the sound of sleigh bells at Christmas and gather with her family and friends in the little white church to give thanks for another year.

She liked to walk for miles, and would encourage her father out day after day to enjoy the snow scenes. So it was nothing special that particular afternoon in December that they were two miles from home and following carriage tracks along the top of the ridge.

She stopped at the very highest point where the tracks

were dug deep into the snow: they were twisted and turned as though the coach had gone out of control. There were deep ruts and gouged-out tracks, perhaps because of horses' hooves, and the snow was flung away everywhere. Emma was afraid to look and only glad her father was there, because at the very height of the ridge you could see to the bottom. More snow was displaced and there was the coach, overturned as she had feared. She cried out and put her hand over her mouth.

Emma gasped, and her father, coming up behind her, panting, followed her gaze, and then he forgot his tiredness and he too stared. Below, the brown horses were lying at unnatural angles and there was blood, bright scarlet, and the snow around was all shapes and turns. Emma hesitated for only a few seconds and then, regardless of the revulsion which came upon her, she began to plunge downward while her father called after her, 'Wait, Emma, the drifts may be very deep,' and since the snow came up to the top of her thighs and impeded her progress somewhat but did not stop her, he too began to lift his legs high enough so that he made progress through the three-foot-high covering. It was difficult to do that, but Emma barely noticed it. Her heart beat hard and even when her breathing shallowed for the effort she waded on through the sea of white, trying to stop herself from worrying about what tragedy she would find.

She did not stop until she had reached the carriage, but she could see then the upside-down coach, and there were people inside. Nobody was moving and they too were lying like rag dolls in confusion, in ways which made her think they would never move again. She took another breath so that she would not let herself break down in tears. There was no room here for such things, she told herself, there must be something she could do. She heard her father's voice. Like any good parent he would have shielded her from whatever disaster he could, but Emma took no notice.

She got down in the snow. Inside the coach there were four people as far as she could make out, and none of them was moving. One door could not be reached because the coach lay on its side. The other was somehow jammed shut, and hard as she tried, and hard as her father tried, they could not budge it. She glanced away as though if she did so when she glanced back the scene would have been some mirage which was gone, but the stillness all around confirmed what she had feared, that there was no one left alive from the accident.

Her father walked all around the outside, and she followed him. There were another two men who had been thrown clear, the driver and another passenger who no doubt had been on top at the front. She looked up back to the ridge where she and her father had seen what had happened, and she thought that the driver must have lost control in the ice and been taken too close to the edge and then had been able to do nothing to stop the accident.

'I must go back for help,' her father said.

'No, let me go. I'm faster than you.'

She didn't listen any further. It wasn't much of a choice, she thought, to stay with the dead or run for help which

3

she knew was beyond them, but it was the only thing to do. She was glad of action even though her legs ached before she had gone half a mile in the depth of snow, and it seemed to her a very long time before she came in sight of the little white town which was her home. She could see the church spire first and it lifted her spirits because she was so tired by then.

She ran up the wide road towards her brother's house. Laurence and his wife had not been married long. She could not think what else to do. It was Saturday afternoon, just after lunch, and most people were still indoors after the midday meal. He would know what to do, he was reliable, he was a lawyer, a good lawyer she corrected herself, glad to think of something which did not really matter here. The front gate was open, it could not be closed because of the amount of snow. She ran up the path, slipping because it had been cleared only that morning and had set hard. She tried the front door and it gave (nobody ever locked their doors), and she shouted and almost fell into the hall as her brother came out of the dining room, staring at the fuss she was making.

On seeing him Emma felt such relief that she wanted to cry. She was too out of breath to cry and speak, so she poured out the story as fast as she could and he listened. He was a good listener, it was part of his job to do that, and he was tall and solid and sturdy and he was a happy man with all his married life to look forward to, and such things made people strong, Emma knew.

Happiness freed you to meet whatever problems arose.

He didn't interrupt, he nodded, his eyes grew wide and his expression stern, his mouth went into a line and when the tale was finished he was already putting on his coat and boots and saying to her, because his wife had come into the hall and heard the tale too, 'Stay there with Verity.'

'No,' Emma said. 'I'm coming with you.'

'There's nothing you can do. They're all dead, you said so—'

'I don't know so,' she argued, 'and I'm not leaving you and Father.' There was no logic to this, she felt he was right. She could hardly use tools to break into the coach, she could not pull dead bodies from it, and her brother, as her father, was trying to shield her, and she knew that it made sense; she might even be a burden to the men in some way.

'Besides, I can show you exactly where it is.' He argued no more. He was already out of the door and he would go to his neighbours and friends and those who had the ability to determine what happened next: the doctor, the firemen, the police.

Verity too urged her to stay at home. Verity was big with her first child and moved slowly, but Emma ignored her and went back through the front door again. She had the feeling her brother could find the place with a few directions, but she wanted to be there trying to do something useful. The men were ready in a very short time and she ploughed back through the snow, feeling not tired now but glad to be useful.

The light was already beginning to fade. Once darkness had set in it would be a lot more difficult to do anything at all. Laurence jemmied open the door, but her initial reaction had been right: the four people inside were dead. The six bodies had to be carried back to the town on a big cart. The rest could be left until another day.

'Are you ready?' Laurence said when it was so dark that she could not see his face.

Emma hesitated.

'There's nothing more to be done and certainly nothing a woman could do here,' he said briskly to hide his emotions. He even turned away.

Still Emma hesitated. 'In a moment,' she said.

He looked at her as he had always looked at her when he was exasperated. As siblings they had so little in common, she thought, and although younger than her, he was forever telling her what to do. The cart left, the men went and she stood. She didn't know why, Laurence was right as usual, she could achieve nothing here, and yet she could not go. Something which had happened here was still going on. She couldn't have explained it to him, he would have said it was nothing but old wives' tales, women's superstition and ridiculous, but he did not linger any further. He was as tired as the rest.

Emma's legs ached. She longed to go, but couldn't. She walked around. She tried not to look at the carriage or the dead horses or the different bits and pieces which had been thrown clear because of the accident. It grew quiet. She was not sure she could find her way back in the darkness. She stood for another moment as she watched Laurence's tall figure fading away into the night and then she heard something, or did she? She listened. There it was again. Crying. It could have been some kind of bird or an animal. Whatever – it was something in distress, and in this temperature it would not last the night.

'Laurence, wait!'

'Come on, Emma, hurry up,' he responded, stopping. 'It's freezing hard and Verity is all alone in the house.'

'Wait!'

He heard the urgency in her voice and did not start walking again. She went round and round the scene of the accident, stopping every few yards, but there was silence. Had she imagined it? Then, but faintly, she heard it again and moved in the direction of the noise. She was getting nearer. It happened once more and she thought if she hadn't moved closer she would have lost the cry altogether, abandoned it as a figment of her imagination. There was finally a very faint cry and she could see in the shadows a small form.

'Laurence!'

He was near her now. Emma got down in the hard snow. A cold wind was cutting across the bottom of the valley. She scooped up the form. It was warm, but only just to her touch.

'Oh my God, it's a baby. Go back to the coach and see if you can find anything to wrap it in.'

He paused as though he would argue and then he went and came back with some kind of huge blanket and they wrapped the child in it and started for home.

*

7

'You came to us out of the snow,' she would tell George afterwards. Nobody lied to him, nobody pretended that he had been born in Mid Haven. His parents had been Irish immigrants on their way to who knows where when exhaustion, poverty and an overturned wagon had claimed them and their friends.

At night she would tell George stories of how his parents had come from Ireland in a very large ship, hoping for a better life, they had got him to the New World and could manage no more, but he had Emma and her father and the prosperity of a town like Mid Haven.

It was indeed a haven, she always thought, with its college, lovely buildings, pretty streets and squares. The New England houses were well built of white wood and it was prosperous. It had culture, education and people like her father, she thought affectionately, people who cared about those less fortunate than themselves.

From the beginning Emma found herself desperate to keep the child. Her father certainly gave the matter no more thought: he accepted George into their household with joy and would sit the little boy on his knee and read to him things which would have been well beyond the child's comprehension, though George always seemed happy sitting there, listening to her father's melodious voice as he talked of the things which mattered to him: philosophy and science. He would read poetry and George would sit quite still and watch the pages of the book and absorb the words.

Her brother, Laurence, said that it was ridiculous, the

child was too young to understand. Laurence had told her that she should not keep the child: she was an unmarried woman, whatever would people think? He should go to a couple who might raise him, but Emma did not take his advice.

'I found him,' she said. She might just as well have claimed him as she would a game, she thought with guilt afterwards.

Her mother had died some months before and their household was silent with grief. She and her father now had something to do besides wish things were otherwise. The child made a huge difference.

'You have no idea what he'll be like,' Laurence said.

'He's a boy like any other,' Emma said.

At least Laurence did not suggest that he and Verity should take George. Verity was delivered of a boy two months later and they had sufficient to cope with, Emma judged. Laurence, she knew, had looked at the child's black hair and blue eyes and milky skin. He was so obviously Irish, and the Irish were not well liked here. They did not stay, they moved further into the country as George's parents had been trying to do.

George was a sunny-tempered child. The first words he said were her father's name and hers, and Emma was delighted every day by his company. She taught him the names of the flowers and trees in the garden. He loved to watch the birds come down to drink from the stone birdbath and take baths, the bigger ones in turn, the small brown birds jumping in and out of the water in game.

George liked to run about in the spring warmth, and for her to run giggling after him.

She could not imagine having had a child of her own and loving him more. There had been a time when she looked on other women's children with envy and wondered why she had been singled out for such a life and wished for a husband and a home and for somebody to shut the bedroom door with them both inside, but it had not happened and yet she had George and he was a delight.

As he got older and went to school, waiting for George to come home each day was one of the pleasures which made Emma's life worthwhile. He would run all the way back because although he liked school he liked to be with her much more. He would fling open the door, throw his schoolbag towards the hallstand and then call her name from halfway between the various downstairs rooms, and when he saw her he would run and throw his arms about her. She did not think that life could be any better.

'You have too much to do,' Laurence said, and sighed heavily as he closed the sitting-room door. Emma looked up. She had been mending George's torn trousers. He loved climbing trees and was forever tearing his clothes.

It had been a long hot summer and although she usually enjoyed the summer it seemed to her that since her father had been taken ill in June the heat had been relentless and the yellow flowers had grown so tall that they had overbalanced onto the lawn. The fruit had not ripened as it should have done for lack of water: the plums had shrivelled stonelike upon the trees and the apples and pears were lost among the many leaves which overshadowed them. The blackbirds had had the best of the strawberries and blueberries because she had not had enough time to pick them.

'Could George not have done that for you?' her sister-in-law Verity had said, and Laurence added, 'What an idle little fellow he is.'

She had tried to distract George from her father's illness by telling him to go fishing or swimming with his friends, but George had devoted himself to her father and would read him to sleep while the bumble bees buzzed their way through the second flowering of the purple chive clusters below, the windows open to the garden.

'What were you thinking of, putting a herb garden there?' Verity asked. 'It's the perfect place for roses.'

Emma could smell the thyme which flowered a delicate shade of pink, the lemon balm which overran the path so that you could not help standing on it and dispersing its clean sharp scent into the afternoons. Her father loved the smell of the herbs; he had said in jest before the stroke which took his power of speech that he loved it better than any flower because it reminded him of Emma's wonderful dinners.

The evening of the stroke, when she had hoped he was getting better, she looked in on him after George had gone to bed. She thought he was asleep. The weather had broken, she was glad of the cooling breeze but was about to close the window against the rain when she heard him murmur to her from the bed. She stopped.

'Leave the curtains open, child, I like them like that. I like to see the rain and hear it when I drop off and it's the relief of it. Leave the lamp off, open the window and let the air in.'

She obeyed him, and the smell of fresh rain on the herbs beneath was calming.

'You haven't called me "child" in years,' she said, going to him, only half able to see how he looked because his face was in shadow. 'You seem a little better.'

'I'm worried, Emma.' He moved about in the bed as though he were uncomfortable, and she went over and smoothed the sheets and coverlet as she had a done a hundred times since he had been taken ill. She wished she could do more.

He patted the bed and she sat down.

'There's nothing to worry over,' she said in her strongest voice. 'Everything's going to be fine.'

'Oh Emma, what a very bad liar you are.'

She tried to laugh this off, but the lump in her throat wouldn't allow it. She shook her head.

'I have nothing to leave you—' he said.

'I won't need anything, Father.'

'It's all been so badly done, and I'm sorry.'

The tears would not hold and began to glass the front of her eyes. She moved herself as though the distraction would stop them, and when her voice came out it was the whisper she had promised herself it would not be.

'You're all the world to me,' she said. 'The best father a woman ever had.'

He shook his head and moved about even more, so agitated. 'I'm sorry for the things I did in my life which were ugly and hurtful. I wish there was some way I could make up for them now, but there isn't. I've had to live with it.'

'You've never hurt anybody,' she said, dismayed that he should regard himself in this way.

He lay back on the pillows and his voice was weaker. 'When you're a young man you think everything you do is right, you're brought up to believe it. It doesn't matter how bad it is because the world is yours and women and children they come second.'

'Please, don't upset yourself. There's no need.'

'Do you remember the garden path at home? The smell of the herbs reminds me of it and your mother calling you into the house for your tea.'

Vaguely she thought she could hear her mother's voice, in a wild cold place and the house where the fires were big.

She had chance to recall nothing more because her father's face and his body began to alter as the stroke invaded him. Those were to be the last words he said.

She had tried not to think about that conversation, she still held that he would get better. She had to hold on to that, there seemed nothing else, but she was reminded of it all once again; she could not tear her mind from the memory. She tried to concentrate on Laurence now, thinking that he might suggest she should hire someone to help in the garden. She was taken aback when he said, 'George should go away to school.'

Emma was so shocked that she didn't know what to say, and took refuge in, 'Father is devoted to him.'

'Most of the time I don't think he's aware of anyone. He's sleeping more and more deeply.'

Emma wanted to shout out loud that he was doing nothing of the kind, instead of which she blinked down at the tidy needlework as though there were more to do.

'Dr Shuttleworth says he won't last the week,' Laurence said.

Emma bit off the thread now that the trousers were finished, folded them and found herself unable to move or speak.

'I thought I would come round later and go through Father's papers. There are so many of them which he's ignored, it could take weeks.'

Emma wanted to scream and shout that their father was not dead yet, but she felt a sudden sympathy for her brother because he didn't look at her and she thought that perhaps sorting papers was his way of dealing with something which men were not allowed to acknowledge hurt them deeply.

'I think that's a good idea,' she said with energy, and she waited for him to look at her, but of course he didn't. He didn't ever seem to look at her directly: he always had such important things to do and so many of them.

He merely nodded and went away home for his evening meal.

He came back almost straight afterwards, as though for once he wanted to be in the house; perhaps he too wished for a way to hold off their father's death and thought, as a man might, that if he were there and the doors bolted death would have no way in. It was a foolish notion which Emma rather liked, but instead of her brother's presence being of comfort it was quite the opposite, and all the time he was there in the study she moved from room to room trying to be efficient and accomplishing nothing.

In the end she went and opened the study door. There were papers stacked beside him and he said, in an attempt at humour, 'I don't think he's ever thrown anything away,' and Emma smiled in acknowledgement of the attempt and moved further into the room as Laurence frowned at the papers in his hand. 'Look at this.'

She went and bent over to look.

'It's really old,' Laurence said, 'just some notes about a lecture he was probably giving. It's from when we lived in England, well, not me obviously, but you and Mother and Father. He never talked about it, did he?'

'You're too young to remember. He did say something before he was so ill, but it was vague. And I don't remember much, just a house set up high in the village where we were. Tow Law Town. A little mining town in the middle of County Durham. We were happy there. He used to lift me up and throw me up high and catch me. He seemed so tall.'

'He was. Is,' Laurence amended.

'So are you.' Her brother was one of the tallest men in the area. Somehow she had always thought it would have made him kinder, that he might hold off life for her, that he might have shielded her and her father as he grew older, but he never had. Perhaps he was the kind of person whose ability to love was limited to his wife and children. It must be, she knew, a great responsibility.

He got up abruptly, in case, she thought, he was about to show his feelings. He said it was late and Verity would be expecting him home. Seconds later he was gone, leaving the desk untidy. Would he come back tomorrow? Would he spend part of each evening there so that she could grow used to him and maybe they would talk more about their early life and she could tell him things which he could not remember? She thought she might like that.

Long after she had imagined George in bed she found him asleep beside her father. She would have left him there, but he sensed her and opened his eyes.

'May I stay here?'

'Of course. I didn't mean to disturb you.'

George looked intelligently at her and then, after making sure the old man's eyes were closed and his breathing steady, he turned to her once again. 'He's going to die soon, isn't he?'

'No—'

'Please don't say that. It's the kind of thing Aunt Verity would say. She told me he would go to the angels last time I saw her.' George raised his eyes to the ceiling, but they were glassy.

Emma smiled at this. 'Everyone dies eventually,' she said.

'It isn't eventually yet,' George said, closing his eyes and turning towards her father.

Emma kissed him goodnight and went off to her bed. She tried not to think about her father dying; she didn't think she could bear it any more easily than George could. She didn't sleep. The night was warm. Usually she loved the fall, but this one was already on its way and she did not think her father would live to see their favourite time of year. She felt as though the leaves, having had too dry a spring and summer, would not turn the usual gold and rust and orange. This year it was as though they had shrunk away, curled up against the wind, shrivelled.

She lay awake until she heard the clock in the church strike three and then she got up and wandered across the hall. George and her father lay as before but not quite, she realized. There was something different. Her father was stiller than he had been. She walked quietly around the bed and then back again, and she sat down softly in her mother's favourite rocking chair and waited for the dawn because she did not want the little boy to wake up and discover alone that the man he had thought of as his father had died in the night.

Judge Philips was a friend of theirs, so although he could have left it to other people, after the funeral was over and the mourners had gone, he lingered. Laurence said to him, 'I expect after all that tea, Judge, you'd like something a little stronger.'

The Judge slid his huge wobbling backside forward in Emma's best chair. She had feared for it ever since the moment he had sat down because it had been her father's chair, and as he rose to his feet she wished for perhaps the tenth time that she had moved it into another room where it could not be so ill-treated. He reached the table where he had deposited what she realized now was the will, picked it up and waved the papers at Laurence and said, 'After you, good sir.' He nodded towards the door.

'Can you read that here, Judge?' Emma asked.

Both men looked surprised and she realized that they were not used to her questioning such things.

'My dear,' he said, 'this is not women's work.'

'Are we to hear second-hand how things are left?'

The Judge looked apologetically at her and then at Laurence, and after Laurence nodded the Judge said, 'There is no mystery to it. Your father naturally left everything other than a few small bequests to his son.'

Emma stared.

'Did you expect it to be otherwise?' Laurence said, and she heard the note of ice in his voice.

She remembered then that her father had said he could leave her nothing. She understood now that he had meant this literally and although she urged herself to put such thoughts from her mind she felt afraid for her future and for George.

'Why yes, why should I not? What about my home?'

'It's the family home, of course,' the Judge said.

'Laurence and Verity already have a perfectly good house just as large as this one.'

'Which will be sold,' Laurence said.

Verity added, 'You didn't really expect to go on living in a huge house like this by yourself? That would look odd to others.'

Emma realized they had already spoken about this between themselves and worked out what they would do. How naïve she had seen.

'I'm not by myself,' she objected.

'Once George goes to school you'll be quite alone,' her sister-in-law said.

'George isn't going anywhere.'

There was a short pause and then the Judge coughed and wheezed, and he said, 'My dear Emma, your brother becomes George's guardian. It will be his decision alone.'

There was another silence and somehow it sounded quite different from any before. Even the shadows which were stealing across the grass in the back garden, the first dead leaves almost lost amongst its abundance, were altered somehow.

'Perhaps you will begin the process of selling our house, Judge?' Laurence said.

George was a completely different child after her father died, Emma could see. Laurence, Verity and their two young sons moved in almost immediately. Verity put their beds in George's room.

'Boys don't need a room to themselves,' she said, 'and besides, George will hardly be there and when Daniel and Charles are a little older they will go away to school too so it would be a waste of space to give them more just for the vacations.'

George retreated to the library, but Laurence decided he would turn it into his study, the better to work at home in the evenings, and the boys were banned from there. If George went upstairs to read the other boys followed him, shouting and playing noisy games. He liked noisy games himself, but not with them. These things mattered, Emma thought.

'George is very quiet,' Verity said. 'He used to be so fond of playing outside. He isn't ill, is he?'

'His father has just died,' Emma said.

Verity laughed. 'Nonsense,' she said. 'Children have little concept of death.'

'I think he has noticed that Father is not here,' Emma said, but Verity was busily moving in her own furniture now that the other house was sold, and disposing of sideboards, tables and bookcases which Emma could not remember being without.

She also employed someone to help in the garden, and Emma came back from the local bookstore which had become one of her own refuges to find her herb garden pulled up and laid in heaps on the path, and the gardener, Mr Burton, saying how stubborn some of it had been.

'I couldn't get my fork in at that rosemary. Must have

been there for years, the stem's all woody.' He shook his head. 'Rosemary should be replaced every two years, and the mint had gone rusty. It shouldn't be in a pot like that, you know, even when the pot's in the ground: doesn't do it any good though it does tend to take over everything, given its way.'

Emma went into the kitchen. This too was no longer her domain: Verity employed a cook. She strode through into Verity's sitting room – which had been the winter sitting room, the cosiest room in the house – and demanded, 'Why did you pull up my herb garden?'

Verity, who was studying the menus for the next week, looked up as though she hadn't heard what Emma was saying.

'The herb garden,' Emma repeated.

'Oh yes. I'm going to plant roses there. Now that Laurence and I sleep in that bedroom I thought the scent would be delightful in the summer as we go to sleep with all the windows open.'

At dinner that evening Emma was almost late. She sat down without apology. They had a formal meal each evening, the children banished to bed, and she could not help but remember the autumn evenings of the years before: her father and George and herself toasting crumpets late on Sunday afternoons when the darkness had come down early over the land and the fire was bright against the hearth tiles.

Laurence, usually first to begin eating after everyone was served, hesitated, smiled at his wife and then looked across the table at Emma and said, 'We've got a nice surprise for you. We're aware that you would much rather have a place of your own, you have grown used to being the mistress here, so I've found a nice little cottage which will be just right.'

Emma, lifting a portion of potato to her mouth, put down her fork, heard the sentence once more in her mind and then over and over.

'A cottage?'

'Charming little place on the edge of town. I'm sure you'll like it. George will be going to school next month and you'll have very little to do for the first time in years. You'll be able to potter there to your heart's content.'

Verity beamed across the table at her.

'The garden is just big enough for you,' she said.

The cottage, as Laurence had said, was at the very edge of town. The land rose directly behind it, so there was no back garden. Verity had been right about the front garden too: it was at least a dozen steps to the door, a vegetable patch to the side where the gooseberry bushes had run wild, but little could have grown there, the house next door overshadowed the space.

At the back there was no place for anything; the cottage leaned in against the land as though it had stood up straight for too long. Consequently it had no back door, just one to the side which led directly into the kitchen.

There were three small dark rooms with stone floors downstairs. The staircase was narrow, she could not see to the top because of the lack of light, but it was no surprise that up there the rooms were better because they were above the surrounding countryside. There were no views except for one window looking away from the town to where the road strung out grey into the distance. The third bedroom was tiny, had no window, and Emma could smell the damp. From the second, if you had opened the window, you could have stepped outside and made your way carefully down onto the road.

Verity, who had insisted on going with her, went from room to room finding something positive to say about each one. 'And just think,' she declared, when there was nothing more to see, 'you don't have to put up with the boys tumbling about you.'

Laurence and Verity's sons were little ogres. Emma had caught the elder one in the garden the day before using a garden spade to bang the living daylights out of some unfortunate frog. The other child wet his bed nightly because Laurence would allow no night light and the poor boy saw creatures coming to get him in the darkness. Often Emma lay awake and heard Verity get up to change his sheets, and a vague smell of warm urine hung about the child all day.

George, insisting on seeing the cottage, though he would be long gone to school in Boston by then, stood in the darkness of the freezing little kitchen and said, 'It's awful,' as though he had been an adult.

He had grown so much lately and had altered in other ways. The joy and light had gone from him, he rarely spoke, and when Emma had explained as gently as she could that he was going away to school, he merely nodded. There was a large portmanteau standing open in his bedroom which Verity was gradually filling with clothes which he would need. He would go directly after Christmas and not come back before spring. Emma felt like apologizing to him, but she didn't see the point.

She alone took George to the station. He did not look at her or speak even when they said goodbye. He turned his back to her and climbed onto the train.

2

'Is that you, Mick?'

They were, Mick Castle thought, the sweetest words that any woman had ever said to any man; it was the mantra of his homecoming and something he looked forward to all day.

He responded, shouting through the hall, before he closed the door, 'Aye, it's me,' and then he made his way into the light of the kitchen, saw the black dog, Hector, get up from beneath the table, tail wagging, and then his young wife busy at the stove.

'You been at the brandy bottle?' he said, kissing the back of her neck.

'No, you fool, it's for the sauce.'

'You smell of it.'

'Well, I did have a little nip. Several little nips, in fact.'

'Let's taste it then,' and she turned around and kissed him, wooden spoon in one hand, her white pinny covered in the making of the dinner.

'Would you like some brandy?'

'Food will be fine when it's ready.'

'You know, Mick, they say there are only two kinds of landlord, those who drink and those who don't, and you're in danger of becoming a Methodist.'

It was true, you lost the taste for booze when you were with it all day and when you saw what it did to other people. He was gagging for tea right now and she made some without him asking, though she did say it would rot his insides at this time of night.

'Tea after six is an abomination to the Lord,' she said in jest, as she poured boiling water into the pot.

'Where's Connie?'

Isabel sighed. 'At her books again. That child will turn into a schoolteacher if we aren't careful.'

Secretly he was rather pleased that his child was keen on learning. Her mother wanted her to be decorative. She spent the evenings putting Connie's hair into rags, so that the child complained she couldn't sleep for the nasty lumps, making her pretty dresses, showing her how to paint and embroider. Connie hated the fuss of standing while her mother pinned new clothes around her and she showed no aptitude for embroidery, painting or singing. She had already refused to learn to play the baby grand piano which Mick had bought so that there could be music in the house.

He went into the big room which was more like a library than a sitting room. Books lined the walls. He had had the bookshelves built to house his father's books when they had moved into the house, just to keep something

26

of his childhood. He didn't have much time for reading.

To be fair there was another sitting room, they were not short of space, but the library was Connie's domain, she loved it, had come to dominate it in some ways. Their child was beautiful, but then she didn't know or it didn't matter to her and yet her mother told her so over and over again. Isabel had rejoiced when their daughter had been so lovely, and so had he, but it was a different sort of loveliness that he saw and that she saw, somehow.

He didn't know what he had done to deserve such things. She was like a fairy being. He was dark and tall and rather spare, while Isabel Hanlon, like her father, was pure Viking, big and bright yellow-haired, blue eyes you could drown in, clean-limbed and long-legged with cheeks like blushing roses, and he adored her.

He had never come across anything which was as wonderful as going to bed with his wife. She was ice and fire, giggles and sweet moans, her hands were soft and caressing and her mouth was moist and tasted of strawberries. She gathered him to her with such completeness that he thought they had been destined for one another, that she had been born to be his and for him to marry her, and although neither of their parents had thought it a match he knew that it was worthwhile.

He had not known ecstasy until he touched her. He had not lived a full life before he met her. He did not care what either of them had given up for the other, that only made it sweeter. They met in that perfect union which only real lovers knew and nobody else was anywhere within that magic circle. Together they could hold the horrors of life at bay.

Their child was small, delicate. She had white blonde hair, grey-green eyes like the sea at Tynemouth on a fair day. He did not dare to call it perfect, yet he had no idea where she had got such looks. She was truly his father's grandchild, though his father did not see her. He had died weeks before she was born. It was, to Mick, a huge loss. He had wanted his father to see him as a father and not just as something his father had not wanted him to be. His father had been a scholar and he was anything but, and yet Connie too had the makings of a professor.

He missed both his parents. It was not a balance between one and the other, and in his dreams he remembered himself as a small child and the harmony which had given way to disappointment when he had turned out not to be a scholar but had followed his grandfather into business. Sometimes he wished to be that child again, but in daylight he went about as other people did. You could not grieve in public, it was not seemly.

Connie soothed him. She didn't acknowledge his entrance; she was sitting at his father's old desk, counting on her fingers. He leaned over and kissed her cheek.

'Now you made me lose count,' she objected, moving just a little away from him, as though inviting his kiss to follow, as if she were only teasing and knew that this was so; his child adored him and for him she was the whole of the stars from the sky.

The dog had followed him in and lay down heavily

before the fire, like a guest who doesn't want to make a fuss. Mick went over and sat in the armchair and then Hector moved so that his face was on Mick's feet. Labradors love to put their heads on your feet. Mick sat there for a few minutes, luxuriating in the fire and the peace until his wife broke the silence, opening the door and saying, 'The dinner's ready.'

'In a minute,' Connie said.

'Now, young lady,' her mother said, a trifle sharply.

Mick wished he could have said, as his mother might have done, 'Come and sit with us – leave the dinner and let's talk and think of other things.' His mother had been the kind of woman who made stews so that it didn't matter whether you ate at a particular time, but Isabel thought differently and her cooking was the kind that would not and should not wait, and the smell of it through the door she had left open drew him towards the dining room. His wife, Mick thought, was given to practical things, she cared nothing for books and her cooking was perfection.

Connie went on writing and looking at her book. Isabel glanced appealingly at him before she left the room. Then she went back to the kitchen.

'You can finish it afterwards,' he said to his daughter.

'I'm stuck. Will you help me?'

'I have to go straight back.' She wasn't stuck, he knew, she just wanted an excuse to keep him at home in the evenings and he wished he could have done so. He was saying these words as they reached the dining room.

'Not again,' his wife said.

'I cannot help it. I've nobody reliable on the door and it's Saturday.'

'One of these days you'll come home for your dinner and remember that you have a family.'

'Isabel—'

'Sit down,' she said, 'before it spoils.'

Mick's pub was the Black Diamond, one of half a dozen public houses he owned locally and the biggest. It was a common enough name in that area. The Black Diamond was the coal which was mined there. The trouble was that coal-mining was already on the way down. At one time the little town had been home to five thousand people and although it was still buoyant enough in some ways it was as though the heart had already been knocked from it, and that was hard because it was his home. He had been born there when the ironworks and the coal-mining and the coke-making were at their most lucrative.

Now the ironworks was failing because the man who owned it, Eden Summers, had moved most of the work to another town a dozen miles away. Mick couldn't think well of him for it. What was it with some men that they cared more for making fortunes than for people? It was as though the town sat on the edge of a cliff, though in fact it sat on a ridge high above Weardale and beyond it the moors petered out into mucky little pit towns before they reached Durham City, a dozen miles away.

The big pit in the town was still open, though there were

rumours that it wouldn't be for much longer. Two thousand men worked there. He couldn't imagine what would happen when it closed: it was too hard to think about.

He liked his pub, especially at this time of year when the nights were drawing in. The men drank there all year round, some of them every night, though most of the pitmen couldn't do that because they were on different shifts, so it was usually Fridays and Saturdays or whenever they could get away.

The place was big. It had been built years ago as a private house, but the man who owned it went off to South America, and Mick had bought it at a knock-down price. Most people rented their houses and those who could afford to buy them rarely bought a big house in such a place. Only the vicar and the doctor owned houses this size, and he had been granted a licence for it.

It was well built: thick stone walls, big marble fireplaces, a number of outhouses, a square yard at the back, but at the front it faced right onto the road beyond the wide pavement, another reason why he thought nobody else would have wanted it.

When he got back it was almost nine o'clock and the place was already rowdy with voices. On Friday, Saturday and Sunday nights, despite his wife's annoyance, he had to be there. Employing other people to make certain everything was all right did not work, he had discovered over the years, though the smaller pubs were in tiny places and he did not have the same problems there. He was big and it was useful to be able to throw people out, though usually there were willing hands to help him.

The men didn't like fighting, but after a few pints the younger ones in particular, not satisfied with hewing coal or quarrying stone all week or sweating in Summers' damned foundry, had sufficient energy to quarrel and then they would break tables, chairs, glasses, bottles – anything they could – and he wasn't having that. They could fight outside. The people living nearby might and could complain often at the noise, but once men were beyond the doors of the pub Mick didn't consider it his problem.

Saturdays were the worst because nobody had to work the following day. He and Ed Higgins, a Yorkshireman who had worked behind the bar for five years, were prepared. Ed, not tall, had been a boxer in his youth, and though he was stouter than he used to be he would not have any brawls in the bars and was inclined to bang troublemakers' heads together and throw them out.

There were three scuffles that night and it was late when they closed the doors and locked up. Ed and Jack Allen, the young lad who helped during the day moving barrels of beer and clearing up and anything else Mick and Ed couldn't see to, finished behind the bar while Mick went into the back to add up the takings. They would wash and dry the glasses and put them away and wipe the table tops. In the morning two women came in to sweep and scrub the floors, the passages, the windows and anything else which Ed thought needed attention.

Mick always meant to stay at home until eleven in the mornings, but somehow it never worked out like that.

There was always too much to see to, a delivery or a problem, and it wasn't right to leave the others to sort it out: they didn't have the kind of experience or the ability to deal with it.

It was after one o'clock when he arrived home. He did not expect Isabel to be waiting for him. The only one who greeted him was Hector, the big black dog. Ulysses, the other black dog who used to stay at the pub overnight until some years previously when armed men had broken in – God only knows what they were doing, nothing was left there – came home with him. They didn't kill Ulysses but he was lucky they missed him. There were bullets stuck in the woodwork. Mick thought the dog had run low and quick and hidden, as his instincts bid him, and Mick decided he would rather lose what there was – no cash, he always took it home with him – than his beloved dog.

So the house was silent. He let the dogs out into the garden and followed them there for a few minutes, but they knew how late it was and did not linger.

He took them back into the kitchen and the minute he made a light he knew that something was wrong. The place was a mess. Isabel always cleared up before going to bed, but the pots and pans were just as they had been before dinner. The warmth had long since died. It smelled of cold grease.

He bounded upstairs. He went straight into the bedroom which he shared with his wife, and there too it was untidy. She had shed her clothes before she got into bed, there was a trail of them upon the floor, and what hit him was the strong smell of brandy. A glass lay on the rug where some of the brandy had run out. His wife was asleep.

'Isabel?' As he drew nearer the stink of brandy grew stronger, and he knew from experience that there was no point in trying to rouse her. She was drunk.

He didn't go to the Black Diamond the next morning. Isabel did not stir. He went downstairs and gave Connie her breakfast and stopped her from going up to see her mother; he told her that Isabel was feeling a bit queasy and needed to go back to sleep.

At midday, the time that the roast was usually underway in the oven and there was the promise of Sunday dinner to come, he went down to the pub and took Connie and the dogs with him. When he got back Isabel had still not been downstairs. He distracted Connie by promising her a walk in the afternoon and finding cheese and bread for her to stave off the hunger, and then he went upstairs and found Isabel awake.

'Are you all right?'

'Mick—' She sounded as though she were about to cry.

'Don't worry about it.'

'Connie—'

'I'll see to Connie. Do you want anything?'

She managed to shake her head.

'Go back to sleep,' he said.

She did. He went downstairs and took Connie and the dogs for a long walk and then he cleaned the kitchen. He had already told Ed and Tom that he would not be back that day. He made up the fire and sat there by it and read to Connie in the evening. When she had gone to bed, he went to bed too – he was exhausted.

In the morning when he awoke his wife was crying.

'I'm sorry,' she said. 'I don't know what happened. I just—' She stopped there.

He took her into his arms. 'Don't upset yourself,' he said. 'It was nothing. Everybody does that sooner or later. It was frustration. You were fed up. I wasn't there and I should have been, that's all.'

'I will try to be a better wife to you.'

'You always are.' He kissed her. He put his arms around her. He held her close. He laughed into her ear. 'You snored,' he said, and she protested and pushed at him, and they both laughed until it was forgotten.

'Connie has stopped attending lessons, Mr Castle.' Sister Luke had tried to put it delicately. Mick looked into the nun's sweet round face and noted that there was regret.

'She became very naughty over a period of time. At first we didn't like to say anything. It's hard when a child looks like an angel and behaves as what can only be described as the very opposite. We did attempt to remonstrate with her, but it did no good and we didn't like to say anything to you – there was such a feeling of failure. Gradually over the past few weeks she has been absent more and more.'

'I don't know what to say,' was all Mick could manage. He felt as if he were back at school himself, sitting there on the other side of the headmistress's desk in the heart of the convent school.

The whole thing made him feel uncomfortable. He was not a God-fearing man, and the statues of Jesus in white looking strangely blonde, fair-skinned and pale-eyed, and Mary in blue left Mick confused. He had had to talk Sister Luke into taking Connie in the first place because he and Isabel were not Catholic. The children, depending on which school they went to, were divided into 'Catholic Cats' and 'Church Dogs', and there were fights on the streets on certain days.

He had thought that the quiet nuns would calm his daughter. It seemed now as though he had been wrong. He had known Connie was unhappy for some time, but was loath to move her because the other school took the children in the town up to the age of twelve, all in one class, and he didn't think much could be learned that way.

'Mr Castle,' Sister Luke looked straight at him from large saucer-shaped blue eyes, 'Connie is exceptionally clever. She is bored at our little school and we have a great many children here who need our help because they are so far behind. She is disrupting the other children. I am going to have to ask you to take her away.'

Telling Isabel was hard, and he had chosen the wrong time. She didn't look at him. She was making the evening meal and her face was red and moist from working at the range, dealing with pans of simmering water and a hot oven inside which was cooking pork with sage. The pans held potatoes and Brussels sprouts and carrots, and somewhere about there was the smell of apples baking slowly with rich butter.

Her bright yellow hair had gone into little damp tendrils about her face where it had escaped from its neat fastenings at the back of her head. She banged about for what seemed to him like a very long time. Then she said, 'And what do you propose to do now?'

'I think she should go to boarding school. There's nothing here worthy of her.'

Isabel stopped what she was doing and turned to him. 'You what?' she said.

'There is no practical alternative.'

'She could go to the council school. It's good enough for other children.'

'Sister Luke says she's very clever—'

'I've seen no evidence of it unless you mean that she'd rather sit with her face in a book on her own than take part in what anyone else is doing or has suggested. She won't even play with other children. I'm not sure that's very clever. I have done everything I can. She'll hardly let me put her into a pretty dress. She does nothing such as girls should. She cannot sew, knit or embroider, though I have tried to teach her. She won't have piano lessons or go to dancing school. She avoids the kitchen. I don't think she even knows how to put the kettle on. It's as if we had the boy you always wanted.'

He was stung and answered too quickly, though he

didn't realize this until it was too late. 'I never said anything of the kind.'

'You didn't have to. It's what all men want, a child in their image.'

Mick stood like a stranger and listened to her shouting at him. How had things got to this and why hadn't he noticed?

'I love her. I don't care.'

Isabel didn't seem to hear this; she didn't acknowledge it.

'Why don't we ask her what she wants to do?' he suggested.

'She's a child. What can she know?' Isabel sounded tired, defeated.

He looked at her and then he said gently, 'Why don't we go away for a few days, the three of us?'

'I don't see how that would help and if you cannot even be here in the evening, how could you possibly manage it? And we are not going to look at boarding schools, so don't think you can persuade me that way. We live in this godforsaken place because of your work and all I have is my child. You will not take her away from me.'

'I wasn't trying to—'

'What else would you call it? You take everything,' she said, and she ran from the kitchen and left the dinner.

He pulled the pans off the heat and followed her upstairs. She was sitting on the bed in their room, dashing the tears from her face.

Connie said from the doorway, 'What's wrong with Mammy?'

'She's been peeling onions.'

Isabel turned her drenched shiny face away from her child. 'You're going to the council school. The nuns won't have you any more.' And with that she got up and went off downstairs, back to the kitchen.

Mick sat where he was.

Connie hovered beside the door. 'Do I have to go to Mr English's school?'

'Unless you want to go to boarding school.'

'Leave here?'

'Would you like to do that?'

In answer she ran to him. 'I don't want to leave you and Mammy,' she said.

That night Isabel turned away from him, and it meant something different than it had before, not just that she wanted to turn over, or that she felt more comfortable facing the wall than the window, or that she wanted him to mould himself against her. She turned away deliberately and somehow he could not ask her to turn back.

He tried to be at home more. In the mornings they had breakfast together, but she had nothing to say. The food was the same as usual, but it had no taste and he knew why that was – it had been cooked automatically without love. How ridiculous that it should taste so odd, so different, so unappetizing. He could not eat it.

He took Connie to the council school. He didn't like the

look of it. It was cold, there was only one classroom, all the children were in it; he did not think his child would flourish there. The rows of desks were soldier-like, and the children were silent. The only heating came from a big stove at the front of the classroom where the teacher sat, and there was a cane on the teacher's desk. He did not want to start off badly with Mr English, but he could not help saying, before he left, 'Could we go out into the corridor?'

Mr English, a small thin man with a bald head, followed him there.

'Don't go using that cane on my child.'

Mr English stared and said nothing.

'My girl is small and will no doubt cause you problems, but you don't beat her. Do you understand?'

It was a few moments before Mr English spoke, and during that time Mick noticed how his body shook and how shabby his suit was and how lined and fallen his face.

'I am not in the habit of caning small girls, Mr Castle,' and he turned wearily and went back to his classroom.

Mick had never felt like a bully before, but he did when he left the school. He knew very well that Norton English had a sick wife, was paid very little, and he had everything to do when he got home because she could barely rise from her bed. It must try him hard to deal with children who were often bigger than he was and with no inclination for learning. Mick pitied him, but did not see what else he could do.

3

MID HAVEN, NEW ENGLAND, 1905

Emma Appleby could not imagine why Judge Philips was calling that afternoon. She was caught up in trying to decide which pieces of her furniture would fit into the cottage. All of it seemed so big.

Verity had come into the room while she was thinking about it, and when Emma told her the problem she said, 'Why then, leave it here. It's a pretty enough room and I like it.'

'I have no money to buy new furniture or for anything else.'

Verity looked at her. 'Oh my dear,' she said. 'I had no notion.'

'I've never needed any before now. Father had accounts at all the shops in town—'

'Do not let us talk about money. I am sure that Laurence will be able to help,' and Verity went away.

Laurence had had a note sent that she should meet him at his office, but when she got there they were both so embarrassed that it was not an easy meeting. His office had oak furniture, including the big green leather-topped desk which had always been in the library at home and now stood between them.

'I had imagined Father always made you an allowance.'

She didn't say anything. Her father had been a generous man, there was no question of her paying for clothes or books or trifles of any kind which she chose. Everything was delivered to the house after being chosen by her and the accounts were sent to him monthly. He had never mentioned it and she had assumed that it was always like that. She had made presents for him, knitted him warm gloves, hat and scarf for the winter, and socks of course, and she had bought plain journals and covered them in lovely fabrics. He had always said if she wanted to go on trips away she had only to say so, but he did not want to go and she did not care to go alone. She had been content to spend her days with him and with George, and she was glad of it now that they were gone.

Laurence frowned. 'I'm not a rich man, I could take care of your rent and groceries and the day-to-day needs, but I'm not sure I could run to furniture. Perhaps you and Verity could find enough things from the house which would do.'

She had said nothing to Verity, pride prevented it, but it did not seem to her that any of the furniture in the house would go into the poky little place to which she was being sent.

She tried to collect her thoughts now and told the Judge that she was the only one at home, and he said that he was glad of that. She offered him coffee and took him into the sitting room by the fire and made small talk until the coffee came.

Judge Philips had not married until fifteen years ago, a woman much younger than himself. She had borne him six children and had died in childbirth. All were boys.

She had done so well, people said, yet Emma could not help regretting that two or three of the children had not been girls; she could not imagine a household made boisterous by six small boys. On the few occasions when she had seen the Judge and his wife, Mary, when four of the children were running around, she had found the noise deafening and had only been glad to come back to the peace, the security of her father's house, to wander through the colours and sweet smells of the flowers in the extensive garden. It had been high summer and there were lilies everywhere, stargazers in white, with pink middles, yellow and a bright shade of orange. Lilies, she thought, were unashamedly brash in the summer; she loved them for it. Lavender edged the paths for the smell as much as the colour.

The garden always calmed her, no matter what the season. She loved the bare winter trees, the first spring flowers, blue and yellow and bright red, the warmth of spiky dahlias each looking like a separate sun in late summer and the roses which bloomed thick and cream, and though she hated to admit it because of what Verity had done to the herb garden after her father died, they had the best smell of all.

The Judge had had plenty of help of course, especially

43

since Mary had died. The gossips said that he did not spend much time at home, but Emma did not blame him for that: he was almost sixty and children were trying even for people younger than he was.

He drank his coffee quickly, but when she offered more he refused, mopped his brow with a large handkerchief taken from his trouser pocket and then stood up and said, 'I've come here to ask you something special, Emma. As you know, your father and I were friends for many years. You are – beyond the age where women think of marriage and yet – I don't need to explain my circumstances to you. Indeed,' he looked down at his well-polished shoes, 'you were very kind and attentive to Mary. I – I loved her very much. I waited for a woman like her for so many years, only for her to be taken from me like that – it was almost unbearable.'

She gave him a few moments to collect himself. She didn't say anything, she had noticed that speech didn't help at such moments, the grieving person didn't hear and left the would-be comforter feeling inadequate, stupid and garrulous, and the words were left in the air somehow for the most interminable amount of time, until one's face had taken to burning.

She realized that the Judge had begun speaking again, and she had to chase the sense of what he was saying. Even then she seemed to lose his words, as though they were disturbed by sounds coming in from the garden, but the windows were shut against the wind. She had never faced a winter without George and her father. She missed them both so much. She drew her thoughts back to what the Judge was saying. She could hear her father accusing her of inattention when she was a child and he was teaching her something and whatever was happening beyond the window absorbed her.

The Judge paused while she was still in pursuit. He seemed better, relieved, as though he had taken all the heaviness from his mind somehow. He seemed to be waiting for some kind of response and since she could think of nothing he finally said, 'I have of course spoken to your brother; I saw him earlier and he has given his permission. I would not have spoken to you so soon, with you in mourning, but I understand that you are moving into a cottage. I can see why you want to leave now that the house has a new mistress, and I'm sure I can offer you something much better than that.'

Whatever was the Judge referring to? She was annoyed with herself for not having listened more closely.

He looked down again. She had never seen him so sheepish.

'My boys need a mother. I was hoping you would think kindly of us.' He beamed at her, his red face, broken veins, suddenly shiny.

To say that Emma was astonished would be inaccurate. She was dumbfounded. This lasted only seconds and was followed by disbelief and then embarrassment. The Judge, happily, did not give her time to speak. He put up one hand. 'I don't expect an answer immediately. I know that a – a maiden lady like yourself will need time to consider taking on such a new life, but I feel sure that you won't regret it. You looked after your father so well, my dear, I don't doubt you will do the same for your old friend.'

'But Judge—'

'No, no. I will take my leave and call tomorrow. Good day, my dear.'

And with that the Judge was gone, picking up his hat from the hallstand and leaving her silent. She wanted nothing but to be alone. However, a door opened and her sister-in-law, Verity, came into the hall with a look that Emma could only describe as arch.

'Well,' she said, 'what did the Judge say?'

'You knew?' She guessed immediately from Verity's face and felt a sudden rush of anger that her sister-in-law had told her nothing, as though it were a treat to be kept to oneself like a wrapped birthday present.

'Laurence sent me a note earlier, to beg me to leave the house to you so that the Judge could speak. My dear, we're so pleased for you – such consequence.'

There was a sudden chill in the air which Emma could have sworn was not there before.

'I haven't given him my answer.'

'You couldn't of course without speaking directly to Laurence. He has promised to come home early,' and with that she went back to what Laurence affectionately and disparagingly, Emma thought, called her knitting: the running of the household.

Emma could not rest, and in the evening when she heard voices, having left her door ajar, she knew that Laurence

46

was home for his evening meal. She had to stop herself from running straight down and blurting out her thoughts to him as if he were her father and she the small girl she had once been. Laurence, she reminded herself painfully, was nothing like her father. She missed her father more and more as time went on. Why was he not still there for her when she needed him so very much?

Having made herself wait for some time, she went down. Verity and Laurence were having their pre-dinner sherry before the fire, the children having been put to bed. Laurence smiled as he saw her.

'I gather we have something to celebrate,' he said. 'Having been obliged to wait for so long, and not exactly in the full flush of youth, you have landed yourself a prize. You are taken aback of course but I'm sure that the Judge has thought a great deal about this. He could have any woman he wants – a girl of eighteen perhaps. It never occurred to me that he would ask you.'

They were so obviously waiting to hear what she said. Their faces were blank for several seconds and then Verity laughed and said, 'My dear, there is nothing to be afraid of. Marriage can be – a constant source of joy and although the Judge is not young I'm sure he has – plenty of vigour.' Verity's face was suddenly scarlet and she took a big gulp of sherry, smiled and turned away.

Afterwards Emma had no idea why she went with them into the dining room, Laurence talked about his day and Verity about hers. She sat, dumbstruck.

Afterwards they had coffee and Verity said to her, 'We

haven't had a wedding in the family for years. It will be wonderful. You and I will have such a good time planning everything: the dress, the guests, the occasion. You could be married in the summer; people will not mind if it is not quite a full year since your father died and the summer is such a joy for a wedding.'

Emma said nothing.

Verity leaned in as though the room was full of other people and she must keep her voice low. 'Being a married woman is wonderful. You will have your own home, you must have longed for that, not just a room to call your own. I know that I put your nose out of joint when we moved here because you had been mistress for so long and it cannot have been comfortable for you.

'The Judge's house is one of the largest in the area and you will be able to change everything that you wish, especially the garden. Just think of the enjoyment you will have with your own house and garden to do with what you please. My dear, you've gone quite pale. You didn't eat anything. Though it will be wonderful to look so slender in your wedding gown – quite as though you were twenty!'

Emma did not sleep. She thought about George so far away in Boston. He had sent her a stilted letter after he got there, the kind of thing she was sure he had been told to write. Perhaps it was even read before he was allowed to post it. It was about lessons, nothing else, and through what was not said she could feel his unhappiness.

She lay that night and made her decision. She would go to the Judge's chambers the following day and talk to him.

The rest of the night went on and on and sleep got further and further from her. She was relieved when day came. She thought the clock would never reach an hour when it was respectable for her to call. Even then it was frowned on, but she did not care. She turned up and the clerks in the office were obviously surprised to see her, but she had to wait only seconds after the Judge knew she was there.

He came out into the hall and greeted her affably. 'Do come through.'

His office, or whatever it was called, was very like Laurence's. She turned swiftly when the door was closed.

'I want to ask you something, Judge.'

'Why of course, my dear, anything.'

His tone was so warm and his eyes so reassuring that she began to think marriage to him would not be so bad after all. It could be her only chance, the Judge was important. The trouble was, she thought ruefully, that he was an old man and the idea of having to share a bedroom and, even worse, a bed with someone whose flesh was sagging and whose teeth had gone brown, whose breath was sour and whose pate was bald – she tried to see it in a good light and couldn't.

She didn't want to sit down, but because the Judge couldn't sit down until she did, he was too much the gentleman for that, she took a chair.

'You need have no worries,' he said. 'Anything you wish for you shall have. I'm not a poor man, as you know, and although my children are boisterous there are plenty of servants and you would not have to do anything you did not wish to do.

'I'm sure you will want to alter the gardens, of course. I know how dear your own house and garden are to you and although I could say nothing it has been hard for you to see the home where you lived with your father taken from you. I have very large gardens and the gardeners will be there to do your bidding. We shall all be there to do that. There will never be any work for you to do and you will have all the gowns that you desire and you will have beautiful jewellery—'

'I have only one concern. George.'

The Judge frowned as though he had never heard the name before. 'The Irish boy. Of course. I understand he has gone to school in Boston. A very good idea. My boys will go too of course, though at present they are rather young.'

'George is like my own child.'

The Judge wrinkled his nose at this and then waved an airy hand. 'You would not think so if you had one of your own. One's own children are so very dear.'

'He is very dear to me.'

The Judge smiled and nodded. 'Yes, well, when you become the mother of my boys you will appreciate the difference.'

'When Laurence and Verity suggested that I should go

and live in the cottage they wanted me to take George with me.'

'I can understand that. They want only their own family and they thought that you would be alone, but you will not be, you will be the wife of the most respected man in the area. How is that?'

'George will live with us then.'

The Judge hesitated. 'I would like to say yes, but I'm afraid I cannot. When he is home during the vacations you would wish to see him from time to time and I feel sure that there are many families who have no child and would be prepared to take him in for a little – help.'

Emma could think of nothing to say. She felt some relief that she could not now marry him. How close she had come to giving up so much for George, and yet she would not have been unhappy because he would have been there, at least in the holidays, and she might even have enjoyed the house and the garden and new dresses, and the Judge might have been persuaded to take her away from time to time because she had always longed to see what was beyond the place where she had lived for all her life, but had not wanted to go without her father. Travel sounded so exciting and she had only been to places in her dreams and in the books that she read.

She stuttered her way out of the house – she must have made the right noises, she could not remember afterwards. It was an icy cold day and the sky was overcast. She made her way slowly back to Laurence and Verity's house and considered what to do. She thought of the cottage, she thought of having no money, she thought of the weeks and weeks when George would be away at school, and she could not help thinking of when George would be old enough to leave her, that he would go away and get married and she would be left alone there in the cottage. Was that a better fate than marrying the Judge? None of it seemed like a bargain, but it was all she had to consider. Whatever would she do?

4

The smell of burning came to him as soon as Mick opened the front door. Black smoke was pouring from the kitchen. He ran, shouting his wife's name. The smoke was coming from the oven. He found a cloth and opened it. Whatever it had been was unrecognizable; it was now a charred piece of meat.

He managed to get the roasting tin on to the top of the stove. There was no other sign of activity in the kitchen, the vegetables were still unwashed in the sink. Dirty crockery and cutlery from earlier in the day littered the surfaces. The milk and butter from breakfast had not been put away. He opened windows in the kitchen to clear the fumes and went out of the room, closing the door behind him.

He called Isabel's name several times and then found her in the sitting room, unconscious. There was an empty brandy bottle and a glass lying beside her.

He got down on to the floor and said her name several times, but there was no response and in the end he picked her up and carried her to the bedroom. Here too was evidence of all the things that had not been done. The bed was rumpled where they had left it. Clothes were scattered on the floor as though she had thrown them there deliberately, some powder was spilled upon the dressing table, a pink satin powder puff lay like an upturned mushroom. He put her down and stared at her unconscious body. What was happening here? How could she do this now, and why?

She would not have help in the house. When he had pointed out that it would free her to do whatever it was she wished to do she said that she didn't want people in their home, seeing the way that they lived and reporting back to the village.

He had not wanted her to be a prisoner there alone on the hillside and besides he had wanted them to make friends with other couples, to have dinner parties and play the married game.

He knew everybody and was great friends with Sam Blythe, the doctor, and his wife Marjorie; the local quarry owner Tom Robson, who was married with two children; and Will Wearmouth, who was just married, the solicitor he had known since they were small children. They had caught minnows in the stream below the village, and stayed out later than they should, making plans for running away as the houses lit their lamps in the cold distance.

Always Isabel had wanted to be alone with her husband. He didn't mind at first because it was fun, but the idea haunted him now. His friends had withdrawn, some of them merely nodded to him in the street and sometimes he and Sam and Tom and Will had gone off into Durham and had dinner there and stayed late, but he had not liked to leave her alone the past year or two because he had begun to realize that things were changing, that she didn't like the loneliness of the house and felt rejected.

The company of other people didn't matter so much now – his friends had children and he was at work most of the time anyway – but it troubled him. He thought back to when they were first married and Isabel was pregnant with Connie. She had been so excited, so pleased. He was setting up the business very young, and there was not much money. There had been no more children since.

She stirred, opened her eyes and winced. Then he heard Connie's voice from her bedroom. He went in. She was sitting, wide-eyed and rather shocked, he thought, on the bed.

'Is Mammy all right? She couldn't get up off the floor.'

'She's fine now,' he said.

The following day he decided to leave work early and collect Connie from school. The doors opened, the children streamed out, tumbling over the steps, boys shouting, running, pushing, the girls in small slow groups, the odd child alone, hanging back. Some of them had dirty faces, badly cut hair, grubby clothes. Their shoes were well-worn. Some of them looked down as they walked.

When they had all gone he waited a little longer and then became impatient and ventured inside. Mr English was sitting at his desk, but he looked up when he heard the noise.

'I've come for Connie,' Mick said.

Mr English looked surprised.

'But she didn't come to school today,' he said.

Mick ran home, panicking. He felt sick. He didn't know what he thought. He didn't notice anything he passed. He dreaded that it would be a repeat of the previous night. Therefore he was surprised and delighted when he opened the door and the smell of cooking met his nose. He paused, took in that all was well, and headed towards the kitchen and the sweet smell of beef roasting.

He stopped short at the door. The kitchen was orderly. Isabel had a glass in one hand and was stirring a pot on the stove, a wooden spoon in the other. She didn't hear him, she was doing a little dance and swigging brandy. Then she sensed him, stopped and turned, affronted surprise taking up the whole of her rather white face.

'Where's Connie?'

She shrugged, went back to her cooking and poured herself some more brandy.

He didn't know what to do, he wanted to dash around the house, searching every corner and cupboard, yelling her name, but it was pointless. Isabel was not so drunk that she would not have been aware that her child was in the house instead of in school unless Connie had sneaked back and was reading in the attic. She had no friends; he could not think of any place but here or the garden that she might have gone.

He ran from room to room. He noticed nothing but that every room was empty. When he had exhausted the house he took in every inch of the grounds outside. He felt sure that had she been within earshot she would have come to him. He went into the stables, the carriage-house, every outbuilding, even the hen-hut.

There were no horses, no hens, no carriages. The buildings were empty. In his desire to ensure an income for his family he had neglected these. She was not there, nor in the orchard where the grass was long and the plum, pear and apple trees were old and bore no fruit, nor was she in the fields around the house. He searched the woods.

He went back to the town. It was dark and he was becoming more and more afraid. Rain began to fall, each drop hard like a gun pellet. He wanted to weep, the pain in his heart was so bad.

Had she run away? Why had she not come to the pub? He tortured himself thinking that she had been taken by someone, dismissed the idea as stupid but he felt guilty that she had not considered coming to him. How long he spent wandering the streets, watching carefully, calling her name down unmade roads and narrow alleyways he did not know. In the end he found himself on the way home, unable to believe that had she been able she would not have returned to her home.

The lights burned in the kitchen, but Isabel was not there. The meat had been taken from the oven half raw, the vegetables, cold, were in their pans of water. He wanted to stay there, afraid of what he might find. He avoided the downstairs rooms. Upstairs in Connie's room no light burned, but the curtains were open and even though the room was in shadow he could see the outline of the shape of his child fast asleep in bed. He wanted to break down with thankfulness, but he didn't want to disturb her. He stood for a long time, watching, unable to believe that she was actually there. Then he made his way across the landing.

No lights burned in here either, but Isabel was sleeping and the brandy bottle, now a familiar sight, was empty; he had no doubt, he did not need to check.

Where was she getting the brandy from? He did not keep such things here. He had never kept alcohol in the house. He didn't drink at home, Isabel had shown no inclination for anything other than the odd glass of sherry in the evening or when she was making the Sunday dinner – or so he had thought.

He went downstairs into the kitchen and opened the cupboards and was still surprised when he discovered empty bottles, dozens of them, not even at the back. If he had been at home at all, had opened a cupboard in the last twelve months, he would have known. How had he not known, he who dealt with drunks daily, who sold such things to people as his living? How had he not smelled it? He examined the bottles more carefully. It was vodka, he should have known by the shape of the bottles, he chided himself.

He didn't want to go to bed. He sat in the living room over the grey ashes of the long-dead fire.

At the Black Diamond the following day he called Ed

into the office and asked him if he had seen Isabel recently.

Ed shook his head slowly and then said with uncharacteristic softness, 'What's the matter, lad?'

Since he had to tell somebody, and since Ed was the closest thing he had to a father, Mick told him what had happened. 'I don't know what to do, Ed.'

There was silence and Ed frowned, and then he said, 'And do you think you'd be that much better off if you did know?'

'What do you mean?'

'Sometimes things are best left alone,' Ed said, and he went back to the bar.

Mick decided that he needed to talk to someone who might know about such things, and the only person he could think of was the doctor, Sam Blythe.

It was mid evening when he reached Sam's house. He had been home first to find his wife in the kitchen as though nothing had happened, making dinner, completely sober, and his child curled up with a book. After that, on the pretext of going back to work, he had gone to Sam's house when the surgery was closed. He knocked briefly at the back door before Marjorie answered it. She looked surprised to see him, but pleased.

'Mick!' She kissed him swiftly on the cheek. He tried to remember when he had last seen her, felt her warmth and kindness, and wished once again that things might have been different, that she and Isabel could have been friends. 'Come in. Sam's just finished.'

'I don't mean to interrupt your evening—'

'Nonsense. He'll be delighted to see you. I'm just about to put the children to bed.'

There followed ten for him glorious and painful minutes when the two little girls and one boy were present. He wished his life were the same, and then Marjorie took them to bed and Sam took him through into the surgery.

'It must be an official visit,' his friend said. 'You never come for anything else any more,' and then he paused and said, 'Sorry, I've had a bad day. I can tell by your face that something's wrong. Is it Connie?'

Mick shook his head. Sam waited, but only for a few seconds. 'Would you like a drink?'

'No!'

'Sit down.'

Mick finally forced himself into a very uncomfortable chair across the desk from where his friend sat just like a doctor, watching carefully for any visible signs, for any clue.

'Isabel's drinking.'

'How much?'

'A lot.'

'How much is a lot? Two or three glasses of sherry or—'

'A bottle of brandy at a time, a bottle of vodka. Connie keeps running off and ... being difficult.'

Sam didn't say anything and Mick wasn't surprised. He stared out of the window to give his friend time to get used to the idea. There was nothing but the backyard beyond, big square flags for its floor, the washing line stretched across from corner to corner. A great wall surrounded it, keeping out the fell, the streets, and no doubt the wind.

'She wanted more children and it didn't happen. I shouldn't have come here.' He would have left, but Sam eyed him, quelled him.

'It isn't as simple as that,' Sam said gently.

'I don't think she cares for me any more. I think she wishes she hadn't married me.'

'And do you wish you hadn't married her?'

Mick glowered at him. After a few moments Sam said, 'People have holes in them which they try to fill and sometimes they can't have the sort of love they crave and so they fill themselves with other things. With some people it's relatively good stuff, the church or gardens or embroidery, and with others it's stuff that destroys them. Either way it's the same thing, obsession, passion, people try to disappear because life isn't what they want or they don't feel as if they should be here, as if they deserve it. Would you like me to talk to Isabel?'

Mick shook his head.

'She mustn't know I was here,' he said.

5

Emma could not sleep. The Judge called the following day. She was not surprised he did so, she had expected it. He must have wondered at her rushing away like that when he had made her such an offer. She made sure that she was not at home and was obliged to listen to Verity, when she finally returned mid afternoon, saying that the Judge had been there. Verity was agog to know what was happening, but Emma made an excuse and said that she would go to see the Judge as soon as she could.

Laurence said heartily over the evening meal that he and Verity were having a dinner party: the guests were to be married couples only. She wouldn't mind having her meal on a tray in her room that Friday evening, would she?

To make it worse, one of the couples was Mr and Mrs John Elstree. John had been one of her suitors in the period before her mother had taken ill and needed care, but then he went away south for a while and came back with a bride.

The night of the dinner party, with a plate of cold food and a jug of water in front of her, she watched the carriages arrive and the people alight, saw the men in evening dress and the women in lovely gowns, and in particular Amelia Elstree in blue, her blonde hair so pale against the gathering evening light and her soft southern voice as gentle as a stream as she spoke intimately to her husband and he smiled at her.

Emma could not help thinking of what happened beyond the bedroom door, of the caresses and the kisses, but most of all how each could turn in the night and be reassured that the person they loved more than anyone in the world was close and they had children from their marriage, people who looked like them, who would go on for them, who would own the earth and satisfy the longings which people had.

Emma got up and closed her door and then her curtains, but she could hear the distant irritating tinkle of laughter. The smell of good food wafted up the stairs and she had seen the champagne brought up from the cellar, the claret decanted, the best cutlery and china washed. She had caught a glimpse of a huge white linen cloth being thrown over the dining table.

After dinner there was music, as Verity played the piano. Emma could not help feeling satisfaction that Verity's playing was so bad. She stumbled through a Beethoven sonata which would have been so easy for Emma, but they applauded anyway because they were her friends. Though it was late when the guests left Emma lay awake in her bed, her stomach having somehow turned into a stone.

She was so upset that she did not sleep. If she had been married to the Judge they would have been there together, part of things. It was as if some tide were sending her irrevocably towards an old man and his brood of children. She thought of his bed and felt sick. Finally, when the dawn broke and somehow reassuringly the birds began their chorus, she fell into an uneasy sleep.

She could hear her mother calling to her in that beautiful accent: 'Bairnie, howay in now. Supper's on the stove.'

She could see the birds in the clear air around the house, swallows or house martins, they had sharp wings and sharper flights, they made a swirling eightsome around the place, wherever it was, they swooped and dived and went up again, managing to avoid one another as though it were a dance, intricate and never to be seen again. Nothing could be repeated.

She could see the land way behind the little village. The moors were covered in a velvet purple and everywhere there were enormous bees, the kind that did not sting, round and furry and buzzing loud, going about their business as they had done for hundreds of years.

It was warm though the sky had cleared and the cold was coming down with the evening and she was running down the road to meet her father as he came back for his tea. He was reaching down for her. They were going home.

She awoke and there was a feeling of loss as though her parents had been so close to her, but she could hear the morning sounds downstairs, she was back in her brother's house. She thought bitterly that that was what it was now: she had no place here. The only place she had was in Judge Philips' house.

She closed her eyes and tried to go back to sleep, but

she could not though her mother's voice and her father's presence stayed with her until she finally roused herself to go down to breakfast.

Her mother had been of Irish extraction. Nobody here had been told of that, she did not think Laurence knew of it. Their mother had been taken by her family to north-east England, where they had lived in poverty as iron-workers and coal-miners. Her parents had come from the same small area. They had met when her father was teaching at the university in Durham and her mother was very young. They went for picnics into Durham in the summer, made sandwiches and lemonade and sunned themselves on the riverbanks.

The Judge was invited to dinner; it was taken for granted that Emma had accepted his offer. He made a joke of asking her again in front of them. Her mouth was so stiff she could say nothing.

Emma watched him chewing his food. His teeth were mostly gone, those that were left were brown with age or black with decay, and his mouth opened so that you could see what he was eating, his tongue was coated yellow and the saliva in his mouth frothed. He drank so much that his cheeks went shiny red. He wheezed when he got up from his chair and his knees clicked because he was so overweight that they objected to carrying him.

Verity brought up the subject of the wedding, but the Judge said that was women's business and he would leave it all to them. Verity spoke to Emma later of how they would decide what sort of stuff she would want for her wedding dress and what kind of flowers would bloom. The Judge said that he had envisioned a wedding soon; he did not want to spend time idle while his bride-to-be lived just across the town.

When it was late Verity said she was going up to bed and Laurence called Emma, as she would have gone too, and they went into the library and he closed the door. Emma was surprised. Was he going to offer her a way out? Had he finally understood?

'I can see that you are worried about this marriage,' he said slowly. 'Is there something else in your life? Is there another man?'

Had Emma been in a different mood she would have laughed. How stupid. How could there possibly have been anyone? There was nothing in her life beyond the house and the garden and a child she considered hers. She would have settled for that, but it seemed that she was not allowed to.

'I thought for a moment that you were going to refuse the Judge, that you were going to take hysterics, and then I remembered how sensible you have always been and I'm proud of you. A hysterical woman is not something to be lightly considered. I know that Mabel Thomas was such a woman and we all know where she ended.'

Emma's breath was all over the place. Her brother was threatening her. Her hands trembled. Her whole body shook. Mabel Thomas was in an institution for the mentally ill. She had been forcibly married to a man three times

66

her age, whom she did not care for, and somewhere between the church and the bedroom she had screamed and thrown herself on the ground and was deemed to have lost her wits.

She had been eighteen and like a cow, Emma had always thought, was given by her parents to a man who had a great deal of money. There had been another man, Emma thought, though she didn't remember the details, and Mabel Thomas had not been allowed to see him again because he was young and poor. She was taken away in a locked carriage and gradually she had faded from people's memories.

'Marriage is right for you, Emma,' Laurence said, smiling a little. 'It is just that it has been such a long time in coming. You will become used to it in a short time; you will wonder why you had no husband and house of your own before this and then you will be happy. And in time you will learn to love and respect the Judge and his children.'

She said nothing, at least nothing she remembered afterwards. She made the kind of noises which her brother thought passed for compliance and then she wobbled her legs up to her bedroom, closed the door and leaned back against it.

'You must come and see the boys now that it is settled you will be their mama, and we will announce our intention to the world,' the Judge had said, and so she made a visit to his house. She had been there many times before, but she looked at it differently and was horrified when she could see herself there imprisoned as this man's wife and regarded as nothing more. Panic set in. She had to get away, she had to get out of here.

Emma could not think how to put any plan into action, she felt as though she had mud up to her neck and was about to be swallowed completely.

Verity insisted that she must have a new dress for the betrothal party, and Emma went along with the idea because she could not think of a single reason not to. In the meanwhile she told herself that if she did nothing she would become the Judge's wife because she had no means of leaving.

She had no money. With a jolt she realized that all she owned were her clothes and a few books which people had given her over the years as Christmas and birthday presents. She was trapped here, suffocating.

The Judge's six children were noisy and ran about unchecked every time she saw them. They ignored her as they ignored all adults, and the Judge, being a man who controlled things outside his home, did not strive to do so inside it, so that everything was turned upside down and in spite of the maids protesting, the boys ran in with filthy shoes, threw their clothes on the floor and turned up when they liked for meals. Emma almost regretted that she would not be there to bring order to such a place, and then she shivered for having even thought it.

Also it had not occurred to her that the Judge was mean. He did not buy her a betrothal gift of any kind, and a quick look at the household accounts showed her that he spent no penny he could avoid. So much for his ideas that she should have everything she wanted. Even her wedding ring was to be second-hand. The Judge boasted of how he had bought it very cheaply for such a good ring when he went into the jeweller's in town.

Verity seemed to think Emma would look her best in a white dress for her betrothal party. It wasn't actually white, it was cream, with horrid little pink flowers on it that not even an eighteen-year-old girl could have carried off, but Verity insisted and Emma was so distracted with the idea of not being able to get away and how tired she had become that she didn't care enough to argue.

On the night of the betrothal party, however, she saw herself in the mirror and thought how ghastly she looked. Verity gazed at her and frowned. 'You're very pale. Do you have any jewellery to go with the dress?'

'I have a string of pearls.'

They had been her mother's, but when she put them on they looked worn and old and yellowed, rather like she was.

'You can't wear those,' Verity objected, and she found some pearls which even Emma realized were expensive. 'They were my grandmother's. You will be careful with them, won't you? They are real.'

They were exquisite, large and had a diamond clasp, and there were pearl drops for her ears. Somehow, Emma thought, they made the dress look worse and herself look older, and as she saw the image in the mirror she thought that Verity had a great deal of jewellery, that her grandmother on her father's side had been a wealthy woman and Verity, being the only granddaughter, had inherited all of it. That was when Emma's face burned because she imagined how much money that jewellery was worth, and she dismissed the idea straight away but it came back later when she had had the congratulations of all the Judge's friends.

They were his age for the most, at least the men were. Several young women were his friends' second wives, and they all had babies. Most of them were having a child a year or every two years, and they also had their husband's children from his first marriage. They looked tired, were very quiet, and none of them seemed happy though they smiled and greeted one another gaily enough.

They were dowdy, the lot of them, she thought, as though they no longer cared about such frivolous things as dress. Their husbands ignored them, clustered together and talked business and smoked cigars and drank a great deal. Emma was inclined to drink a great deal too, but she was not offered of course – the ladies seemed to take nothing stronger than lemonade.

The Judge's house was large and the rooms were filled with dark clumsy-looking furniture. The maids slept in the attic in horrid bare little rooms which reminded Emma of the cottage. They must be freezing in winter and stifling in summer. The single beds were old, and there was something so awful about a single bed, she couldn't bear it. Emma was horrified. Her father would not have kept servants in such places. That was another thing she thought she might have achieved had she been staying: she would have fed them well and given them heated rooms and decent clothing and presents for their families, but it could not be enough to hold her – she could not give up her liberty even to save other women.

On the evening of their betrothal party the fires were small, the food was modest. Nobody else seemed to notice. Emma did not think she betrayed herself. Her brother came to her smiling and said he had known all along how sensible she would be, just as she had always been. He kissed her cheek, the first time she could ever remember. She wanted to scrub her face with nettles.

The party finished and they went home. She was first upstairs, wanting to rid herself of the stupid dress which made her look ridiculous. She thought of Verity's idea of her bridal gown covered in more roses and felt sick. She took off the pearls and the earrings and strode into her sister-in-law's bedroom to replace them. When she opened the top of Verity's lovely wooden jewellery box she was taken aback at the glitter of diamonds, rubies and emeralds.

She put down the pearls and then in her mind she saw herself taking the box itself and running away in the night, and just as she took the box in her hands the door opened and Verity came into the room. Emma put down the box very carefully.

'I have just put the pearls back.'

'My grandfather brought them from some far-flung place where the boys dived for them which is why they are all different. They mean a great deal to me.'

'But you have other jewellery which you wear.'

'It is all from my grandmother. She loved rubies and sapphires too, and I have a lovely diamond necklace which I never wear. It would be quite out of place in Mid Haven, but Laurence has promised to take me to Boston in the spring and there I will be able to buy new gowns to match. Such finery,' Verity said. 'You must come with us. The Judge I'm sure could take time away. We will go dancing and shopping and stay in a fashionable hotel. What do you think?'

It was the first time Verity had made her feel like an equal.

'It sounds perfect,' she said.

There was to be no sleep for Emma. She paced the floor, sat by the window watching for the dawn and wondering how she would live out her life in this place with these people. When the dawn finally came, she made up her mind. She must steal Verity's jewellery. All she had to do was walk into the room after she had packed a bag, secrete the box in her bag and leave.

She could not do it. There must be another way to come by sufficient money to get her out of here.

The following day she approached Laurence in his study. It was Saturday, he was working at his desk at home and she said that she needed some money. She did not like to ask, but there were some gifts she wished to buy for people who had been good to her. He looked puzzled and she hated that she had to ask, that he had not offered.

'I'm sure the Judge will be more than generous when

you marry. I have so many people to keep, I can't afford to be open-handed.'

Emma was stung. 'He has shown no signs of it so far,' she said, and then wished she hadn't.

Laurence frowned, but she was so angry that her cheeks burned. She felt she had put up with so much from Laurence lately.

'That would hardly be delicate.'

'I doubt anyone would call the Judge delicate.'

Laurence's face darkened and she thought how little he was like their father.

'Don't you remember what our parents were like?' she said, she didn't care now, she was beyond that. She wanted to try to summon any regard that he could ever have had for her; she wanted to probe beyond the distance where he had put himself. 'They were happy together. Do you really think I could be like that with a man twenty years older than I am?'

'I can't see what difference it makes.'

'How would you feel if Verity was sixty?'

'That's quite different.' He was not looking at her and his mouth had gone thin.

'And what is the difference?'

'I'm surprised you need to ask.'

'Tell me then.'

'I'm not going to do anything of the kind. You forget yourself.'

'You're the one who has forgotten,' she said. 'We used to talk about home—'

'This is the only home I know.'

'You treat George as though he doesn't matter because he's Irish, yet our mother was Irish, Kathleen McLoughlin.'

Laurence's eyes blazed though he said nothing, and that was the first time that Emma thought they had eyes the same colour, deep green like emerald fire.

'Her parents left Ireland for a better life, just like our parents left Durham, to make things better for us.'

'And they did,' Laurence said.

'And now you're destroying what there is between us by insisting I marry that old man.'

There was silence. Emma was stunned at herself. What on earth was she doing, challenging her brother like this? She wanted to run from the room, she wanted to cry, ached to, or at least move her gaze from his, but she wouldn't let herself; she held his eyes with her own.

'I have insisted on nothing,' he said softly. 'I'm trying to help you, I'm a better man than my father.'

Emma wanted to hit him.

'How could you say such a thing?'

'Because it's true. He was never as good as you thought he was.'

'What do you mean?'

'I went through all his papers after he died and some of them made very pretty reading. Believe me, Emma, I want you to marry a good man who will look after you.'

'What papers? Where are they?' Emma was reminded of the last conversation she had had with her father. She had not forgotten what he had said about wishing that he had behaved differently.

'I burned them.'

'You're a liar!'

He moved. She thought he was going to come around the desk and hit her for the first time since they had been small children, and she thought at that point if she had moved too, if she had shown fear of any kind, he might have done it, but she stood there.

Nobody said anything for so long that Emma began to tremble. She couldn't control it, her whole body was in shock. He picked up a pen and threw it down again and he looked at it and at the desk and then back at her and he said quite clearly, 'I have never lied to you, whatever you think of me. I burned the papers because I didn't want you to find them. I didn't want you to know what kind of a man he was and I wasn't ever going to tell you, and even though you accuse me of awful things now I won't.'

'Why not? Why should you try to shield me from the truth if you think it's so, and what kind of being do you think I am that you should take from me the right to know?'

'Because I care for you,' he said, and that was when Emma cried.

Emma was even more angry now and determined to leave. Laurence had treated her like a possession, like something he could control, and he had talked of their father in that awful way. She thought how happy they had been as children and she wondered how he could do such a thing. She had made him angry and he had not cared what he did or said.

The next day she went into Verity's bedroom and lifted the lid on the jewellery box. Verity did not even lock it or put away the valuable things. She had so much trust, and why should she not? There was little enough crime in New Haven, no one had much worth stealing. When the people went out to church they did not lock their doors.

There was a further problem. Such distinctive pieces would surely arouse suspicion should she try to sell them locally, yet what else could she do?

Frustration became her main mood. Emma put the pearls from her mind, but the idea surfaced again when she went to bed. She could not steal from her family. Her worse self told her that they had stolen from her – her house, her future even. That was petty, she argued. She fell into a doze about an hour before they usually got up and it was as if the almost sleepless night had made all the difference. When she awoke from this doze she could see everything clearly before her. She had no alternative; they had left her none. She waited until Laurence had gone to work, until Verity was gone to the shops with a brief goodbye, and then she went upstairs.

Emma could not believe the person who picked up the pearls. Further over on the window ledge was a box into which Laurence emptied the loose change from his pockets, and since there was a good pile she took that too. She stowed the pearls in the bottom of her suitcase and she put only what was really necessary on top, a few clothes, fewer books, her mother's pearls, she didn't see the irony quite, and then she left. It would be some time before they knew she was gone. Verity was going to have lunch with some friends and she would no doubt stay there half the afternoon, gossiping. The roads were dry and the streets were deserted. She took the first train to Boston which was the nearest place she could take a ship for England.

Boston was so big that it frightened her, but she found her way to George's school and her heart lifted. She longed to see him, he came home for such short periods and no matter what she said or did he had nothing to say. Things would be different now, Emma thought resolutely.

The school was a lovely place as schools go. It was laid out on generous grounds, the campus covering a large hill. The buildings were grey and there were plenty of grassy places for the children to play games.

She was directed to the principal's office and impressed upon him that she would very much like to see her nephew, she had come so far and indeed his aunt was very ill and one could not say such things in a letter. The principal was all kindness, yes of course she must spend the rest of the day with George and bring him back after tea.

The boy who came into the principal's office was almost a stranger: taller, thinner, he looked older and his face was set. He did not smile or look anxious or seem pleased to see her. He mumbled some form of greeting and did not look her in the face. It was as though he had become resigned to his fate and no longer cared. He was not interested in why she was there, perhaps she had just wanted to see him, such things did happen at prep schools, she knew.

The principal said little except that he would expect George back at six. Emma was euphoric for a few moments. The minute they were outside and walking past the triangle of grass towards the school gates George stopped. He looked away at the playing fields.

And then he said suddenly, but with vehemence, 'I wish you hadn't come here. It makes it worse. I'm in trouble all the time. I hate team games and I hate math and—'

'George—'

Still he didn't look at her. 'I would rather have been in that awful little cottage than here, at least I would have been with you, but I can't because my Aunt Verity wrote and told me you're going to marry that smelly old man and I'm to be sent to live with other people. I knew how it would be. I just wish you hadn't come, that's all, because I already know and I don't want any tea and you can just go home and marry that – that fat old bastard and I don't care. I'll go and live with other people and I hope I never see you again!'

Bastard was the worst word he could think of, she knew. He was trying to shock her, and suddenly he was all child, he didn't look so big or so old. He was about to run from her, she thought she heard the intake of breath that was almost a sob and he lowered his eyes as children do when they are about to cry, so she said quickly, 'I'm not going to marry him.'

George didn't look hopeful, he didn't even look up.

'I'm not going to live in the cottage either.'

That was when he looked at her, light beginning to dawn in his eyes which still gleamed with unshed tears.

'I hope you didn't leave anything valuable when we came out because you're not coming back here. We're going to run away.'

He didn't believe her, she could see for a few seconds, and then he looked dubiously at her. 'How can we do that and where to?'

'We're going to England, to where I was born, to find my family, to some kind of life which will suit us better than this.'

George hesitated for just a second. 'Let's get out of here,' he said.

She booked them into a small hotel. They did not eat in the dining room where she thought a single woman and a boy might be remarked upon; they walked a long way before they found a tea room, and there they had sandwiches and cake. She only hoped she had sufficient money to get them to where they were going.

She had worried about it, had carried the pearls in her pocket onto the train, but she might just as well have had a sign which read 'I have stolen jewels from my brother and his wife', she was so certain it was obvious on her face, but nobody noticed. That was the thing about trains:

nobody looked at you, nobody talked to you, nobody saw anything or anyone. Nobody heard how hard her heart beat, so that her heart and the train went together, and that in the end was comforting.

She was a different woman by the time she got to Boston and its intricate streets, by the time she had gone into the first jeweller's and told them a story about her husband dying: 'I need to sell these, they belonged to my grandmother.' She offered the pearls and saw greedy eyes.

She came out of the shop when he made her a low offer. She walked a long way before she came to another jeweller, and this time she was more nervous than she had been with the first because his response was the same: he offered her a small sum. Despairing, she almost came out of the shop, but as she opened the door to leave he called her to come back and then he said apologetically, 'I am sorry, ma'am, I did not realize how fine they were and I could give you a little more.'

He had a better face than the first man, she thought, or perhaps it was just that she needed him to be a finer man.

'They're valuable, I know they are.'

'You'll find with jewellery that when you buy it it's expensive; when you sell it back to a jeweller it's worth very little.'

'I could go to a pawnbroker.'

He shook his head. 'You wouldn't do as well.'

'I need the money and I will find someone who will pay,' she said, and he looked at her once again and then he went into the back of the shop and came out and he counted out the money in front of her.

She wasn't sure whether it was enough, but what could she do? She thought he was right and that everyone would cheat her and the more desperate she looked the worse it would be. She picked up the money, stuffing it into her purse.

'I am only trying to make a living,' he said, and she heard the accent and looked harder at him.

'Are you English?'

'Irish.'

'So am I.'

He looked her up and down and she said, 'My mother's family were from Derry, but they went to England to try and better themselves.'

'So many do,' he said, 'but we both made it to the New World.'

She managed to ask directions and discovered where the Cunard offices were, and it was only when they reached them that she was intimidated. They looked luxurious, all mahogany and brass, and inside everything was hushed. When she went further in people were being attended to by smartly dressed men behind huge desks; when her turn came and the man smiled politely at her she wanted to get up and run. She asked the prices, she asked when the next ship was sailing, and then she excused herself. She hurried George outside.

'We can't do this. It will take almost everything we

have. There'll be nothing for us to start again.'

George looked down. 'We can't go back to Mid Haven and I'm not going back to that school. I'll run away. I'll get myself to England if I have to,' he said, and she began to regret that she had brought him up to behave this way, to argue like a lawyer, to think like an adult. It was not what she had intended.

She wanted to cry. Her eyes smarted and the pavement was cold and the streets were dark and narrow. It began to rain, cold and hard, icy on her face; it was relentless. Whatever had she been thinking of to bring them here? All she had thought of was getting away. Practicalities had not come into it.

The evening was getting darker and colder. She turned around and went back inside the Cunard offices. She saw then that her decision was made, that she had done the first thing in her life that she knew to be wrong. It was already too late.

The ships were pictured, hung up all around the room, and had wonderful names. Theirs was called *The Saxonia* and was sailing to Liverpool in three days' time.

They would go third class; she would keep as much of her money as she could. She agreed. They went back outside. The night had cleared, the stars would soon be out. She turned away. She felt like an entirely different person from the one who had left Mid Haven. She would never be the same again.

The ship was enormous, she had not expected it to be frightening and it should not have been, she reasoned.

People were walking towards it and suitcases were on trolleys and those helping were milling about. She breathed freely for the first time in months and then, just as she was about to go aboard, she heard her name spoken behind her and her heart did horrible icy cartwheels. She dragged George back so that he complained, and when he was completely shielded only then did she turn to face her brother.

'I knew I would find you here,' he said. 'I should have known, I should never have told you about the papers I found. How predictable you are, Emma, running for home from the nearest port on the first ship.'

He had never seemed quite this big before and he made her feel like a criminal, and then she remembered that she was, and she didn't know what to say.

All she managed with trembling breath was, 'I can't go through with this marriage, Laurence.'

He said nothing and then she collected herself rather better and knew that there was little to lose in honesty now.

'First of all you took our family home, then you sent George away to school, and finally you would have liked me to be gone from your sight in that awful damp little cottage. Couldn't you bear the sight of me?' Again he said nothing; he watched her as though she was talking in a different language.

'And then the Judge. Dear God, Laurence, did you really think I would let you do that to me?'

She waited longer this time and her eyes were searching his face.

'I did the best I could.'

'You didn't want me in your house. Did it not occur to you that my happiness might be important?'

'Duty must come first.'

'Really? Then where was your duty to me?'

'I thought I'd done it, I thought your independence was enough if you couldn't marry and then when you had such a good offer of marriage, I assumed that was what every woman wanted.'

'To a man of her own age whom she loves.'

He shook his head and didn't look at her any more. Then he smiled. 'Does anyone truly love in marriage? It's all there is for women.'

'No!' Emma hadn't realized she had spoken so loudly until people around them broke off conversations and stopped moving to listen. 'I won't have that. It's not good enough.'

'I see.' He was so quiet that Emma was even more afraid and she could feel George close in against her back as though he were afraid he would be dragged back to school if he moved even an inch.

'You didn't believe me when I said I hadn't lied,' Laurence said. 'You can't go to England: there is nothing there any more. All you have is here. I haven't told anybody that you've left, I told Verity that George hadn't been well and you had insisted on going to see him. I told her that I had taken her pearls to be cleaned. She was more worried about the damage that would be done to them than anything else. Do you still have them?'

'Of course not. How do you think I got this far?'

Laurence stood like a waxwork, he was so pale. Emma did not remember ever having seen him so upset.

'I can't believe you stole from us, your family.'

'There was nothing else to do.'

'I haven't told anyone that you ran away and if you come back now no one need ever know. I'll make up some kind of story about the pearls and you can marry the Judge as planned and George can go back to school—'

There was a muffled sound of despair from behind Emma and George pressed himself into her back and put his arms around to her front so that she doubted she could move even if she chose to.

'Please come back.'

She could not believe that her brother was begging her and then she saw that he did not want his name tarnished, that he did not want the town to know that she had run from him and from Verity and from a whole way of life, and that he would have to go back and tell them.

'I can't do that,' she said.

'I can't believe you would be so irresponsible as to do this,' he said. 'There's nobody left in England. You have no money. How on earth will you survive?'

Laurence looked around him as though help would appear from nowhere or as though somebody was waiting to grab her and the boy. Emma stepped back. George automatically did so too.

At that moment she sensed a presence behind her.

George let go. She turned around. The man was wearing naval uniform.

'We are leaving soon, Madam. You must come aboard.'

'I'll be moments,' she said, and suddenly she felt righteous, gleeful.

Laurence was pressing his lips together as though he would have liked to have said a lot more but was resisting. 'You can't do this to us, Emma, and you can't take George into that damned wilderness. You can't condemn him to poverty. Here he would have education and opportunity. Have you not given any thought to that? Come along now. I've bought tickets for you both. We could be home before dark.'

What a lovely thing to say, it was the kind of thing her father had said, but he had not used it like this, he had not tried to persuade her to go back to a life she could not stand. She had to remind herself then that she had been right to leave because under Laurence's gaze and his lawyer's constructive argument her mind was wavering.

Laurence gazed at the officer and he hesitated, but as Emma tried to turn and follow him Laurence said, 'She's not going anywhere,' and he tried to get hold of her arm.

In that moment all Emma knew was that she needed to be free. She tried to drag her arm from his hold and when he didn't let go she protested and the officer came back.

'Is this your husband, madam?'

'No, of course he isn't. I'm Miss Emma Appleby. If you look down at your passenger list you will see it and I have the papers to prove it if you care to look.'

'Is there a problem?'

'No.'

'Yes, 'Laurence said. 'This woman is running away. I am her brother and have come to take her home. I'm sure you wouldn't stand in my way.'

The man considered for a second and then he said, 'The tickets are paid for, sir. Her papers were checked and everything was made right at the Cunard office and the lady has the freedom to come on board if she so chooses.'

'I do,' Emma said, having finally wrestled her arm free.

George was standing well away towards the ship and she knew there was no chance that he would agree to go back.

'I'm going,' she said.

'Very well then,' Laurence said. 'Go to England, and when you get there remember what I said because you will want to come back to your family, you will long for your home so much, and you will realize how stupid and foolish you have been and you will regret everything that you have done.'

The tears which had been so long in coming filled Emma's eyes and began to spill over. 'If we had not been from the same family we could never have been friends. Why don't you go home to your wife and children and your wonderful life and leave me to what I am trying for? I know that you never loved me even though I wanted you to so much. Goodbye, Laurence.'

Then she turned from him and marched George before her on to the ship. She didn't look back.

6

Mick got used to going home to no dinner, the cold rooms and the way that Isabel had stopped doing anything in the house. He employed various maids, but they would only stay for a few weeks at the most. Isabel had taken to living in the sitting room and drinking all day.

He decided to find out definitely where she was getting the spirits from. He remembered what Ed had told him about leaving things as they were, but he felt as if he had to do something; he needed to know what was going on.

He watched her carefully: it wasn't difficult any more, she so rarely went anywhere, but he had to keep a close eye on things now and he knew when she left the house in the late morning. She wore a hat with a veil and he suspected something which hid the wearer's face.

She was fairly sober at that time as she had not yet begun the afternoon drinking session, and he watched her from a distance. She went around the town, not through it; she followed the road which led almost to the fell and then, with a quick glance, to make sure no one was watching, she went swiftly in at the side door of the Red Lion. It was a farmers' pub: a lot of the local men who owned small businesses went there as it served good food. It was owned by a man named Henry Atkinson.

There was nobody about. Mick slid in after her, hovering there by the door in the cold, draughty passage, listening to the loud voices. It was market day, the day of the week when the farmers came in to go to the local mart where sheep and cattle were sold, and where they paid their accounts and met up and talked about the prices and the government, and where they would sit down to eat pies and peas and drink beer.

She could not have gone in there, into any of the doors which led to the various rooms, and so he reasoned she must have gone upstairs. He watched the narrow steps disappear into the soft gloom and then very slowly he followed because there was nothing to dull the sound of his tread. When he reached the landing the doors were closed. There was a thick carpet all the way along the hall which muffled his footsteps. He stood quite still.

There was soft conversation and chuckles of laughter, and he froze. He could hear his wife's voice, noises from her such as he hadn't heard before, keening, a kind of moaning and a man's voice urging her, or himself, on.

Mick wanted to burst into the room in rage; later he didn't know how he had stopped himself, and he only just held back as though there were a brick wall between himself and the room and not just a stout door. He couldn't help remembering the words that Ed had told him, that it would not help for him to know. Ed had been right.

Only a stupid man would force the door, only a man who had lost complete control would part them amidst his wife's whimpering and grab the person whom he could blame for what was happening and choke the very life from him. And then what? Would he kill her? Would he beat her senseless? Would he be able to explain to his daughter what he had done? Would he be able to explain to the law? What would be left? It was too late for anything like that, and he had known it for a long time.

He pictured his daughter. If he went in there now it would be because of his pride and not for any useful purpose, and it would make things worse. Telling himself that almost made him laugh – the idea that things could be any worse. The truth was that they had so obviously been this bad for a very long time and it was only that he had not discerned it. He was ashamed.

His wife had gone to another man for what he could not give her, and there was nothing he could do. This was not something which was happening for the first time; it sounded familiar, regular, everyday almost, gleeful, confident, and that was the worst thing about it. This was not a special event, it happened all the time.

Her voice was lifting now, she was beginning to beg and after it to make soft and then louder noises of slow gratification. She was enjoying herself, she was being satisfied in a lingering way as though it were what she lived for.

Had Isabel's guilt sent her to drink? Could she not live with the person that she was, with the person who would do this, who could not help it? Did the drink soften the idea of her betrayal? Could she excuse herself somewhere in the middle of the brandy haze? He understood now at least in part. His wife was living lies and two lives which she could not reconcile.

He slid down the wall. Suddenly there was nothing but the floor; he needed something to hold him, something to gather him to it, and the soft flowered carpet eased him.

She had never done this in their bed, even in the first days when he had loved her so much and physicality was everything. She had not taken on that tuneful yearning noise, that tone of ecstasy and lust: she had been young, eager, funny, and it was lighter than this. He had thought she was happy with him. He had thought what happened between them was wonderful, but it was not this. It was love. He didn't think this could be said to be love. It was something quite different.

Down on the floor, listening to her voice lifting and then screaming with pleasure, Mick felt the tears run down his face. How surprising. He had not cried when his mother had died, he had not cried when his father had died, and now, when he was realizing that his wife did not care for him, perhaps never had, because he could not do this to her, had not even done this in the time when Connie was conceived, he was crying. He was not a man, he was just a thing, left outside and unwanted. Had she ever really wanted him? Did she want this man or was it brandy she wanted, vodka, the sweet never-to-be land that gloated and tempted and was always there in pink hues of cloud above the ground?

It sounded so real, the screaming now; it went on and on and the man's voice still soft as though he were in control. This man knew what to do as other men did not and Mick had a horror that people could be held to such things.

He thought he would never forget the screams of his wife in ecstasy. He couldn't move, he sat there as though nobody would come out of the room, as though his child would not come home, as though his wife would not return, and in some ways she had left forever.

The tears had turned into grateful sobs beyond the door, though they were quiet as they must. Why must they? Nobody should know, it was too shameful. She did not love him, maybe she never had loved him, he was not worthy, he was not adequate, he had spoiled her life, taken something from her which she needed and this was the result. She could not help it, he felt sure.

When the screaming had stopped, when it had slowed and taken on the music of satisfaction, of completeness, there was laughter again and finally silence. And after that he heard the man's voice. He did not know him well, but they had met occasionally through business and possibly, he could remember now, socially. It was Henry Atkinson, who had clipped, almost aristocratic tones such as northern people did not have. He was from a good family, moneyed business people. How long had Isabel loved this man? How long had she been giving herself to him so completely?

He was older of course, he was married and he had

several children as far as Mick could remember. He was educated, erudite, even said to be fascinating. Mick had been at one or two dinners when he had spoken; he had been charming and was held in high esteem by powerful men in the area.

His wife's family had also been wealthy and respected; Mick could remember seeing Henry's wife, middle-aged but slim and fair-haired, pale-skinned and blue-eyed. She must have been incredibly beautiful at twenty because she fairly took your breath away now: a sweet mouth and gleaming white teeth and a perfect skin. Her shoulders were pearly, she wore an expensive gown, her lovely throat and neck glittered with diamonds and she was talking to all the right people. He had never met her socially, he was very far below them, had seen them almost from afar, had kept within his own circle.

Mick stood up, managed to get to the stairs, he even got down them without much noise though he doubted anybody would have noticed, so caught up in the sublime minutes after sex were they. He got out of the building and was fine. He didn't even need to take deep breaths. He understood now.

He waited across the street, just down the side of the alley. When she came out she went into the street and up the road and into a perfectly respectable off-licence. She came out with a bag – not a big bag, just large enough to hold two or three bottles of spirits. Why had he thought she had to go to a pub for such things? There were several places which would sell her spirits and think nothing about it, and enough of them so nobody would think there was anything untoward. He went to the school gates much too early and again Connie was not there and he went home and waited.

Isabel came back, but she didn't come upstairs; she went into the sitting room and began drinking. He found Connie later on, in a nearby barn with a book. She greeted him as though this happened every day.

'Oh Daddy,' she said, 'I'm reading about King Arthur and his knights of the round table and about Guinevere. I don't think very much of her, do you? It's so obvious that Lancelot is not the sort of person you would marry. I would have stayed with Arthur if it had been me.'

He gathered her to him and it was not for her, he thought with dismay, it was for himself. He held her there until she complained. He heard the bright brittle note in her voice. She did not know what was going on, she only knew that things were not as they should be in her young life.

Together they went back to the house. Isabel was drunk by then. He made a meal for them with what he could find and he took Connie up to bed. He read to her and when she fell asleep he went back to the pub. There he took a bottle of whisky into the office with him. How pathetic that he should employ the same kind of means as Isabel did to keep himself sane.

Ed came to him. Mick's hands shook, he couldn't even pour out the first glass of whisky. He watched like somebody detached as the golden liquid flowed over both sides

94

of the glass and his hands shook so much that he couldn't stop. Ed, horrified, watched and put out both hands.

'Come here, I'll do it. You're spillin' it, yer clown.'

Never had Ed spoken to him like that, so gently, as if he were a child. Ed took the glass and the bottle from him. He handed the glass to Mick who downed it quickly. Ed poured him another.

When Ed came back, much later, he looked at the second drink he had poured. It was almost untouched. That was one thing that was good, Mick thought savagely: he himself would never take to drink in a big way.

He went outside for the air. Nell Whittington, the local whore, was still hanging around. He could see her standing back in the shadows, but there was a half moon and the twisted curl of her hair gave her away.

'Come in,' he offered. It was a cold night, but she hesitated.

'I need to make some money.'

'I'll give you some money.'

'I don't want no charity,' she said.

'Oh howay,' he said.

She had been a pretty woman once, but disappointment and loss and the deep lines in her face made her well past forty-five and he didn't think she could be older than that.

He took her through into the office, sat her down, found another glass and poured generously. She looked at it.

'You in need of company?'

He nodded.

Nell drank her whisky, looked doubtfully at the money he took from his pocket. 'You want me?'

He hated to offend her. 'Nell—'

'All right,' she said, and he even thought he heard relief as he pressed the coins into her hand.

'How are the bairns?' he said.

She looked severely at him. 'You know they're fine, you're always asking our Larry and givin' him money and drink for nowt.'

'Do you wish I wouldn't?'

'Nay, I don't wish nothin', at least nothing you can do.'

He wished there was some other way he could provide for them which was less clumsy than this. It was quite a lot, at least she would think it was a lot, she wouldn't think it was guilt money either because he had always thought he should help her more, it was just that somehow he couldn't help everybody.

'I don't want it.'

'Oh, take it, for God's sake, it makes me feel better.'

She shook her head and laughed a bit.

He said, and softly, 'Have you ever had a man that you really liked?'

Nell stared at him. 'You mean close like?'

'Aye.'

'Nay, savin' your presence, you're all bastards really.'

When he laughed and didn't reply she smiled.

Mick laughed more and shook his head. Nell watched him. 'Your wife, she's beautiful.'

'Aye.' He stared down into his whisky and he had the

feeling that Nell understood completely without him saying more. 'We didn't know, either of us, that there is no such thing as love. Only for our bairns. She's a grand little lass is yours, different though.' She got up.

'You want more whisky? Something to eat?'

'No, thanks.'

Her husband had died down the pit and was blamed, and she got no money for it. Instead she left her children with her drunken brother at night and gave herself to the men as they came out of the pubs. What else could she do? Take in washing? Scrub floors? What was the difference but for pride? Whoring paid better, he knew, and she had two children and a leaking roof in the windswept little house at Road Ends where there was nothing to stop the howling winds from the fell. Her husband had been no good, had beaten her when she wouldn't let him touch the children; her brother was a drunk. She had been so pretty, so fresh and young.

'Nell—' He stopped there, he didn't want to insult her because he liked her, she was doing her best.

She hesitated by the door. 'I know.' She looked hard at him. 'We go on but we want to scream. You do a lot for me. If you get fed up you know where I am.'

She was right, he had lost hope that night and a lot of other things as well. He went home eventually, as he must because of Connie and Ulysses, who had stayed at the house that day, and Hector, glad at last that he had given up his watch at the pub, sighed as they walked, knowing that he would be back to the house and all would be well and he would see Ulysses and there would be comfort, a fire, warmth and a rug. Only there wasn't any more, and Mick didn't care somehow.

The dog sighed again when they got there. The house was cold and it looked unfriendly. No fire burned, no supper was ready. The kitchen was undisturbed and Connie was in bed. Isabel of course was drunk. He left her on the floor in the living room and went to bed.

After that the world narrowed and was strange, as if it were all happening to somebody else. He could not keep the house and the pub and the child and everything working and going round and round as life should. He kept falling over himself and his grief until all he could do was go to work and make sure Connie had something to eat.

It was as if Isabel died that winter and with her all his hopes and dreams. The future had gone away, there was nothing on offer except to get up every morning and try to keep his life turning, his child by him.

Connie, in unspoken agreement always went back to the house after school now, as though she knew he could not stand any more. He didn't want it that way, but it was all there was.

He couldn't bear to see the house as it had been. He neglected it. He ignored the garden, he watched in some satisfaction as the lawns became meadows, as the fields around it grew and were empty, as the house decayed and was thick with dust and his wife slipped further and further into the land of lost hope and he into despair.

He kept up a lilting voice for his child, but he knew that he didn't deceive her.

It was as though his child was alone when she came home from school, so he left a dog there. At night, while Mick worked in the office and drank whisky slowly, Hector would nudge a warm moist nose into his hand. It was all the pleasure that Mick had. When he heard the thumping of the dog's tail it lifted his heart just a little. Hector was always there, as Ed was always there, except that Ed went off to his little house a couple of doors away for sleep and sustenance, if he ever ate anything, which Mick doubted.

Ed's gift to him was constancy. Nothing else got done. Somehow Mick didn't want the women there who cleaned; he couldn't stand it. The house and the pub sank beneath the weight of his sadness and nothing came to alleviate it.

7

TOW LAW TOWN, 1906

At first Emma had faltered. The journey had been so long and every day she had told herself a hundred times that this was a very bad mistake and she would end up going back to New England and admitting that she was wrong and marrying Judge Philips, though now that Laurence had gone back and told his tale the Judge would not have her, the town would never accept her. These thoughts had driven her on. There was no going back. She was three thousand miles away, across an ocean. There was some relief in that.

George had spent the days on board ship running about the decks with other children and getting to know the crew so that they called him by name. He ate hungrily and slept well and was a good sailor. When they landed in England and boarded a train he was up at the window most of the time in case he should miss anything which they passed. It was all new and he was determined not to miss a second of it.

A savage wind bit her ankles as Emma got down from the train, holding George's hand so tightly that he objected.

'Is there a hotel?' she asked the stationmaster.

'There's nowt like that here, lass,' the stationmaster said.

She didn't know what to do now. They had eaten sparingly for days. All she had left were her mother's pearls and in the end she knew she would pawn or sell them, but she did not know what awaited her so she had clung to the comforting idea that she still had funds.

She had thought Liverpool was a lot nearer than it was. It was meant to be in the north but this place was a lot further north, not so very far from the border with Scotland and on the opposite side of the country. She had forgotten or not known any English geography.

She had finally reached her destination and it was indeed the very middle of nowhere. There was nothing for miles but this little town. It should have been spring, but showed no signs of such. When they had stepped from the train a keen biting wind was hurling big flakes of snow about. She could not believe she had been so stupid as to bring George to this godforsaken place.

'We need somewhere to stay,' she said to the stationmaster, but even as she spoke he had turned his back and was walking away.

She was beginning to feel that she had come here for no better reason than her own stupid will. The voices from the past which had urged her were silent now, making her feel foolish, making her panic. Her memories did not include this windswept road. Had she come to the wrong town? It was nothing more than a few streets set on a bleak hillside, the houses small, shabby, badly built, crouched low there as though trying to get beneath the bad weather. The main street was wide and an icy wind rushed through as though it could not wait to get to the moors. Surely she had not been born here? But her memory told her that she had.

The station was deserted. She could not stand here any longer. It was growing colder and the light had already faded from the day. She picked up her bags and began walking in what she thought was the direction of town. The street was flat where she stood and the railway crossing was at the bottom of it. On either side the street rose sharply into hills and there were houses snaking up it and public houses, lit up. She thought she should go and enquire about a room, but men hung around the outside of most of these establishments in spite of the weather as though they did not get to spend much time outside, and she dared not approach them.

She thought about how her window at home looked out at the street and the trees and the white wooden houses. Here tiny terraced houses ran for as far as she could see down the main street and around the corner, away out of the small town. The other way the houses stretched off down a hill. The afternoon was turning into evening and little rooms were dimly lit. Net curtains were drawn across the windows and other curtains on top to keep out the draughts no doubt, she thought.

She began to walk up the main street and along it. It wasn't busy. Most sensible people were inside and she was so chilled that she longed to join them. George was beginning to falter beside her. She must find some place for them to stay and soon, yet she continued to walk. Finally she came to where the road turned and there on the corner was a big well-lit building. The sign read The Black Diamond.

Emma gathered what courage she had left, took George's hand for comfort and ventured inside. The smell was the first thing that hit her, the smoke of cigarettes and a fire, stale beer fumes sour-sweet and unwashed bodies. The second thing was that it was busy, full of men. They lined the place like wallpaper; they stood, lounged, took their ease, yet few of them were sitting. They wore grimy caps and their faces were creased and either pale or dirty. They smoked and they had big glasses in their work-worn hands.

They were intent on the conversation and at first they ignored her. She moved beyond the hallway and into the room on the right. Men sat at small round tables playing dominoes and a fire beckoned, though she could see it only beyond their legs. The air was grey-blue with smoke, almost orange with tobacco fumes, and the smell of beer was thick enough to choke you. As she left the doorway and moved nearer to the bar the conversation became less of a hum and more of a broken rhythm.

The men were not like those she knew. Their upper bodies were well developed, their lower bodies less so; they were mainly short in stature. They wore old suits, the material tired and in some cases mended or in holes.

A well-built oldish man standing behind the bar was staring at her.

'You cannot come in here, love,' he said in a low, almost embarrassed, voice.

Emma took a deep breath amid the silence. 'Do you have rooms?'

He went on looking at her, but perplexed now. 'Nay, lass,' he said.

Somebody laughed.

'Aw, give the lass a room, Ed,' some wit ventured. 'We could take turns.'

Emma understood the implication immediately and her face burned, but nobody laughed. What a strange code they had. It wasn't polite to say such things in front of a woman, he had gone too far. The barman didn't look at her and all the noise died. Even the fire was silenced. And then somebody said, 'Shite, Bill, bugger off,' and the tension was released.

'I will pay,' she said.

He shook his head and went back to polishing glasses as he had been doing when she first came in. Emma looked helplessly around her.

'You can come home with me, pet,' somebody said, and they all laughed.

Then somebody else said, 'Why lad, she's old enough to be thee mother. Leave the woman alone.'

'Isn't this a hotel?' she said loudly to gain the barman's attention.

'It's a public house,' Ed said.

George's fingers tightened. He was very tired.

'Are you the owner?' she said.

'I'm just the bar keep.'

'I'd like to see the owner. Is he here?'

Ed looked at her and there was bitter humour in his eyes and the way that his mouth straightened. 'Mr Castle doesn't see people, love.'

'Tell him I would like to see him. Now,' she said.

'He—'

'Now,' Emma insisted.

The man didn't look up. He disappeared into the back and conversation started around her again. She could hear the clack of dominoes, even the fire burning. The men turned their backs as though she was not there, as though they had been at some kind of concert and the entertainment was over.

It was a short while, though it seemed longer, until Ed came back and then he beckoned her beyond the bar and out of the room and down a dark hall and finally into the light, into a room where a good fire burned. He went out and shut the door behind him and Emma felt trapped for a few seconds. Then she put down the bags that she was still carrying, that she had carried for so very long, and she eased her fingers against the pressure that was gone, and suddenly she was grateful for George, who was standing as tall as he could.

It was a very small room and there was not much in it but a desk, a chair, a fire and lights and a man sitting behind the desk. That was all. Emma had never seen such a bare room. It was very odd. It was so obviously an office.

There was a large bureau, but there was not even another chair, as though he never had visitors or as though nobody was ever asked to sit down. How odd, she thought. A pool of lamplight covered the desk and he was writing, though he looked up after Ed had gone, after the door was closed.

He sat back in his chair, the pen still in his hand as though it were a permanent fixture. He was not old because his skin, beneath several days' dark growth of beard, was smooth, his hair was thick and black and fell forward, but his eyes were dulled and half closed as though she had suddenly lit too many lamps, almost colourless and certainly lacking in expression.

It was strange, but somehow he looked timeless, as if he had lived a great deal and cared for little of it. He was very thin and his shabby clothes hung off him as if he were poor or simply didn't consider food or dress important. She thought he might be tall, but it was difficult to tell when he was sitting and she was standing. She couldn't help but think little of his terrible manners, that he didn't get up or offer her a seat, but then why should she expect such things in a backwater such as this? Normal rules did not apply. He didn't look at her as one or two of the men had. There was nothing lascivious about it, he just considered her.

'What are you doing here?' he said, with the emphasis on the 'you', as though he could not understand her presence. For the first time Emma remembered the way that her mother and father had spoken. There was a lilt to his accent that she had missed all her life since losing them.

His voice was the voice of the fells, the sound of her childhood; it was the wind in the trees and the smell of the heather and the song of the moors, something indefinable, something sweet.

You're tired, she told herself.

'I need somewhere to stay.'

He sat back in his chair and the light hit his face, and Emma thought she had rarely seen such a closed expression. Then she noticed the cigarette burning in the ashtray and the whisky in the glass and a bottle, half empty, nearby on the desk.

When he didn't say anything Emma, trying to be brisk, said, 'It's a very big place, you must have rooms.' Even she could hear the desperation in her voice.

He shook his head.

She wished she could have cleared her throat. This man didn't know how bad things were, that she had very little money and could go no further. She couldn't let him turn her away. 'Anything would do. Please.'

'We don't let rooms. There's nothing suitable upstairs, it's all a mess. You'll find somewhere but there's nowt here. It's a tip, and as for the rest of it . . . Nobody could stay here, it isn't fitting.'

'It's a blizzard out there, so I don't have much choice, Mr—?'

'Castle. You are?'

'Emma Appleby. I need a room. George is very tired and so am I.'

'You can't stay here.'

'I will not go on.'

He sat back in his chair. 'What on earth are you doing here? Are you American? You sound it.'

'I come from New England. I want to find my family.'

'You're a very long way from home.'

'This is my home, Mr Castle.'

He smiled and it reminded her of Laurence, it was such a cynical grimace. 'Nobody wants to call this place home. It's the kind of place people live when they have no alternative.'

'And what makes you think I have an alternative?'

'You need to find one. I'm sorry but we don't have rooms to let. It's just a pub and I have a lot of work to do as you can see. Goodnight, Mrs Appleby. I wish you luck.'

'It's Miss,' Emma said, but he didn't seem to hear.

He had dismissed her. He went back to writing. She could see that the barman had been correct, this man was not interested, he did not care what happened to her as long as he didn't have to deal with it.

She turned around and dragged George out and then as she reached the hall she stopped. There was a narrow passage which led out the back way or the bigger hall which led to the front. She could hear the men laughing and talking. She did not know what they were saying, she didn't understand and she didn't care.

There was the back door beyond that she could leave by, or she could go out the front. In the passageway there was no light, but she knew what it was outside – heavy snow. She looked up and saw a big staircase, straight, none of that fancy turning which she had seen in some houses, and there was something about it which appealed to her. The way that it led up into the darkness did not put her off or frighten her; it was the way ahead. Beside her George's body sagged. She stood for a moment and then she looked about her.

She made as if to go towards the stairs, but George tugged at her arm. 'What are you doing?' he whispered. 'We can't go up there. They'll find us.'

She heard a faint growling, a low noise, and when she turned in the shadows she saw movement and then through what light there was from the bar, a big black dog emerging from where the owner had sat. The dog's claws must be short, he must get lots of walks on hard ground, she surmised, for there was only a faint clip-clopping of them upon the bare floorboards.

She hadn't noticed the dog, he had not moved or made any sound when they were in the office; he must have been under the desk. How discerning that he knew she was not a threat or perhaps he was sure that his owner would take care of it.

He was a very big dog even for a Labrador, Emma thought, slightly worried: a square head, a thick neck, solid shoulders, substantial legs and body and enormous paws. Lots of people would have backed off at that point, and she thought the dog was waiting to see whether she would back off, or whether he would have to threaten her further. It was his job to do so. The dog held her gaze steadily while he considered, and she watched his white even teeth. But she wasn't afraid; she thought it was only bluff.

Her first instinct was to run, but that was stupid, she knew. Nothing made a dog run after you like taking to your heels, and in such a place she was bound to fall and after that she wasn't sure what might happen: it would depend on the dog and a dog that size could make a terrible mess of one smallish person and a child.

She took a deep breath. The dog stood, watching her. She gestured to George to stay still and keep silent, though she didn't think she needed to. She waited for the man to appear, but perhaps he was not aware of the dog, perhaps he was so used to the low growl from the animal's stomach that he took no notice.

She stopped, shrank back, waited, but nothing happened. The dog was crouched low as if he would spring; she could see the raised hair on the ridge of his back. Then she remembered her father's dogs from her childhood, how they had been just like this, and she got down very slowly, all the time keeping her gaze on the dog, easing her body to the floor. She was looking straight at the dog now; she watched its ears which had been laid back come forward in curiosity, but still cautious, and she said, in a voice barely audible except to the animal: 'Silly old thing, it's only us,' and then she beckoned, both hands outstretched but confidently.

She could see the dog relax because she was on his level. His tail began to wag. And remembering her father, her eyes filled with tears. The animal came to her and she said into its ear, 'We're going upstairs now, but you mustn't tell anybody,' and then she kissed him on the forehead. He tasted so beautifully of dog, all pheasant and partridge and autumn and bounding through the heather and swimming in ponds and coming back with a duck in his mouth. He smelled of warmth and vitality and she could not help hugging him. The dog accepted the embrace, was patient, and when she let go she was only afraid for how boldly and noisily he thumped his tail on the floor. Nothing might bring the man sooner, and yet she could not be sorry.

She picked up the bags and slowly she made her way to the bottom of the stairs. She need not have feared. The dog, sitting down now, watched her, making sure that she was safe, while his tail swept the floor in big arcs. She and George tiptoed up the stairs and the dog stood up at the bottom; his tail had gradually ceased to wag, but that was just because he was waiting until she reached the top of the stairs. Then he turned and disappeared into the darkness at the back of the pub.

She opened the door of the first room she came to. George, only half awake, stared and Emma followed his gaze by what light there was through the huge window which dominated the room.

The night was clearing and she could see her breath, it was that cold. It was a big room and must have been lovely once. There was even the vestige of some flowered wallpaper. The curtains, when she tried to close them, wouldn't move and as she pulled harder one of them came down with a crash and she moved just in time as, together

111

with whatever had been holding it up, it plummeted to the floor. A big carpet covered the middle of the room, but it was uncomfortable under her feet: plaster had fallen from the ceiling and it crunched as she moved.

She could hear the faint noise of merriment. It was just a hum and comforting in a strange sort of way. For a few minutes she wondered if the owner might come upstairs for any reason whatever, but he didn't, and she began to relax and thought herself foolish for being nervous. Why would he?

The bed had been stripped but she did find some blankets and pillows on the floor in the corner. There were various pieces of furniture, all large, which she dared not explore, they looked so intimidating. Finally, trying to reassure George, they lay down and he went to sleep.

Emma wondered again what she had done. How on earth had she got them to this place? She wished now that she had never left. She wished she had put up with the marriage plans. Even the Judge looked safe and secure from her present situation.

When Emma awoke she thought she was in her bedroom at home, and then she opened her eyes and was disillusioned. Sunlight was coming into the room and showing every mark on the windows, which hadn't been cleaned in years.

One of the curtains lay in a heap where she had pulled it off in her attempt to close them; she could not now think why it had been so important. The other curtain hung half off. They were velvet and at one time had been dark raspberry-coloured. They were moth-eaten, almost in holes, and they had gone orange where the damp had reached them.

She turned over. George was sleeping. She was desperate to use a chamber pot. She slid from the bed, got down and looked underneath it. A large green object was there, dusty when she recovered it from the floor, but clean.

Relieved of her problem she went across to the dressing table where a jug stood in a bowl. The water in it smelled foul because it had been standing for a long time, but nevertheless she rinsed her hands, wiping them on her dress because there was nothing else.

The day was bright. The room somehow looked worse in daylight. The furniture, like the curtains, had been good once. Now it was battered, had had no polish, had lost most of its handles, some of its doors. A thick layer of dust covered every surface.

'I'm hungry.'

She turned around as George spoke. She was so hungry herself that she felt sick. The bed was bad too, the mattress stained and sagging. The blankets which had covered her in the night were also in holes.

She ventured from the room, George close behind her. There was nobody about, it was a wide landing with various doors off it and a long passageway from there, and she followed that and when she pushed open the door she found narrow backstairs, no carpet, and so dirty that she almost slipped on the thick covering. When they reached the bottom they were right beside the back door. Rooms led off on either side. One was the kitchen.

A greasy smell pervaded the air. She followed the smell to the back of the house and opened a door. The room was full of smoke and somebody was coughing. It was the dirtiest kitchen that Emma had ever seen, and when she could make out the barman of the night before he was ladling something from a blackened frying pan onto a plate.

Emma backed away noiselessly and beckoned George beyond the back door. It was sunny, but the wind driving the snow tore up the road and almost knocked her off her feet. She drew George in against her.

They began walking back down the main street, partly because it was shielded from the wind but partly because she could remember having come past shops, and if she went either of the other ways beyond the Black Diamond there seemed to be nothing but houses going along flat to one side and down a steep hill on the other. She could see some sort of church across the road and another at the far side, but the rest of the town, such as it was, was back where they had come from the evening before.

There were shops on either side of the road, but they were not the kind of shops where you could buy anything to eat unless you were in a kitchen and had a range at your disposal. There was a hardware store and a shoe and boot shop and an apothecary's and a butcher's. The butcher's had a good smell coming from it, and when she and George ventured across the street there were pies in the window.

She left George with the bags and ventured inside. There was a queue. As she joined it every woman in front of her turned around and stared and they looked at one another. They wore what was almost a uniform: shawls to keep out the wind (very sensible, she thought), stout boots and dark-coloured skirts and blouses, and it was only at that moment that she knew she stood out even before she spoke.

These people were poor. They weren't wearing rags, but their clothes were well-worn, and in colours which would show no dirt. She must have looked very stylish, though she had thought her clothes modest when she was in Mid Haven. Her hat, which was well made, had ribbons, and her cherry-red coat was fitted to her figure. Her black leather boots had little heels on them, most unsuitable since she had left home, and she had black leather gloves neat to her wrist. She had never felt so out of place.

She could see the dead animals hung up in the back room and another butcher further inside cutting up a pig (at least she thought it was, but she didn't like to look too closely). She didn't understand much of what the women were saying; they kept up some form of banter with the butcher. He was a well-built man who obviously liked his own meat and pies.

There were two seats in the shop, as though he encouraged people not to leave and even when they were served they would sit down as though they had been on their feet for hours, which they probably had, she thought. Their faces were worn and some of the women had children around them or in their arms, and more children played outside.

It was difficult to tell what age the women were: they had deep lines in their faces and broken veins, probably because of the weather. Their heads were covered with scarves, like pictures she had seen of women in hot countries, as though for modesty, but here she thought it probably had more to do with the biting cold wind. Their clothes were shapeless and their figures were either skinny or very fat, their bodies like balls on their thin and buckling legs.

Under the gaze of the local women Emma could feel the blood rushing to her face. They had no manners, but then they did not often see someone like her, she thought in dismay.

She heard shouting. It sounded loud, though she could not hear the words, and for some reason it drew the attention of most of the shop. Several of the women went back to the doorway and huddled there together, pushing for a better view. Emma had a bad feeling about it and she was right. When she had asked them, very politely, to make way and they did not, she shoved because the noise had increased and it was taunting.

When she got outside she could see three children and they were throwing stones at George. Others stood back jeering. She could not make out the words, but she understood what they were doing. George had taken it well so far, but he had picked up a large stone to fling back at them. Emma made short of the space between her, George and the crowd.

'Put that down this minute!' she said.

George, not used to her raising her voice in that way,

turned and dropped the stone instantly. Emma swung round to the children. She felt six foot tall, she was so angry. But she didn't do anything, she just looked at them. Silence reigned.

One of the women came out of the butcher's.

'Are you shoutin' at my bairns?'

Emma very slowly took her in.

'Are these children yours? Do they usually throw stones at people because they don't know them?'

More women came out of the butcher's. Curiosity, Emma thought, was a bad onlooker.

'Foreigner!' somebody shouted.

Emma stared them down and went back into the butcher's as though nothing had happened, but this time she said curtly to George, 'Come with me.'

Finally she reached the front of the queue; by then most of the women had gone. The seats were free, but some women lingered outside, talking and darting sideways looks at her as though she were the subject of their discussion. She asked him for two pork pies.

'You're not doing my business any good, Missus.'

'It's Miss,' Emma said. 'Miss Emma Appleby.'

'Is that right?'

'That's exactly right.'

'Is it now?' He glared at her. 'We don't want the likes of you around here with your bairn. We have enough whores as it is, even if they make themselves look like fine ladies. You're no fine lady. You get out.'

Emma didn't know what to say to that, but the crowd

was pressing into the doorway again and the butcher was a very big man. He made as if to come round to the front of the counter so she retreated. She was horrified by what had happened. She didn't move quickly but the crowd jeered more. Emma walked very slowly, George by her side, until they were a long way down the street.

It was only then that she noticed a woman had followed her and she turned.

'What do you want?' she said.

'Are you the competition, pet?' the woman said.

'I don't understand.'

'Well, you didn't get them clothes round here unless it were from a man.'

'I'm an American,' Emma said. 'I came here to find my family and it's nothing to do with any man.'

The woman looked familiar to Emma, though she couldn't have said what it was about her, just that she thought they had met before, but it was clear they had not. The woman was short like her, and she had lived in this place or somewhere like it, Emma could tell, because she had careworn eyes. There was something brave about her, she kept on looking straight at things even though she had long since seen enough.

'Do you know the Applebys?' Emma said.

The woman's face changed at that point and she was no longer even remotely friendly. 'There's nowt left for nobody to come to. You might as well go back to where you came from.'

'I have no money and I need some place to stay.'

'Can't help you there. There's no livin' here for the likes of us except up against a wall. If you've come down in the world, pet, I'm sorry for it, but you'd make more in Bishop Auckland or Durham where the men have money. It's mining here and the ironworks and nowt much else, no plump pockets, just dark alleys and pennies, you see.'

Emma didn't know what to say and beside her George moved about as though he half understood and wished he didn't.

'There were hotels at one time, but the coal's almost gone and the ironworks is doing badly, people don't come to stay any more. You'd have to get a train out of here to Bishop Auckland or Durham: plenty of hotels there.'

'Is that far?'

'Oh aye, quite a long road.'

The woman walked away. Emma wanted to question her further, but was exhausted, and still they had had nothing to eat. She and George picked up their bags and went further. There was not another butcher's and even if there had been her courage was almost gone, exhaustion was setting in. There was no pawn shop but she had nothing left other than the pearls and several books so it didn't matter.

She had brought only her favourites, even slim volumes were heavy, but when the weather had been bad and she had almost turned back she would read the poetry of Emily Dickinson or Walt Whitman, and be cheered by their words. The books had been gifts from her father and it would take a great deal to make her part with them. She comforted herself with the idea that nobody in a place like this would have heard of American poets, much less want books by them.

She didn't want to go back to the Black Diamond. She couldn't think what to do next. She tried to be cheerful for George's sake, but suddenly there was nowhere to go. The street went down to the railway crossing and then up the hill, and beyond that there were pubs and churches and one or two shops – ladies' clothing and another which sold yarn – and that was all.

She badly wanted to look for her grandparents' graves, if only to reassure herself that this really was the place they had lived. In a way she hoped it wasn't. She could not bear to think that she had reached the right place, that she had come thousands of miles to this, but if it was not then whatever was she to do?

They went to the graveyard. It was, if such a thing had ever been, a perfect place for the dead. It was high up and clean, and there were no sunken places where a sudden rain shower could flood the graves since it sloped down into fields. Nothing was soaked or neglected, nothing had sunk, and the sun came out and it turned the stones butterscotch in its own bright warm way in remembrance of the dead.

There was a good view of the fields as they went down into the valley beyond the horizon and at the other side was the little town and its pits. She thought that if you had to be buried somewhere, and indisputably you did, it was as good a place as anywhere.

The wind keened over the gravestones as though in affection, and she looked for anybody of her name, but she couldn't find them. It was not that big a graveyard, she thought, and yet they eluded her. Had she come to the wrong place?

It was George who found the first. He danced about, ran, stopped, read, started up again, and she was glad of him there, darting about like a sprite. He shrieked her name and pointed and she went over, slowly at first, not that she thought he was wrong, but because she feared he was right. He was. The gravestone read: *John McLoughlin, father of Kathleen.*

It was her grandfather and she could see that her mother had erected the stone. She knew that her mother had left the town after her own father had died; she could not have done otherwise. She had put her name upon the stone as though it would bind them together still, and there it was. Emma could not help tracing a finger upon the indented stone where her mother's name was inscribed, even though her mother was not buried there.

How far away she seemed. How could she have left. But she had a husband and a small daughter and there was a new world waiting for her. Emma thought of her parents and of their delight and of their success in finding Mid Haven.

She knew that she had been right to come back here where her grandfather was buried. George pointed and she saw her grandmother's name. They were side by side not underneath or on top. They were equal in God's eyes and in the eyes of everybody who came there, and she liked that.

As she stood there snow began to fall again. It was typical somehow, she thought: it was meant to be spring, but here in the middle of freezing nowhere no leaf seemed to be stirring, no shoots from the ground. She felt as if she were a small child again, putting out her tongue to catch a flake of snow upon it, and somebody was laughing behind her and encouraging her, and she knew that it was her mother. She had not felt as close since her mother died.

George searched further, but Emma found the Applebys, in the far corner of the graveyard, where most older people appeared to be buried: her other grandparents, their gravestones very plain, almost hidden in shadow, nothing but names and dates, Mary and James. After that she felt at home: all four of her grandparents lay here.

The day grew worse. Emma and George walked back to the Black Diamond and into the kitchen. Emma had decided that she would be bolder. Here she found vegetables in various stages of decay and these she peeled and diced and put onto the stove with water and some salt and when the soup was almost ready she saw the bartender standing in the doorway.

'We thought you'd gone,' he said.

Emma didn't answer. She found bowls and plates and spoons and knives and she knew how good the soup smelled and that he was a man who would object to nothing if he could fill his belly. He produced a loaf of bread and some butter and all three of them, without a word, sat down to eat.

Ed ate rapidly. Emma got up and poured more soup into his bowl. He looked at her with grateful eyes.

'I don't know your full name,' she said. 'I'm Miss Emma Appleby.'

'Edward Higgins. I'm from Yorkshire.'

'Do you have family, Mr Higgins?'

'Nay,' he said, and something about his tone stopped Emma from asking more.

She gave him a third bowlful and George a second, and there was even some left for her to have seconds. She was quite proud of the soup, though it was nothing but vegetables, water and a little butter added at the end.

He went back to the bar, thanking her awkwardly and saying, 'You cannot stay here. Mr Castle is due in soon and he won't stand for anything.'

Emma told George not to go anywhere near the bars or the men. She said he could go outside or up to the room where they had slept.

She began to clean the kitchen. She was not used to grime and she could not sit there and endure it. Under the sink she found cloths, a scrubbing brush, washing soda and a big bar of hard yellow soap. She heated up some water and even found a bucket so that she could wash the floor. She was pleased with the result.

She scrubbed the surfaces, even on top of the cupboards; she threw out all the food which had gone off, and there was a lot of it; she turned out the cupboards and scrubbed those too. She threw out the awful rugs which covered the floor and were heavy with dirt. She took the brush and soapy water to the walls, and she had almost finished the floor when she heard a sound and saw the boots and looked up at the owner. She thought he might have seemed less emaciated or more friendly in the daylight, but if anything he looked worse, white-faced as though he never slept, eyes narrowed against the daylight. He had a half-smoked cigarette between his fingers and looked around in wonderment.

'What in the hell are you doing still here?' he said. 'This isn't a bloody orphanage, you know.'

Emma got up, her dress was dragging because it was wet, her forehead was sweaty and her hands were sore. He was glaring at her.

'I told you last night to leave,' he said.

His voice had gone very soft. Emma didn't trust that. She knew more about men than she knew about women because she had lived with her father for so long and with Laurence and she did not mistake the dangerous note behind the softness.

At this point her hair, which was also damp, had come loose and rather a lot of it was in her eyes. She pushed it away with a wet sleeve. 'We have nowhere to go. I know that can't mean anything to you but – I could work if you would let us have the room upstairs. You're not using it and – and it would mean a lot.'

He looked baffled.

'We – we travelled to Boston and took ship to Liverpool

and then trains and then – we got here and then the money ran out.'

'You came all the way from America to this?'

Emma almost laughed. 'I know,' she said, 'isn't it ridiculous?' and then her voice broke. 'There's nobody left. I thought I had people here. I don't know why. My mother was an only child and so was my father and they're all dead. There's nobody left for me.' She rubbed her hands on her skirt which was sopping wet.

He looked at her quizzically. Then he glanced around the kitchen, not as if he saw it, but as if he saw it differently.

'Do you want a barmaid?' she asked.

Now he looked disparagingly at her. 'Even if I did I don't think you'd make much of one at your age and I don't want a cleaner either, so leave that lot alone.'

'The place is filthy,' Emma objected. 'I've never seen anything as bad this.'

'It's not your concern. Take your bastard and go.'

'He's not my bastard!' Emma said and then she heard herself shouting and at a man who suddenly seemed so big and so bad-tempered.

She burst into such tears that she couldn't see. Her dress was by now stuck to her very thin form, her hair had gone into what her mother used to call 'rats' tails' and worst of all somehow she managed to knock over the pail of dirty water which she had just used to scrub the floor. The lukewarm water went everywhere, all over the floor, all over her feet and all over his feet, though to her surprise he didn't move, as if things like wet feet were irrelevant.

'Why does everybody think such a horrible thing?' she demanded.

'Where's your husband?'

'I haven't got one.'

'Women round here that have bairns have husbands unless they're whores,' he said and walked out.

Emma slopped down the passage after him and even into the room which was his office. She had never done such a thing before, she couldn't think why she was doing it now, but she felt such rage that she could not hold it in as she was used to doing.

'Don't you say things like that to me! I'm tired of hearing such dreadful things. My father and I took that boy in after I found him in the snow. I'm taking care of him.'

He looked surprised and not pleased. 'Well, it doesn't look to me as though you're making much of a job of it, bringing him all this way for nowt.'

'It wasn't for – for nowt!'

'Then what the hell was it for? What are you running from?'

'My brother arranged a marriage for me, with an old man.'

He stared. 'They have arranged marriages in America?'

'Not like that!'

The room resounded to their voices, and she could hear her own lifted in argument and she wasn't afraid. She realized then that after the way Laurence had treated her she had stopped being afraid of men, no matter what their power.

'It must have been pretty bad to make you run away like a spoilt bairn.'

'He wanted rid of me. So here I am. You don't use those rooms upstairs for anything. What difference does it make to you whether we're up there?'

He looked at her. 'You slept up there?'

'It was better than outside, though not much. The whole place is disgusting. What did you expect me to do, disappear into the snow in the middle of this stupid little town?'

There was a long silence. Emma sniffed again, really this crying thing was terribly messy, but she felt much better. She pushed back her wet hair. 'And I made soup and Mr Higgins said it was very nice.'

'Did he now?'

'Yes, he did.'

She waited and she thought he was going to ignore her, to sit down and begin on his work – there were a lot of papers – but he didn't. He eyed her. 'All right,' he said evenly, 'you can have a room upstairs and you can have the kitchen, but I don't want you anywhere else and I don't want that bairn in the bars or in anybody's road. Do you understand me? You can have a week. And stay out of the shops and such, they don't like strangers, especially not women with bairns on their own.'

'He's called George and he's twelve.'

'You will find somewhere else before the end of the week.'

She nodded wordlessly, and then she marched out of the office and back into the kitchen. She washed the kitchen floor again and then she went upstairs and found dry clothes. Nobody said anything; nobody put her out. The night came down, not as rapidly as it did at home, but softly like a thief just after four, and she liked the way that it hesitated and came down like a blanket. The noise from the bars did not really intrude, but she closed the doors and she and George sat down beside the kitchen fire.

She heard shouting and other noises – a clattering, and then the sound of breaking glass. Emma opened the door and ventured into the darkness of the hall and a rare sight met her eyes. Men were fighting both in and out of the pub – she had never seen anything like it. She had read of hand-to-hand combat without weapons, but she had not thought it was so noisy. Men screamed and shouted one another's names and cursed, and it was not anything scientific like boxing, she imagined, where there were certain rules.

Bloody fists punched heads and stomachs, one man picked up a chair and broke it over another's head, but instead of going down on the floor the man merely stood for a few seconds and then turned to take vengeance and they grasped one another and grappled and went heavily against the wall. Another man held his opponent down on the floor with a chair leg while smashing him in the face with an almost square fist. Chairs and tables overturned, and glasses smashed, raining like diamonds against the lamplight.

Mr Castle and Mr Higgins were fighting at either end

of the room and one of the windows had been broken. Emma thought somebody might have gone through it and been badly injured, but it looked as though somebody had fired rocks at it from outside as they were visible on the floor and the glass was lying everywhere in shards.

It did not stop the men from rolling in it as they pushed and pulled and punched. One big square man got hold of a whisky bottle from behind the bar, smashed it on the bar top and tried to push it into Mr Higgins' face. Emma screamed and pointed, and Mr Castle heard her, reached him and knocked him over before he got any closer. Another man ran right in front of her with a knife in his hand and she put out one leg and he fell over it. He went down hard and fast.

Emma was amazed at herself. This place was nothing to her, neither were these men. Why then did she already feel as though she belonged here? If anybody had told her that she would be fearless in such circumstances she would have thought they were mad. Somehow it was basic stuff, like which side you were on, and she was on the right side and the winning side, she could see, as various men were thrown from the door and Mr Castle and Mr Higgins and one or two others stood triumphant in the middle of the floor. She was pleased. She wanted to cheer. How odd. How barbaric.

Then it started up again, but she could see that the worst was over and that the intruders were half-hearted now, some of them punch-drunk, none of them able to do any real damage, either to the men or to the place. She went back into the kitchen and shut the door and leaned against it as though she thought they might get that far. It went on for a long time and she could hear Mr Castle's brutally vile voice.

She didn't exactly know what he was saying, which was just as well, and then she heard his voice raised in thanks to various men and the outside doors slam. After that it was quiet. She wanted to hover in the kitchen, called herself a coward and went out into the hall and through into the bar.

The place was a mess such as she had never seen. She could not help staring at the broken glass which was like a raised carpet on the floor there was that much of it. There was blood, little pools and trickles. Not a single table or chair was upright and many of the chairs were broken. The floor was strewn with broken glass and swimming in beer. Mr Higgins pulled a chair upright and sat down.

Emma went to him. 'Are you hurt?'

He grinned in admiration. 'Nay, lass, I'm fine, thanks to you.'

Mr Castle stared at her and then said, with a touch of humour, 'Help with many fights, do you?'

'Well, he, well, I—' Emma felt embarrassed at her part in the conflict.

Mr Higgins sighed. 'I'm getting too bloody old for this, Mick.' He screwed his eyes up at his employer, winced and brought bloody knuckles across his cheekbone.

Realizing that neither man was badly hurt Emma went back to the kitchen and brought a big brush and shovel and bucket and she began shovelling the glass into the pail. Sweeping up glass covered in beer was a very difficult thing to do, but they all helped. George came through and put the chairs upright, and he and Mr Higgins took the broken bits outside because they could burn them next time they had a bonfire, Mr Higgins said.

When all the glass was gone – and Emma was careful because she thought of the black dog and she didn't want him to get any glass in the pads of his paws (she still kept finding tiny little particles in among the beer) – eventually Mr Castle came to her and he said, 'You've washed too many floors today. Go to bed.'

She tried to protest, but he shook his head.

'In the morning it'll be dry and any glass that's left you can sweep up then if you've a mind.'

She could not help saying to him, 'You won't let the dog in here.'

It made him smile. 'He's safe in my office and no, I won't let him through. Go to bed and take George with you. He's dropping.'

She hadn't noticed that George's face had become paler and paler, but he was still there, chatting brightly to Mr Higgins as though he cleaned up after fights every day. She went over and collected him and they went wearily up the stairs.

She was so exhausted that she didn't care about the grubby sheets, the dark room and the curtains on the floor. She covered George and herself with blankets and they slept.

8

It was very late when Mick got home after the fight. He was always late home, it was always the darkest middle of the night, it was always silent. He liked the silence, the getting away from the constant sound of the men's voices. Not that he minded – they paid the wages, they provided the money – but the silence that greeted him in his house was like velvet to his ears. He went to sleep to the sound of it, but not yet, not before he checked that Isabel was safe, that Connie was safe, that he had done what he could and was content to leave it until another day.

Connie didn't look like his child these days, Mick thought, more like some wild creature from the hilltops. She had hacked at her hair with a pair of blunt scissors, it would appear. It hung, dirty blonde, about her face. She looked like a boy except that she was too fragile to be any such thing, and in spite of the ragged clothes there was a grace about her which made her unmistakably Isabel's child.

It was on his lips a dozen times to say 'Aren't you cold?' because Connie wore nothing on her grubby feet and a boy's shirt and trousers, much too big – where she had got them and what colour they had originally been he had no idea. But he had never tried to alter anything she was, it was bad enough for her having to live here like this. The familiar feelings of guilt swept over him in such waves that he was surprised to find he was still standing.

He thought briefly of the woman who had invaded the Black Diamond, strange, middle-aged, prim little soul. Plainly dressed, plainly spoken, too thin to be pretty, too white-faced and long-nosed with her hair scraped back, and then he remembered her eyes. She had lovely eyes, deep green.

And then he thought that his marriage had made it impossible for him to see any woman in a good light, but she had shown courage tonight such as he had not seen before. He thought of the way that she had shouted back at him and he thought of the long voyage across the sea.

She must have had tremendous faith to have done such a thing and even though it must have been so very hard she had made it here. He wondered how bad things had been that a middle-aged spinster would leave everything she had for something as uncertain as this.

He never went to bed without looking in on his child. She was the only good thing to come out of their marriage. She wasn't asleep. He always hoped that she would be, but he knew now that she waited until he came home before she slept.

The lamps blazed in her room. It was cold, but at least it was clean. It was the one thing he insisted on, that his bedroom and her bedroom and the bathroom should be clean, and that Connie should have meals brought to her room. They had long given up any pretence of meals in the dining room.

The bed was huge and Connie was tiny, huddled there under her blankets.

'Did you go to school today?'

She rolled her eyes. He asked her every day, even on Saturdays and Sundays. It had become a standing joke.

'Of course I did.'

He hadn't mentioned boarding school to her in a long time. Now he did. She didn't reply. Mick sat down on the bed and knew how tired he was, his body ached for night after night and day after day of conflict and business and trying to get things right and failing so badly here at home and from the bruises and knocks which he had endured, trying to take control of the Black Diamond away from the intruders.

'What is the point of school?' She looked directly at him and both her face and her voice were filled with scorn. She reminded him of his mother: she had the same fine and rather acid intelligence. 'I can read, write and add up, all of which you taught me before I went to school. The rest of it has been a waste of time,' she said, her mouth going into a thin line. And then she stopped.

He had hoped she wouldn't notice but he hadn't seen his face in the mirror. She stared. Her eyes got wider and wider.

'You've been fighting!' she said. 'You're bleeding.'

'Where?'

She touched his cheek.

'I think it's somebody else's blood,' he said. 'Some of the Crook lads tried to smash up the bar.'

'Is Ed all right?'

'It's Mr Higgins to you and yes, he's fine. Now go to sleep.'

She said something else, but it was inaudible. And then she said again what he had not caught. She didn't look at him when she said it, as though she were ashamed to betray any affection. 'I will never leave you here,' she said harshly, 'to her and to this.'

She sounded like an adult. It hurt him so much, the child being mother to the man. It was not to be borne and yet it reminded him what he was doing, how much he loved his child. She flung herself at him, then away from him, towards the pillow which she grabbed. He tucked her in, kissed her, saw her comfortable and then he left the room, softly because he knew that she would sleep now. He threw off his clothes and fell into bed; he didn't even notice that Isabel wasn't there.

There was food now at the Black Diamond. Edward Higgins practically lived there. He had a small house, Emma had discovered, two doors up, which he went to when the night was old and he was exhausted, so he didn't sleep at the Black Diamond, but he was always back early in the morning. Emma wasn't sure whether this was a good thing or not. She didn't like the idea of being alone there, but since the boss, Mr Castle, stayed until the middle of the night there were actually only about four hours when she and George were alone. She did worry that somebody would break in, but when she voiced this to Mr Higgins he laughed.

'Why is that amusing?'

'Nobody's going to break in here, love, not these days. We had one break-in and after that Mr Castle made sure that there's nowt to take – and it's the middle of nowhere. And also folk know now that we won't have it.'

So, the Black Diamond was as safe as you could get, she thought. Mr Higgins was two doors away, the streets were silent by then, she quite liked the old house, its creakings in the night became her comfort. Knowing that Mr Higgins would be there for breakfast, more prompt than ever, she made pancakes.

Pancakes were cheap. There were hens at the back of the pub. She liked hens: they had always kept them at home and all she needed after that was flour and water. Mr Higgins recommended beer. She didn't know how he knew, but after she used beer she knew that it was the answer to the best pancakes, and she would put butter on them and sugar, and Mr Higgins could eat a great many of these so she would make stacks of them. After Mr Higgins appeared, shamefaced, with sausages from the local butcher the pancakes seemed even better. The sausages would bake slowly to golden brown in the oven and the pancakes were delicious.

She fed the hens with leftovers, such as they were, boiled up, and the hens seemed to like it. They had their own space out the back and she almost envied them. The view looked down beyond the moors, into the little fields and small grey farms which made up the land. The hens had a great big field. She remembered having once heard someone say, 'The way to keep your goat happy is to give it a very big field,' and she thought that was true of everything, be it goats, hens or people. They could have laid waste to the rest of the garden out the back, but they did not because they had about a quarter of an acre to themselves and a wire fence between one and the other.

Nobody said anything. Mr Castle acted as though she and George were not there. Mr Higgins came in regularly and eagerly for his meals.

As soon as the customers began to come in at noon every day she would retreat to the back and there she taught George his lessons. She was aware that he saw no other children and was afraid that he would become lonely, so she decided to enrol him at the nearest school which was just along the road. It was a big, rather gloomy-looking building. She had seen the children going in.

George didn't object to the idea when she suggested it to him, and she thought that she had been right: he needed the company of other children. She took him there on the following Monday morning.

Inside it was freezing, the floors were bare, the walls high, and when she found the door which led into the classroom she was worried.

There were great rows of scholars. This room too was

bitterly cold and worst of all at the front of the class a middle-aged man was attempting to remonstrate with a child, a thin and badly dressed child, whom she assumed at first to be a boy. To her astonishment the child was actually laughing and swearing at him and evading his grasp quite successfully, dancing around him as though it were some kind of boxing match, while he stood, thin, shabby and bewildered.

The children shouted too, some of them were standing in the aisles, others on their desks or chairs and Emma winced at their language, glad she did not understand all of it, in their thick guttural voices. George stood, gaping. The child was tiny, dainty, and that was when she knew that it was a girl.

'Come on then, you old bugger!' the child taunted him. 'Make me do it. Go on!' Her voice was light and rather elegant, she barely had an accent and her eyes shone, but there was something hard and withdrawn about her, her tiny fists clenched and when the man put out both hands in despair she laughed and ran away, down the aisle and beyond where George and Emma stood.

She was half-starved, her rags hanging off her in spite of the chill and her limbs so white beneath. She was dirty and her eyes were huge and dark. She stared at them for a few seconds and then turned and ran out of the door.

The schoolmaster seemed not to notice them, he stood there confused and then he shouted, 'Silence!' and he picked up and waved the cane at the other children. Gradually, they subsided and peace descended.

George drew nearer to her. The schoolmaster noticed them, but Emma withdrew from the room. She marched George out of the building and there she took great breaths of air as though there had been none inside. She led the way back to the Black Diamond and into the kitchen, which was thankfully deserted. There she made tea and they sat by the fire.

'You don't want me to go there?' George said anxiously.

'Certainly not. It was chaotic. I've never seen any school like it.'

Mr Higgins came in; he had taken to doing so from time to time before the customers arrived and he would buy foodstuffs for the meals. He seemed to have some arrangement with the butcher and with the men who went fishing. Having questioned him on this matter Emma discovered that they drank at the pub and Mr Castle was happy for him to make bargains of this kind so that their beer was cheap or free.

Other things which she needed, such as flour, coffee, tea, sugar, butter, cheese and milk, Mr Higgins would provide. It was an unspoken agreement. He bought these and she cooked and now he had all his meals with them. She thought he was beginning to look better for it. He ate breakfast, eggs and bread, had a cheese or meat sandwich for his lunch (he called it his dinner), and in the evening, early for him because he had to see to the bar nearly all the time between noon and late in the evening, he would hastily consume fish and vegetables – Mr Higgins did not believe in vegetables and Emma had had to go to the greengrocer and take what she could get, mostly potatoes, carrots, Brussels sprouts and what they called turnips. The greengrocer had a very large garden behind his shop and a very big attic for storage and a cellar too. It was important to have vegetables, though she didn't recognize all of them. What was unfamiliar she baked slowly and none of it was a disaster.

Mr Higgins was mesmerized by Emma's baking. She couldn't think why. She made bread, she made cakes, as she had before Verity and Laurence moved in and with them a cook so that they were more grand than before and her talents were not needed in the kitchen.

She liked the cooking and baking; it was familiar and she spent more and more time at the stove. She liked the hot water, the ovens, there were two of them, and the way that she could put pans over the fire, but best of all was the top oven where she would bake bread almost every day. It brought Mr Higgins in from the bar and she would smile and give him a big chunk of still-warm loaf thick with butter to eat as he went back to his work. He even smiled sometimes and he always thanked her.

Also he liked her coffee. At least she could get good beans. She found a grinder in the cupboard, old, brown and square, and the smell from the beans as she ground them mixed with the smell of bread baking made her close her eyes and think of herself at home when her father was still alive and everything was bearable.

It was ridiculous, she knew, but Mr Higgins was not

much younger than her father would have been now, she realized, and she wanted him there in her kitchen. She wanted to put good food inside him and for him to prosper. He had had a hard life by the look of him and sometimes he was very tired and she wondered why Mr Castle employed someone of that age to run his pub when Mr Higgins was so elderly, but she soon saw why.

Mr Higgins had found a home there. She wanted to laugh at this until she saw that she and George had done the same and that in some ways Mr Castle was running 'a bloody orphanage'. She had not thought him sentimental, yet he got a lot for what he gave. Mr Higgins was very good at running the place, the men liked him, the beer flowed, and she was keeping the place clean and she had no wages.

She had no money at all. She had to apply to Mr Higgins for her trips to the shops, but since she spent so little and he benefited so much he didn't seem to mind. She had not quite ignored Mr Castle's command not to go near the shops, but she only went when she had to because she was aware of people talking about her. Their voices dropped as she drew near, they looked down or away, but the shopkeepers endured her because she had money. She was grateful to the poachers who frequented the pub for rabbits, pigeons and brown trout.

The end of the week had come and gone, and while she had half waited for Mr Castle to say something to her, in her heart she knew he would not. Everything had altered after the fight, so the end of the week was not noted in any way. They went on into the second week and the third, and she even made the room upstairs more habitable for herself and George. Mr Higgins put up the fallen curtain and she found decent sheets and bedclothes, and she stopped worrying about where she would go from here.

Emma became more and more conscious of the fact that she hadn't been to church since she had left home. That Sunday she determined to take George and made her way with him down the narrow lane to where the parish church stood above the fields which led to the dale. She was not late, but she had not wanted to be early because she knew no one and wanted to take this slowly, but as she and George sat down near the back of the church she was aware of heads turning and of whispering, and of people staring and trying not to be seen doing so.

The church was very well attended and a great number of smart people sang and prayed and listened to the sermon and endeavoured to keep their children in order and their babies from crying. Most of it was from the cold, Emma could not help thinking. The church smelled damp, as though despite the warmer weather which was trying to produce spring, and mostly failing, nothing penetrated the stone.

She found the sermon long and the vicar was the kind of man her father would have referred to as 'a church emptier'. He was not a learned nor a kind man, she thought, listening to him telling people that they would go to hell unless they did a great number of unpleasant things, like not enjoying their lives one little bit.

You obviously had to be miserable, Emma thought, to go to this man's heaven. She was bored. George was even more bored. He fidgeted, and the look of relief on his face when the sermon ended was so obvious that she had to hide a smile. George was used to a man who would tell the children stories to keep their interest, to encourage his congregation to live varied and interesting lives, to make them happy before they went home to another diffi-cult week.

These people were poor, they worked hard, the men were either pitmen, quarrymen or ironworkers. They lived in tiny houses. They worked shifts and their women had to be up no matter what time it was to see to their needs and to the needs of their many children. The church here was gloomy and filled with a dark-grey light, yet when she and George stepped outside after the service finally finished she could not believe what she saw. It was raining, light spring rain, and through it the sun shone and beyond sun and the rain a perfect rainbow arched above the little fell town.

The vicar did not even come outside to shake his parish-ioners by the hand. Emma was ready to make her way back to the pub. She was not prepared for the woman who came up to her as she was leaving and said, 'Excuse me.' When Emma heard her, she stopped and turned, summoning a smile to her lips. The woman said with an effort, 'My husband is not the kind of man who turns people from his church but I'm afraid I must tell you that we don't like women of dubious morals to attend our services. It wouldn't be right for the rest of the congregation.'

Emma was so angry that she could feel her face burning. The woman was ugly, Emma decided. It was not her looks, it was the expression in her eyes. The wind blew her hair about and it fell loose in wisps about her bonnet. A going-to-church bonnet, Emma thought, and then thought herself frivolous.

'You are a – a single woman with a child and – you live in a—' She couldn't bring herself to say the word, so Emma helped.

'I understand it's a public house,' she said.

'A dreadful place.'

'Well, actually it's not that bad if you ignore the spitting and swearing and fighting,' Emma said, and she turned away and walked George off down the path to the road.

'There isn't spitting and swearing, at least not much,' he said. 'It only counts as spitting when you spit on the floor, Mr Higgins told me.'

'Mr Higgins tells you too much,' Emma said.

George ignored this. 'And even though we saw that fight Mr Higgins says there isn't as much fighting as there used to be when he first came here because he and Mr Castle bang their heads together regularly and everybody knows except the Crook lads. Mr Castle makes people bleed. Mr Higgins says he's a really good fighter. He could have been a professional pugilist, Mr Higgins says.'

'Thank you, George,' she said.

'As for the swearing—'

'Thank you, George,' she said again, and he laughed.

Mr Higgins was in the kitchen when they got back and George related what had happened. Mr Higgins shook his head. 'I don't hold with too much church,' he said, 'and you couldn't go to the Catholics either, or the Methodys, and as for the Presbyterians—' and he went back to the bar, shaking his head.

Emma found after that day that she didn't want to be there at the public house. She wanted not to care what people thought, and such people, but it was difficult to feel that she had made so bad a start. She wished she could make some kind of money somehow so that she could find a small house of her own. She wasn't sure she even wanted to stay here, she felt just as out of place as she had done in Mid Haven, but there seemed no help for it.

The warmer weather had come even to this place, though it was not what she was used to. The seasons had no definite times. One was very like another. The cold intruded even now, whereas at home – she tried not to think about that. In the garden at the house – Laurence and Verity's house, she insisted to herself – all the trees would be in bud and some of the flowers would be giving out pink and purple colour, whereas here the cutting wind came straight down from the fells and there was little warmth.

People huddled over their fires even though the nights were getting lighter, and now and then she heard the lambs in the fields, and sometimes on the breeze there was a sudden softness which could be there one day and gone the next. You couldn't rely upon any kind of weather, but she was getting to understand that and even to like the unreliability of it.

If you didn't know what the day could offer then you couldn't predict anything and there was an excitement to it and she quite enjoyed the way that you needed to make fires all the year round, but she was sure that if summer did not arrive she would wish very much that she was back in Mid Haven, though not the Mid Haven she knew but the Mid Haven that had been before her father died.

She liked the way that the two men plus the young man, Jack Allen, ran the pub. It was competent and mostly organized, and she knew from what Mr Higgins said that Mr Castle had other public houses, and though they were smaller – some of them had been somebody's front room or parlour or somebody's house – they were now officially his. He had built up the business and though he displayed no sign that it made money she felt sure it must, and it no longer seemed a strange way to make a living. She thought he was shrewd.

But still she wanted something more than the life here offered. George did not like to go upstairs without her at bedtime, and although she was almost sure nobody would get past Mr Higgins, Mr Castle or the black dog who roamed the hall, she was not quite happy when George was out of her sight with the noise from the bar, the men sometimes raucous towards the end of the evening. She didn't trust anybody totally.

There were often fights, but she had grown used to that too. Mr Higgins would throw people out and though not a tall man he was big sideways and it was not flab, she thought, and after the big fight Jack was there to help.

He seemed a nice lad, from a few doors away, smiled a lot, didn't say much, but he would do whatever was required of him. George took to following him around, and although she didn't like to tell George all the time what she required of him, and she remembered that Mr Castle had said George wasn't to go into anywhere other than the kitchen and upstairs, George needed male company and Jack was a good lad. He kept George out of the pub when it was busy or there might be trouble, she realized, having heard Jack say, 'Not now, lad,' because he was grown up and George worshipped him, 'you just go and get on with your lessons and when you're done we'll go outside and I'll show you how to play cricket.'

Emma knew nothing of games, but once or twice on a fine day she would see Mr Higgins and Mr Castle outside playing cricket with George and Jack. It was a rare occasion, mostly they were too busy, and she would keep herself back at these times so that George could enjoy their company.

Jack also taught George soccer (they called it football),

and she was glad of the respite and would go upstairs out of the way and read. She had only the books she had brought with her. She longed for new reading material, but there wasn't another book in the place and she had no means of acquiring more.

Most of the men who came to the Black Diamond were content to sit by the fire and play dominoes or darts, or just quietly drink their evenings away; she had seen enough to know that, but she did not go anywhere near. She had a feeling that their staying here depended upon them not being seen or heard.

It had not occurred to her that people – men in particular – would talk about her or that it would matter to any of them. Mr Castle had been right, she was a middle-aged woman and she was the only one there at night and though there was no wrongdoing of any kind it made her angry, but then she knew what small towns were like: had she not lived in one all her life? Mid Haven was as different from this place as it could be, but in some ways it was very much the same.

The nights were now soft enough to leave the windows open when she went to bed. One particular night she couldn't sleep for pondering her problems. She could hear from below the men's guttural accents and their harsh laughter. She waited until it had quietened and thought then that she would sleep, but she didn't, and in the end she took a candle and went downstairs.

A low growl, slow and venomous, met her and the big

sleek black dog emerged into what light there was, a halo from his head to his tail. She could see his bared teeth. She reached the bottom of the stairs and then got down to him.

'Hector,' she said, 'it's just me. Are you pretending to be useful?' He recognized her voice, or understood what she said, and the growl ceased. She pulled his silky ears and to complete his discomfort she kissed him on top of his shiny head. 'What are you doing here? I thought you went home with Mr Castle.'

'I haven't gone home yet,' a voice said from the darkness, and she jumped.

'Oh, I nearly died!' she said.

She hadn't seen him in days. Sometimes she caught a glimpse of him; occasionally they passed in the hall and merely nodded as though they were neighbours. She moved into the doorway, into the light, and he sat just as he always did amidst an ocean of papers.

'Hector stays here now at night. Ed lets him out in the mornings. You aren't afraid of the dog?'

'I understand dogs. It's people that are the problem.' She liked the idea that Hector was there when she was alone, and she thought that Mr Castle was a better man than he appeared to be, leaving the dog there with her for whatever reason.

Mr Castle sat back and studied her. Not in the way in which a woman might object to, even though she was wearing a nightdress and shawl.

'How long are we to have your company?'

She didn't know what to say to that. 'I didn't mean to

put upon you and I do know what people are saying—'

He looked surprised and then nodded. 'Sit down.'

Emma hesitated. There were two chairs, that was a surprise, though it couldn't claim to be a comfortable chair, it was hard and unyielding.

'Do you want a drink?' he offered, picking up the whisky bottle which seemed ever present.

Emma couldn't help her surprise, but shook her head. 'I went to church and it didn't work—' She paused there, watched him shake his head. 'What else was I supposed to do?' she protested. 'If I had somewhere to go and live I would.'

Hector came over and put his face in her lap and she stroked his soft warm head.

'He's a lovely dog,' she said.

'I have half a dozen at the different pubs. They're named after ancient heroes. Ulysses stays at home and looks after my wife and daughter.'

'Is he black too?'

'Aye, they're brothers,' and the dog, hearing his voice, left Emma and went to his idol. Mick caressed his ears.

'Labradors are the best,' Emma said.

She wished Mr Castle goodnight and went back to bed, feeling quite comforted somehow between the man and the dog. Hector went with her. He seemed to think it was his duty. She heard the dog lie down rather noisily at the side of the bed and give great sighs before he went to sleep. Somehow so did she.

*

Summer eventually arrived, such as it was: high winds, rain, the flowers by the roadsides lay low, battered by the wind, but dandelions studded every place where grass was allowed to lie in the little town, round faces making pools of colour. Sometimes, when Emma and George went walking, if they went by the allotments just outside the bottom end of the town down in the valley where it was more sheltered, men were working diligently, they had dug over the ground and planted it with potatoes, carrots, cabbages, cauliflowers and Brussels sprouts, and as the year advanced Emma saw the neat rows of greenery waving in the wind.

There were leek trenches, currants and rows of gooseberry bushes, and she liked to see the progress of such things. She wished very much to have even a small patch of ground where she might be long enough to make such progress.

It was George's birthday, he was thirteen, and on that Sunday she determined they would celebrate. She wrung a cockerel's neck – he was eating too much and was a plump bird. She said to Mr Higgins that they were to have a special meal, so even though they were busy on Sundays she prepared it. Mr Higgins got Jack to see to the customers, and they sat down mid afternoon when it was quieter and most of the men had gone home to their Sunday dinner and a sleep before coming back for the evening session.

They were in the middle of this meal when the back door burst open and there stood the child that she had seen swearing at Mr English and running from the class-room. The child hovered. Whatever was she doing here and how did she know where they were or who they were?

'Shut the door,' Emma advised her. 'There's a terrible draught.'

Though filled with curiosity Emma was determined to act as though children she didn't know turned up there every day.

'Do sit down,' she said. 'Would you like some pudding?'

The child didn't say yes or no. Emma went on serving the sponge pudding with syrup to Mr Higgins and then to George, and because she was ignored the girl slid into a chair.

'Would you like chicken first or just the pudding?' Emma asked her.

'The pudding first and then chicken.'

Emma duly served her a large portion and had to stop the child from eating it before she served herself.

'You must wait until everyone has some. Then we will all eat together,' she said, half expecting the girl would ignore her, but instead she put down the spoon she had picked up, sat back in her chair and watched as Emma served out the last of the pudding.

After this she gave the girl what was left of their meal, heating it in a pan over the fire first. The girl demolished it quickly.

They left the table for easier chairs. Mr Higgins went to sleep and then apologized and got up, thanked her and went off back to the bar.

'Would you like to go outside and play a game with George?' Emma said.

The girl looked disparagingly at him, but George just went on returning the look stonily and in the end they went.

Emma was more and more aware of George having nobody his own age, and then she saw Mr Castle arrive and the child fling herself at him, and she realized that this tiny ragged girl was his. She was astonished. Finally he stood back and the girl went to George and Mr Castle came inside, awkwardly.

'I didn't mean for her to bother you.'

'She's not,' Emma said easily. 'She's eaten and she seems happy.'

He glanced out of the window.

Emma had no idea what to say. His face was completely unreadable.

'What is your daughter called?'

'Connie.'

'She goes to Mr English's school.'

'Not often,' he admitted.

'She isn't happy there?'

He looked at Emma and she explained what had happened.

'I have offered to send her away to school, but she doesn't want to go. I don't know what else to do.'

And that was when Emma had the idea.

'I'm not going to send George there,' she said. 'I teach

153

him myself. I'm not a teacher, but I had a sound education. I could teach Connie if you like. My father was a scholar. I know some Spanish.'

She didn't know why she said such a foolish thing, it was just that the idea rushed into her mind and confused her.

Mr Castle began to laugh. She was amazed. She hadn't seen him laugh before very often, it took years off him. He really wasn't so very old, probably not as old as she was.

'How could I refuse?' he said.

'Mathematics and literature and I play the piano.' This was ridiculous in a way, because although there was a piano in the bar she had never touched it. She didn't think anybody had played it for years and though her fingers had often itched to do so she didn't dare.

'I don't think Connie is at all musical,' he said.

'You say that now, but you know everybody is musical given the chance and everyone has enormous talent. It might be worth a try, or – or would Mrs Castle object?'

He hesitated, but she could see that it was mostly surprise, and then he said, 'I don't want Connie here at the Black Diamond.'

Emma was rather taken aback at this, she hadn't expected such delicacy about his child. He was right of course, she didn't want George here either except that even she acknowledged it was harder for women and even worse for a girl, but she couldn't suggest that she should take George to his house. Whatever would his wife think?

'I own a building just up the road, it looks straight on to the moors,' he said.

'I don't understand what you mean.'

He stood silent for so long that she became impatient, but when she began to speak he said, 'You could live there and teach the children.'

Emma looked at him, it was a scathing look, she knew. 'Alone?'

'Not necessarily. You could have a dog and Jack lives a couple of doors up and – and I would come by every day and, and bring Connie to school—' He stopped there because he had not meant to say such a thing.

'A school?' Emma hesitated. This was taking the idea much further. She thought in general that was what men did best, they took the idea and ran away with it faster than you had thought. 'I don't know whether I could manage a school.'

'I didn't mean anything general, just that—' and there, she thought, he ran out of ideas.

'You cannot have a school for just two pupils,' she said. 'It's ludicrous.'

'Then what do you suggest? There's nowhere to send either of them.'

'I could tutor them at your house though it would be most days and—'

'No,' he said definitely.

He was silent again and she had no idea what to say, she felt so out of her depth, so far from anything she knew.

'The other house would be better.'

Practicality came to Emma's rescue. 'You'd have to pay. I don't have any money.'

'I had already realized that,' he said drily. 'Why don't we have a look at the building tomorrow? We could invite other people to send their children. There isn't much here, you said so yourself, just the nuns and Mr English. We could charge people.'

And wasn't that just like a man, Emma thought. Money in everything. 'Nobody would come. The people here – they don't like me. Most of them don't even speak to me. I'm a stranger, and an incomer, even though my parents came from here.'

The children burst in and Constance Castle, looking like an ordinary child, said to her father, 'Can I come back tomorrow? We have plans.'

9

The house stood alone with a high wall around it to stop the winds from disturbing the building or its garden, Emma thought, with some satisfaction. It was big and solidly built, the kind of house which most people wanted when they dreamed of families and the future, and yet it was empty.

She followed Mick Castle through the black iron gates and into the grounds and there she liked everything she saw. She wanted to run about like an excited child among the trees and the overgrown flowerbeds, but it was enough to watch Connie and George do that.

The view was of the tiny square fields below, the grey stone walls, and the very bottom of the valley where the river just at that moment caught the sun and turned white.

Inside, the rooms were big, the kitchen contained a huge stove and all the rooms had big wide fireplaces. It was very cold. She shivered, and he noticed and said, 'I'll send you plenty of coal.'

'Mr Castle—'

'Connie means everything to me,' he said, and he didn't look at her, as though the cost of saying it had been huge.

'In that case I will do all I can to make her happy and to teach her as she should be taught,' Emma said with some dignity, and went into the next room.

The morning sun was already taking the worst of the cold from the rooms at the front and Emma thought what it would be like to watch the sun rise in such a place. She could already see the children there, not arranged in silent groups as they had been at Mr English's school but crowded around the kitchen stove, eating cake and drinking milk and her reading them a story. She knew it was an idealized version of what she wanted, but she felt so good that morning and did not hurry. He did not seem to need to be away and went after her around the place with slow steps as though it meant something to him, and watching how his face changed she said, 'You were born here?'

They were upstairs and he was at the window as though he could take deep breaths of clear air. He smiled just a little at her perception and nodded and turned. 'In this very room.'

It was the room with the best view, the one she had thought she would take for hers and every morning push back the curtains and see the dale spread out before her as though for her to take possession of the day.

He went off into the other upstairs rooms as if he didn't want more conversation. Emma accepted this and said nothing. She thought particularly about the garden and saw in her mind healthy children running about outside, making snowmen and snowballs in the winter, being shown the way that the garden came alive in the spring, sitting outside while she read to them in the summer, under the trees which edged the garden and sheltered it from the road, and watching the falling leaves while she explained the seasons to them and how things worked.

There would be picnics and perhaps even something where she could let the parents and public come in, stalls to raise money for some cause – perhaps her own if most of the children could not pay for their education – and in the autumn – would it be like the fall at home?

'What about furniture?'

She had not heard him come back in. She had not considered something as mundane as what she would need. When she didn't say anything he added, 'Desks?'

'There won't be any desks.'

'Chairs?'

'Yes, lots of those, some of them comfortable, and I will want a very big long table for the kitchen and benches so that the children can sit around it. I will also need quite a lot of beds.'

'It's going to be a boarding school?'

She heard the surprised note in his voice and realized that she had not known until that exact moment that it would be, that she would want children there who needed to be with her for whatever reason.

Mr McConichie's shop was one of the most exciting places Emma had ever been to. It was up at the top of the main street, just before you got to the Black Diamond, so it was a place Mr Castle knew well since he went inside and greeted Mr McConichie with the usual laconic 'Now, Bert', which Emma had discovered was the way men around here greeted their fellows.

'Mick,' Mr McConichie nodded.

Mr Castle introduced them and Mr McConichie looked as if people came into his shop every day looking for lots of furniture especially as Mr Castle told him exactly what was going on. Emma was not used to this much frankness.

'No desks though,' Mr Castle said.

'Just as well, don't have none,' Mr McConichie said. And then he looked curiously at Emma and said, 'Could order some in.'

'It's not going to be that kind of school.'

'No?' Mr McConichie said, a little surprised.

'It's going to be a very special school, an academy such as we have where I come from. It will be called Miss Appleby's Academy.' Emma was inspired by her own idea, and Mr Castle seemed pleased, and even Mr McConichie looked approving.

'Place needs more schools,' he said.

Delighted at this sudden enthusiasm Emma beamed at him. 'You think so?'

'Lord, yes, keeps them young 'uns off the streets and out of my shop. They're never done thieving things, those lads. They comes in here in twos and one talks and t'other takes handfuls of things. They think I don't see, that there's summat wrong with my eyes.'

'I need a table and some chairs,' Emma said.

Mr McConichie had a long wide pine table and benches for either side. He had a great number of easy chairs to choose from too, and George discovered a dappled rocking horse and urged Emma to buy this. It was very expensive. Mr McConichie, who obviously didn't have a possible sale for a rocking horse every day, looked hard at her and said he could do her a good deal. Emma remained firm. She didn't think Mr Castle's purse could be expected to run to such lengths.

He had bedroom furniture. Emma baulked at the idea of second-hand beds.

'Could get some new 'uns,' Mr McConichie said. 'How many you wanting?'

'Six singles and one double, I think.' Emma was unused to dealing with men like this, but she liked it especially when Mr McConichie quibbled about delivering the furniture and Mr Castle said, 'Howay man, Bert,' which she took to mean 'you can do better than that', and Mr McConichie said that since she was buying so much he would deliver it free to her door.

'And bring it inside,' Emma insisted.

Mr McConichie told her she was driving a hard bargain, and she said how on earth was she supposed to get the furniture inside without help, and this he allowed.

Next they went to the hardware store down the street which smelled of paint and oil and the general fustiness which Emma knew pervaded such places. She bought chalk, a dozen slates, pens, paper, ink, cutlery, crockery and various kitchen utensils, bowls and pans and matches, and after she had ordered all this to be delivered – Mr Barron had a horse and cart so that wasn't a problem – they went further down the street and past the Cattle Mart Inn and up the hill and there was a drapers which sold pillows and blankets and sheets and pillowcases.

All this was to go on Mr Castle's account at the various shops and Emma was embarrassed about how much she was spending. After that Mr Castle said he had to get to work and gave her the key to the house and told her that he would tell the butcher and the fishmonger and the greengrocer and the general grocer that they were to give her what she needed. She tried to thank him, but he hurried off as if he were being chased.

Alone with George in her domain she wandered around, amazed at how things were turning out, while George ran about upstairs, saying, 'Can I have this bedroom?' and 'Can I go and have another look outside?' and when she had allowed him out into the unseasonal cold weather he dashed back and said, 'We've had coal delivered and kindling.'

The coal had been unceremoniously dumped in a huge glittering black pile, great big pieces, not far from the back door but to one side so that it did not impede anyone's entrance, but Jack was there and he began to knock at the big pieces with a hammer so that it was small enough to go into the buckets he had found or brought with him.

Emma discovered old newspapers in the bottom of the kitchen cupboards; she tore these up and opened the door of the range and proceeded to twist the newspaper into butterfly shapes – George was entranced by the idea and eager to help. She put good thick sticks on top and finally a little coal. She lit it and stood back, closing the door to allow it to pull and watched in sheer joy as the flames licked their way around the coal and began to give out a little heat.

Various things had been left in the house, but they were all in need of cleaning and she set to straight away and scrubbed the pantry shelves and all the cupboard shelves.

Mr Barron arrived with his horse and cart and brought in the brushes and pans and buckets and cutlery and crockery and all the other things she had bought from him and put as much of it on her new big kitchen table as he could because Mr McConichie had arrived almost at the same time. There was a slight contretemps about whose cart would stand nearer the house, but when she remonstrated with them they took it in turns and she thought how fast men were to help when they were being paid.

Later, tired out, she and George went back to the Black Diamond to eat and sleep. Mr Higgins had already been told that she was moving out. He said he would be sorry to see her go, he would miss her, and she said that he would miss her cooking and he laughed and said that was true too. She also said that he must come to the schoolhouse and he could eat with them there, it was not far, and he looked much brighter at that and said was she sure she wouldn't mind.

He told her she could take the chickens which he had always considered a dreadful nuisance and he would build her a run and make sure they couldn't get into the rest of the garden and wreck it.

The following morning she took their clothes and a few books and other bits and pieces and moved into the schoolhouse proper. She ventured out to the shops and there boldly put on Mr Castle's account tea, coffee, sugar, flour, yeast, butter, lard and such vegetables as could be had, and she had already decided to grow her own vegetables when she got the garden going and maybe even fruit if the climate would stand it in the spring. Here and at the other shops people looked queerly at her, but she remained brisk and decisive and ignored them.

Mr Castle arrived mid morning and she was able to offer him coffee.

'Do you think I could grow fruit here?' she asked.

'You would need a greenhouse and even that might not stand.'

'A glasshouse?'

'Yes, but in a sheltered spot. The best place would be beside the wall down there.'

He pointed. They were in the kitchen at the time and she thought his knowledge showed that there had been such things before, or perhaps at one time he had made plans for what there might be in the future. The future, she thought, was a very shy child which could grow into a snarling monster. Had it been that way for him?

'I would like apple and pear trees, espaliered against the wall, and currants, and could I not grow plenty of vegetables?' she said.

'I suppose you could. Jack could come and help, he's a good lad. He could turn over the soil and dig, you couldn't do all that yourself, especially if the scholars were boarding. The soil's heavy here, but the frosts are keen and break it up. It's good for potatoes and turnips, and you can keep brussels sprouts and cabbages in all winter, and sometimes even the roses bloom at Christmas.'

He had a faraway look in his eyes as he said this, and Emma realized he was not just talking about what she could do now.

'You need a dog.'

He spoke carelessly, but in the evening when he brought the dog she saw that it was the dog she knew and she saw how he got down to the animal and cradled its ears with his hands and spoke softly and very close to the dog's face, and she saw how the dog watched him and she saw later how the dog watched him leave as though he would never see Mr Castle again. Did dogs regret people? She felt sure they did, and she got down as Mr Castle had and she said, 'Hector, he'll be back and you'll be here and though you might miss him I need you now to look after George and me. Will you come into the other room? There's a good fire.' When Hector followed her in and settled down by the fire George got down beside him on the newly bought rug (from the same place as the bed linen came from – she had gone back for so many things she needed) and went to sleep on the dog's stomach, and Hector did not move as though he knew that George was just a child.

When it was late she roused George and took him to bed. The dog was waiting by the door and though she let him out he would not go until she went with him, as though he without her and she without him was no good, so she followed him into the garden and the sky was lit with stars so very bright. When he had done what she thought he had to do he came and sat by her to show her that he was ready to go inside, and they went back in together. Hector waited at the bottom of the stairs, and when Emma had locked the door and felt safe she said to him, 'Hector, would you like to come and sleep in the bedroom? I would feel so much safer if you were there.' He followed her up the stairs, and when she climbed into bed he lay down with a great sigh on the rug (which she had bought of course when she had bought the one downstairs) and went to sleep. He snored. She liked his soft, snuffly snoring. It was so reassuring.

George, having gone around all the bedrooms, kept changing his mind about which he wanted and in the end he just looked at her and said, 'I'm not sure. Could I sleep with you just until I get used to things?' and she said that yes, he could of course if he chose, and it was such a comfort to have the child and the dog there, and even the wind moaning outside as it made its way from the heather down the valley to the dale and beyond made her feel good. She was growing used to it. She even liked the great silence of the house.

It groaned as old houses sometimes do and she was not afraid. Houses have their own sounds and their own ways and in a coalfield sometimes there are abandoned pits beneath them and the fields beyond the houses go up and down in ridges and that is how you know that there was, or is, a pit nearby. It might alarm some people, but when you are born and bred in such a place you don't really mind, and Emma felt like that then, that she was born to live here.

The ridges are like the waves on the sea where some think we all came from, and that is familiar. The waves in the sea and the waves in the fields can lull you to sleep and that was what happened to Emma on that first night. She had thought she would be so afraid, but she was not.

The following day Emma had a visitor. She heard a banging on the door. It was late afternoon, the sky had been deep grey for hours and she was reluctant to open the door because it was growing dark. She thought she could not stop answering the door at that time, but she hesitated when she did so because she recognized the man who stood on her doorstep.

He didn't give her a chance to say anything, but launched into something which she felt sure he had rehearsed and said it so quickly that she understood he was afraid of her reaction even though they had not met properly.

'Miss Appleby? I am Norton English, the master at the

school. I would like to speak to you if it is at all convenient. I understand from the talk in the place that you are attempting to start a school. You cannot set up a school here. We have no need of another, we have two already. There is no cause for you to do this, I doubt you have any qualifications and I cannot see why you would do such a thing when there are no pupils.'

If this had been said in any sort of a convincing manner Emma would have shut the door on him, but by the end of his speech the sweat stood out on his pale forehead, his thinning hair plastered to his head, which was shiny with moisture. He had no coat. He was ill-shod and his shirt cuffs were so frayed they were almost two pieces of material. His hands shook.

'I remember you, Mr English. Do come in.'

Evidently he had not expected any degree of hospitality. He stood on her step as though rooted.

'You have a child. I saw you come into my school. I would be willing to have the boy even though he appears to have no father.'

'Mr English, I wouldn't send Hector to you and he's a Labrador,' she said. 'Come in, do.'

Mr English, thus summoned, meekly followed her into the kitchen.

She gave him tea and apple pie, sat down across the table from him, watched him looking at the enormous piece of pie like a starved schoolboy who wasn't sure he should, before attacking it with appetite, and then she said, 'I'm not trying to steal your pupils, but it seems to me that schoolmastering is not your true calling.'

Mr English looked long at her. He was finishing up the apple pie.

'Unfortunately,' he said, 'it was all the work I could find.'

'You do not like it?'

'My wife is very ill.'

Emma enquired as to the nature of Mrs English's malady and discovered that she was in constant pain from arthritis in her feet and hands which was crippling her.

'She cannot hold a knife or a fork,' he said, 'and she finds walking difficult. We live on her parents' small-holding a mile away.' He smiled briefly. 'She was going to run the farm and the sheep – she knows so much about these things – and I was going to teach and we were going to have children. None of it seems to have worked out and the teaching is all we have.'

Emma absently cut him another piece of apple pie even though he protested, and she poured more tea and said, 'Could you not sell the place and move into the village?'

'It isn't ours to sell. Like her parents were, we are only the tenants. I need my job, you see, and when I heard that Mr Castle was paying for this new school I knew that he would take his child away from me. He has problems at home, you know, his wife drinks, it's become common knowledge, and though I don't like to say so, I feel certain that it is affecting their child.'

Emma called Jack, who was working in the yard, and asked him to keep an eye on things while she went off to see Mrs English; then she loaded up a basket with food, and hoping she didn't seem like a condescending busybody she followed Mr English's lead down a dirt track.

It felt more to her like three miles though it must have been nothing of the kind. The fell was one of those places which was lovely to look at, but not much fun to be on. The road was narrow and stony and full of potholes and wove its way amidst stunted bushes and grass. It ran for miles on either side and she could see nothing beyond stone walls and the odd tree, and the wind cut into her ankles even though the sun shone.

When she got there she was appalled at the state of the buildings. Even the small stone house, though picturesque she was sure in the daytime, was falling down and the outbuildings had no roofs. There were broken stone walls everywhere and the grass was long right around the buildings. You could not have grown anything there, it could have nourished nothing but sheep, the land was so rough.

They went inside and it was no different. If there had been a light of any kind Emma would have been able to see her breath, she thought. Mr English explained that he would have been home by now, Mrs English could not see to the fire or make a light and there was nothing more than a dull glow in the grate.

'Is that you, dear?' Mrs English said, as though it might have been somebody else.

'I've brought you a visitor,' he said.

He lit the lamp which cast nothing more than lighter shadows and a tiny woman was to be seen on a couch in the corner of the room, swathed in shawls. Emma made her decision instantly. She said who she was, and added, 'Mr English has allowed me to invite you to stay with me for a day or two.' She did not look at Norton English's face at this point. 'We've come to take you up to the academy.'

Mrs English stared. 'What is the academy?'

'It's the new school. When we have more pupils Mr English is going to help me there.'

He didn't answer. It was bad enough, Emma thought, that he was obliged to carry his wife most of the way back, but he seemed willing enough and it was no surprise, Emma thought as she swept the two people out of the house and away down the track towards the lights of the village.

'What in the name of God are those people doing here?' was Mick Castle's question when he came to collect Connie and found Mr and Mrs English gracing the kitchen fire.

Emma bustled him into the little room she had made her study at the back of the house. It looked over the yard to the side, but when she worked there she could also see the gates and anyone who should enter, though the noise Hector started up would have alerted anybody to visitors.

'It's just for a visit,' she explained as she closed the door. 'Have you seen where they live?'

'He has a perfectly good job and—'

'He has nothing of the sort.' Emma surprised herself with her vehemence, but she cared. She could hear her voice shaking. He was not reassuring. He was big in the room. Emma had forgotten how large men were, just by their very beings, and he was scruffy and ill-shaven and carried with him the odour of the bar, cigarettes and beer, which while it might have been attractive to some made her want to wrinkle her nose and complain.

'The schoolroom is an appalling place. Who could learn anything there? The children are disruptive and Mr English cannot control them.'

'That's his problem.'

Emma stared at him, held his gaze. 'Is it really? Is this the kind of education you want for the children here? It won't do!'

He returned the gaze, his face cool and sarcastic. 'I see, and do you think you would like to have forty children here?'

'Why not? The place is big enough'

'You're overreaching yourself.'

'Nothing of the sort. Do you think any of those children wanted to be there? They were sullen and badly dressed—'

'The people here are poor.'

'They're poor because other people keep them poor and if they had education they would not be poor for long. They could then do the things God intended them for, not live out their lives in this godforsaken hole while rich people leave them in grinding poverty.'

Emma had never made such a speech before. She didn't know whether to be proud of herself or not. She could hear her voice, loud and booming in the air.

'I cannot afford to keep the village,' he said.

'You can afford to keep your wife in spirits all day,' Emma said, and then was horrified.

He stood for several seconds, and Emma thought of the people being thrown out of the pub and wondered what it felt like, and then he turned and would have left the room. Somebody who was nothing to do with her whisked round and stood against the door. She tried to hold his gaze.

'I'm sorry,' she said. 'That was unforgivable of me.'

He looked down at the unprepossessing hat in his hands which must have been years old, it was falling to pieces. 'No,' he said, softly, 'you're quite right of course.'

She faltered, and then she said, 'Mick—' for the first time, and then her voice gave out and her resolution and she stood away from the door and he opened it with a kind of jerk and left the room.

When she went into the kitchen both he and Connie had gone. She pretended that nothing mattered, she gave Mr and Mrs English the stew she had made for dinner, but later, when his wife had been shown to a clean bed in one of the downstairs rooms which Emma had designated a bedroom, hastily made ready, she and Mr English sat at the kitchen table and he said to her, teacup in hand, 'I could not help seeing Mr Castle's reaction and I don't blame him. We have no right here. We must go in the morning.'

'You will do nothing of the kind. We must have a doctor

for Mrs Castle. I will go and see Dr Blythe. What did you study?' Emma asked.

'Classics.'

'Then how did you end up here?'

His thin face managed a smile. 'I'm a pitman's son, Miss Appleby, I did not fit in. I could find no work. I married Jane and began to try to teach these children. There is much evidence here of Roman occupation, of times gone by and—' He stopped. 'All that was wanted was basics and some of them are not very receptive. Most of them lead the kind of life which you cannot imagine. Their mothers often have many children, they live in tiny, bug-ridden houses, their fathers drink, the men are foul-mouthed and have no compunction about beating their wives and children.

'These children are always hungry and cold and afraid – how can they learn anything when they come from such conditions? The people are often very superstitious. They have no learning themselves and they don't see why their children should. The children leave not being able to read or write and not knowing that they can count to more than ten on their fingers.'

The following day Emma went and sat for a very long time in Dr Blythe's surgery among the shabby-clothed people who had colds and coughs and the more seriously ill ones who waited patiently in the stuffy little room lined with benches. Eventually it was her turn, and she was summoned by Mrs Blythe into the doctor's room. It was large and, from what she could see, well equipped. Sam Blythe was well dressed; everything was clean.

He greeted her by name, asked her to sit down and then enquired what he could do for her.

'I want you to come to the academy. I have Mrs English staying with me. She is far from well. She cannot afford to pay you, as you must know. But she must have attention. Will you come?'

The man shifted uneasily in his chair.

'You have three children, Dr Blythe. Are you intending to send them to the council school or do you have other plans?'

He didn't speak.

'You have few alternatives,' Emma said. 'If you become my school doctor I shall allow the first to attend free of charge. I can offer Greek and Latin, Mathematics, English Language and Literature, Botany, Exercise and Domestic Science.'

Still the man was silent.

'I believe your eldest child is almost six and not at school yet. Surely you wish for him an education.'

'My wife teaches him at home.'

'Is your wife a classics scholar?'

'Are you?'

'I have on my staff a classics teacher, a very clever man. In the meanwhile I would very much like you to see what you can do for Mrs English. She is in a great deal of pain which I feel could be alleviated with some help from you.

Please come as soon as you are able,' and she nodded and left.

Emma did not know what to do about the council school in spite of her brave words, and Mr English went off as usual the following day. That afternoon, however, when Mrs English was nodding by the fire, she took George by the hand and made a visit to the schoolroom.

Mr English looked pleased to see her. He introduced her to the children. Nobody said anything. A lot of them didn't even look up. She told the children to come forward to the fire, she had the desks pushed back by the bigger boys, she got them to sit on their coats, arranged them as well as she could so that they could see both herself and the fire and hopefully feel some warmth. She had Mr English throw as much coal onto it as he could so that there was soon a moist odour of long-unwashed clothes and bodies, which Emma ignored.

She read them *Hiawatha* by Henry Wadsworth Longfellow. They sat in perfect silence. Then she put them into groups and got them to play games, such as the one where each person in turn in the circle must add on the next piece of the story and each person had two minutes.

Several of the children could not do this and hesitated, they were shy or badly spoken or had never been encouraged to speak up, but they began to lose this as the story went on and Emma wrote it up on the blackboard, each group in turn.

They became competitive, shouting that their story was the best, laughing and vying with one another, and Emma let them. She saw Mr English hesitating, but he did nothing since she had their whole attention.

Emma did not like to admit to herself that it was the first time she had taught a huge roomful of children, and if anybody had said that she could do this she would have hesitated, but the time for hesitation was gone and she knew instinctively that if you were to get up in front of a crowd like this you had to take the room, to own it, to entertain as well as teach or you would lose them, and once you lost control of forty children you would not easily get it back. But she taught them.

She forgot that she was small and an incomer and that nobody liked her. She was so engrossed in holding their attention that she became the teacher she wanted to be that day, and when she saw how easily she had achieved it there was a feeling inside her which flowered and grew until her whole being was alight. She had been born to be a teacher and had never known it.

When the sun came spilling into the room she decided that they had had enough of being inside. She showed them how to play softball though all there was at the front of the classroom in a cupboard were two cricket bats and some suitable balls. She divided them into two groups: Mr English took one, she the other. They were fiercely competitive and shrieked and shouted and used very bad language, quite unconsciously, but Emma said nothing. She was so glad to have held their interest all afternoon. When four o'clock came she let them go home and they wandered unwillingly out of the door.

One boy, quite large, who probably would not be at school much longer, lingered at the front of the class and even came to her and said, 'Will you be here tomorrow, Miss?'

'It's Miss Appleby. What are you called?'

'John Wearmouth, Miss.'

'Well, John, Mr English and I will put our heads together and maybe have an outing soon. What would you think of that?'

The boy's eyes were larger than ever.

'That would be grand, Miss,' he said, and then he turned and ran out of the room. He wore thin shoes on his feet which would not last many more days, Emma thought.

She gazed around the room.

'We need another stove in here for when the weather gets bad,' she said. 'I will speak to Mr Castle about it.'

This was pure bravado. She had seen neither Connie nor her father since she and Mr Castle had disagreed, and she was certain she had overstepped some mark and wished she had not spoken to him as she had.

Dr Blythe duly turned up that evening, rather late and looking tired, but he gave Mrs English something to dull the pain. He went off without a word and when it was late Emma sat over the kitchen fire and thought badly of herself for all the interfering things she had done in the past few days.

10

It was two more days before she braved the Black Diamond, and even then she had to force herself to go. She didn't want to see Mick Castle, but as soon as she stepped through the back door she saw Ed in the passage. He greeted her cheerily.

'You must come to lunch on Sunday,' she told him, and his smile widened.

The door to the office stood open and Mick was sitting there just as usual. Emma knocked softly on the open door. He didn't even look up, but he said, 'You can come in. I'm not biting anybody today,' and then he glanced at her. He seemed more unkempt than usual, as though he hadn't slept in days.

'Isn't Connie coming to school?'

'You didn't really think I'd keep her at home because you shouted at me. She runs away, very often. I don't know whether she would actually stay with you even though she seems to like the idea.'

Emma suddenly didn't know what to say. She remembered how she had barred the door and called him by his first name, and it was as though everything was altered somehow. She felt her face begin to burn. She remembered how she had felt about John Elstree. Foolishly, ridiculously, she wanted to stay here in this horrid little office with this scruffy man and hear him say that he was not offended.

'You will bring her then?' was all she could manage.

He said he would. Still she hesitated.

'Something else?' he said.

'I need a stove for Mr English's schoolroom for when the autumn comes. Those children cannot work in the cold; it isn't good for their concentration.'

'You cannot—' he said, and then didn't go on.

'I know. I'm an interfering old spinster, but I cannot stand by and watch things go on when with a little effort they can be changed,' and she left. Her face did not cool down all the way home. Her heart raced and her head panicked.

When Connie came to the school it was different from when she came to play, Emma thought. She was hiding against her father, not quite to the point of touching him but leaning in, as though she were a shadow of him, though she looked nothing like him. His wife must be very beautiful, Emma thought: the child was tiny, graceful, she had delicate features, curling blonde hair, wary though deep-blue eyes and was wearing a dress, coat and boots, not the ragged garb she had been in that day at the school.

Connie spied the dog and went over to him. Hector got up, wagging his tail.

'Do you know him?' George asked, going across, faintly resenting the girl's apparent knowledge of the dog, yet too well-mannered to show it, Emma thought.

'He's one of ours,' Connie said, hugging the dog posses-sively, and then she too seemed to realize what she was doing and drew back a little.

When Mr Castle had gone, saying he would return for Connie at four, Emma took the children and the dog for a long walk, pointing out to them the valley beyond and the fields and telling them all about the farming year. Then they came back and sat in the warmth of the kitchen and she gave them milk and biscuits which she had made the day before and they did some reading.

She was very pleased with the standard reached by Connie, which was well beyond her years; she told the girl so, and saw her face shine. They did some writing, describing the walk they had had earlier and the things they had seen, and read out to her what they had written. They did spellings, also things they had seen while they were outside.

After they had eaten their midday meal she gave the children aprons – well, tea towels knotted around their waists as aprons.

'What are they for?' Connie asked, and Emma thought how different she was already from the child who had run from the schoolroom. Her face was open, ready for new ventures, and Emma was glad. She thought it was something about that warm kitchen, the dog, the range and how confidently her father had left her, that made this easy and simple for the girl.

'We're going to bake cakes. There's the recipe. Have you learned about pounds and ounces?'

'Only in sums.'

'Well, this is the use for them,' Emma said. 'You and George can find the ingredients in the cupboards. The oven is hot, I will help you with the measurements if you need it and show you how to measure it all out and how the scales work, and then we will mix the ingredients together in a bowl and put them into greased tins, and I will put the cakes into the oven and we can time it, when they will come out.'

Connie clapped her hands. Emma gave them each a wooden spoon and the three of them made cakes. She let them do the weighing and mixing themselves, watching from the other end of the big pine kitchen table while they flicked flour at each other and giggled, but eventually they got the cakes into the oven and the smell of them as they baked was for Emma the best part. Connie wanted to open the oven to look at them, but Emma explained why they would sink and how the heat would escape from the oven and the temperature would drop.

When they were ready she took them out, turned over the tins with a cloth and dislodged them so that they ended up on wire racks to cool and then were eaten with glasses of milk. When Mr Castle came back at four to collect her Connie ran to him, explaining in hurried words all the things that they had done that day.

Mick could not believe the difference in his daughter. She had never been so animated before, and this was after just a few hours in Miss Appleby's care. They sat in the kitchen as he had never done before. His memories of kitchens of late had all involved Isabel and her drinking, but he found that he was happy in the warmth of Connie looking so pleased, Hector asleep by the fire and the children describing their walk over the warm dry fields, either of pasture or filled with wheat or barley, the birds they had seen, the different kinds of trees, and how Miss Appleby planned to feed the birds in the garden when the weather turned colder so that they could see them more closely.

He thanked Miss Appleby and took Connie home, only to see his child change before they got back to the house. He was loath to leave her there. She went in, her mouth set as usual and the joy gone from her, but when he would have left her in the long echoing hall and she would have gone either to her room to bed or to his study to read, he said, remembering, 'Miss Appleby plans to take boarders. I know that we live here and I wouldn't want you to feel that I was keen to get rid of you—'

She had already heard what he meant and turned a hopeful face to him so he stopped there. 'Could I really go?'

His heart sank. He knew that he should have provided better for his child, that in a way he had put her mother's welfare ahead of hers and that it was not right. He couldn't remember when the switchover occurred, when he had known that Connie was being damaged because Isabel could not cope, was drinking, retreating, was taking part in their lives less and less.

He thought he had denied this to himself, he had hoped that it would improve, had thought that her child might move her, might alter her behaviour, and it had not and he could not have known this, he told himself over and over. Why had he then not known when it became injurious to Connie, when she became unhappy? Had he been so caught up in his own unhappiness that he did not see?

That week Connie went to Emma's school every day and by the end of the week Mick had asked whether she could stay, and Emma agreed. A sign was made and painted and put up, and it read 'MISS APPLEBY'S ACADEMY' in black letters on white and then in smaller letters '*Boarders and Day Pupils*'.

The room was dark, it was early morning, the curtains were closed and the draught howled through them from the open hillside. The fire was dead, black and grey ashes in the grate. Isabel looked clearly at him for the first time in many weeks.

'So you're taking her away from me,' she said.

He had thought he was prepared for this. 'She needs other children, she's lonely here.' He thought he might appeal to the mother in her.

'The whole world is lonely,' Isabel said, gazing down into the pretty teacup which held her gin. The brandy was long gone. Now it was bottle after bottle of gin, he couldn't stop thinking of how he had once thought gin smelled exciting, the juniper berries seemed to hold promise, now the smell of it made him feel sick.

The cup was white with a gold line around the rim and some kind of flower on it. No doubt it had been a wedding present, they had had dozens of teasets and he could remember thinking how foolish it seemed, he had never imagined that his wife would use them up in quite such a way. When she was very drunk she dropped them or fired them at the walls. Sometimes they lay for days in pieces where the girl who saw to the house had neglected to pick them up and Isabel had not noticed.

'You shouldn't take her away from me, she's my only comfort,' and Isabel began to cry, enormous tears which once had moved him. Now he only marvelled that she could do such things at will. 'She's all I've got. You're never here. You've got your new woman. You never come home to me.'

He was amazed. He stared.

Isabel gazed at him. 'I heard all about her,' she said. 'The schoolteacher. You've given her my child!'

Isabel began to shout at him. He could not remember now how it was when she was sober, what she used to say to him, how much in love with her he had been. She was not a pretty sight with spittle on her lips and the dim look in her eyes and her thin voice lifted as much as she could lift it when she called Emma Appleby a whore.

'And she's – she's an American!'

That made him laugh and Isabel was all the more enraged when he laughed at her. He didn't do it often, the situation had long since ceased to amuse him. She threw her cup at him and after it the teapot which matched it. He watched it smash against the fireplace and thought with regret of the many tea sets which had gone the same way. Then she got up. That wasn't good.

She flew at him and tried to sink her nails into his face, but he held her off quite easily. She was so thin, she had not eaten anything but dry toast for months and the drink had left her emaciated. He couldn't understand how she had lived this long, but he would have given anything for her to last even one more day.

He didn't let go of her until all the fight was gone from her skeletal body and she slumped against him, sobbing, and then he moved her carefully back to the sofa which had become her refuge and he left her. The maid – he couldn't even remember her name, there had been so many – was hovering beyond the door.

Connie was standing in the hall, fully dressed, her suitcases beside her, and he thought she must have heard it all. Not that it was the first time, she too had become used to such scenes, but she was white-faced and there were tears in her eyes. Her hands were folded across the front of her belted coat.

'Am I still going?' she said.

He picked up her suitcases, they were heavy, he suspected, with books.

'Open the door,' he said.

Connie stared at the size of the room. It was the same as her room at home, but there were three beds in it. It had not occurred to her that she would have to share with anybody and although she had never thought of her room as being large she saw now that it was and she had had it all to herself. Here the furniture was cheap, the wardrobe looked insubstantial, there was a small chest of drawers beside each bed and no dressing table, which she was disappointed about. She had not thought that having her own room was so important.

'Who else sleeps in this room?' she enquired of George.

'Nobody. What have you got in there, rocks?' He nodded at her suitcase and then stopped trying to move it.

Connie pushed it over and opened it. There was a book-case along one wall. She carefully decanted the books and began to arrange them. George, without being asked, helped her until they were all in and the suitcase was empty. George seemed less interested in the other suit-case and she was not surprised, it contained boring things like clothes. Also, her mother's silver-backed mirror, hair-brush and comb. She had stolen them from her mother's bedroom which had not been used for a long time. She could not remember the last time her mother had ventured up the stairs even to kiss her goodnight. It made her want to cry.

She had thought she would have a dressing table on which to put the brush and comb, but it was no matter; she opened the case and put them carefully on top of the chest of drawers, the mirror face down in the middle though there was no lace-trimmed dressing table such as her mother had at home, the comb on one side and the brush on the other. She expected George to comment; she thought a girl would have done, but she didn't know any

187

boys beyond brief acquaintance at school. He didn't say anything and she liked that.

He waited patiently, watching her as she put her belongings into the drawers and the wardrobe and then the two children went downstairs together. For the first time Connie worried about what she had done in coming here. She had left her father to her mother, something she had promised him she would not do. She felt guilt suffuse her body like cold drenching water.

Miss Appleby had greeted her warmly, but it was not long before Connie wanted to run out of there; she thought to ask instead of just going. Miss Appleby merely said that she should put on her outdoor things.

'Would you like to take Hector with you? He's always ready for a walk.'

Connie had never walked a dog before by herself and even though she knew Hector well, she wasn't sure how to respond, but all Miss Appleby said was, 'He won't leave you.'

She knew, but she had needed to hear it. She was happy to take the big dog out with her, and set off away from the school and towards the edge of the town, and Hector stopped and sniffed as they went along, but Miss Appleby was right, he didn't leave her. She had also thought that George might want to go with her and she would have found it hard to object, but she hadn't wanted him there. Not that he had asked or even looked as though he wanted to go, but once she was outside she rather wished she had asked him.

She became conscious of being lonely then for the first time ever. She had always liked being alone and now she didn't. She walked for the first half an hour and every step of the way she wanted to go back, and once she had turned back her steps increased in speed until she was practically running by the time she reached the gate of the schoolhouse and she was out of breath and Hector's tongue was hanging out.

Nobody said anything other than had she had a good walk, but George brought her a book to look at: it was about dinosaurs, and they sat together at the big kitchen table and drew pictures of dinosaurs while Miss Appleby told them all about these creatures who had roamed the earth long ago.

Her father did not come back at teatime. She seemed to be the only one who had expected him to and she realized with a jolt that she always saw him every day; no matter how late he came home he went in and kissed her goodnight.

When it was bedtime she didn't have to take herself to bed, Miss Appleby gave her a warm milky drink and saw her upstairs, left her to undress and said she would come back to tuck her in. Connie was not used to being tucked in, but when she saw Miss Appleby pushing in the bedclothes around her she thought it was so comforting. Miss Appleby even kissed her goodnight and said, 'I hope you won't be lonely your first night here. We leave the bedroom doors open so all you have to do is call if you are afraid or miss your parents.'

Connie was about to announce bravely that she was never afraid and then didn't because she did feel rather strange away from home for the first time, but as soon as Miss Appleby had gone George came in and sat down on the bed. He told her that Hector slept on the landing and snored, and that made her giggle.

George said goodnight and left the door ajar. She soon fell asleep. She did stir in the night, not quite sure why she was where she was or where it was, and her bed was smaller than she had been used to, but she was aware of the covers being tucked tightly around her and then she lay still, and Hector was indeed snoring. She fell asleep again, listening to the comforting sound of the dog.

The first night when Mick went home after Connie had left he realized that he had a routine, that he always stopped by her bedroom before going to bed himself, that he only stayed there because he was aware of her sleeping in the same house.

He went into Connie's room as usual that first night and was aghast for a few moments to find that she was not there. The whole place seemed to echo with silence. He had not even paused downstairs to see where his wife was; for months now she had slept ten or twelve hours at night in the same place on the sofa.

He couldn't bear it. He left the house and went back to the Black Diamond and slept in a chair. His office was still warm from the heat of the day. He found himself on the floor on a rug. He thought of Connie at Emma's house, safe at the house where he had been a happy child, and he was almost happy himself.

When he awoke he could hear soft rain upon the window. He was stiff from lying in the same position for so long, but he felt rested and energetic. He couldn't remember the last time he had felt like that. It was morning, the curtains were not closed and the sun was shining as the rain ceased. He never slept long and well. Knowing that Connie was safe had affected him more than he had imagined. He got up, stretched a bit and opened the door. He went into the bar.

The smell of stale cigarettes and beer began to disappear as he opened the windows. The sun and wind made their way through the room and hit his face, and he took a few deep breaths before leaving the window open.

He watched the newly made-up fire and set the kettle over it, and when it boiled he made tea, sat and drank it slowly. The sun coming into the room showed up the dirt and the dust and he was astonished. How had it got like that? He used to have women in to clean. He felt sorry, remembering how he had dismissed them without a word, not caring at the looks on their astonished faces.

They had been widows, women who had children and needed what work they could get. It had not mattered to him somehow. He was ashamed. He went into his office, and in there the mess was worse, and then to every room in the place. Curtains were falling down. Mouse droppings littered the floor. The bar wasn't too bad, Ed wiped the tables, but since Miss Appleby had gone nobody cleaned anything.

He did go home that morning and it was there that he noticed for the first time how shabby his clothes were, how unkempt he looked, and then he laughed into the mirror and knew what the problem was. He cared that Miss Appleby should think he was respectable. It was ludicrous. He was not interested in her as a woman and yet because she was looking after Connie and he respected her somehow he felt that he needed respect in return. It didn't matter, she would see to Connie anyhow, it was her way, but somehow what he was doing was not enough. How appalling.

He washed and changed and went back to work. He didn't shave. It was defiance somehow. He wasn't even sure how long that would last.

Somehow it seemed important to let the doctor see Isabel again. Sam came to her, was gentle with her, and even the house seemed to like him: the sunshine fell softly through the window and turned the dust and dirt to magic, and Isabel seemed younger and her voice was pretty because Sam was there.

Sam didn't say anything to Mick while they were in the room. He spoke directly to Isabel, his voice like a violin, notes tripping up and down so that anyone would have been glad to listen. Isabel drank her gin and smiled at his face and his tones and then she fell asleep amid the concert of Sam's performance.

'You could have her committed, you know,' he said, watching her carefully.

'Oh Sam, how could I?'

His friend looked at him in some exasperation. 'She's getting worse. You know she is. Why did you think anything would get better? What did you expect? You know better than to think that such things as alcohol are the reason for madness—'

'She had everything, a loving family, a lot of money, beauty, intelligence, wit . . .'

'Some people are just different. I know that sounds ridiculously obvious. Your wife is very ill – accept it. Because it comes in a form people don't like they call it idleness or cowardice. She needed something to dull the fear, to smooth the hours. Drink is not the problem, it's what many people think is the solution, and it isn't, and other people who don't have the same problems think that if people like Isabel give up the drink they will be fine, but it isn't true: they take on something else if they do.

'They need something, they need medicine of some kind, something to dull and pass the hours because each minute crawls, each second is a lifetime to some. She drinks because she cannot bear her life, because she's in some dark place all alone and if she didn't drink the chances are that she would end it. I'm sorry, but it's part of her make-up, part of her mental derangement. It isn't to do with you or with Connie.'

'Are you sure?'

'Of course.'

'Liar,' Mick said. 'You know damned fine it could have been childbirth.'

'It could have been but don't you think that's just men loving how they can blame women for everything which goes wrong?'

'That's a nice argument,' Mick said.

'The medical profession knows little and what it doesn't know it makes up.'

Mick shook his head and sat down and closed his eyes.

'If she had had tobacco or opium at her disposal it would have been the same.' Sam paused.

'I can't stand it. I love her.'

'You love the woman you married. Nobody would recognize her now.'

'At least I got Connie out.'

Sam accepted the change of direction. 'Does she like being with Miss Appleby?'

'I think it's too soon to tell, maybe it'll be all right for a while and then she'll hate it like she has other schools. What are you looking at?'

Sam was staring at him across the room. 'You do know people are talking?'

Mick lifted his eyes to the heavens. 'There's nothing for them to talk about.'

'She lived at your pub.'

'Not with me. I went home. She's an old maid, give me some credit. She's plain and prim, and I don't think she even likes me.'

'People won't send their children to her if you spend time there.'

'I go to see Connie. And besides, they have very little choice. Norton English is a clever man, but he can't control children, and nuns are, well, nuns. Miss Appleby will run a good school.'

'And you're paying for it?'

'One of the best deals I ever made if Connie is happy,' Mick said.

One Monday afternoon that autumn George and Connie were sitting over the living-room fire reading when Emma saw a well-dressed woman coming up the road and turning in at her path. The woman wore dark but expensive clothes and was smiling politely.

'Good day, Miss Appleby. I am Mrs Summers. I would like to have a word with you.'

Emma wanted to suggest that it might wait for another day, but there was something determined about Mrs Summers' mouth that made Emma think the woman might try to insist, and so she gave way and invited her in.

'My husband is Eden Summers, he owns the ironworks here and is on the council. We are very much involved in the church. I understand you attended while I was away. I'm sorry that the vicar and his wife were apparently so unwelcoming, but you must understand that if you intend living here you have made a very bad start. You have upset a good many other people by setting up a school. You are an incomer, Miss Appleby, and have taken a great deal on yourself without leave from anyone.'

All this before they had even sat down, Emma thought wearily. She had been going to offer Mrs Summers tea, but after this long speech Emma sat down with the woman and then couldn't think of anything to say. But it wasn't necessary. Mrs Summers merely paused for breath and then carried on.

'Mr English is paid to teach the children here. It is hard to believe that you went to the school and taught the children, unasked and uninvited. You must not attempt to usurp his position here. It is a small town, everyone knows everyone. I'm only sorry that you took it into your head to imagine that we needed another school. If you had made enquiries before plunging into this matter without asking anyone you would have been better informed. I'm sure I don't need to say anything else. You will naturally take down the sign and perhaps find somewhere which needs your services. It will not, however, be here.

'You have no right either legal or moral to stop me from setting up a school here,' Emma said. 'I am educated and—'

'Not in England. Do you intend to beggar Mr English by your conduct? How is he to make a living if you steal his pupils away? Have you no concern for anyone other than yourself? I understand that the Englishes live here with you. Do you know how that looks?'

Emma just wished that she would go.

'This place needs him,' Mrs Summers said. 'It does not need somebody from a foreign land coming here and trying to teach her granny how to suck eggs.'

'I am not from any foreign place. I am English. I was born here.'

That stopped Mrs Summers. She stared.

'My father lectured at Durham University when he was a very young man; my mother came from this place, they had a house here, my grandparents are buried here.'

Mrs Summers had gone white.

'My father won a place to teach at a New England college and my brother was born there. I was born a few houses along from here. I even remembered the view. I left here when I was a small child and I wanted to come back. I did not think to be so ill received.'

Mrs Summers didn't answer immediately, but when she did there was an expression on her face which Emma was surprised to see. It was pity. She watched the woman pause and it was as if the pity was not real but just a front for some kind of different feeling. It was almost like watching someone eat a piece of chocolate cake: it was a triumph, an enjoyment. Mrs Summers was pressing her lips together so that she would not smile and the pity was completely gone. She spoke slowly as though she relished what she was saying.

'Your father was estranged from his parents, Miss Appleby. When he met your mother he walked out and left his wife and three children for her. After you were born there was no way they could have remained here. He had to claim you as his own; she had to endure the stigma of being an unmarried mother in a pit town until he did so. His wife was so ashamed of what he had done, his parents were broken-hearted. Three small children, one of them only a baby, four months old, I think. He had been conducting a clandestine affair with your mother when his wife was pregnant with their third child.'

Emma stared. She didn't know how long she went on staring. She wanted to deny such terrible things, to claim them as untrue. Her father could not have done such a thing. She remembered how gentle and caring he was.

'Your parents were never married, how could they be?'

Stupidly all Emma could think was how horrified Laurence would be if he discovered that he was illegitimate. So stuffy, so righteous. And then she remembered what he had said, that he was a better man than their father had been. Laurence knew, or at least he knew some of it, and yet he had not told her. He had risked her leaving. No wonder he had been so upset at the docks in Boston. He had tried to shield her because he knew how much love and respect she had for their father and he had gone about it the wrong way and this was the result. Emma could not help knowing that if she had been his brother rather than his sister he would have said something.

After that she had a desire to cry, long and hard, to run away so far that she need never come back, but she had done that once already and it seemed that it had caused more problems. Since she could do neither of these things she sat there, trying to keep a civilized expression on her face.

Somehow she rose to her feet. 'Thank you for coming, Mrs Summers.'

'I'm sorry to bring you such ill tidings,' the woman said, smirking.

'Not at all,' Emma said stiffly.

Nothing else was said. It seemed an interminable amount of time before her visitor got to the front door and during that time Emma tried not to hurry her along; it seemed that the distance between there and the outside door was a hundred miles and Mrs Summers' steps slowed and then lagged and it took several years before they reached the door. Emma grasped it, hung on, even though her nails were breaking against the wood and her breath had left her.

She ushered the woman out. She wished at that point she had stayed in New England and married the Judge and not known any of this. Did Mick Castle know? He might have done, but would not connect it up. Men would not, could not, see things like that. He was only grateful that his child had a teacher and some care.

The door was finally closed. She turned around and leaned against it hard as though Mrs Summers was about to break in, and when her breath had gone in and out several times and nothing happened she allowed her body to slide into the nearest chair.

Then she heard the sound of the children and was obliged to pretend that all was well. They were eager for supper; they knew she had had a visitor. Connie had known it was that awful Mrs Summers who tried to keep everybody right, and they had waited. Mr English came back from school and Emma had to admit that he was looking much better now that he was well fed and he and his wife were well housed.

She paced the house long after everyone was asleep and then she took Hector outside. He stayed by her. How strange that the dog should comprehend when the children had not. They were self-absorbed as children always were. Hector followed close by as she walked around the garden, and watched the moon. It was the same moon that her parents had seen, that her grandparents had endured after their son disgraced them. What was her father like as a young man? She could not think of him as negligent. She could not accept that he would have done such a thing as to leave a woman who was his wife and with whom he had fathered three children. It must be wrong, and yet she saw in her mind Mrs Summers' shocked and satisfied face. It was true. It must be true.

She remembered his caring of George. How she had brought the baby into the house in a blanket and he had accepted him so freely. Did he not think of his own children? Emma thought she could never have left her husband and three children. Was it not the same? Were you not bound irretrievably to the person you were married to by the Church and the law, when you had lain with them, spent so many days with your offspring? Was there no joy? Was there nothing to hold you? However did you walk out and leave three children and the woman you had sworn to stand by? She could not reconcile it with her idea of how things were meant to be or how things had been.

For the first time she wished that she could have spoken to Laurence. She went to bed, but did not sleep. She tried not to see her father in this new light; she tried not to believe what he had done. She tried to comfort herself, saying that he was not that man, and then she remembered Mrs Summers' face.

She lay watching as the dawn came early and then she got up and started the fire in the stove, sat over the hearth in her night things with a big blanket around her, and when it was alight she put on the kettle; when it finally boiled she made some tea.

The tea made her feel better, at least for a while, and then the children were awake and she was glad that she had no time to think, but later in the day after Jack arrived she sent him with a note to Mr Castle. She had no one else to confide in. Mick Castle might be able to help, she thought.

By the time he had come to see her Mr and Mrs English were alone by the back-room fire with the door shut, the children were in bed and she was exhausted though she didn't know it until the room was quiet and the house was silent and there was only Mr Castle and Hector and herself and the door was closed. She burst into tears.

'Emma?' He hadn't called her by her first name before and she wished he had not done so now. She held up one hand, palm turned to him, even backed away slightly as though he had made steps towards her.

'It's all right,' she said, 'I shall be fine.'

'What is it?'

He drew nearer, and she wished he hadn't and then was glad he had done. She turned a tear-stained face to him as she would never have done with another man, and she didn't even understand how she could do it when he was there; it was just that she had had nobody to turn to since her father had died, and then she saw her father flawed and broke down.

Mick stood back since she didn't seem to want him there, though that wasn't quite true, but it was enough to hold him beyond her and she was perhaps grateful for that.

'I heard such awful things about my father from Mrs Summers.' She couldn't get her breath.

He didn't say anything. She waited for him to question her, though it was the last thing she could have stood and in a way she wished that he had been less sensitive. If he had ploughed in at that point she would have retreated, perhaps even apologized, and the moment would have passed and she would have stood alone, and she would have managed it. She thought for a second, I would have been fine, and then she knew that it was not so.

'Tell me what it is.'

'That my father – it isn't true – that my father walked out on his family, ran away with my mother. He can't have done it.' She waited for him to say that it was not so, that he knew nothing about it, that it could not have been, but he did not and when the time went forward and still he did not she found the tears dripping. 'Did you know?'

He stood silent until she could have screamed and as

the silence went on she felt worse and worse. And she could see comprehension in his face.

'I didn't make the connection,' he said.

'Why not?' She glared suddenly at his white face, his dark eyes.

'It's a common enough name in these parts. How could I have known?'

'He did then.' It was almost a question, but she didn't want it to be.

'As far as I know.'

'And how far is that?' She was glaring at him again as though it were his fault.

He looked down, as if the floor held fascination.

'I know the family.'

'Are they here?' Emma was aghast. It had not occurred to her that her father's infamy mattered here, yet it would, she saw, that kind of thing mattered for years and years, perhaps even for generations.

'Some of them.'

'The wife?'

'She died.'

'Oh God! The children?'

'One of the girls moved away. The other girl lives here. The boy, he's here too.'

Emma's hands were shaking. She could not look at him. 'Tell me about them.'

He hesitated. 'I don't know about the one who moved away. The girl married a pitman. She's widowed with children. The boy is here too. Larry.'

Emma stared in disbelief. 'Is that Laurence?'

'That's right.'

'Is he married?'

'No.' There was a pause. 'He sits by the fire in the Black Diamond in the afternoons.'

'He's a drunk then.'

Mick said nothing to that. Emma could not believe that her father had called both his sons by the same name. She knew that some people did such things, but surely that was only when one son had died. Was that how her father had felt?

'My brother is called Laurence,' she said. 'I'm sorry, I shouldn't have asked you to come here, but I had no one else. You said the daughter was widowed. Is she very poor?'

'Emma—' he stopped. 'How do I say this to you?' He said it by walking away, standing beside the window, looking out though it had been dark for hours and there was nothing to see but shadows. 'Nell Whittington is the local whore.'

Emma stared at his back and couldn't think of anything to say and then asked, 'Why does she do such a thing?' As she said it a memory half came back to her, something nudged at her mind. She was too upset to work out what it was, but it niggled there and would not leave.

'She used to be a dressmaker but her eyes failed. Workmen here, they make good money and when they come out of the pub most of them still have copper to spend, especially on paydays.'

What Emma said next really upset her. She didn't know

how it got past her lips. 'Do you think people know that we are related?'

'Some of them might have worked it out. It didn't occur to me so maybe not to them either.'

'They will know now,' Emma said bitterly. 'I'm sure Mrs Summers has told everyone.'

There was a long silence during which Emma could see a big moon rising in the sky in the garden.

'I never had a sister before. I always wanted one, I disliked Laurence and he always despised me. To think things should come to this. Mrs Summers thinks I should leave.'

'I don't think you should go anywhere,' he said.

'But whatever am I to do? People didn't like me anyway, but now—' She couldn't think beyond how appalling the whole situation was.

He said nothing more and she thought he was right: the best thing to do when you didn't know what to do was nothing.

When Mick left she went outside with him and Hector stayed at her heels, even though his idol was present. He was her dog now. Mick Castle looked at Hector. Then he got down and took hold of Hector by the ears in such an affectionate way and Hector licked his face, perhaps in apology or regret.

'Good boy,' Mick said, and then he walked away. Neither of them said goodnight.

It was very late when Emma went to bed, and it took all

her courage: the last thing she wanted to do was lie in the darkness thinking, but there was nothing else to do at this time of night so she went, and then she stared up at the ceiling and she remembered the woman who had spoken to her outside the butcher's. She remembered what the woman had said.

Was that Nell Whittington? The woman must be older than she was, but not that much, and yet she had looked so used up and her eyes were defiant and full of sorrow. Emma went over again and again the scene in the front street so soon after she had arrived here. She had not given that woman a moment's thought since.

She was guilt-stricken and sat up in bed, as though there were more she could do upright, and then lay down again, but she could not put from her mind the image of the woman whose face she had recognized. Yes, she thought now, she had seen her own face looking back at her, even though they had different mothers. She and Nell looked alike.

So Mrs Summers had been right and all the awful things she had said were true. Mick Castle had confirmed them, but she had not accepted what he had said as completely as she did now. She did have family here; it was what she had wanted, but to find them in such a way, in such awful circumstances, and to know that her father was not the man she had thought him was, a bitter blow.

There were two bars in the Black Diamond, the bigger one looked out over the main street and was the lighter of the two rooms. Not that it made much difference, but the other room looked out across the yard, where she had hung clothes when the weather was dry and windy, even in the cold. At this time of day the place was not full, but there were quite a lot of men, most of them older, some playing dominoes. She could hear the clack as the dominoes were put down on the table or turned over the other way. Where the room got the light two men were playing darts.

Some of the men sat on their own and even though she had not seen him before she could see immediately the man who was her half-brother. It was the way that he sat, he looked just like Laurence, so exactly like him that she was taken aback. She couldn't think what to say or how to approach him. He was Laurence without the fine clothes and attitudes; Laurence as he would have been had he been poor and neglected.

She began to understand just a little at that point why her parents had emigrated, but she could not reconcile herself to the mess and pain that they had left behind. They had thought of themselves only. Would she have done such a thing for John Elstree? If he had offered to leave his wife and children for her, would she have gone with him? She didn't think so and then she thought that she had no right to judge.

She knew nothing of men. She had not even been kissed. If John Elstree had kissed her and held her in his arms and assured her of his love would she have lost her mind and gone with him? Knowing that she had no life in the little New England town, would she have left?

Her half-brother sat with a cigarette in his dirty brown fingers. He looked like somebody who had given up: his face had caved in, his cheeks were sunken and had deep wrinkles as if somebody had taken chunks out of his face. He was older than Laurence, and she felt a sympathy such as she could never remember having felt for Laurence because there something defenceless about his whole body. He sat by the fire and the light of it played on his face and it was filled with sadness.

'Are you—' she spoke very softly, 'are you Laurence Appleby?'

She thought he didn't hear her, but it was just that he hadn't noticed her approach him, and then he looked up and her impression was that he was so like his namesake that she didn't know what to say.

After that she didn't speak and he went back to regarding the fire as if it were his only friend, his gnarled fingers clenched around the tankard they held.

'I think we're related,' she said.

He looked at her as though he thought she might be speaking to somebody else, and then stared.

'Did you know we had the same surname?' she said.

He didn't say anything, he just looked disbelieving and something else, as though his interest or even basic curiosity had long since been sated.

'Our father was the same man.'

'I never had no father,' he said roughly, taking a great pull at the half-smoked cigarette which he held as though it were a part of him, turned in toward his hand. 'He buggered off and left me mam. She had two other bairns, lasses, older 'n me.'

'But your name—'

'It was his name.'

'His?' As far as she knew her father had not been called Laurence. There was a glimmer of hope in her before she remembered it was his middle name.

'That's what she said. She said he were a soldier, but it weren't true, he were a bastard.'

'He was a scholar.' Emma couldn't help correcting him.

Laurence shook his head. 'A hewer. But clever like. Me mam said he were always at his books. He didn't like work.'

It was her turn to stare.

Emma wanted to deny it. Her body felt as though her stomach had been pulled out of her and there was an enormous hole and she would never eat again.

'He knew how to talk, me mam said he could talk anybody into owt. He had another lass and she were expectin' and that were why he left us. After the babby were born he were here for less than two years and me mam on her own. They went overseas where nobody knew them. Me mam said he were a rare talker – he talked her into marrying him and t'other lass into going with him and runnin' off with him.'

The babby. It took Emma some time to realize that he was speaking of her. He said nothing else and she could think of nothing more to say to him. She staggered out of the bar. She went the back way, past Mick's office.

Ulysses came after her, and as she was crying nuzzled his wet nose into her hand. She went out into the yard, she needed the air, there were so many things she needed to get used to. She took a lot of deep breaths, trying to absorb what had just happened, and then she heard movement behind her and glanced back.

'I'm going to find out where Nell lives and go and see her. Do you know her?' she asked as Mick followed her into the yard.

'You shouldn't,' he said. 'It isn't going to help.'

'I'll just ask somebody else if you don't tell me,' she said, wiping away the tears with the knuckles of her hands.

Road Ends, Emma discovered, stood apart from the rest of the village. It was about half a mile away.

The view was clear across the valley. On a fine day like this it was blowy because the wind had nothing to stop it. When she reached the very end house she saw how poor it was: the windows were rotten, the walls were crumbling, the door had no paint. She banged upon it and when it opened she had the weirdest sensation of all.

The woman who opened the door looked so exactly like her that it was like looking into a mirror, and Emma couldn't think of anything to say. She had been right, this woman was her sister. It made her feel worse. As with the brother, Nell looked older because of what she had been through, no doubt, Emma thought, despairing and adrift. She had always thought she looked like her mother, but the resemblance here was so strong that it was undeni-

210

able. Nell was dressed in dull cheap clothes. There was a smell of broth on the stove, of vegetables cooking.

She didn't speak, she just stood there in an attitude of defiance, her eyes blank and huge black smudges under them, her cheeks bright with broken veins. Beyond her, two children were sitting close to the fire. They were silent. The room was damp, dank. It made Emma shiver even to be there. The anxious look conveyed a message to Nell and her face filled with dismay.

'Do you remember us meeting outside the butcher's in the main street? I'm Emma Appleby. May I come inside?'

The wind was making her dress cling to her ankles. There was nothing to stop it, no other buildings around here. These terraces beside the road must have been built for a special purpose some time back and they had wonderful views for miles and miles, but up there on the tops the weather was king and a cold wind whipped across the bare land.

'What for?' Nell asked, half closing the door as though Emma would attempt to push her way inside.

There was no point in putting off what she had come here to say.

'I think we have the same father,' Emma said.

She expected to see surprise, even denial on the other woman's face, but Nell merely looked down as though she had suspected it, as though she had known all along and was bitter about it. She went white but tossed her head as though to get rid of the information, as though it didn't matter one little bit.

'It's nowt special round here. Lots of lasses don't know who their bairns' fathers are.'

'May I come in?'

'Nay, what's the point?'

'Do you remember your father leaving?'

Nell looked as if she wasn't going to answer, she stood back even further and closed the door so that it was no more than a crack from being shut, and then she said, 'Aye, I remember him going on living here after he left my mam and how she begged of him not to go, and him and her just over the town, and then she heard they had a bairn. She was so ashamed she couldn't keep her man. People called it her fault.

'She never looked at another man. She was having our Larry at the time and Larry wasn't normal, he's a bit simple. Him leaving, that finished my mam off and I think Larry is like he is because of it. He was the only man in the family and the youngest of us. She went cleaning to other folks' houses and left us until the day our Larry set the house on fire. It weren't much, but it stopped her going far until we got older.'

'I knew nothing about you.'

'Well, now you do,' Nell said and she closed the door the inch or so it was ajar which was as effective as though she had slammed it in Emma's face.

11

When Emma got back to the house Mr English waved a piece of paper in her face.

'I got a letter from the authorities. I have to go and live in my house and run the school by myself or I'm going to lose my job,' he said.

Emma made up baskets of food and clean dry bed linen which she and the children carried and they helped Mr and Mrs English back to the house on the fell. The house smelled damp and as though out of humour the rain began to fall. George shovelled coal from the coal house and staggered in with bucketfuls and Connie, who had with pride learned how to lay a fire, sorted out paper and sticks and soon there were fires burning in the down-stairs rooms. Emma decided that she would talk to Mr Castle and get him to send them some more coal.

Mr English and George moved the bed into the big kitchen and pushed the table and chairs right to the back wall. The table folded down at both sides until it was no more than a few inches across, the chairs went under-neath. This, Emma thought, would be a permanent sick room for Mrs English. She sorted out the lamps too and heated food on the stove. She determined that next time she came she would bring thick curtains to go over the doors to keep out the cold this coming winter. When they left, the children and Hector ahead of her, Mr English said, 'Thank you, Miss Appleby, nobody could have done more.'

When they got back she put the children to bed. She went into the garden with Hector and the stars came out. She heard the gate but Hector wagged his tail so she knew that it was only Mr Castle.

She told him about the Englishes and that they would need some coal and he said, 'Do you want me to keep the whole bloody village?' and Emma lost her temper and retorted, 'Well, somebody has to in this godforsaken place. They have nothing.'

'They have a lot more than most people.'

Emma was shaking with temper. She had never felt so angry. Her cheeks burned and her hands had made themselves into fists. She tried to swallow and then she said, 'They need coal.'

'All right.'

She would have turned away and gone back into the house, but when she half turned he got hold of her and to her astonishment brought his mouth down on hers and it was exactly right. Emma didn't hesitate for a second. Having never been kissed before she found it was the one thing that mattered. She wanted it to go on and on.

She felt his hands on her back and drew closer. There was no part of her that reminded her who she was or what she was trying to do in her life. No respectable inkling saved her. She slid her hands up his body to his shoulders and it was the comfort as much as anything that she needed and the reassurance somehow that somebody cared to be that close when nobody had done so before. Her gratitude would have sickened her had she given it a moment's thought, but she didn't because she was so intent on his sweet mouth and the closeness of him was such exquisite joy.

She had long imagined what a man's body close to hers would feel like, but she did not know that she would immediately feel ownership, some strange kind of assurance that he was hers, when she knew he was nothing of the kind. Her imagination had not taken her anywhere near what it felt like to have him there; his body was taut and lean and his mouth was better than she had ever thought anything like that could be. She was immediately shameless and gave her mouth completely and drew him very near as though, she thought later, she knew all about such things.

Perhaps you instantly did, perhaps it was instinct, it certainly was hunger, and she was not the woman who did not take advantage of a situation when she could. It was as if she had loved him, longed for him, and it was not so. She didn't think she had for one second thought lasciviously about Mick Castle, but maybe she was pretending to herself because she had no intention of letting him go, of letting him go home, of letting him go not just out of sight but even inches away from her. He was her captive, he was all hers at that moment.

*

For the first time in her life Emma turned the key in the lock of her bedroom door. Hector, who was usually to sleep by the bed, accepted that he must stay in the hall. She heard him lie down, slump there, and that was the last thing she heard outside the room.

There was no light, but then she had not closed the curtains, and shadows of every hue decorated the walls. All she knew was that somebody wanted her and he was not a stupid young man who cared about his place in society and he was not an old man with foetid breath and a desire for younger flesh. It was nothing like that. It was just that he was there and she had known how he would feel, that she would not be uncomfortable or old or out of place or that he had any motive beyond the meeting of their bodies. The honesty was entirely disarming.

Mick's skin was smooth and firm and his mouth was gentle at first and so were his words and then he was just what she needed him to be, no more or less, he didn't expect things she didn't know or intrude. And he was hungry and that was fine. She had been hungry for twenty years.

He didn't even lie and tell her that he loved her. She knew very well that he reserved that for Isabel. She didn't care. She was glad he was warm against her in her bed. She liked the way that he gathered her close. Being against him was the safest place that Emma had ever been.

She had never had too much chocolate or too much wine, and she thought it was high time that she had too much of something, but she didn't think she could ever have too much of Mick Castle. Even when his body had completely satisfied hers she didn't let go of him. She was afraid that he would disappear into the darkness like so many hopes and dreams, that everything went the same way, that all was insubstantial.

He had very good instincts, she thought: he didn't let go of her, he held her there every second and his hands were gentle as though he knew exactly how much she needed him and if he didn't she told him so and made him laugh quietly, his breath sweet upon her face and his voice the sound of her dreams. She thought she would never get enough of any of it. She wanted the night to go on and on as a night never had, because he kept away the horrors of the darkness, the reality of her life, all the things she felt she must shoulder and hold up and go back to – they were all gone now that he was there. She felt safe, she told him she felt just as secure here with him as she did when Hector was in the room and he laughed so much that he had to hide his face against her neck.

In the darkness he stirred. Emma came back to consciousness slowly, having finally fallen asleep, and heard him say softly, 'I have to go. It's almost dawn.'

Emma opened her eyes, not sure where she was or what was happening and then she remembered and she was aghast at herself and smug and she felt stupid and a whole host of other feelings ripped through her so that she was obliged to discard them. She listened and he was right, some bird had decided that the day should begin. How irritating. Worse, how impossible. She felt cheated. It was like one bite of chocolate cake and then somebody snatching it all away when you had never had chocolate cake before and were desperate to eat the whole thing yourself.

'It's pitch-black,' she said.

He chuckled against her. She thought it was the most beautiful sound she had ever heard. He kissed her neck and then he kissed her throat and just when she waited for him to kiss her again he drew back. She let him. She didn't want to and then she was afraid.

'Mick—' and when he started to get out of bed she said his name more urgently and he came back to her.

'You don't want the children to find me here.'

She let him go again and then she said his name again and he laughed and he said, 'If you don't stop saying my name like that I will never be able to go.'

'But—'

'I will come back.'

'Do you promise?' She had always thought badly of women who might say such things to men, it was ridiculous and pathetic, and Miss Emma Appleby, that school-teacher and righteous woman, would never have lain in her bed naked with a man and said such things.

'I promise,' he said, and he kissed her so full on the mouth that she thought she would always remember it afterwards.

She hadn't realized that that was exactly what she needed him to say. She didn't ask him to say it again, but she held the words in her mind and tried to believe in them though she knew that nothing good ever lasted.

He dressed and then he leaned over and kissed her again, and just when she thought it would never end he stopped and held her face in his hands for a few seconds and then he was gone and he had been right, the dawn was breaking grey and heavy in the sky and the bird had stopped singing.

Mick got home before the light, but even then he caught that curious pink-and-grey dawn which few people are awake to see. He opened the front door. The shadows were softer and were mingling with the breaking of day, and just as he closed the door, noiselessly as he had thought, he heard Isabel's voice from the sitting room, 'Mick, is that you?' just as she had always done and he went into the sitting room and she was on the sofa there, gazing at him, and it was the stupidest nearest thing to those pictures of the Sleeping Beauty when she awoke after a hundred years. Where had the prince gone who kissed her?

She looked crumpled: the dress she wore was grey with age and sweat, but when she lifted her face she looked young and beautiful, the way that she always had, and her eyes were filled with tears.

'Where were you?' she said.

'At work.'

'Where is Connie?'

'She's at Miss Appleby's. Don't you remember?'

'I want her here. I'm so tired of everything.'

She leaned against him and would have fallen had he not caught her and so he held her in his arms and when she fell asleep he carried her upstairs and into their bed for the first time in months. She went on sleeping as though everything were all right.

Emma awoke in a kind of blissful languor. She could hear the children making a noise downstairs, moving about, but she lay there and thought about the night and what his body had felt and tasted like and how good he was close against her. She had to get out of bed when she heard Hector begin to bark outside her door, so she put on some clothes hastily – the ones she had scattered the night before – and opened the door.

'Couldn't you have let Hector out?' she said to the children as she went past the kitchen and flung open the door.

She felt like someone different: she could have laughed and shouted for joy and run around the garden like a small child with a new toy. She had never felt like this. Somebody had wanted to be close and it was somebody that she cared for. She cared for him. That had not occurred to her. She had thought it was hunger and neglect and the need for someone to acknowledge that she was a living, breathing woman.

She let the sunlight fall on her uplifted face and smiled. She didn't care what she had done, she was so pleased, so grateful, she mattered in the way that men and women mattered to one another in the most basic sense and she had given up hope long since that such a thing would happen to her. She went over every moment of the night and then she wished she could see him, she wanted to run to him, to tell him how she felt. She walked around and around, and then she stopped when she was almost beside the gate.

Something else was different and it had nothing to do with Mick or with the night. She couldn't tell what it was, she stood a few moments longer, but she couldn't rest so she went back and put on some shoes and walked all the way to the gate and there she saw the sign, MISS APPLEBY'S ACADEMY: *Boarders and Day Pupils*. Somebody had daubed in big white letters right across the sign WHORE. As she stood there, shaking, Jack arrived. He didn't say anything, he just looked and then he said hastily, 'Don't worry, Miss, I'll get rid of it.'

She nodded and went back inside and tried to be normal with the children, but as she sat down to breakfast with them, she couldn't eat – all she had was a cup of coffee. She thought of how the dreams had gone wrong and of what she had done last night, and guilt and horror swept over her. She should never have come here. She had achieved nothing. She would have been better staying in New England and leading the life which Verity and Laurence had wanted for her. She had been mad to do what she did. Nothing could be worse than this. She felt dirty, used, stupid. She had slept with another woman's husband and in a place like this where everybody knew everything.

She excused herself to the children and then she went back into her room, but the memories were as warm as the sheets and everything here reminded her of him. She stripped off her clothes and then she poured water from the jug into the bowl and she washed her body vigorously until it showed red in protest and even then she cried because she was so ashamed of herself.

She had lost control. She was indeed her parents' daughter. She was no better. She had prided herself on knowing who she was, but the woman she had thought she was would never have done such a thing. Even when she was dried and in clean clothes she didn't feel any better. She sat down on the bed and wept until her eyes were swollen and raged bitterly at herself.

What had given her the right to do such a thing? And as for Mick Castle all he wanted was a willing woman, someone's body to make him feel better because his marriage was a travesty. She tried not to blame him for that, men were weak, hadn't her father demonstrated that so very clearly?

Had someone seen or was the word on the sign just a coincidence? She didn't think it could be. Somebody knew that she had taken another woman's husband into her bed. She made herself wash her face in cold water. She had to go downstairs and see the children and thank Jack for his help though she didn't know what to say to him.

The children were easy: she gave them some difficult sums to work on at the table and she went outside. Jack was still busy. She dragged her feet over to him.

'Jack—'

'It's disgusting, Miss, that's what it is,' the lad said, and at first for a second she thought he was accusing her and then she saw he was angry with whoever had done this. 'Nobody likes change,' Jack said, 'this is because you tried to do summat different. It's nowt to do with you. Don't you think it.'

'You know, don't you?' Emma said, and she watched the heat rise from his shirt collar up his neck to where his brown hair was cut short.

'What folk do before you're in a place is nowt to do with you,' Jack said, and then she realized they were talking about quite different things. 'I've heard what folk say and because of Nell, and there's nowt wrong with Nell but what happened and it weren't her fault they call you the same. Don't you take no notice, Miss.'

She smiled at his back. He couldn't see. He was a lovely lad, kind, loyal, and he liked being part of her small family, she could tell. He often stayed when he needn't have. He played football with George and Connie and when he didn't have to go to one of the pubs to help or back to his mam to see she was all right he felt at home here and Emma knew then that that was what she had wanted to do.

She wanted children and young people to find some place to be themselves and to grow. She didn't feel better about herself after that, but it did make her feel more calm, and when he had done everything he could to remove the lettering and not managed it, he went back into the house with her to sit down for a little while before he tried again, and he stayed until he had to go to the Black Diamond.

She wondered if he would tell Mick and whether Mick would come storming up here, but she thought, no, Mick would think too that they had been seen and he could not come back. Perhaps they would never be like that again, and it was for the best. She lifted her chin and brought herself under the rigid control in which she had always kept her obviously foolish nature. She swore that she would never do such a thing again and hoped to be forgiven for this one slip, this one time, but it seemed so awful to her that the single memory was tainted and spoiled.

When Mick awoke Isabel was staring at their bedroom as though she had never seen it before.

'It's such a mess,' she said.

It was just as usual. He had not observed that the wallpaper was hanging off, the dressing-table drawers were open and the wardrobe was spilling clothes. The sunshine coming in through the big gap in the curtains showed it all up.

'How do you feel?' he said.

'Sick. Suddenly yesterday I felt so ill and I – I retched and retched and then I felt worse and I was going to have another drink and – and I couldn't somehow. I was on my own with that stupid girl – was she meant to be looking after me? I got rid of her and then I went outside, I saw the state of my house, my kitchen. What happened to it?' She began to cry. 'How did I get like this, Mick?'

She moved forward and he took her into his arms for the first time in months. She stank of gin and vomit and sweat and her hair was tattered and tangled.

'And you?' She drew back and traced the beard and his face. 'What happened to you?'

'Would you like something to eat?' he said.

'Is there anything?'

They got out of bed. She stood for a few seconds and then collapsed. The girl who looked after Isabel – he could not even remember her name – was back in the house by then. He sent her for the doctor.

Sam looked across the bed at him. Isabel had fallen into an uneasy sleep.

'She should be in hospital.'

'Can't I look after her here?'

Sam stood for a moment and then he said, 'Get rid of the drink, if there's any left. Don't let her out. Give her water and stuff that's easy on her stomach. You must stay with her. If she has another drink it could kill her.'

'I won't go anywhere.'

'And get somebody to sort this place out,' Sam said roughly.

Mick didn't come back. Emma hadn't expected him to and there was relief in her as well as a stupid disappointment, and she was even able to blame him for not coming back to her. She tried to concentrate on teaching the children. Jack had spent all morning trying to get rid of the paint on the defaced sign, but in the end he had taken it down and that was how she felt. As though everything were finished. The afternoon and early evening crawled by. She thought that he might wait until the children were in bed and she hurried them there. They looked at her strangely, but once they were in bed there was nothing to do. She couldn't concentrate to read. Perhaps he thought she was cheap, maybe he had a problem at work, or maybe Jack had told him about the sign.

In the end she went to bed and cried. Hector, allowed back in the bedroom as though nothing had happened, slept on the rug by her bed. She began to think that it had not happened at all, that she had been so desperate that she had imagined the whole thing. How shameful, how cowardly, how base.

She didn't sleep. She turned over a hundred times and then went downstairs into the black of night, tried to bring the stove back to life, and after she had done so she waited a long time for the kettle to boil. She was still sitting there, the tea she had made gone cold, when the day arrived and all she thought about was what the previous dawn had been like, how happy she had been, and how she had felt so empty when he had gone.

Mick did not leave the house for a week. Jack took a note to Emma – only to say that he had been detained and would she go on looking after Connie, he would be in touch. He sent other notes to the Black Diamond and to the managers of the small pubs he owned nearby. People would just have to manage without him.

Jack also took messages to the women who used to clean the pubs and the house, to ask if they were paid more whether they would come back. Two of them must have had no other work because having been dismissed with pay but without a word they came back to the house. They said nothing, they brought with them cleaning equipment and soon, beyond the bedroom, Mick could smell polish, hear general noise. The windows were opened to the day and Mrs Dexter, a widow with two grown-up children, bustled in despite being asked not to come into the room and brought tea on a tray for Mick and Isabel.

'I could come in here and clean next if you can move Mrs Castle to the back bedroom. It's all fresh in there. I've put clean sheets on the bed, there were plenty of them when I looked, and I'll get the bath hot and she can get out of those clothes.'

'Mrs Dexter—'

'Now, Mr Castle, don't you worry. I won't be telling tales abroad. I nursed my Bill for months before he died and I know all about sickness. You should have sent for me sooner. I don't know why you didn't,' and off she went.

Isabel sat up and sipped at her tea, but she looked helplessly at him. 'I need a drink.'

'You can't have one.'

'Mick, I have to.'

'Drink your tea.'

She threw it at him. Luckily he had been expecting

227

something of the sort and avoided it and since Mrs Dexter had not yet changed the bed he didn't worry about the mess.

When the bath was ready he carried Isabel in there, discarded the dress which she had worn for so many weeks that it could almost have stood up by itself and soaped her emaciated body. Every rib showed. She cried. He washed her hair and took her out and towelled her dry and put her back into a clean bed, not the one she had got out of. He could hear Mrs Dexter clattering about in there and singing 'Jesu, Joy of Man's Desiring', slightly off key.

Isabel wouldn't eat. She wouldn't drink anything, she turned away from him and then back to him and she tried to get free, tried to get out of the room, she did everything she could think of to find herself some spirits, but he didn't leave her, didn't let her, and she cursed and shouted and he wondered why he had not tried to do this sooner or would it have been impossible, the way that she was? What had changed? He could not work it out.

'I hate you,' she shouted. 'Why are you doing this to me? Give me the bottle. I know you have it.' She ran at him, kicked him, thumped him, tried to hit him anywhere she could, but he didn't give in.

Then, just as he thought she was getting better she came to him, smiling and saying very softly, 'I only need one drink, just one. I will give you anything you want.'

She cried and pleaded and then she pulled off her clothes and offered herself to him for just the one drink, just one. She wouldn't eat. She threw everything back at him. In the end he didn't let Mrs Dexter into the room, he took food from her and cups of tea. He lost count of the tea Isabel threw at him. There was tea on the bedclothes and on him and on her. There was food on the bed and on the floor. When he wanted to open the curtains she wouldn't let him, so he had no idea what time of day or night it was. He urged Mrs Dexter to go home, but she didn't.

'I've got nothing to go home for, Mr Castle, my bairns are grown and left and I think you could do with somebody here.'

This was undeniable. He wanted to say something, to apologize, to offer her money, but he didn't. She knew all those things. When Isabel slept sometimes Mrs Dexter came in and watched her and he would go off to his room and doze. It was never for long, he couldn't rest, he knew that Isabel needed him.

He tried not to think about her with Henry Atkinson and most of all he tried not to think of himself with Emma. He got on with what he was attempting to do. He kept on offering water to her parched mouth and eventually from sheer thirst she took it. She wouldn't have anything else, but at night she began to breathe and sleep easily and on the fourth day she managed to get some buttered toast down.

She gazed at it as she ate it, as though she had never seen it before. He wanted to ask her why she had done what she had done, but he couldn't; he must make do with what was happening now and try to keep going.

Day after day she demanded gin. She threw water at

him, she threw the pillows at him. When she slept he stood by the window exhausted, but ventured down into the kitchen. The house was transformed. Mrs Dexter was scrubbing the floor, the windows gleamed, the surfaces were spotless, and on the stove something smelled very good.

'How is Mrs Castle feeling?' she said with a slight smile.

'A little better, I think.'

She crossed herself.

'The things that are sent to try us,' she said. Then she sat back on her heels and surveyed him. 'What about a bath for you and a razor and some clean clothes?'

He didn't say anything, he hadn't thought about himself like that, he had been concentrating on Isabel for so long, but he nodded. He went back upstairs. The other woman, Mrs Hobson, was hanging out clothes in a stiff breeze so it was probably Monday morning and when he went to the other window the garden was such a mess in the cold day, there wasn't a flower in sight anywhere. It made him want to cry.

He bathed and shaved and changed his clothes and stared at himself in the mirror at how different he looked, and then Isabel appeared in the mirror and he turned round quickly, fearing that she was angry or had found a bottle, but she just smiled at him sadly and said, 'I'm hungry.'

12

It was ten days before he went to see Emma, and that was ostensibly to see Connie. Not surprisingly the first thing Connie said was, 'When can I come home?'

He was able to reply, 'If Miss Appleby has no objection you can come home in the morning.'

It was late, he had meant to come sooner but he couldn't get away from Isabel, and Ed had come by with the problems from the Black Diamond and other managers had done the same because he had not been near the other pubs and there were things they could not manage on their own. He didn't want to take Connie back home now. Isabel was never at her best at this time of day: having come through several hours without a drink she was exhausted.

Connie was pleased and went to bed early the better to pack her things and wait for the morning.

The children in bed and asleep, left alone with Emma, all Mick could say was, 'I'm sorry. Isabel needed me.'

And the sensible woman he had fallen in love with looked at him with glittering green eyes and crimson cheeks.

'She needed you? Oh well, that's very good then, isn't it? I hardly recognized you when you turned up here. You look almost like a gentleman. You're not the man I remember. You're not the man I took to my bed.'

He glanced at the door of her study, but it was firmly closed and in fact her voice was lower than normal and that worried him, Emma usually shouted when she was angry.

'She couldn't manage without me.'

'I hate that. I hate how I manage. I hate these women who can't do without men. I hate them and I hate you. Go away.'

'Emma—'

'Just go. I wish I'd had more sense than to let you touch me. I wish I had never had anything to do with you other than business.'

He tried to put his arms around her, but she backed away.

'Do you know what someone wrote upon the sign? Whore! That's what I am, I'm your whore. At least I was, but it will never happen again. Jack took the sign down for me and he's always here, thank God, to see to things. I'll get him to take Connie home in the morning. Don't come back here.' She would have left the room, it was such a good exit line, and she tried to sweep out and then he pulled at her arm and the door didn't open because he put a hand down on it.

'It isn't like that,' he said softly. 'My wife is mentally ill. What do you want me to do, put her in an institution? Do you think I want to be there? Do you think I haven't thought about you every day and every night? Do you think it's easy for me?'

'I think you're younger than me and handsomer than me and that I'm, I'm—'

He pulled her to him and then he kissed her and it was balm to him. He felt as though now he could go back into the private place in his head where he loved and was loved. It was short-lived. She wrenched herself away.

'I'm not going to do this again. You have no right to come here and expect it. You're married. Very married so that don't have room in your life for anyone else, you barely have room for your child—'

'I love her.'

'Words are all very well, Mick, but you left your child here for ten days while you saw to your – your wife's needs. She's what you really care about.'

He stared at her. 'What can I do?'

'You can come here and act decently and not treat me like your whore.'

'Don't say that.'

'You may come and collect Connie in the morning if you choose. You have no right to anything more here. You may keep me at present, something which I hope to change with paying pupils, but I am not available to you.'

'I never thought of it that way.'

'Good. Then we know exactly where we are. Now go back to your wife.'

She went out of the study, giving him no option but to leave.

*

This time was better, Emma thought. She congratulated herself that she had put him from her, that she had successfully left him and that he had gone. She heard him leave, she didn't see him, she went upstairs and he would not follow her there. She didn't even cry she had such good control of herself. Then she shook and shook, and called herself names for having gone anywhere near a man in the first place. They were all alike, they were all like her father or they were like Laurence or they were like Mick Castle, expecting everything while giving nothing.

She went to bed and fell thankfully into sleep. She was back in New England in her garden and her father was still alive and she still believed in him and the scent of the herbs was coming up from the bed below the window and all was well.

Mick went back for Connie early the following morning. He and Emma didn't look at one another. She was very bright. He said little. Connie was excited at the idea of going home. There at least he had got something right because Connie saw her mother come out to see her and her face shone with joy and surprise and she said, 'Mam!' and ran into Isabel's embrace and heard her mother laugh and then Isabel took her child into her arms and hugged and kissed her and told her how much she had missed her and said how she should tell her everything which had happened at Miss Appleby's school.

They went in, they spent the afternoon together, they ate dinner, it was so civilized and all the time he thought about Emma. He didn't want to, that also made him feel guilty. Was he never to feel anything but? Everywhere he went, everything he did, he was always meant to be somewhere else, to be doing something else. Even now he worried about the pubs, the business, whether it was going on as it should be – it probably wasn't.

If he had been three people he would have managed, but most of all he remembered the hurt look on Emma's face, the way that she had made him go, he had to sit here and pretend that he felt as he had felt before when Isabel had been his wife and everything had been better.

It had not been perfect, he admitted now, it never had been perfect, and why should anything be but for the fact that most things were so godawful that we were deserving of something perfect in our lives, just one thing, and he thought the night he had spent with Emma had been that. How bitter she had been! He thought of the words and the way that she had looked at him and he was amazed and rather proud of her. He thought he would never forget the way that her lovely green eyes shimmered when she was angry.

It took all the strength he had not to run out of the room and out of the house and over the village to the place where he had been born. Being with Emma somehow was the completion of all that. And he felt now that he came third. What a strange place to be. First there was Isabel and then there was Connie and even to himself he was third. What was he to other people? Nobody took any notice and why should they, though he wanted to run about and shout and say, 'What about me? Don't I matter?' but he couldn't do it.

Men were supposed to take what they could get and be grateful for it, he thought. They had to be strong, so he sat there and stupidly all he wanted was whisky and there wasn't any.

Connie didn't want to go to bed, even when it grew late, and after a day such as this he was so tired. He didn't think he could stand any more. She stayed up and stayed up and Isabel let her and they sat so close together and talked and from time to time Isabel looked at him with love.

Finally he carried his child to bed, she was almost asleep and she was so happy, the smile on her face should have made him glad too, but he was not. He laid her down in her bed and Isabel covered her up and it was better than it had ever been before. Sleeping, their child looked angelic, she was safe here.

He made the excuse of taking the dog out, though normally he would just let Ulysses out, since Isabel had been so ill he had not liked to leave her even for a second and now the dog waited at the back door, surprised when Mick went with him. Mick thought of Emma across town, what was she doing? He wanted her very much.

He stayed outside for so long that the dog was circling, wondering what in hell he was doing out there. So he went inside and settled Ulysses by the dying sitting-room fire and he thought how odd it was that Isabel no longer lay there as she had for months, the smell of gin everywhere, and the awful thing was that he didn't care. That wasn't true, he just wished things differently. He wanted to be with Emma.

He went upstairs and into the bedroom and there his wife was, no different than she had been before everything went wrong. She was beautiful again, young, she held out her arms to him. He tried to think how it would affect her if he refused to sleep with her, if he seemed not to want to be there, but he couldn't do that to her because she was so needy, he had done everything, he had brought her back to this, he could not desert her now.

She was ready for bed. She was wearing a nightdress that he had long since assumed had been thrown out. It was one she had worn years before. It didn't hide her body. It gave a shimmer to her skin and he had loved the way that he could see the slender curves. She looked at him from beneath her lashes and he went cold. He didn't want this any more. She was not as she had been. She had been ill, that was what Sam would tell him, but it didn't matter. He had no place but this to go and he didn't want to be here.

His wife was beautiful, but he could not help comparing her with the schoolteacher across town. She smelled of chalk and pastry and lavender water and he wanted to smile at how attractive that had become. He remembered her smiling but mostly he thought of how she had achieved so much from so little. It was her determination that he loved and then admitted that it was also to do with her body which fitted so perfectly against him and the hunger on her which was so very desirable and her hands which touched him and were like fire.

His wife smelled of the perfume he had bought for her when he had loved her. My God, it was gone, every feeling he had had for her except pity, but they were married and she was moving towards him and he knew what he must do next. He had to. If he didn't then all the work he had done to bring her back to her life had been in vain and so he smiled and picked her up in his arms.

She was so light, she weighed nothing, as women wanted to, how stupid and yet it also made him think of Emma, the way that her breasts almost filled his hands, that had been a surprise, they were small but perfectly round and he remembered the catch of her breath because it was all new, the wondrous way she looked at him because she thought it might be love and in any case she needed him.

When a woman needed you like that, her lips apart, her body yielded, and you had seen her in McConichie's ordering furniture, somehow it was wonderful. He loved her for her independence and the memories of her demanding warmth for other people and knowledge for the children and trying to do so much for others. He had never seen it before like that in anybody.

She risked things which were not for her financial gain. How strange that was and new except that when he gave himself credit for anything he was aware that he had chosen to try and do the same, even in a small way, it made him feel so good, to help other people.

He liked that she could do so much, that she had come

here in search of some bloody stupid dream, that she had failed and not cared and gone forward so many times and that he had been a part of it. He remembered when he had first seen her and how she had crept upstairs with George. He had the feeling now that he had known what she was doing.

Hector had padded softly into the hall and Mick thought he could remember how he had waited to see what she would do with a growling dog. He didn't hear what she said or even what she did, just that Hector had come padding back to him, tail wagging, and Hector rarely made mistakes with people, or perhaps it was only with hindsight that he knew this.

Even then he had been fascinated, finding her soaked, her clothes stuck to her slender body, washing the kitchen floor. He was astonished at her determination and wanted to know more about her, to be a part of her life, because he had suspected that she was going to do something different, and unpredictability in women was not something he had ever seen before.

But yes, he thought now, his mother had been like that. She didn't care that people would castigate her for her behaviour, she had gone ahead and done what she thought she should, and Emma was so like that.

He made love to his wife because she expected it, required it, had come back to him and he should do it, but all the time he was aware that she was not Emma, that it was not fun, that she did not giggle afterwards, that she did not tell him that she loved him. She didn't.

Had she ever? He had always been, he thought now, the lover and not the beloved. With Emma it was equal. How many women could offer that? And then he thought of Henry Atkinson and decided that perhaps they all could with the right man.

He and Emma Appleby were equals. And it was the first time he had known anything like that except that his parents had been like that too. How had they managed it? Was it luck? Was it just that they happened upon earth to meet one another and marry and there was nothing more to it? How was that and why had it not happened to everyone? Why were some people so lucky? Why did some people have that and some people have nobody?

There were those like Ed who lost everything in a single day when his wife and child had died of influenza, and they never found anything more other than work to help them. And there were women who had no man for years and years and yet had to endure. Where was the balance, where was the justice in it? There was none.

Some people had the nights with nothing to comfort them other than bedclothes and the darkness. You got through it if you were lucky and that was all.

That was what he did now. How awful, how presumptuous, how superior and patronizing, and he hoped Isabel did not know that this was his lot when he was in bed with her. He no longer loved her. He could not love two women at once and she had been too much trouble. That made him feel awful, guilty. His duty towards her was because of Connie and he even had to remind himself of that.

She had never put him first, even when he had met her before they married. Nobody but Emma Appleby ever had. He had come first with her and she was first with him and always would be, but he couldn't tell her. She was not his whore. My God, what was that? Was a whore just the desperation of a man who couldn't stand his life? If so, then whores were the best of women in a sense because they needed the money, they did it for no other reason and men needed the sex. It was nothing but a transaction and maybe that was how it should be.

No broken hearts, no broken heads. Nothing lost. It was so stupid. Emma was his whole life now and he could not have her. Did she think of him? Perhaps she did not. And that was good, that was how it must be, but he remembered the silk of her skin and the joy of her and how she had laughed. She had never had a man before and yet she was sophisticated enough to enjoy it.

Isabel slept. It was a normal sleep and he lay there, holding her and thinking of Emma in her bed in the house where he had thought anything and everything was possible. Now nothing seemed possible. Everything was turned to dust. He didn't even care as much as he had for Connie and that really was bad. He lay awake all night, he watched how the shadows changed in the room and he heard the owls calling to one another in the garden. It should have been wonderful, but it wasn't.

13

Sometimes George could not help thinking back to what his life had been like before he came to England. He shuddered when he thought of his uncle and aunt and their two children, though he felt sorry for the boys being treated in such a way, but he was not altogether happy with his new life here in England.

He knew that it was stupid to think so, he had escaped from so many things, but he missed the company of other boys, the way that he had been friends with them when he was younger, before his father died and everything had gone wrong. He was ashamed to admit to himself that he wanted more, he thought after all his Aunt Emma had done it seemed churlish to ask for more, but as often as he tried to dismiss the idea the more often it surfaced in his mind.

He wished in some ways that he still lived at the pub. When he ventured back the first time he had the chance Mr Castle was off somewhere on business, Mr Higgins was busy behind the bar and Jack was away helping at one of the other pubs,

'And you shouldn't be here. Your Auntie Emma woulnd't

like it,' Mr Higgins admonished him before he got on with his work.

George ventured into the village. It was Saturday and he was bored and had needed to get away from the house. There he found some boys playing football, in the usual way, with jerseys to mark the edges of the goals at either side of the back lane. He watched them and the ball went through the jerseys more at one end than the other, mostly because that side was only three.

They ignored him. He hoped they might ask him to play but they didn't so in the end he went nearer and offered,

'You're one down. Can I play?'

They stopped, they looked at him. Then they all moved slowly towards him. George tried not to panic, tried to read their faces but he wanted to run.

'Wee's he like?' one bigger lad asked another.

'A furriner. From the lasses school.'

'It's not a lasses school,' George protested.

'Are you a lass, like?'

George was already realizing that he had lost this game before he started.

'I can play football,' he said, 'and cricket.'

'Can yer now? You sound as though you cannot. You sound like a lass.'

George would have left at that point but that the biggest of them came forward and hit him. George shouldn't have been astonished but he was. He tried to defend himself, he thought of Jack saying how to do so, he was sure Mr

Higgins would have known and he would have copied them but he didn't remember anything but how he felt. Felt he was going to be sick, never eat again, be unable to come back to the village like this from the academy. It was a humiliation and a defeat. He was on the ground his lip was bleeding and he wanted to cry.

They jeered. George got up and seven of them stood there so there was nothing to do except go home.

He tried to get upstairs in order to wash his face before his Aunt Emma saw him but she was not easily deceived. She called his name, said,

'Wait a minute. Turn around,' and as he did so she looked severely at him.

'Have you been fighting?' she said. 'Come into the kitchen and sit down.'

He was only glad that the kitchen was empty other than the two of them, he put up with the warm water on his face, he endured the lecture about how fighting solved nothing but afterwards he couldn't wait to be away and the moment that she found something else to do he escaped.

It was the end of the afternoon by then. He went to the Black Diamond, there didn't seem any place else to go. He found Mr Higgins in the kitchen and though he was certain that Mr Higgins didn't want to hear it he blurted out the story, finishing lamely,

'And my Aunt Emma says I mustn't fight. She says it doesn't solve anything.'

Mr Higgins poured out tea, gave George some bread

and jam, and they sat down at the table.

'Women don't like fighting. The trouble is it's the only way men resolve their differences in the end,' Mr Higgins said. 'It doesn't sound as if it was much of a fight.'

'It wasn't,' George said miserably.

'You can't take on seven lads, George man, the only sound thing to do is run away. Remember that.'

George felt a bit better then. He drank his tea and ate his bread and jam and then Mr Higgins took him out into the yard and showed him what to do next time. It was, Mr Higgins said, 'dirty fighting', but as far as he was concerned you couldn't afford to worry about things like that. He showed him how to kick the other lad between the legs and also how to knee him in the same place and how to duck in under the other boy's chin and bring up your head hard and then how to dodge and how to weave, and most important of all how to beat your man before you started if you got a chance. No matter how tall he was you thought of yourself as the bigger and the better fighter. Two you might manage, especially if you could scare them. Sometimes, if you showed yourself very good, a number would run away. You had to judge it.

George found the whole of the next week very trying. He determined to go and confront the boys who had treated him badly but he was so afraid that he lay at night looking up at the ceiling and wondered what it would be like when all seven of them laid into him. He tried to tell himself that it was not cowardice not to go back, that even Mr Higgins would think him stupid for doing such a thing, but he could not rid his mind of the humiliation of lying on the ground in the back lane and of how all the lads in the village would know.

It was a very long week in some ways. In others it was too short and by Friday night it was galloping and George sweated in bed so much that he had to throw off the covers and he lay there for hours wishing it was not Saturday. He only went to sleep by convincing himself that he would not go and that it was the right thing to do.

When he awoke early he changed his mind and the time crawled past. He let it go until mid afternoon and then he walked slowly over the road and down the hill and into the back lane on the edge of the village where the lads as usual were playing football. He thought they were the same ones, there were certainly seven of them. They noticed him immediately and stopped and there was hilarity. George's lower lip shook.

'Can I play?' he said. 'You're one man down.'

'It's the lad from the lasses school,' the one who had knocked him down said and then another lad came out from behind, taller than the others and he looked across the ground between them and he said simply,

'Why aye, you can play, Geordie lad. Howay,' and George recognized him as John Wearmouth, one of the big lads he remembered from going to Mr English's school and his Aunt Emma had read Hiawatha and they had told stories. John smiled at him and the others fell back.

George, feeling defeated and relieved at the same time,

couldn't move for a moment or two but he knew that his moment had come, he was 'Geordie lad' now to the other lads in the village, John Wearmouth had said so. His joy was brimming over ten minutes later when he scored a goal and the others clustered around him, yelling in triumph.

Emma went to visit Mrs English. She took George and Hector with her. Connie had not come back to school even after three days so Emma declared a holiday. The weather was cold and fine. Hector, always keen for a walk, dashed about through the scrub, chasing the smell of rabbits. George was silent. Emma knew he missed Connie but perhaps he was so used to losing people by now, she thought sadly, that he didn't ask where she was.

George accepted what happened. She wished she could do the same. After forty years of being alone her body craved Mick Castle and she was disgusted. She had thought she was a repressed, middle-aged woman. That was gone, she had never felt so vital or so needy or so angry with anyone. She thought that if she had had a weapon to hand she would have killed him.

She had awoken the morning after she had told him she would have nothing more to do with him and the loneliness settled over her like a carpet, it was so heavy, so dark. She tortured herself thinking of him taking his wife to bed. Was that what he had done? Of course he had. The jealousy that she felt after that almost felled her. She sat and cried and then was angry with herself. She had been better off without him, better off without any man. All they had brought her so far was grief. She would put him from her mind forever.

She set to cleaning Mrs English's house as though the skies might fall if she didn't. She scrubbed floors and polished what furniture there was and brought great buckets of coal into the house, though there was enough already for the living-room fire. She had made and brought cake and a stew and some bread.

Had she still had any sense of humour she would have laughed at the stupid woman who kept herself so busy because she missed a man who had used her. And just once. Somehow the just once made it worse. It could not even be thought of as anything lasting, anything that mattered. She could have clung to the idea that he had cared enough to be there, to have forsaken his wife even just a little.

She could not go back to thinking of how very good it had been, the best night of her life. It was not that in her mind any more, it was a mistake, an error of judgement, a stupid lapse. She told herself that she should have known how it would be and avoided it.

Worse, he had turned up at her house looking so much younger, clean-shaven and smart with shiny hair and calm eyes, and she had hated him the more for that. It was as though she had loved someone else and he was obliterated from the earth. This man looked almost rich, he looked sophisticated, a successful businessman. He was not hers, he never had been, her scruffy northern man had vanished, perhaps she had only conjured him.

When Mr English came and told her that the school was just as bad as it had been before he met her Emma had an idea, one she had hoped to put into operation long since.

'Why don't you bring them to my school for a visit and we'll go for a walk?'

'What, all of them?'

'You could call it a nature outing.'

'But it's cold,' he said.

Emma could have cursed Mr English's lack of imagination. Were all classical scholars this way?

'You could talk to them about the geology of the rocks and tell them about the various seasons and I could make food for them and we could do the Romans, how they came here and all the marks they left on the land in the north.'

Mr English brightened up at this idea. The Romans were the saving of him, Emma thought.

'Has Mr Castle's little girl come back to the school?' he asked. 'I understand that his wife is much better.'

Emma went home, determined to think about her venture and to forget all about Mick Castle and his family, only to find him on her doorstep with his child.

'I'm sorry I didn't bring Connie back sooner—'

'There's no need to apologize, Mr Castle,' she said smoothly, and she thought it was easier now that he had turned into this different person. She thought, in one way

I am like Isabel Castle, I have no friends either. She could have felt sorry for Mick had he not gone to bed with another woman to combat his difficulties and she was able to congratulate herself for this thought and the one which followed, which was that if she had had a pan within reach she would have hit him with it, right round the head.

Connie took her suitcase back up the stairs with her and George followed eagerly, so he must have missed her a great deal, Emma thought. And not least of all was the fact that Mick Castle was paying the bills. She must carry on being civil to him, no matter what. That required several deep breaths, after which she told him about Mr and Mrs English and the scheme for the pupils to spend a day with her.

'You took down the sign.'

'Jack couldn't get the paint off. He did offer to paint over it, but it seemed nothing more than an invitation so I left it.' She said goodbye to him briskly and went inside and stood against the door, breathing heavily as though she had run a long way.

The nature-study day was cold but fine. It wasn't easy. She deputed several older girls and boys to look after the rest so that they were in small groups and then Mr English stopped from time to time to tell them about the landscape and the history of the area and Hector ran about wildly, being patted all the way along.

At the furthest part of the walk they came to what Mr

English called 'a sharp sand quarry' and he launched into the history of iron- and steel-making, and after that Emma decided they had had enough and took them all back to the schoolhouse for soup and cake. They sat as well as so many of them could, one lot in the kitchen with her and the other lot in the biggest sitting room with Mr English, and naturally the boys went with him and the girls stayed with her and they had a pleasant afternoon.

Things went backwards. That was the only way Mick could think of it, but Isabel, in her very clean house with her very clean kitchen, no longer cooked. There was no need because Mrs Hobson did the cooking and Mrs Dexter was very keen on polishing and dusting and hanging out the clothes. The smell of warm ironing greeted him one afternoon when he came home early, worried somehow that he might find Isabel comatose on the sofa, with empty bottles and the sweet disgusting reek of gin, instead of which his wife sat like a statue in a very neat dress, staring out of the window.

It was a lovely clear day He asked Isabel if she would go for a walk – Ulysses would go with them – but she refused. He asked her if she would like to go into Durham and look for new clothes; it had been so long since she had had any and the dress she wore was years old.

She looked at it in surprise, as though somebody else had decided what she would put on, and he had a vision of Mrs Dexter reaching into the wardrobe – Isabel no longer got up for breakfast as she had done before she was so ill

– and encouraging her to wear the prettiest of her dresses. Mrs Dexter was trying to please him for some reason and had picked out the dress which men might like.

'Shopping?' she said, as if he had suggested something improper.

'We could stay at the County and go dancing. We used to do that, do you remember?'

'I didn't care for it then,' she said. 'How could you possibly have forgotten?'

Exasperated he said, 'What would you like to do, Isabel?' and her lips twisted and she said, without moving, 'I would like just one large glass of gin.'

It was the first time since she had been so ill that she had mentioned it.

'Sam says another might kill you.'

'Dr Blythe is a liar. Besides, how would you notice? You have your woman.'

The awful thing about that was it was literally true. He not only loved Emma Appleby, he had gone to bed with her, so nothing rescued him here. Excuses would not do, he hadn't even made those to himself, though he had tried. He wanted to say to her that she was the only woman in his life, that he cared just for her, but it would have been such a huge lie that he couldn't utter it.

The evenings were endless. He tried not to go back to work, he was there less now than he had ever been and there were so many problems: there were fights, the beer did not arrive or was off, the pubs were becoming fustier and neglected and at the Black Diamond Ed had influenza and had taken to his bed. There was only Jack he could trust, and although Jack was nineteen Mick had taken to getting Jack to go to each of the pubs in turn to report what was going on.

He remained at home where he and Isabel sat at either end of the table and did not make conversation. Mrs Hobson's culinary delights did not much stretch further than corned beef pie and potatoes, or fish with parsley sauce – he hated that most – and there was no roast on Sunday because she insisted on having that day off and he could not blame her. He had thought it might encourage Isabel to cook, but they had bread and cheese on Sunday. She made no comment.

Sunday morning arrived and with it fine weather. He had always hated gardening, but it would give him something constructive to do since he did not feel he could go to work on Sundays any more, but the ground was solid with frost, there was nothing to be done outside.

He and Isabel had hardly slept at all and that was because when he had spoken softly and reached for her because he thought he should, she had said in a strained voice, 'Don't touch me,' and turned from him.

The way that she had told him what she really wanted had altered everything. He got up and went downstairs and wondered what they should have for breakfast and suddenly there was a knock on the front door and a half-grown boy with a note in his hand which he said was from Mr Higgins. He read it swiftly. Jack had been hurt in a fight and Ed was ill. Could he come in to open the Black Diamond?

There was nobody at his house on Sundays and he had reserved it so that he need not leave Isabel. He slipped upstairs and found her sleeping well. She would probably sleep for hours, she did so now once she got off, and it had been several days since she had slept for any length of time. He practically ran into the village and found Ed at home, ashen-faced in his tiny sitting room, holding a blanket around him.

'How badly hurt is Jack?'

'He's at home. Got into a fight. I was in bed. There's nobody to open up and in any case it was too much to ask the lad to do everything himself—'

There were people to help at every pub. Mick had carefully organized this.

'Nobody came in,' Ed told him. 'You know what folk are like.'

'What about the other pubs?'

'I don't know. I wasn't there,' Ed said shortly. He tried to get up, swayed, and Mick helped him back to bed, offered him tea, but Ed had a drink of water and lay down.

First of all Mick went to Jack's house. He cursed himself. The boy was in bed, whey-faced where there were no bruises. He tried to sit up, he tried to say that he was sorry. Mick sat down on the bed and shook his head. 'Don't be daft, lad,' he said, 'you did your best. I asked too much of you.'

'Nay, I didn't get it right, Mr Castle. And now – now what am I going to do?'

'You're going to get better and I'm not going to let you try to run things.'

'You won't get rid of me?' The boy looked scared.

'You're the best worker I ever knew, saving Ed Higgins. Lie down, go to sleep and stop worrying.'

He sought out Sam and discovered that Jack would be all right.

'He's lucky. He could have been killed. They kicked him. They didn't aim very well, but next time they might.' There was a look of censure on Sam's face, though he tried to hide it.

'There won't be a next time,' Mick said roughly. 'I'll employ more people.'

'Won't that make it worse?'

'What do you want me to do?' He glared at Sam.

'I want you to put Isabel into the mental hospital where she should be.'

Mick swore, turned aside. Sam went on looking doggedly at him.

'Her illness is ruining everything. How bad do things have to get before you let me do that? Think about your child, man.'

Mick was so furious that he turned on his friend. 'God damn you, Sam, what the hell do you think I've been doing?'

'You're putting off the inevitable and Connie is suffering for it and so are you. Put her away.'

'I cannot!'

Sam eyed him for a long while, so long that Mick couldn't hold his gaze. 'This was not your fault.'

'How do you know that? Maybe I made her ill with how I went on.'

'Nonsense,' Sam said in the brisk way that his patients had come to rely on.

Mick didn't say anything to that and his friend and doctor eyed him for even longer this time and then he said softly, 'What are you not telling me?'

'Nothing.'

'Lies won't help.'

'I have to go.'

'Mick—'

But Mick strode out of the surgery and slammed the door.

He went to houses in the village where people were of various help but the influenza had taken down a lot of them. Eventually he managed to make sure there was somebody to open up the other pubs, but nobody from the Black Diamond. He opened the place himself.

Sunday was the busiest day of all, the only full day the pitmen had off, and many of them came as soon as he opened. They would drink all day, but some would have several pints, go home for their Sunday dinner, sleep it off and be back in the evening. It was very late indeed when he finished, closed up, went to see Ed.

'I'll be up tomorrow,' Ed offered, but Mick could see how ill he was.

'If you aren't better tomorrow I'll send for Dr Blythe.'

Ed couldn't eat, Mick made him some tea and he sat up for that, which Mick took to be a good sign.

Finally he went home. It had been such a bright sunny day, though most of it he had only seen beyond the windows of the pub, and the night had turned cold and clear. Ulysses enjoyed the walk back, Mick dreaded what he might find.

The house was silent and he thought if she was in bed then there would be no noise, he had convinced himself and he would be able to sleep. Having had no sleep the previous night it was the only thing he cared for but he could tell as he stepped inside that that was not the case. He didn't understand how he knew – nothing was altered, the house was clean and even smelled of the lavender polish which Mrs Dexter favoured, but when he drew nearer the sitting room there was the now familiar smell of gin.

No light burned in there, he had to make one, and what he found was no surprise. A gin bottle lay empty on the floor and another further over and then another and the whole room was permeated with the smell of juniper. Isabel lay on the sofa, breathing shallowly.

14

Mick carried his wife all the way to Sam's house. He had nobody to help at that hour and he did not want anybody to know what was happening. She was light, but her clothes, breath and body reeked of gin. The surgery was closed of course, but he went to the back door and managed to hammer on it in the darkness. He was sure Sam was often called out at the front door or the back, and indeed Sam did not look very surprised as he opened the door, but he looked dismayed when he saw who it was. They put her to bed, Marjorie helped and said she would keep an eye on her and Sam took his friend downstairs and into the sitting room.

Sam went across to the oak court cupboard and took a bottle of Glenfiddich from the upper bit with the neat little door and glasses from the underneath where it looked as though many such things were housed, judging by the glint of the crystal.

'I don't need that,' Mick objected.

'Yes, you do.' He poured the golden liquid and handed it to Mick.

Mick downed the whisky and said, 'How can I still like the way this tastes?'

'Why can't you be honest with me?'

All Mick said was, 'More,' as he held out his empty glass and Sam filled it.

Sam sat down in his chair by the fire and contemplated the blaze for a few moments. He waited.

Mick could speak when he too had contemplated the blaze and his insides felt warm with the second glass of whisky.

'She has a lover.'

It was, he thought, the very last thing that Sam expected to hear. Somehow he didn't have to look at Sam to know this. The silence and the way that Sam sat so still and then moved about in his chair told him what his friend thought.

'She isn't happy with me, I don't think she's happy with Connie.'

Sam said into the silence that followed, 'Somebody else?' He looked not surprised as Mick had thought he would, rather his look was caustic. Mick couldn't hold his gaze.

'He lives here. His business is here.'

'How long's it been going on?'

'Years, I think.'

'How do you know about him?'

'I went after her one day and – and heard them together.'

'Christ,' Sam said.

'He's married. He has several children.'

When Sam did speak it was not what Mick expected him to say.

'Isabel is killing herself. Would you rather she were dead than with somebody else?'

Sam got up and helped himself to an enormous whisky. Mick listened to how the liquid sploshed into the short squat glass and how Sam put down the decanter with a bang that might have shattered it.

After that Sam was brisk.

'You and Isabel are staying here and if she changes at all you must shout in the night; if she vomits and chokes you yell at the top of your voice, do you hear?'

The bedroom where they were was in the front. It was a regular detached stone house, the kind of house which children would draw, and there would be a mother and a father and maybe even a dog and an even number of windows upstairs and down, a door in the middle. Mick felt a sudden pang for his black Labradors who were at the various pubs and at Emma's house, sleeping. Only perhaps they weren't, perhaps they knew that there was trouble and they were keeping watch. He hoped so.

At the front there was the kind of garden which even if he had not seen it before – and he had seen it many times – he would have known. It had at the far side a wall which divided the front garden from the back, and at this side all the flowers grew in beds which were so neat and divided up by paths, and they were even and regular and everything was in oblongs or squares as if designed by somebody who loved mathematics.

Sam did. Maybe Marjorie did too and they gardened

together. He envied the regularity of it. What must it be like to grow vegetables and pull mint from the ground for Sunday lamb dinner? To know that every day and every week you would be doing the same thing, and it would be usual, normal; you would go on and on and perhaps you would live a long time so that the pattern became ingrained and you expected nothing more and in time your children had children and you saw them and saw how everything was supposed to work. He thought it must be the greatest luxury of all.

There was a new wooden bridge with a little stream and beyond it lay an orchard and beyond that there were fields and he could hear the cry of a pheasant even now. The orchard was filled with bare fruit trees and long grass. He wished he could turn time back just a little to the only night he had spent with Emma when foolishly things had seemed possible.

Mick did not think that he could hate a man more than he hated Henry Atkinson, but somehow there was nothing to do but leave Isabel in the capable hands of Marjorie Blythe and go to see the man. Mick had protested and apologized and said he would send someone to care for her while he was out on this unexplained mission and Marjorie had said, 'How stupid, who could know more than I do?'

So he had left Isabel there. He didn't know what to say to Marjorie. How could he? He hadn't slept, he hadn't eaten. Marjorie, to be fair, had not asked him why he ate nothing and then, the morning well advanced, he went to the White Hart, one of Henry Atkinson's most successful ventures.

It was midday and the unforgiving sun showed him that this public house was as good as his, better perhaps. It had a light atmosphere and the man behind the bar was genial. No, Mr Atkinson was not here and would not be for some days, and Mick was envious that Henry Atkinson could do this when he could not: go and leave it to other people and know that everything would be all right.

He enquired as to where Mr Atkinson might be since he needed to see him on business and the barman eagerly announced that he had gone to Durham city where the brewery was; so Mick then got on a train and went to Durham.

Henry Atkinson's family and his wife's family were rich, two of the public houses in Durham were owned by him and some in other villages, so it was not easy to find where he might be. Mick went to several before he found the one he wanted. In any other circumstances it would have been a pleasure to be in the public house where he finally discovered the man he was seeking. It was one of those pubs which were set in a place which had been a drinking habitat for hundreds of years.

At the front it did not look much, but there were half a dozen small rooms, all leading into one another. Each of them had a a tiny black fireplace, corner seats and windows which opened into another room, and each led back to the bar. He was not surprised to find that Henry Atkinson was there and he said he would like to see Mr Atkinson if it were at all possible, and when he was refused he pushed people aside and went into the back and there was the man his wife adored.

He was nothing like the idea of a man who women could not resist. He was not particularly tall, he was not lean, he was not young, he was not anything that Mick could ever have envisaged Isabel would have cared for and he was not a person you could compete against. If she loved this man she could never have loved Mick, he knew. Henry was grey-haired, middle height, middle-aged, ordinary, not fat or thin, nor was he particularly well dressed. He did not turn Mick from the room as people said, 'He pushed his way in' and 'Sorry, Mr Atkinson.'

Instead, Henry Atkinson said, 'No, it's all right,' in a calm manner, so Mick assumed he had no idea who his visitor was.

Mick was shown to a small office, not so different from his own, by a man he had thought of as his rival, but he was nothing of the kind. This was the man Isabel loved: a man with watery blue eyes, red-rimmed, possibly from spending too many hours at his desk.

'I'm—'

'I know who you are,' the man said, and he had an ordinary voice and that was strange somehow. He looked levelly across the distance between them and said, 'Mr Castle. I was expecting you sooner or later.'

Mick stood where he was and didn't say anything. He

couldn't think of anything to say, he wanted to strangle the man sitting there, it was only somehow the insignificance of his body that disconcerted Mick. How could you knock a little old man like that about his own office and gain any satisfaction from it when he was looking at you almost with polite dismay?

He was intelligent though. He looked down and then back up at Mick as though it cost him an effort and then he said, 'I'm so very sorry. None of it was meant to hurt anyone.'

Mick laughed. 'Well then, what it was for?' he said.

'I love her, you see.'

'I have bad news for you then. Your relationship with my wife has ruined our marriage and it has cost Isabel almost everything. She is very ill and you have caused it, you with your lack of restraint, with your greed, with your self-indulgence. She is drinking herself to death and I don't know what more to do.'

Henry Atkinson looked puzzled and then he looked sad and strangest of all he looked lost.

'God, I feared this would happen.'

'This is the second time she has been like this. The first time I managed to stop her and to get her well again and now—'

There was a long silence as though Henry could not bear this any more than Mick could and Henry shook his head and looked around for something to distract him and he said, 'I heard that she had been ill and I wanted to come to her, but of course I couldn't.'

Henry sat where he was for a moment and then he got up and went to the fire and kicked the ashes back towards the grate.

'How long have you known her?' Mick said.

'Twelve years.'

Mick stared and could not reconcile the idea of what the man was saying with the man himself. He was not aggressive or difficult or predatory, you could pass him in a street and not notice him, with his thin covering of hair on his head and permanently furrowed brow.

'But we've only been married for eleven.' Mick stared and stared and then he realized what it meant and he could have stood there for days. He had not understood, he had not known that the greatest reason for his life had not been of his doing, was in fact nothing to do with him.

Henry Atkinson threw him a look of apology. 'I didn't know until the child was born that she was unmistakably mine.'

Time passed. Nobody moved. Nobody spoke. From somewhere there was a great wall of hurt and he resisted it and then he went numb. It was the only defence he had.

'Would you like to sit down?' Henry Atkinson asked him kindly.

And then Mick lost his temper and slammed Henry Atkinson up against the far wall of his office as though that might help. Henry didn't complain, he just let go of his breath as though it hurt.

'How could you do that? How could you use another

265

man in that way? Didn't you know what would happen? Didn't it occur to you that I might find out?'

'Of course it did.'

Mick let go of him. 'And didn't that matter?' He was looking down at the little man. Henry Atkinson seemed to have shrunk and put on ten years since Mick had walked into his office.

'It was a risk I had to take.'

'Fond of taking risks, are you?'

Henry shook his head and Mick saw in disgust that he was actually crying, his head turned aside as his eyes closed, like a schoolboy caught out in a prank.

'Why on earth did she marry me?' Mick said.

Henry shrugged. 'She liked you. I think she thought you were a younger version of me. I have to say that I encouraged her. She was almost bound to conceive at some point. We were just grateful for the timing.'

Mick found that his hands were clinging to the front of Henry Atkinson's untidy desk. Papers spilled towards him as he held on but they didn't go any further.

'I am married as I'm sure you know,' Henry Atkinson said. 'I have six children. Their mother is an excellent woman of her kind. The arrangement suited us very well, Isabel and me, except of course that you are not a younger version of me. I think she thought she could endure it and for a while she did and it seemed that no harm was done but—' he stopped there and looked at Mick sympathetically, 'forgive me – I think she found you dull, in the way that you live.

'She found your friends worthy and earnest, the last thing that younger people ought to be. Frankly, she didn't adjust well to marriage or motherhood. I held out hope, I wanted her to be happy. I would have given her up if she had been content with you. I do love her very much and despite what you think I would have given anything for this not to happen to her. If she had had other children it would possibly have been better. I know she feels like a failure, though I didn't make her feel so and I'm not saying you did either, in fact, knowing you as a decent man, I'm sure you didn't.'

Mick concentrated on his breathing. It did seem as if it would stop at any moment, it was so irregular.

'The whole thing has proved too much for her,' Henry said. 'I didn't realize that she had become so dependent on spirits. I'm sure you think this affair has been frequent and easy for us, but it hasn't. We have tried to stop seeing one another; I did attempt to give your marriage a chance. After you were married I hardly saw her for months and months together, but always we came back to one another. With an addictive nature such as she has she cannot give things up, even me. I adore her. I have asked her to go away with me and she has always refused. She was so convinced that she could make the marriage work.'

Mick stood and looked at the man. Henry Atkinson was not his wife's lover, he was so much more than that. He was the father of Isabel's child. Mick wondered what his other children were like and marvelled that a man who had six children already would need another, but then it had not been need, it had been indulgence.

How could one man have seven children and two women and so many other men have no children at all and nobody exclusively their own? Nobody who ever really loved them? You cannot shout unfair, he thought, it was unseemly to do so, pity was the worst thing ever and yet it seemed that men like Henry Atkinson could take the world and other men could only look on and wonder and commit sins like envy and jealousy because their lives seemed like nothing in comparison.

Had she thought when she met him how stupid he was and how much she needed to marry, and because he was in the same kind of business as Henry she could manage it? Was that really how it was?

Had she never loved him? Perhaps she had liked him once. He remembered every single word which Henry Atkinson had said. He did stop to consider that maybe it was not so, but nothing came to his aid, everything came down complete and stinging.

She had loved nobody but Henry. She had wanted nobody but Henry. And she had to marry because Henry was right: a woman would conceive when she should not. There were so many women who were childless, who looked at other women's children and gazed into cradles with envy. They were not the future, as he was not. He had not thought that he would end the line and he could not accept that Connie was Henry Atkinson's child, and yet she clearly was since she resembled him so much.

Did Mick love her in spite of that? No, he loved her because he had brought her up as his child and she adored him.

When he saw her the very next time she ran and threw her small self into his arms and he could never accept that she was another man's child, she was his, she was completely his daughter.

He buried his head against her golden hair. She smelled of the fells and the dogs and the sweet sweeping wind, the way that it got down among the low-lying gorse where the grouse flew and the pheasants plodded across the fields in slight confusion as though they had never got used to this cold and unforgiving place, and yet they lived and their cries rent the silence so very often in the early mornings and the long slow afternoons and he was always glad of it. They had made a place and however many of them were shot they survived, and sometimes their brash colours lifted above the tall summer grass in the fields. Like the people, they were always there.

15

'I'm going to close the academy.'

Mick frowned. Emma didn't look at him when she said the words, she did not want him to flatter himself that it was because of him that she was leaving. It was nothing of the kind. He had only come that day to tell her that his wife was ill again and to ask humbly if she would take care of his child over the coming days, and she had agreed for now and then she had told him that it would be tempo-rary.

'There's obviously no need for it. Nobody else has come and Mr English is perfectly capable of teaching the chil-dren what they need to know. He's a very good man. Connie is bright, she can go away to school and enjoy that. Thank you for your help.'

She thought he might have said something, that he might have protested. He just stood there like somebody totally defeated. Of course it was daylight and the chil-dren were around and she had deliberately told him when he could not respond any way other than politely, but he didn't seem to be able to manage that. She glanced at him to find that he was watching Connie as she ran about the schoolyard.

Emma was scandalous by village standards, she had lived in a pub, lived alone with a dog and a child, she was convinced that every woman in the village knew she had been present at a fight in the pub and God knew how many of them suspected she and Mick had slept together. Who would send their child to that kind of care, that level of morals?

The trouble was that she had no idea what she would do, where she would go. She had no money and every time she thought of leaving she felt sick. She had found and lost love here with a man who cared only for his wife. She did not want to stay here and watch him struggle any longer.

He didn't even argue with her – he didn't say anything.

Emma couldn't think what to do next and the following day, while the two children were doing their general knowledge questions – there were always three up on the board first thing – she heard a knocking on the door. When she opened it she saw Nell standing there, two badly dressed and not very clean children beside her. Emma was too astonished to speak and as she went on staring Nell faltered and looked down and Emma could see that it had taken all of her courage to come here. She must have needed something very badly indeed.

'Will you take Eddie and Rose, Miss Appleby?' Nell produced a fistful of silver coins and then put them back deep into her skirt pocket in case anybody should see.

Emma didn't know what to do except to shake her head.

'Don't they go to Mr English's school?'

'I can't send them there.' Nell turned her face away in defiance, Emma could see the hard set of her jaw.

'I don't think he would turn any child away, he's a good man and a fine teacher.'

'It isn't him, it's other people. They won't have their bairns mix with mine. I've had bricks through my windows and cow muck pushed through my letterbox and rubbish left outside my door. The women, they shout at me on the streets. I could have done other things, taken in washing and such, they say, I didn't have to resort to what I do, but it pays a lot better and it means I can be with my bairns during the days and when our Laurence is there at night – it works, you see.' She looked at Emma and then her eyes blanked and she half turned from her and said, 'I have their husbands because they don't want them and I do things for them that they won't do and there's nowt wrong in it, it's just the Church teachin' that folk mustn't enjoy things, like heaven was going to be so wonderful . . .'

Emma didn't know what to say to this. She should say that she was leaving, that the school was closing, but having remembered how Nell had shut the door in her face and how Nell looked at this minute, Emma found it impossible to do so. And there was also a kind of triumph that Nell had come to her, she had not thought it would happen and she couldn't help being pleased that it had.

'Come in,' she said.

'No, I mustn't.'

'If the children are to have lessons here they must see

272

what it's like and whether they care for it and be introduced to George and Connie. And so must you.'

'Miss Appleby—'

'I think you had better call me "Emma" since we are so obviously related.'

'It won't do you no good to be associated with me. I need the bairns to read and write, I want other things for them than what I had, but I can't come in.'

Nell was ready to turn away having relinquished her children's hands, but they stood very close to her.

Emma touched her very lightly on one dirty hand and she smiled into Nell's worn face and said, 'You and Laurence are all the family I have here and I really want to get to know you.'

Nell looked disbelievingly at her, stood for a few moments longer, tried to disengage herself from the children, and when they wouldn't move forward she gave in and entered the room cautiously. It was mid morning and the first thing Emma got all the children to do was wash their hands before they had their milk and cookies. Washing for the two girls was not something they did often, Emma could not help reflecting, watching as the water clouded and their fingers emerged, nails still grubby but hands white.

Emma busied herself, having urged Nell to help them, and they watched at a distance as George poured milk into mugs and Connie proudly carried the still-warm cookies on a big plate and put them in the middle of the table.

'What are cookies?' the bigger girl asked.

'Biscuits. Do you like biscuits?'

She glanced at her mother.

'It's from the French,' Emma explained. 'It means twice baked. Isn't that nice?'

They sat down. The biscuits were nothing more than sugar, flour, butter, egg and vanilla essence, but they were golden and fresh. She made tea and leaving the children at the kitchen table to get to know one another, she took Nell through into the sitting room.

'How much will it cost?' Nell asked. 'And I don't want no special rates. I know that people don't send their bairns here and that you must need the money.'

Emma hesitated. 'I know it's none of my business, but if you don't have to live where you do live and how you live, why do you do it? I'm sorry but—'

'No, I understand what you mean. We're mucky and the house is falling down. I just can't seem to manage all that I have to do and our Laurence too. I get tired. Besides, I've saved every ha'penny I could for a long time so that I could manage summat like this. I can tell you now that this is like a prayer answered for me. Will you take the bairns and show them better things? I need you to.'

Emma considered and then she nodded, and since Nell had been frank she was as well. 'I have to have a reason to stay here,' she said.

Nell frowned at her. 'You weren't going off some place?'

It was at that point Emma saw that Nell had her father's eyes.

'Is summat the matter?' Nell asked.

'We look alike.'

'I don't look nothing like you, Miss Appleby.'

'You look very like me, only better, thank goodness. I hope that isn't insulting, for I'm plain and you are very comely, the same thing but different. Will you stay for lunch?'

'Lunch?'

'Dinner. Stay, please. It will give the children a chance to get to know one another and afterwards if you have time we could take them for a walk.'

'Mine seem never to go nowhere. I'm frightened to let them out because of how folk talk at me, shouting and that.'

'We'll take a nature study walk,' Emma said, and she thought how many times saying this had got her out of a difficult situation. In such a place there was always something fresh to see.

It was strange, Emma thought, as they took the children down the long valley into the dale, but Verity had never meant even a tiny portion of what Nell meant already and yet they had nothing in common. Nell did not talk much and had no education, Emma wasn't even sure she could read or write, but just having her there on the walk and seeing how Nell's children became more bold, running ahead, throwing sticks for Hector, laughing and shouting with George and Connie, Emma thought, this is exactly what I intended, this is right.

She could learn to love Nell, in fact, she thought, I

already do. Nell moved in some way like their father; there were so many things about her which were like him and yet it grieved Emma because she could not say this, she could not easily be glad of it, and yet it was what they had in common so she could not help but be pleased.

If Nell had had any advantages at all, she thought, she could have achieved so many things. Nell knew about the birds, she spied a kestrel soaring above and she was the one who spotted a sparrow-hawk on the way home. She had special names for the trees and the flowers and told Emma of them, and Emma found herself laughing and glad. They had the same sense of humour, they even paused at the same time and would begin to speak together. They were so alike that Emma was charmed.

When they were quite by themselves she said, 'Will you pick up the children at teatime?' Nell hesitated and then she said, looking straight at Emma, 'I will pay for them to stay with you, I think they need to get out of the place where we live.'

Remembering it, Emma agreed, though she said nothing except, 'If they wish to stay that's fine, but if they miss you so much that it's unbearable we'll have to talk about it.'

'I've already talked to them and explained that they can come home if they want, but they should stay here for a week and try it. If they are homesick I will come for them. I'll bring their clothes, I didn't like to – to presume. Here.' She gave Emma the purse which she had put away earlier, dodged around the corner of the house and came back with two big bundles, and it was not until she had gone that Emma opened the purse and saw that it contained a great deal of money and she understood that Nell had needed to forgo so many things to make sure that her children had an education. Emma was half inclined to call her back, but she didn't, she just watched Nell's thin figure as she walked away.

No insult to Nell, she thought, but she washed all the clothes, she bathed and scrubbed the two little girls thoroughly and disinfected their hair and combed it carefully for nits. She put them into voluminous nightgowns and told Connie that they were her responsibility. 'They will be in your bedroom.'

Connie's lips went into a thin line. 'I liked having it to myself.'

'Yes, well, now you won't. You must look after them, Connie, they haven't left their mother before. If you have any problems you just come across the landing and tell me. I'm relying on you.'

'Do you know what their mother is?'

'I know that men have made life so difficult for women that when they are widowed they have very little choice. They do what they must do to feed their children, and that's what Nell does. It's not what she would have chosen, but many women lead lives they would never have wanted. Do you understand?'

Connie stood for a moment and then she kissed Emma suddenly on the cheek and ran upstairs and no more was heard that night except that Emma thought she could discern Connie's calm voice through the ceiling a couple of times when the children went to bed. She hoped George didn't feel out of it and when she went up she looked in on him. He was still awake. She kissed him. 'It's getting very female around here. Are you all right?' she said.

'Can Hector stay here with me?'

She said he could and Hector lay by George's bed, but later, when George had gone to sleep, Hector padded across the landing and lay down by her bed just as he always did. She was not afraid with Hector there, but she did spend some time regretting Mick Castle before she went to sleep. She was glad that she had been given an excuse not to move on.

16

Isabel lay with her face turned to the wall in the spare room in Sam's house. It was the smallest of the bedrooms, the double bed in it took up most of the space and Mick wished he could be anywhere but here.

He remembered her running from room to room when he had shown her the house they could have when they were married, the house he would buy if she liked it. She had loved the garden, the way the house stood apart from the village. He had been so much in love with her that he had not noticed there was anything amiss.

And when she had become pregnant he had thought his world complete.

She was still sleeping. She would awaken and demand gin soon. He stood by the window and worried about what to do. It was mid afternoon. He heard Marjorie softly open the door.

She glanced around, at the bed first, no doubt to check on the patient – she was a doctor's wife before anything else – and then at him by the window.

'You have a visitor.' No wonder she looked surprised. 'Mr Atkinson.'

Mick stood for a few seconds and then he said, 'Could

you ask him to come up?'

Isabel stirred just as Henry Atkinson came into the room. He flashed Mick a grateful and apologetic look and sat down on the bed so that when she opened her eyes he was the first thing she saw. He looked at her with such joy, Mick thought. She smiled back as he had not seen her smile in years and her eyes shone brilliantly, he couldn't tell whether it was with joy or tears.

'What have you been doing?' he said.

'I missed you.'

It still hurt to see the way that she looked at Henry, she loved him so obviously, touched him delicately as though he were about to disappear and she would never see him again. She was not aware that Mick was in the room, she could have been anywhere at any time, there was only Henry for her.

'You have got to stop doing this to yourself, my dearest, or we won't see one another again this side of the grave.'

'I don't care any more.'

'What are you punishing yourself for?'

She gazed at him. 'I want to be with you. I want to be your wife.'

Henry Atkinson didn't say anything at first and when he did his voice wobbled. 'I cannot give you more children. If you had been going to have any you would have done so by now.'

'I want your babies, I want to be fat with them.'

She turned away from him. Henry sat there for a very long time and she went back to sleep. Henry got up like a man of eighty; it wasn't age, it was disappointment, disillusionment, frustration. Mick felt as though Henry had not the right to such feelings as these. Henry did not raise his eyes.

And stupidly, somehow he wanted to reassure the man. He stood, horrified at himself, and then Henry Atkinson looked at him and the eyes which held his were glassy with tears.

'I'm sorry, I know I look like a fool and a lot of worse things, but you see I didn't intend this. I thought she had grown to love you. You can't imagine how many nights I lay awake and envied you when you were first married, especially after there was a child. You must believe that I did try to keep away. My wife loves nobody except our children, and sometimes I even wonder about that. She seems to have no capacity for love. I could have loved her, at first I thought there might be a chance for us, she was so beautiful, still is.

'The children were packed off to school the moment they were independent. I missed them so much. I own a great deal and am seen in business as a warm and clever man, but in my house I have always been a nuisance, you see. The marriage was arranged by our parents and she never wanted me except when she wanted a child. I had no other use but making money and I was allowed near her no longer after she was pregnant. My children have grown away from me, my wife wants us to give up the business and move to London.'

He glanced at Isabel before wandering out of the room

as though he wasn't certain where he was going and it was not until Mick heard his feet on the stairs, the brass rods clinking, that he let go of his breath.

Nell's daughters became almost as dear to Emma as if they had been her own. She did not favour them, that would have been unkind and unjust, but she thought that they even looked like her and she had not imagined that she would want a child to do so, and then she thought, yes, she had when she was younger and John Elstree had been a possibility.

She had seen a pretty house in a wide street with lots of trees, her husband coming home to her in the evenings, how they would sit in the garden when it was summer or over the fire in the winter and talk about the children when they were in bed. It would have been blissful, she thought – and most unlikely, her sensible self could not help adding.

She heard nothing from Nell, and the little girls did not talk of her or of their home, or show any signs of wanting to go back. They seemed to revel in good meals, clean beds, the company of Connie and George, and they especially liked Hector.

Emma was almost insulted for Nell that they appeared not to miss her, until one night a snivelling child appeared, and then another, and they cast themselves upon her calling loudly for their mam. She assured them that they would see Nell very early the next day and she took them back to bed and talked them to sleep.

Neither did she see Mick Castle. Jack came now that he was better. Nobody else came to call. She went out only for groceries, and after being stared at and whispered about in the shops she stopped going and asked Jack to drop in orders from the various shops who delivered. It was so much easier.

Nell turned up on the Monday morning after Emma had sent a note with Jack, and her daughters heard her and rushed through and they went straight into her arms. Emma had a sudden pang, but then she was just so glad because Nell was laughing and the girls were trying to tell her all at once what they had been doing and she was saying, 'Don't both talk at once, I can't hear you,' and they were able to tell her what had happened and George and Connie too related what they had done. Emma could tell by Connie's voice that she had accepted Nell and all that Emma had said, and she felt that she might be doing some good there.

When the children went off for their mid-morning break to play in the yard, Nell's gaze followed her daughters, and then she said, 'I think I might be expecting.'

They were playing some kind of chanting game which she did not recognize. Emma felt her insides sink, the sickness of shock hit her. She looked at Nell, but her half-sister went on watching the children, almost as if she had said nothing

'Are you sure?'

Nell smiled and shook her head.

'Why don't you come and stay with us?' Emma said.

283

'I've spent enough time here, you must sicken of me.'

'Give up the house. I would love to have you here. I always wanted a sister and I've never had anybody other than a brother who didn't care for me. Please, Nell, come here.'

'It wouldn't be right.'

'Why not?'

Nell looked fondly at her with slight exasperation as people do when they are related, and Emma wished she could make a picture of that look. She had never seen it on anyone's face before.

'Who would send their children to you when you housed the local whore? It's bad enough my children being here.'

'They didn't send them anyway,' Emma said. 'And I don't care any more. I want a family and you and the girls, that's what you are to me.'

Nell shook her head sadly. 'There's Laurence.'

How could she have forgotten him, Emma wondered, and yet she knew why she had dismissed him from her mind. He made her think of her own Laurence and of how much he despised her, how he had never wanted her around him. It was not fair, she knew.

'He can come here,' she said.

'He cannot. It's too much for him to work out. It would upset him to the point where he couldn't bear himself and then—' Nell stopped. 'I can't do that to him, I have to keep the house going.' She looked bravely at Emma and then said she must be off and went out into the yard to see the girls before she left. She looked at Emma in the pale evening light and she said, 'I never thought to have anybody to help,' and Emma watched her as she walked away, with her cheap clothes and her determined gait.

Emma had put the children to bed and was taking Hector out to splash his boots, when she heard someone running towards her. Hector had already stopped, but he was not growling so it must be somebody they knew. She had a few brief moments when her heart – damn it, didn't she learn anything – lifted because she thought it must be Mick, but a younger, slighter figure emerged from the darkness. It was Jack.

'Summat's happened, Miss, to Nell Whittington like, and Mr Higgins, he said you must come to the Black Diamond. I'm to stay here and watch the bairns, that's what he said, and you must take Hector with you to mind you on the way.'

She wanted to ask more, but the urgency in his tone forbade it, so all she did was pull her coat from a peg behind the door and run with Hector beside her. The dog didn't seem surprised at all, as though he knew what was happening. How did Labradors know such things? Could he hear the alarm in Jack's voice? Of course he could? She reasoned, and the dog's presence made her feel better.

She ran as fast as she could, she didn't know that she could run so fast. She saw how people's heads turned as she went past them regardless, how she stepped into the road with the black dog keeping perfect step, though she knew he could have travelled much faster without her.

The wind, she only just noticed, was cold and screaming through the village, and soon there was nobody except herself on the street and she could hear the pounding of her feet on the buildings across the road.

Men were outside the pubs and they watched her and they shouted, she had no doubt it was rude remarks, but she didn't care, she had long since stopped regarding them as anything important but a source of income to Mick and therefore for the school, so she hoped that they drank themselves senseless and smoked themselves hoarse.

It seemed such a very long way though it could have been but a few minutes. The crowd had cleared, men, some with pints in their hands, standing back in a big circle. They would not have seen her, they could not have noticed, she was so small by comparison, they were so big sideways, feet planted apart, giants of men across their chests from the kind of physical work they did every day, but she shouted at them and not in a ladylike way. Miss Emma Appleby of Mid Haven would scarcely have recognized the screaming banshee who shrieked, 'Get out the way!' in a strong carrying tone that brooked no defiance. She would make a schoolteacher yet, yelling like that.

Surprised, they moved, and it was like the Red Sea parting, so many of them and yet to her all alike, big boots moving aside, and when she got past them she realized why the space had cleared. There was not much light, but she could make out Nell, slumped on the ground. She got down beside her.

'Nell? Nell. Are you all right?'

She knew it was the stupidest possible thing to say to a woman who so obviously wasn't, but she couldn't bear that Nell should be hurt or ill.

She thought at first that perhaps it was best to leave her there, perhaps it was best she were not moved, and then she realized that it was not a fall, not an accident. She got down further, kneeling on the ground. With awful timing it began to rain, cold hard drops like sleet and the wind behind it, but she didn't care how her hair stuck to her face and how soaked her clothes became because it was immediately obvious to her that Nell was badly hurt. There was blood, a lot of it – the back of Nell's skirt and the pavement beneath and around her sticky and thick with it. Hector hovered. One man moved, another said something jeering, and the big black dog turned with intent and the growl that came from the depths of his throat was sufficient to quell any movement, any noise. He crouched, low and dangerous, his jaws apart and his eyes glittering.

Emma turned. She wanted to shout at them, why had they not moved Nell? but then they knew nothing and perhaps they did not like to or maybe more likely they did not want to get involved, they only wanted to see and to be able to talk about it later over another pint.

'You!' Emma pointed at one young man, at least she thought he was, it was difficult to see, his cap was pulled low, 'Pick her up and bring her inside.'

'But—'

'Do as I ask.' Emma stood up and they all moved back slightly, and then the young man moved forward.

He picked Nell up. The men stood further back and Emma turned in the doorway and she took them in with one sweeping glance and said, in their language, 'Have you buggers got nowt better to do than stand there, gawping? Get the hell away home,' and she turned and followed him inside, Hector at her heels.

The pub was deserted. She had never seen it like this. She got the man to carry Nell into the bar and there he put her down on a long settle.

'Has somebody gone for the doctor?'

'Mr Higgins went straight away, Miss.' He stood back a little way. 'Is she going to be all right?'

Emma said nothing and he melted away into the night. By the bar lights she could see the cloth of Nell's skirt and the blood making its way on to the seat. Emma had never felt quite so helpless, Nell looked so very small. She was not large herself, but this sister showed that she had not had enough to eat when she was a child, that she had not had the care that children needed and deserved. She had needed so much resistance to the things which had gone wrong in her life and it had been too much. She opened her eyes and saw Emma and smiled. 'How are the bairns?' she said.

'They're asleep. What happened?'

Nell shut her eyes again. 'Lost the baby.'

'Oh God, Nell, I've only just found you. I never had a sister before, only a stupid brother who never cared if I lived or died. Please, Nell, don't leave me here, on my own. I haven't anyone but you. Please don't—' She started to cry. She knew it was stupid, she knew it wouldn't help Nell, she wanted to stop, but she wanted so much to have this sister she had just found, for them to be together, to have history in common, to laugh and to grow old.

Emma stared. 'Nell?'

There was no reply.

Emma had seen her father dead and her mother dead, but she had not been with someone as they died. She had always thought there would be some time, that you might have some decent conversation, some indication that it was going to happen, not that it would be like this. She had not thought that you would know instantly when the life left the body, but she knew, and still she sat there for a very long time, waiting for Nell to open her eyes. Emma willed her to be there not just for her own sake or the sake of her children but for the sake of her half-sister who had only just learned to love her.

She had the feeling that if she sat there, holding Nell's hand like this, eventually Nell would sit up and say that she was all right, and she would take Nell home back to the schoolhouse and in the morning she would be able to take the children to see their mother. It would be a surprise and she would never let Nell go back to that tumbledown damp hovel at Road Ends, and somehow she would persuade Laurence to come and live with them too. It could not be that difficult. Why had she not insisted before?

She had not wanted to take over, to make Nell feel small or unimportant in the way that they had both at different times been made to feel. She wished now that she had insisted, that she could somehow have helped Nell, given her ease and time, and for them to sit together like families never did and people wanted to. She wanted to have time with Nell and now it was over.

There was a noise behind her, but Hector who was sitting on the floor beside her did not growl and she assumed it was either Ed or Jack, and then she turned just a little and saw the two men in the doorway, Mick and Dr Blythe. She did not move and after regarding them for just a second she went back to what she had been doing.

Dr Blythe moved forward and she said, 'Stay there.'

'Emma—'

'Goddamn you, don't call me by my first name,' was the only thing she could get out, her voice breaking like the surf over rough sand. She couldn't remember how to breathe, she couldn't take in what had just happened.

'I have to see—'

'You don't have to see anything. A blind man could see from there that she's dead. Could nobody have brought her inside when it happened? Did they have to leave her out there on the pavement to bleed to death?'

'Emma—'

It was Mick.

'Shut up!' she said. 'You useless bastards,' and she started to cry. 'How can men do such things to women? How can you do it? How can somebody like this be left to such a fate? It isn't right. Did nobody want to help her? Did nobody offer? All she had was two children and a man who was deranged. Could they not have done something? It isn't right, it isn't fair.'

She drew even closer to Nell. Nobody moved. She took her sister into her arms. Nell was so warm, even then Emma half believed she might come back to life, that she couldn't leave so quickly, and in a way it was just like when an animal died. She could remember one of her father's dogs in just the same way: one moment there and the next gone, as quickly as that. It was the only time she had seen death close up, her father's beloved friend, light gone, spirit fled.

She began to cry. She held her sister in her arms and began to sob for all the things that Nell had wanted and not had, for all the times that nobody had been there for her, for all the long days when she had seen to her children and to her brother, alone and not complaining, and taken men up the alleyway for money. Emma didn't think she could bear that her sister had died.

It was Hector who moved. She didn't tell him to stay away and shut up, but then she didn't think he would have taken any notice. He stood up and came the tiny distance between them and then he put his chin on Nell's stomach, and the tears ran down Emma's face in great streams as never before.

17

Sam carried Nell's body upstairs and put her into the bedroom where Emma and George had slept. Emma didn't want to leave her there. The place was full of memories: her arrival, her despair, her becoming part of the pub itself. She loved and hated the damned place and now Nell was there and there was nothing left.

'Is Jack with the children?' Mick asked her as she sat on the bed.

'No, I left them on their own,' she said savagely. And then she thought of something. It was very late. 'Laurence. He'll have gone back to Road Ends.'

'I'll go.'

'No, you'll frighten him. I'll go myself. You should get back to your wife,' and she got up and strode out the room.

She had not gone far when she heard his footsteps and turned. 'I don't need your help. I have Hector.' She indicated the black dog at her heels, as though he wouldn't have noticed.

'For God's sake. Sam's gone to see to Isabel.'

'He couldn't manage without you before. Where's the difference?'

'The difference is that it's cold and dark and you shouldn't go all that way on your own.'

'You think worse could happen to me?' She laughed and then choked. 'You think I care?'

'You should think about George if anything did happen.'

'My God, Mick, do you ever think about anybody except children and your wife?'

She set off again, ignoring him. He didn't follow her immediately, but she wasn't far past the end of the street before he caught up with her.

She did not believe that Nell was dead. She had the feeling that she would get there and Nell would open the door and they would meet again and everything would be all right, but the wind was so bitter with nothing to stop it. She cried all the way. It didn't matter, the wind dried the tears immediately. The man beside her said nothing and she didn't speak to him, she didn't care whether he was there or not. She wished she'd never seen him. She wished she had not had to face any of this.

When they reached the house at Road Ends everything was silent. Emma went up and hammered on the door, but there was no reply. She shouted Laurence's name, but nothing happened and when she tried the door it was locked. It being the end house it was not far from there to the back door, but when Mick tried it it was bolted from the inside.

There was no light of any kind.

'He could have gone back to the pub,' Mick said. 'We could have missed him.'

'He wouldn't.'

'How do you know?'

'I just do.'

They walked back round to the front and Hector stopped and his hair did not stand on end and he did not growl, he knew Laurence and his tail began to wag just a little, as though he was not certain he should be pleased that he had realized who the man was, and Emma spied a figure in the darkness well beyond the houses. She set off very slowly. Mick didn't follow and Hector sat down beside him. The figure began to move away and then further so she stopped and called.

'Larry, it's me, Emma.'

He moved and then turned as if he were going to run, and she called again but more softly,

'Nell is with me.' He stopped. She didn't want him to misinterpret. 'She's back at the pub.'

He didn't run. He turned slowly to face her though she couldn't see his face.

'She's not here,' he said. 'She comes home at this time.'

'She isn't going to come home tonight,' Emma said, and hoped and prayed that her voice didn't falter. It did, but only after the words were said. She did her best to swallow her grief. The night was not a decent covering for it. Even here as the year grew towards its finish there was no place to hide. She thought she could learn to hate summer when there was not a decent covering for people's grief, but autumn and winter were kinder, dark and cold, and sent you inside to sit over the fire and take comfort.

'Who's that?' Laurence asked.

'It's Mr Castle. He didn't want me to walk all this way by myself. Will you come back with us?'

'Nell says I mustn't leave the bairns.'

'They aren't here,' she reminded him.

'Why not?'

'They're with me, at the academy. You remember.'

'I want Nell.'

He might not have understood, but he was not to be easily deceived, Emma thought. He faded against the shadows of the long building which was the dozen houses that stood there. Emma didn't know what more to say and Mick came and stood beside her.

'Larry, it's me, Mick Castle,' he said gently.

Laurence didn't move. 'Where's our Nell? And the bairns?'

'The bairns are at Miss Appleby's school,' Mick said, 'and Nell's at the pub just now. Would you like to come back with us?'

There was a long silence during which Emma felt despair hit her like a huge stone. She was never going to get past this, perhaps none of them would. She didn't know what more to say.

'She's had an accident,' Mick said.

As they stood not knowing what more to do since Laurence didn't respond, Hector got up from where he had been patiently sitting and he went halfway to Laurence. Laurence saw him, and Emma could hear the smile in his voice because he had long since known Hector from the pub, and he said, 'Good lad, good lad.' He got down and Hector went to him, tail wagging with great confidence. Laurence got right down to the dog and then he put his arms around him and he said, 'Oh lad,' and Hector, in fine acknowledgement that dogs knew more than people, suffered the embrace which Laurence took him into as he had suffered other embraces from the children at the academy, from them all really, Emma thought. Hector knew his duty and did it gladly, and she loved the dog for it. Emma and Mick waited and waited and after a long time Laurence emerged from the shadow of the building, Hector walking slightly behind and keeping to the shadows as though in protection.

'Our Nell's hurt?' Laurence said.

'Aye,' Mick said.

'But she always comes home,' Laurence said, 'always comes back. I stay here with the bairns and she comes back later and she's always in the house and we go to bed and I can hear her, making up the fire for the night. I can hear it when I'm upstairs in me bed.'

'Come back to the pub with us,' Emma said.

Laurence did. Emma did not pretend to herself that he was fooled, that he imagined when he got there that he would see her and everything would be all right. Nothing was all right and never had been, and their experience of life had been so hard that Laurence did not expect anything to change for the better, and it hadn't.

When they reached the pub he stopped quite a long way from the building and he turned to Mick and he said, 'Where is our Nell?'

'She's upstairs.'

Emma put a warning hand on Mick's sleeve, but his fingers came down on top of hers as though in reassurance.

'I want to go up and see her.'

'I'll come with you,' Emma said, and because he trusted her he went and her heart did incredibly awful things, thumping hard and moving around in her chest. She didn't want to see Nell's body; she didn't want to think that her sister was dead.

Laurence watched the landing as though something were about to crash and destroy the building, and in a way, Emma thought, he was right.

'Where is she?' he asked.

She took him into the room, and she thought that Nell no longer looked as if she had been alive. She waited for him to shout and moan and cry, but he did none of that: he stood for a few seconds inside the door and then he very quietly made his way across to the bed and he sat down on the edge of it, as she imagined you did in hospital, and he watched Nell.

He looked as though he were waiting for her to wake up, but he was not, Emma could see. He was just sorry and nonplussed that someone he had loved so very much was not there any more. He sat for so long that Emma's feet went to sleep, but not the rest of her; she thought most of her would never sleep again – why would she, when Nell was dead? How could you find and lose someone so rapidly? It was so sad, so awful. It was the bottom of life.

Larry looked at her, and there was something completely comprehending about him.

'She's dead.'

'Yes.'

He sat there and cried, and Emma waited and she wondered why she did not cry.

At that point there was an intrusion. Mick was standing in the doorway, as if everything were normal.

Emma glared at him, and he looked back at her in such an even way that she could not hold his gaze, though she was appalled.

'I thought you might stay here with me tonight, Larry,' Mick said. 'Why don't you come downstairs and have something to eat?'

It seemed to Emma such a stupid thing to say, but it worked. Laurence got up and went with him and she followed into the bar. It was empty. The men had gone home. Why would they not? It was over, the whore was dead and there was nothing to keep them there.

Mick went to the bar and smiled at Ed. 'Laurence and me, we're hungry.'

Ed nodded and told them to sit down and he would bring them some food. Emma went through into the kitchen with him.

'What have you got?'

'Stew. You showed me how to do it. I'm not half bad,' he said and he put it in the range. While it heated she wanted to cast herself upon his chest and be made to feel better, but she didn't. She stood there and the stew gave

298

off a good smell, so at least she thought, I can teach cookery if nothing else.

Laurence and Mick sat down by the fire. Laurence ate. She tried not to notice that Mick didn't eat. Ed brought beer. When Laurence had had enough to eat – for once he didn't drink much – he lay on the settle and went to sleep. Just as she thought that she and Mick could sit there almost forever while Laurence slept and it was comfortable by the fire, he said, 'Would you like me to see you home?'

'Jack will stay with the children.' She sat gazing into the fire and then she said,

'I don't want to leave Nell here without me.'

'I'll sit up. Nobody will touch anything.'

She didn't stop staring at the fire, as though it held her somehow, as though it were all there was to look at. Then she said softly and desperately, so that he wished he could take her into his arms, 'How could it have happened and why didn't they do something?'

'People are afraid of things they don't know.' He sat for a few moments and then he said, apologetically, 'I need a drink. Would you like some whisky?'

'I don't know, I never had any.'

That was invitation enough. He went and found a bottle behind the bar and poured it into little glasses and brought it across. She didn't drink it: she just held the glass in her hands and smelled it from time to time. It was comforting, he knew, and if you closed your eyes you were in Scotland, staying in some lochside hotel, by a grand fire, and there were dogs asleep as Hector was now and the brass of the bar glinted in the firelight. In the morning you would awake to mist and that day you were to climb a mountain which you could see beyond the loch from your hotel window, and when you went to bed you heard the soft lapping of the loch in the wind. You could look forward to the day and all would be well. He was enjoying this vision, just getting to the part where Emma was there with him and they were together, when she said, 'I'll have to try and persuade Laurence to come and live with me.'

'That might not be easy,' Mick said.

Emma wanted to go upstairs and see her sister again and he went with her.

'Can she stay here until I talk to the vicar?' she said.

'Would you like me to go?'

'No, I would like to do it myself.'

Laurence awoke, they could hear him moving around downstairs and they went down immediately, thinking he might have forgotten what he was doing here, but he was merely sitting over the ashes of the fire. Mick had been putting coal on it all night, but had felt too drowsy to move for the past hour or so. He had just watched Emma looking at the blaze as it died down and he tried to commit to memory every part of her: the small well-worn hands, her straight hair (he had never seen such straight hair, and always put up so neatly out of the way as though it were nothing but a nuisance).

No expensive lotions could ever have reached Emma's

face, so that every mark could be seen from what she had suffered in her life. She had never been beautiful, but her skin looked so soft to him and her eyes so steady that he loved all of her, every inch, every move, every time she spoke, every breath she took.

Her dress was worn, though at one time it had been a deep blue, and her body was skinny, and then he remembered that it wasn't when you touched her, she was satin and silk below the shapeless dress. She was the dearest person in the whole world and he wanted her so much that he thought he might die for lack of her.

He wanted to be with her, so that each second he was not there mattered to him. All else bored him; he was desperate for her presence. The world was grey and unnatural without her, but he understood what she felt for Nell, that her world was the less without the sister she had found, and he was angry for what Nell had had to put up with and he wanted to change things for the better, and he knew that Emma's school could do that, she was right. They would keep and look after the little girls and whatever other children were sent to them. They would try for a better world for them; that was how it was meant to be.

By the next morning Emma's feelings for Nell intruded and she was so aware of Laurence, how hurt he was, how he grieved. She must put her own feelings aside and think of him.

'Can I not stay here?' he was saying.

'Wouldn't you like to see Edie and Rose?'

Laurence shook his head and Emma knew that he did not want to leave Nell. Indeed he said nothing more and she could hear him as he climbed the stairs, and after that there was silence.

In the end Emma told the two girls that their mother had died and gone to heaven. What on earth else could she say? She was surprised by their response. They both stood for a few moments, taking in what she thought they could not understand, and then they turned and ran away. She left them to get used to it, if anybody ever got used to loss – she didn't think they did other than those who believed in heaven. She would say anything to ease their grief and heaven was such a lovely idea, but later Rose, the elder child, came to her in the kitchen when she was preparing the evening meal and said, 'Can I talk to you, Miss?' (In vain had she told them she was Miss Appleby and she had given up trying to persuade them to call her that.)

Emma turned from the stove and regarded the child's serious face and encouraged her to sit down at the big table. When they were seated close, Rose said, 'We're worried about me mam.'

'Worried?' Emma didn't understand this. 'Why is that?'

'Well . . .' Rose looked down at her thin fingers in some dismay, and then she said, 'Our dad died, you know, ages ago like. Do you think he went to heaven, Miss?'

'Yes, of course,' Emma said readily. She couldn't think of anything else which might satisfy the child.

'We don't want me mam to go then.'

This was not what Emma had expected, and she waited for the explanation. But the child said nothing more and went crimson in the face and her bottom lip wobbled as though she would cry.

Emma said, 'Why not?'

'Because me dad used to knock me mam around and we don't want him doing it up there,' and she pointed to the ceiling.

Emma had to stop herself from gathering this child into her arms, and she also had to stop herself from smiling.

'It isn't like that up there.'

Rose waited for a moment and then she raised doubtful eyes to Emma's face. 'Are you sure, Miss?'

'Absolutely positive. When people go to heaven they become lovely like angels.'

'Even me dad?'

'Even him. It's there for all of us.'

Rose looked all over Emma's face to make sure she was not being deceived and Emma had to hold her expression still to meet the child's needs. For such young people, she thought, they knew a great deal.

Rose went off, seemingly pleased with this, but within hours the younger child, Edie, wanted her mam and cried to go home until she cried herself to sleep on Emma's lap. Emma didn't blame them, it was how she was feeling herself.

She apologized to Jack for leaving him there with four children, but he seemed unperturbed.

'Me mam came over and stayed until late and then I watched her home, but I didn't leave the bairns.'

She thanked him, told him how kind he was and watched his face glow. There was nothing better than a lad who was responsible in a crisis.

'Would you wish to become a teacher, Jack?' she asked him, and his face lit up.

'Do you think I might, Miss?'

'I think you would make an excellent teacher,' she said. 'I will help you as much as I can.'

He went home to see his mam, Emma thought, to tell her of the teaching, and then came back almost immediately to catch up on various jobs, so she left him to mind the children again and she went to the Black Diamond. Mick was still there, sitting watching Laurence who had spent a lot of time upstairs with Nell's body and was now stretched out, asleep in the bar.

'Shouldn't you be with Isabel?' she said, and he looked up. He seemed so tired, so drawn, pale and with a dark shadow where he had not shaved.

'I'm going to take Larry back to the schoolhouse,' she said. 'I think he will be better when he sees the little girls.'

Mick didn't get up immediately when she sat down, and she had a terrible desire to touch him, but of course she didn't. She gave him what she was not convinced was a bright smile and watched him as he walked towards the door. When he had gone she looked down and hoped that Laurence would sleep for a while, but he awoke at that moment, looking confused.

At first he thought she was Nell and said her name, but she shook her head and told him flatly that Nell was dead, as she had promised herself she would, hoping it was the best thing to do, hoping that in time he would accept the idea. She hoped in time that she would accept it too.

He then insisted on going upstairs to sit with her and it seemed fruitless to try to persuade him otherwise. Ed had come in, and he looked so pale that it was obvious he had not slept either. After a long while Laurence came downstairs and wanted to go to the house at Road Ends because Nell must be there, and she found herself following him, trying to talk to him, and Laurence picking up speed when he knew she was trying to stop him.

When they got to the house he had a key and undid the lock rapidly and then he went inside and shouted Nell's name. Up and downstairs he ran. Emma stood by the door and watched him until at last he stopped, exhausted. It took time – she thought he was never going to halt the blind scurrying – but in the end even he could finally understand that Nell was not there and neither were the children, and that was when he came back to her and stood, disconsolate. She waited. He stood for a long time; all the while she could hear the cold wind blowing across the fields towards them.

'Come back to the schoolhouse with me. The children are there.'

He looked hopefully at her. Then he nodded.

It was slow progress because every moment he thought

that he might have missed something, she could tell; that in some corner he had not seen, in some cupboard where he had not looked, in some small part of the backyard Nell was there, hanging the clothes out in the stiff breeze, seeing to soup over the kitchen fire. Or she was about to come home, it was night and he was there by himself with the children and he was waiting for her footsteps, for the way that she alone could make him feel safe, her breathing and her presence, and perhaps she would even call softly up the stairs and tell him that she was back and all was well.

She would not care about the men who had taken her up the alley and had her body, however briefly. How could she do that? Emma wondered. How could you be so desperate? Yet thousands upon thousands of women had done so, and it was nothing worse than having a man like the one she'd once seen in the street who asked his wife if she was fucking mad, Emma had heard them, she a pace or two behind him as he shouted, wondering whether he might hit her.

Did men really hate women so very much? Some of them did. She had heard of one man who took his wife into the backyard in the stinging wind and pulled all her fingernails out with some implement while her children watched.

Nell made her money from their bodies and from her own, and it was much better than what many women had. How hard was that, how impossible? Did not women deserve better? Emma felt sure they did.

When they finally reached the academy Laurence hesitated as they went in by the gate. He did not expect Nell to be there, Emma thought, but the girls came to him, shouted his name, Uncle Laurence, Uncle Laurence, and they wrapped themselves around him, and he lifted them both up into his arms and said their names and kissed them.

18

The undertaker had been directed by Dr Blythe to the schoolhouse from the Black Diamond where Emma had left instructions. She could see that the first thing on the man's mind was money. He did not seem happy to be there and gazed around the room she had made her study with great curiosity, as though he had not seen a woman in a study before. Perhaps, she thought, he had not.

She had two dozen girls coming from the council school that afternoon. She had suggested to Mr English that all the children should learn hygiene and cookery.

'Hygiene?' Mr English as a classics scholar could not envisage this, she could tell. Even now she had the Englishes to stay at least once a week: it gave Mrs English a change, and she knew that Mr English liked being there.

Mr English was sitting in the most comfortable of her chairs and Mrs English had fallen asleep after tea and cake in a way in which Emma hoped she did at home, but she thought that it was the noise of the children which Mrs English liked, perhaps the rhythm of their talk and laughter sent her to rest.

'Hygiene is the most basic thing of all,' Emma said, 'and as for the ability to cook, everyone should know how as we can't always rely on someone else for this.'

She could see that Mr English was still not convinced these things should be taught in school. Tomorrow she would have the boys here for the same kind of lesson and that was going to be much more difficult. On top of this she had Nell's funeral to arrange, the girls to console, and each day she had to prevent Laurence from going back to Road Ends because he was still convinced that Nell would come home.

He nodded over the fire while the freezing rain fell. She was even guiltily pleased when he went off to the Black Diamond in the early afternoons. She did try to make him eat first, but Laurence was reluctant to put anything inside him which would impede the effect of drink.

'I don't know how you intend to do this, Miss Appleby,' the undertaker, Mr Crouch, said now, urging his fat form down into Emma's only armchair in her study, as though he might be staying for some time. 'But somebody must pay and I don't suppose the parish is going to do it with any willingness in light of the kind of woman Mrs Whittington was.'

'I imagine that might depend on how many of them were making use of Nell's services,' Emma said.

Mr Crouch fairly spluttered over the tea she had given him, and she only hoped he would choke. She was worried for the sake of her hearthrug; she didn't want Mr Crouch's spit anywhere near it.

'There is no problem about money,' she said, 'and I will

let you know about the funeral arrangements.'

She did not want to approach the vicar, but since Nell had been Church of England it was the right thing to do. She went the very next morning and was seen inside by his wife, who pursed her lips together as though she had just devoured a lemon. Mr Inman's study was dusty and his carpet was grimy. Emma was rather pleased that his wife was a shoddy housekeeper. She sat down unasked and waded in anyway.

'You may know by now that Nell Whittington has died. I would like you to conduct her funeral. Something simple will do; she has two children and a brother and it need not be a long service, just enough so that those who cared for her will understand.'

Mr Inman stared at her. 'I'm sorry,' he said.

'Are you? Why?' She held his gaze unflinchingly.

'I'm afraid I won't be able to hold a funeral here for – for Mrs Whittington.'

'Really?' Emma said.

'I'm very busy this week and we have no room for such a service.'

Emma had expected this. She was beginning to wonder if she would ever again have positive feelings for any man other than pity for her half-brother which at this moment seemed as far as she could go.

'That is a shame.' Emma got up. 'You see, it would have been nice because I believe that the family Nell comes from, my family, was of your religious persuasion.'

She waited.

'I cannot think how that would have been possible,' he said.

'Can't you?' Emma said. And then she looked straight at him and she said, 'You are a disgrace to your cloth, Mr Inman, and I shall be writing to the Bishop of Durham to tell him so.'

Mr Inman got up stiffly, his face was beetroot, so that Emma feared for his heart.

'I don't want women like you and Mrs Whittington in my church and the Bishop will understand.'

'Will he, indeed? And do you think God understands?'

'You are blasphemous, Madam,' Mr Inman said. 'Kindly leave my house.'

Emma got out of the house as slowly as she could; she did not want this man or his wife to think that there was any triumph in their horrible brand of Christianity and so she slowed herself down; her steps would have seen her through a cathedral, down the chancel to the aisle and with stained-glass windows all around (which she would have admired).

Mr Inman had a neglected front garden: it was full of weeds and everything was dying there in the cold winds. He was no gardener, there was little division between the paths and the beds, and Emma could not help noting that all the roses had gone wild. And since gardening was so close to God, she believed, that made Mr Inman the worst of clergymen. She thought of her father saying this of another man and then remembered that her father had left his wife and children. It was difficult not to judge and yet she must not. She was not through with her own life yet. And you never knew what you might do.

Emma felt tired. She decided to leave the children with Jack while she went to see Sister Luke. Jack would talk to them so that they felt he was one of them and funny with it, and they trusted him and would put up with him reading to them or telling them how to behave. It was a rare quality to have children believe in you as they did in Jack.

He was patient and kind and explained things with that certain something she could not define, she only knew that every good teacher had it and afterwards the children understood and that was what mattered. They clustered around him and he liked that, telling them things which he knew, but he must know more before he could be a schoolmaster and a good one, Emma realized, and she was the person to help him.

She had talked to the boys about cleanliness, how important it was and how they should try to help their parents as much as they could. She didn't mention their mothers by name, she thought it might be too much for boys in a traditional pit village where men worked hard outside the home and women inside it, but to her surprise nobody sneered, no boy looked at another and sniggered. Afterwards, Jack said to her, 'You got that right, Miss.'

'Did I?' She was astonished.

'Oh aye,' Jack grinned, 'you made washing sound manly.'

*

Sister Luke received Emma with better grace than the Inmans had done. She smiled and offered her a seat and the pale sun shone in that day. Emma sat in the chair and said wearily, 'I need a service for Mrs Whittington, will you help me?'

'Oh dear,' Sister Luke said, 'I'm afraid I cannot. She was not a Catholic.'

Sister Luke looked old, in the merciless light of morning every crease in her face was enhanced.

'Are you – are you allowed to retire?' Emma asked suddenly, and Sister Luke smiled and said, 'Oh yes of course, we are looked after. We have a place by the seaside just outside Sunderland which is very restful. I love the sea.'

She sounded as though she was looking forward to it; there was a trace of wistfulness in her voice and Emma thought that it was hard being a nun, and then she thought at least Sister Luke had chosen her celibacy, and then she thought further and that maybe she hadn't, perhaps her family could not afford to keep her. Catholic families were prone to sending unwanted women into convents. It was as bad as everything else, she concluded. Emma felt as exhausted as Sister Luke looked.

'I don't know where to turn next. The vicar was obstructive,' she said.

Sister Luke nodded. 'I think he might have mistaken his calling,' she said. And then she straightened and looked directly at Emma. 'I wish I could help you.'

A church which could not offer help when someone

had died was not much of a church, Emma thought as she made her way back to the schoolhouse.

That afternoon, Emma decided to go and see the Methodist minister, Mr Ogilvie.

Mr Ogilvie did not look surprised to see her. 'Mrs Ogilvie is at a chapel meeting,' he said, as though the whole thing were little to do with him. 'Come in, Miss Appleby, do.'

Emma was astonished. She had never met the Methodist minister formally, they had done nothing more than nod at one another in the street, and yet Mr Ogilvie greeted her as though they were friends.

'I have a problem,' Emma said.

'Of course, of course,' Mr Ogilvie said, as though everybody said the same thing, and Emma had no doubt that they did. There was something about this man which made you want to break down and tell him all your problems.

He was not fat, he was not thin, he was not tall, he was not short, he was not jolly, he was not sober, fatherly, brotherly or anything which Emma could have understood, but the moment she went into the house, was it a manse or whatever – she couldn't remember – it was just that she had a feeling that she was at home here, it was so restful, so easy. It was a place for poor souls to ease themselves and she was grateful. She was half inclined to ask Mr Ogilvie if he and his wife adopted disillusioned teachers who had nowhere to go.

Mr Ogilivie ushered her into a study that was full of

books, had a decent fire in the grate and a lot of papers on the desk.

'Do sit down, Miss Appleby. I would offer you tea, but I have no idea how it's made and since Mrs Ogilvie isn't here I cannot do anything for you that way. Let me guess.' Mr Ogilivie sat back in his chair, made a steeple of his fingers, frowned, pondered, and then he said, 'You can't persuade anybody to bury Mrs Whittington and you think I might do it.'

'Exactly,' Emma admitted, sitting down and then getting straight back up and extricating a Charles Wesley hymn book from beneath her before she sat again.

'She was not a good woman, is that it?'

'I suppose it depends what you mean,' Emma said. 'She was left alone with two children, she had no money. She did the best that she could.'

'I'm sure,' Mr Ogilvie said.

'Will you help me?'

Mr Ogilvie sat back in his chair and looked straight at his visitor, and then he said, 'You could have her buried, you don't need a service.'

'I need a service to take her children to,' Emma said. 'I thought you would understand. And for her brother and for her and for me.'

'Children do not go to funerals,' Mr Ogilvie said.

'These two will. I want them to remember something good about her death, so don't offer anything if you think that way. I will find somebody to help.'

Mr Ogilvie held up both hands in protest. 'You are a

remarkable woman, Miss Appleby, and I admire you for your courage. You will have your funeral and you will bring her children.'

Emma couldn't believe she had finally succeeded.

Mr Ogilvie said, 'They must remember her well and I will speak of her well and you will come and you will bring them and we will bury her. They do have somewhere to go?'

'I have taken them into my school. Mrs Whittington was my half-sister, you know.'

I had heard something of it,' Mr Ogilvie said.

At that point Emma heard the outside door. Mr Ogilvie called out, 'Olivia, we are in here,' and she came through. She was a pretty woman, not at all young, but comely – that was the word for her – like a bird, sprightly and pink-cheeked and smiling as though she had done a lot of smiling as the wife of the minister and become very good at it.

'Miss Appleby,' she said, 'how are you? I am so sorry for the death of your sister, how very hard for you,' and she came across and shook Emma by the hand in a way which Emma had never seen before and much admired, where she took your hand and then put her other hand on top so that you felt comforted immediately. 'I shall put the kettle on,' she said.

She made tea and she gave Emma sponge cake which was very good.

As Emma left she turned at the door and said to them both, 'You are very kind. Thank you. I don't know what I would have done without your help.'

They stood there like a pair of beaming lights. She had no idea what they said or thought after she had gone, but she was so grateful that she didn't want to go. She made her way down the garden path and onto the pavement with some regret.

She felt warmed by the Ogilvies and she thought that it was strange how Methodism had saved her. John Wesley had had all the right ideas. She thought she would have liked him; he had united people who had no one to help them.

'What an unusual woman,' Olivia Ogilvie said as they stood and watched Emma disappear into the evening.

'Yes.' Her husband considered for a few moments. 'A brave woman.'

His wife looked at him and smiled. 'Absolutely,' she said, and she took him by the arm. 'Come inside, it grows cold and we have much to discuss now that you have offered to have a funeral for Mrs Whittington.'

'I am a lucky man to have you.'

'Indeed you are,' she said, and they laughed together.

He nodded and then he walked into the house feeling that John Wesley might have been pleased with him. He hoped so.

19

The day that Nell was buried was cold and wet. The wind blew straight from the moors and kicked at your ankles and made you wish you were comfortable by the fire. Emma had not been inside a chapel before and she had thought it would be plain, but in her eyes it was neat and orderly and she liked the way that the upstairs was a gallery and she enjoyed the clear glass in the windows where the rain fell and battered upon the ground, it seemed a fitting accompaniment to the words that Mr Ogilvie said. She could not remember having been so moved by a funeral before.

He spoke of Nell as though he had known her, as he probably had, since it was such a small town. He said that she had been born there, was a child of the earth and a good woman and had done everything she could to look after her children. This, Emma thought, was very true, but she admired him the more for having said it.

The girls clung one at either side of her and George seemed to have grown taller. Mick in a good suit, shaved, bathed, hair cut, looked almost respectable. Also Mr Higgins and Jack and Laurence, though she was convinced Laurence still expected Nell to come home.

The service brought her comfort too, but in a way she

had had so little of Nell that she thought she might always find herself in the graveyard, talking to someone who was no longer there and thinking of the days and months and even years they might have had together: summer with picnics and the children playing in the fields, and winter by the fireside talking, especially when the girls were in bed. She had wanted to make things so much better for Nell and now it was too late. She could not even weep.

The girls hid their faces in her skirt, and what she wanted to do was go back to the schoolhouse and carry on with the teaching.

The best thing about it was that she would be able to go to Nell's grave and take them. Mick had bought a stone, which would be erected later, with Nell's name. It said, 'Beloved mother of' and both the girls' names, and 'sister of' and Laurence's name and her dates, and it seemed to Emma that she had lived such a short time, but that was only because they had not known one another for a decent amount of time. What was a decent amount of time? She wondered. She did not think you could tell. When you didn't love people even an hour was too long and when you did love them a hundred years would not suffice.

She took the girls and George home, and when they got there Hector was waiting outside. How had he got out? Dogs were like magicians, she thought, and she didn't really want to know how he was there, just that he was, wagging his tail upon the cold wet ground, his eyes welcoming, his mouth open and smiling for her.

It was beginning to rain again.

20

Mick went to see Henry Atkinson. Henry owned a fine hotel in Durham across from the County Hotel in Old Elvet, which was the best hotel in the town. It was called the Three Tuns. It was not particularly pretty, but something about it gave the people who went there a feeling of belonging.

There was no view unless you counted the houses across the road or the stabling behind. Mick could see what drew people to the Three Tuns Hotel. It had comfort, fires and intimacy.

Henry seemed surprised to see Mick and he looked ashamed. He greeted Mick as though he had been the lord lieutenant. 'How can I help?' And then, less audibly, 'How is she?'

'Sober.' Mick sat back in his chair. He wanted to add more, that she was horribly, horribly sober and that he couldn't bear it and he might kill her, kill himself, die of frustration, die that he couldn't spend the night with the woman he loved, but he thought of Connie and he couldn't say anything or change anything.

Isabel was not easy to appease. 'I want her here with me,' she had said.

'Well, you cannot have her,' he said. 'It isn't going to be just what you want. This is also about Connie's happiness.'

She laughed bitterly. 'I'm done trying for happiness. I was trying to build a bearable life around me.'

'Connie has her own life to lead. She will come home on Friday nights and go back on Sunday nights and that is all you can expect. If it won't do then I'm sorry.'

'You put her first,' Isabel said. 'How can you put our child before me?'

'I have always put you first, but you are an adult and she is a child and she has suffered.'

'We've all suffered,' Isabel said. 'I am trying to build the life I thought you wanted, where we could be together.'

'We cannot be together all the time. Connie has established herself at school and—'

'That's all you care about,' his wife accused him. 'Miss stuck-up Appleby and her precious little school.'

He said nothing.

'Why do you do this?' Isabel asked.

'I don't know what you mean.'

'Yes, you do.' She looked so directly at him that Mick wondered if there might be evidence on his face of his love for Emma. 'You know that Connie isn't yours, you're too intelligent not to, though you pretend. You know that the only man I ever loved was Henry and yet still there is in you the decency to try. What do you do it for?'

'I want us to be a family. I want to have night after night and day after day.'

'We had that and it didn't work.'

'You always wanted Henry.'

'I still want him. I don't drink when I'm with Henry, you see.'

Now he tried to concentrate on what he had decided to do, a final attempt for a decent life for the three of them. Here, confronting Henry Atkinson, he was beginning to feel that he might be able to manage something.

'You said that your children were in London and that you wished to be there. If you could be there, if you could sell out, would you be reasonably happy?'

Henry sat back in his chair. 'How could that be?' he said.

'I would buy you out.'

Henry was no longer sitting back in his chair, he was on the edge of his seat and his eyes were wide with amazement. He sat for a few moments longer and then he shook his head and said, 'I should give up the love of my life.'

'Perhaps it's time. You have had so much for so long.'

'You wouldn't think that if you were married to my wife.'

'You certainly wouldn't think that if you'd been married to mine,' Mick said, and Henry smiled in acknowledgement of the justice of this and nodded his head. 'I would have married Isabel had I met her first.'

'Oh, I don't think you would. I doubt her father had enough money to tempt you.'

'That's not fair,' Henry said with some energy, 'and neither is it true.'

'You seduced her, knowing that you couldn't marry her.'

Henry looked straight at him. 'And you have never done such a thing?' he said.

Mick tried to keep his countenance, but he could feel how his neck burned against his collar and then his face joined in, and Henry laughed.

'Will you sell your business to me?' Mick said.

'I'm surprised you think you can afford it.'

'Name the price and let's see.'

Henry did so.

Mick got up. 'I'll talk to my solicitor and my bank.'

'Wait just a moment,' Henry said. 'What will happen to Connie?'

Mick had spent a lot of time considering. 'Connie is my child,' he said.

'I could take her.'

'You have six children. Why would you want another?'

'They're all boys,' Henry said with mock sadness. 'Can't you see her in a beautiful dress and all the men in the ballroom drooling?'

'Connie is a scholar,' Mick said in disgust, and he left.

After Nell's funeral Emma worried about Laurence. He took to wandering about outside day after day. She left him for the first few days and then gave in. She trod over the wet grass in the garden, and there he was, standing beside the fence which looked down and out across the neat square fields of the dale, waiting as though Nell would come back up for him, and then she saw he was waiting because she would not come.

'Do you really think she's gone to paradise, Miss?' he said.

'I told you. We're brother and sister and you can call me Emma. I think if there is paradise then Nell deserves to be there.'

'I don't think there's owt,' he said. 'I think it's all like this bastard place. I wish I could pull our Nell out the ground. She's always looked after all of us. I couldn't manage it. I couldn't do what should've been done. There weren't nobody like our Nell, 'cept you.'

Isabel was trying very hard to make life good for the three of them and because of this Mick couldn't deny her anything. Every Friday evening he picked up his child and took her home, but he did not pretend to himself that Connie wanted to be there.

Connie would walk so slowly that he wanted to shout at her, she lingered by every tree, gazed at every view as though she had not seen it before, she kept turning back as if she would run away once again and then she looked at him and set her face such as he thought a child should not need to, and she carried on up the now weeded drive and tidied garden, mown lawn and shining windows. She didn't notice any of these things, he thought: she was concentrating on the mother she did not wish to go to.

Isabel would hear them and come out of the house and down the steps and take Connie into her embrace in a way that he had rarely seen before. But the child was like wood; she did not relent even a little, she did not look at Isabel until his wife looked anxiously at him. He always smiled encouragingly.

Isabel made splendid dinners. They tasted like cardboard. He saw every mouthful which Connie ate and she chewed as though she had to get each piece of food into her very carefully.

'So,' Isabel would say brightly, 'what are you doing at school?'

And Connie would tell her, and a lot of it, Mick could see, was Mr English's doing, and he was glad of it, as on the Friday when her enthusiasm overtook her sullenness and she announced, 'We're learning about the Romans. They did a lot in this area, you know, Mr English says so. He takes us on walks. They had forts here and at the top end of Northumberland they built this wall to keep out the Scots. Hadrian did it. Mr English says we can go there by train and Miss Appleby has been telling us all about the flowers around the wall and how Northumberland has a great history and lots of castles and we are to go and look at some of them.'

Isabel's eyes had already begun to glaze over with boredom and Connie, even in her enthusiasm, knew it, Mick could see. She went on like a circus animal performing. She told her mother about the way that Mr English was going to teach her Ancient Greek and all about Mrs English who sometimes came to stay because Miss Appleby wasn't happy about where they lived and they were going to move into the village because the smallholding produced nothing and Mrs English had terrible arthritis and Miss Appleby had found them a house and Mr English was so pleased because it was between the council school and the academy and therefore was perfect and it was dry and Mrs English was so pleased that she cried.

That Sunday night when Connie went back to the academy she flung wide the door and exclaimed, 'I'm back!' and George and the two girls and Hector dashed into the kitchen as though she had been gone a month. Connie flung herself at Emma and said, 'What have I missed?'

When Mick was about to leave, Emma went outside with him, and as he was about to take his leave she said, 'Try not to mind.'

'I'm glad she's found somewhere she loves.'

Emma folded her arms across her breasts and said, 'She's the perfect scholar for Mr English. He thinks she will go far. He's going to teach her Latin.'

'And Ancient Greek, so I hear.'

'Really, how very wonderful,' and she smiled right into his face.

21

A tiny house next door but one to the academy had become vacant. Emma had gone to take a look at it. She saw the woman moving out, knew that her husband had recently died and she was going to Stockton to live with her brother and his family. She had no family of her own, she said. Emma sympathized.

The woman, Mrs Henshaw, looked sadly at her little house. It was, she said, owned by Mr Barron, one of the few houses which were not pit houses. Emma asked whether she minded saying if anyone had spoken for it and Mrs Henshaw said it would be too small for almost anybody, it only had an up and a down. She showed Emma inside. It had indeed only one room downstairs, but it was a very big room with a lovely fireplace. Mrs Henshaw proudly showed her the oven and the boiler and the little whitewashed pantry on the end which had a tiny window overlooking the yard.

'There was plenty of room for me to nurse Mr Henshaw down here. You can easily get a bed in. He never went upstairs the last year,' Mrs Henshaw said, and she sighed.

Emma asked about the rent and it was very little, so she did something interfering. She went to Mr Barron's shop and asked him if he had anybody in line for the place and he said, no, most people had pit houses and those who didn't were looking for something a bit bigger.

'Do you know of somebody that might like it?' he said and Emma said she thought she might but she wasn't sure about the rent, she thought it was a lot for two rooms and nothing but a shared backyard, coalhouse and outside lavatory, and Mr Barron said that it was getting well known that Miss Appleby drove a hard bargain, but he would think about it and if she wanted she could let him know, but he couldn't wait forever. Emma said she would sort it out that very day.

She went to the council school and couldn't help thinking how much it had changed. It now had two big stoves right in the centre of the room and Mr English had arranged his scholars and their desks in a circle right round them so that nobody was cold.

He didn't stand at the front as he had done, the cane was gone and the blackboard had been relegated to the shadows by the far wall. Mr English sat among his pupils and told them stories of ancient Greece and Rome and he taught them maths by making it about how many fields and how many houses and how many streets they could count and multiply, subtract and divide, and he made up problems such as how long it would take Mary, who lived in Wesley Street, to walk to Thornley, the little village in the valley, if she walked at so many miles an hour. Emma was very bad at maths and thought it would have been a lot easier if Mary had stayed at home and read a book by the fire because it was raining.

He read to them every day, exciting tales of far-away lands, and told them stories which he had begun making up about children like themselves so that they were eager to hear about them.

He combined history with geography, about the kings who fought over Northumberland, and the border reivers, and he told them that their names were very old and that their ancestors had fought not just Scots against English but Scots against Scots and English against English and that in this very area they had come screaming across the hills on horseback, taking away cattle, looting and thieving.

The children found this very exciting, Emma herself was rather taken, and wondered whether the Applebys had been involved. She was very pleased to find that they had been.

She sat down by the fire and told them bible stories. She had brought with her brownies which had cocoa in them and tasted like chocolate. There was a square each – it had taken some doing for all those children, but she was determined that they should have a treat, and she had ordered milk for everyone. She and Mr English had coffee and brownies, and he said he had never tasted anything quite as good.

While they were having this break she told Mr English about the little house and he shook his head and said he didn't think that Mrs English would ever leave the small-holding which was where she had been born. He wasn't sure the school board would like him to move, and Emma said that she didn't think it was any of their business, but of course they would say it was and he must put it to them that Mrs English would die if she were left there.

It was true of course, and he agreed, and once he had eaten his brownie he seemed to view the whole thing in a different light. He would put this to them and said that if he was in the village he could spend more time at the school and they had to be glad about that.

Emma thought she had never seen Mr English so content. He was a real schoolmaster now, a very good teacher. The children listened when he spoke, he didn't have to command or punish, they liked him, she could see by their faces, and he was relaxed and would laugh with them and do as much for them as he could.

Emma stayed a while and he told them about the moon and the stars and also about the constellations which were to do with their birthdays, some thought, and there again they were keen to know which was theirs and the black-board came back into play.

Two big boys pulled it forward, because it was now on wheels, one of Jack's better ideas, and she drew for them the Plough and the Great and Little Bears, they thought that was funny and she told them what to look for in the skies at night. Emma could picture them standing outside their houses in the street, or perhaps behind where every-thing was quiet and dark and there was nothing between themselves and the stars. The stars were something to try for, Emma thought. Why not?

She asked Mr English if he thought they should have a picnic for all the scholars on the first good day, and she would bake for them. The children thought it was a very good idea, though as she suggested it the heavens seemed to open and the rain came down and stotted off the roof and all around the building, and it seemed so funny at that moment that they laughed.

She did not forget Nell. Daily she took Laurence to Nell's grave. She would not have gone so often, but he insisted. It became part of his life, just as going home from the Black Diamond day after day had been his routine. Now he lived at the academy, had his own room and Emma was trying to persuade him to eat, but he couldn't. All he wanted was beer and the sight of Nell's grave, so she had to take him there.

Mick had given her Jack in the same way as he had given her Hector. Jack was an exceptionally clever lad and she thought Mick had done it deliberately because he wanted the boy to do what round here they called 'better himself'. Jack's mother was very proud of what her son was achieving. She greeted Emma loudly whenever she saw her, for the benefit of her friends and neighbours, and Emma would smile and tell her that Jack was the brightest lad in the world, which of course he was, and Mrs Allen was fairly glowing at this. 'Eh, Miss Appleby,' she said, 'you're a grand lass. Giving my Jack such an opportunity.'

*

Mr and Mrs English moved into the village. Mrs English did not worry about the smallholding.

'I've had more than enough of it,' she said, 'and to be fair the owners were glad, I think; they need somebody young and in good health to make it work.'

Mr English got home a lot sooner now that he didn't have to trudge back to the farm, and Mrs English said privately to Emma, 'He goes out, you know, to the Black Diamond and drinks whisky there, very bad for him, with Mr Castle.'

Twice a week Mr English went to the pub, and Emma had Mrs English to the academy to see the children and Hector and to sit over the fire or by the window at the back where the view was the best that Emma could remember, even at home in New England which she had thought she loved so much. But it was only a memory now; this was home.

Mrs English loved looking down upon Weardale and the little farms which were so like the smallholding, but she liked best going back to her tiny house where she and Mr English slept downstairs and when the weather was bad they built up the fire and lay there in the darkness watching it before they fell asleep.

22

It seemed strange to Emma that she should have dreamed this place and made it her reality and now that she thought she had come home she dreamed of New England and her father and mother, at the same time she dreamed of Laurence and Verity as they were when she left, and she awoke one morning and missed New Haven and her past life for the first time.

Why did she care now? Why did she regret leaving what she had not been able to bear? It was not the reality of the present she yearned for, rather the future that could never be: marriage to John Elstree, being part of Verity and Laurence's circle. She would have loved that, she could have stayed there and known nothing of her family here, and though she had achieved so much, the loss of Nell was affecting her in ways which she had not thought of: it made her want other people for her family. She wanted somehow to bring it all together and have it fixed, have it work and it wouldn't, and she was sad that morning.

It was strange therefore that when she went to open the front door in the middle of the day she found Mrs Jones on the doorstep. Mrs Jones worked at the post office. It was a place Emma managed to stay out of mostly. She had no one she wished to write to and the post office was the main source of gossip in the village. Mrs Jones and Mrs Dunwoodie discussed everything and everyone there, according to Mr Higgins, and because it was a service everybody must use there was no escape.

Emma's only knowledge of Mrs Jones was that her mother had complained when she married that she 'found the only Welshman within forty miles'. Most of the people who hadn't spent generations in Durham were Irish and Mrs Jones's mother was not an admirer of the Welsh. Mrs Jones was called Eve and she was a broad-hipped, bonny-looking woman with thick black hair and dark eyes, and there were those who said she painted her face.

'I thought I had better bring this personally,' she said, 'rather than send it in case it got lost on the way, because it is not an ordinary letter. It comes from America, the address is on the back.'

Instead of handing the letter to Emma Mrs Jones turned it over. 'It comes from a relative of yours, I gather, who lives there. It isn't properly addressed to you, you see, just the village name, and though he had an idea that you had come here there is no mention of where you are living and I was concerned because I would have thought that if you had some family in such a place you might have let them know, it would be only common courtesy after all, and that in time, seeing how things are here, you might want to return home.'

Emma wanted to slap her for her curiosity, for her rudeness. She did not know whether she thanked Mrs Jones; she only knew that within half an hour of its reaching the post office the whole of the village would know of its existence and as much as Mrs Jones had discovered about her past life. There were those who would already be hoping she would leave. She panicked and closed the door while Mrs Jones hovered, doubtless hoping for more information which Emma might feel obliged to give.

Once inside, Emma felt her hands trembling. She could hardly hold the letter; there was no way in which she could have opened it. She put it into her pocket and then changed her mind and went into the study and pushed it into the top middle drawer of the desk, which she then locked as though somehow that would make it go away.

She left it there and tried to forget about it. The rest of her day was so full that she almost did so, but when she went to bed she couldn't rest. Why would Laurence write to her now? She thought he would only have written with bad news, but then they were so far apart why would he write to her at all? She knew that she would not sleep until she had seen what it was about, but she had the feeling that she would not sleep after she had read it either.

She tried to talk herself into waiting for the morning, hoping that she would sleep first, but she couldn't. She put on a shawl and went down, and there by candlelight she unlocked the drawer and held up the letter as though she might be able to see through the envelope and not have to open it. Then she tore it open and spread out the thin sheet and even his handwriting made her want to weep: he had almost exactly the same way of making his letters as she did – they had been taught together by their father. It was quite formal.

335

Dear Emma,

I hope this reaches you. All I remembered was the name of the village.

Verity was ill after you left, heartsick about her pearls and aghast that you had gone and that you had stolen her most prized possession. She blamed herself and I had to assure her that it was nothing to do with us. You have always been willful and forward and all those things which women should not be, but I had no idea until you left that you would steal from those who love you.

The pearls were her grandmother's last gift to Verity and I do not think she will be able to forgive you for what you have done unless you come home and make it up to her. As we are aware you sold the pearls to finance your escapade and cannot presumably get them back I have to ask you for information in the vague hope that they might be recovered.

Do you remember the jeweler you sold them to? Was this in Boston? I shall go to Boston and try to find them, though I fear they have long since been lost to us. I shall therefore require you to pay the price which the pearls were worth: a great deal more, I have no doubt, than you managed to sell them for.

If you do not send the money which you owe us then I shall come to England and inform the appropriate authorities and they will have you arrested for theft.

In which case you will be shunned by all who know you in the place which you have presumably tried to make your home. I have no doubt that by now you have discovered the kind of man that our father was. You should be ashamed that you have been cast in the same mould and either you must return or you must send the money. I will give you six months to do either one or the other and if you do not I will bring down the law upon you.

Hector had come downstairs and shuffled into the room; he looked puzzled as to what she could be doing in the study at this time of night, but he settled himself under the desk as he had taken to doing when she worked.

At this point Emma lit a lamp and sat down to compose a reply. She had to stop herself from writing the way that she felt, to put in the anger, and after that she sat still for a long time in the cool and silence of the night and thought hard about what she must say.

In the end she put her feet on Hector's warm sleeping body and wrote to Laurence and Verity, saying how sorry she was that she had done such a thing as to take the pearls in the first place and that of course she would send the money for the pearls as soon as she could raise such a sum, but it was such a great deal of money that they must give her time.

She told them about her school and about how George was progressing and that she did not feel sorry for having come here since this was truly now her home, but she wished them well, she hoped they would have a good future together and that the boys would grow up well and happy and they could be proud of them.

She felt so much better when she had finished this and sealed it. She would get Jack to take it to the post office. She felt that she would never want to go there again and then she went back to bed.

In the morning she went to the graveyard and told Nell's headstone all about it. And the thing she had been holding at the back of her mind came to the front as she thought of Nell. Money. She had none except the money which Nell had given her. It was a great deal, but Emma had been hoping that money would pay for things which she did not want Mick to have to pay for, but now it would have to be saved towards the cost of the pearl necklace.

She apologized to Nell and Nell would have said, Emma felt sure, that the children would have had no one to take them, look after or educate them if Emma had not run away from New England. It was sound reasoning, but Emma was not sure she did not feel huge guilt that she must use the money in such a way.

She needed a great deal more than that. She had no idea how she was to achieve it. Nothing else brought in any money. The idea of leaving and starting again in another place was impractical. She must take on more pupils, people who might pay. The trouble was that she could not go out and talk to people because she felt that most of the village was still against her. She didn't know what to do; it made her tired just to think about it.

23

Mick left the bank with a lighter step and then thought ruefully to himself of how much money he now owed. He didn't want to think about it too much; he felt as though he had put his entire fortune on the spin of a roulette wheel. People did such things, for instance, people in London who were feckless and reckless. Then he laughed at himself. He didn't know anybody who would take such a risk and yet he had accused Henry Atkinson of being a risk-taker; maybe you had to be to go forward. Sitting comfortably at the fire was never going to get a man anywhere, certainly not into the kind of trouble which he had just leapt into.

He didn't want to go to any of the public houses, either the ones he already owned or the ones he had just bought. All it had taken was a good solicitor and Henry's signature and then his own, and it was done. Everything mattered now.

He was excited too. He wanted to go back and tell Isabel. He thought he had just ensured their future. Surely now she would see how much the family meant to him. She had tried hard and he was not going to let anything stand in his way. With Henry Atkinson in London, and temptation elsewhere, Isabel would remember her marriage and her child, at least he hoped so.

It was four in the afternoon when he reached home, and as always he half thought she would be drunk, but his wife was asleep by the fire. The coal shifted in the grate as he walked into the sitting room and she heard it or him and sat up and looked vaguely at him.

'Is it that time already?' she said.

'No, I came home early.'

Isabel sat up, an enquiring look on her face. Mick didn't know what to say; he had no idea what her reaction would be.

He took a deep breath. 'I've bought out Henry Atkinson.'

She looked for several seconds as though she didn't understand and then she said, 'Why would you do that?'

'Well, he told me that his children are all in London and that he misses them and that if he could he would go and live there and—' Mick stopped. He waited for her reaction, for her to shout and scream, and when she didn't he didn't know what to say.

'How could you afford it?' she said.

It was not something he would have thought she would be concerned about. 'I can't. I went to the bank and they agreed to lend me the money.'

'They must think a great deal of you.'

'I'm a good talker.'

'You always were.'

'I know it isn't perfect, Isabel, and I'm sorry. I wish it was, but it was the only thing I could think to do that might help.'

'Yes, I can see how you might,' she said. 'I think it's very brave of you.'

'You've been brave and I know what it's cost you and I want to try and do everything I can to help.'

She drew nearer and kissed him, but neither of them was used to that kind of affection and it was awkward. He didn't know what to say or do, and neither did she.

For days and days after that they maintained a charade that things were better and Mick began to wish that he had not tried to be so clever and correct things which he was not certain would ever be corrected. He went to work, she stayed at home, and in the evenings they sat together over the fire as he had always wanted them to do, and it was the most uncomfortable way that they had ever lived.

Sometimes deep in the night they drew close and that was the worst of all. He was aware of every sound, of every patient breath his wife took, of how thankful he was when she let him go when it was over, and she would turn from him and he would turn from her, and the relief was such that it hurt him. He did not think that she felt any better.

She stumbled to make the kind of meals which she had made when they were first married and he told her how wonderful they were, and they were not, and he didn't think that she believed him. She grew thinner and paler week by week and around her was a band of unhappiness. They tried to talk.

'Isabel—'

'No, don't say anything.' This in the middle of the night when even the birds were silent, even the rain didn't fall.

341

The bed dominated the room; it had grown and was not a refuge any more. During the warm days it was sweaty and during the cold days it was icy, and however near they drew they could not warm one another or reassure one another, and nothing made any difference.

Mick had not thought anything could be harder than to have his wife drink. To have her not drink was worse. Sometimes he thought he could see through her, and although she tried to hide beneath smiles and talk there was somehow no place for either of them to go. She was anxious when he left and when he came home. She worried that the butcher would forget to call, that there would not be sufficient potatoes for dinner. She cleaned and cleaned so that he hardly dared step into the house for the shine on the windows and the doors and the hall floor. Even Ulysses looked confused and hovered outside when he got the chance for fear that his paws might leave prints on the black-and-white tiled floor which Isabel washed every day.

From her kitchen she turned out miracles. The food got better and better. Each night he was required to tell her how wonderful it was, that he had not tasted anything which could surpass it in the whole of his life, and between his home life and his debt to the bank and the way that he didn't seem to be able to manage all the pubs and keep on making money at the rate which his debts demanded Mick was only glad when he fell asleep. It was like being in a deep dark hole where nobody could reach him.

Isabel didn't sleep. Often he would wake to find that

342

she was gazing wide-eyed up into the darkness. She began to roam the house at night, like a polite ghost, never making a noise for fear of disturbing him, so that he noted every second, every movement, the way that she would open the curtains just a little to see if there was a moon. What else could she be looking for?

He found concentration difficult when he was at work. It should have taken up every moment, but he kept thinking of her, scrubbing floors and washing windows and ironing bed linen. He dared not suggest that Mrs Dexter and Mrs Hobson would be happy to help. He was still paying them even though they objected to his largesse. He felt guilty and told them it made him feel better and they would never know when he needed them. Isabel wanted no one in her house, it was just as if it had always been that way.

When Connie came home at weekends the house was so clean that the sheets crackled. Connie looked in wonder at the elaborate food on her plate.

'It's boeuf en daube,' her mother said. 'You do like it?'

'Oh yes,' Connie would say, and indeed Mick was certain that it was delicious. His head told him so, but his taste buds seemed to have given up and the meat stuck in his throat. Connie chased the stew round and round on her plate, and when her mother was not looking and had gone into the kitchen for extra bread, she did not hesitate to scrape the contents of her plate onto the floor beneath the table where Ulysses must have thought all his birthdays were upon him. Mick knew, and she looked at her father apologetically. He simply shrugged.

Ulysses could end up very fat if things did not get better was the only thing he could think of to cheer himself.

Something compelled Mick to go home just after noon on that particular day several weeks later. He was tired, but had convinced himself that things were good. Connie was happy at school and Isabel seemed resigned to accept this. There was peace at home: it was not an entirely happy peace but he had settled for it.

When they had been happy – or when he had thought they were, at the beginning their marriage – he could not wait all day to see Isabel again and would go home during the day. He didn't often do it any more. Work had become his refuge, but for some reason on that particular day he could not stop himself. He just told himself he was being stupid, but his feet took him back to the house which he had bought when they were first married, when he had been so much in love.

Taking over Henry's business had made an immense amount of extra work, and he was spending a great deal of time in Newcastle and in Durham, making sure that what was going well in the business went on doing so and what was not would slowly be brought up to the standard of the rest.

In business he knew that there was nothing as effective as one's own presence for making sure that things went well. In the end, with a business too complex for him to see to himself, he had to rely a great deal on other people. He would learn in time the people whom he could trust and replace those who were unreliable. Until then he must work, making sure that everything ran as it should, so he did not understand the feeling that compelled him to go home when he should have been in half a dozen other places at once. It was just that he had tried so hard for so long.

He had briefly considered moving, but it was too soon and he was not convinced that Isabel would enjoy the city. He did not care for it himself, but he had the idea that they might be able to buy a summer cottage on the coast in Northumberland, and that she might be excited by this. Since nothing had gone wrong that day with the business and he knew Connie was safe at school, he thought he might go back and talk to her about it and they might even take a trip to have a look and see if there was anywhere which would do.

He was tired of course, but he was always tired now. He didn't expect to be happy. And then a small jolt of warm feeling made him remember kissing Emma and realizing that no matter what had happened she did care about him, and he must concentrate on his family and his work.

He knew something was wrong when he opened the door. There was nothing in the house which was disturbed, but the whole place seemed to have about it an air of loneliness, a silence so complete that it could have been death. Then his ears strained and he heard a very light footstep, and then another, and Isabel came down the stairs.

She looked as young as she had been when they had first met, so lovely and full of life that he was taken aback and realized at that moment how much he had loved her.

She wore a velvet coat with matching hat and gloves in a mid-blue colour which made her hair look more golden and her eyes bluer. The gloves accentuated the slenderness of her wrists and arms. He had forgotten how very beautiful she was.

He was so surprised she was going out that he stopped just inside the front door, and the flood of daylight seemed to contain them both.

'You look lovely. You're going shopping?' he asked, in wonder.

She hesitated, and looked dismayed. 'No.' She shook her head.

He waited for her to tell him what her mission was. She looked at him and there was a hint of pity in her eyes. He waited such a long time for her to speak that he had to prompt her. 'Where are you going then?'

'I wish you hadn't come home. Why do you have to make this so difficult?'

'I don't know what you mean. Are you all right?'

She shook her head and the lovely little hat which perched on top of it moved precariously.

'I'm leaving you,' she said, and she looked down and then glanced at him and her eyes were like sapphires.

'Oh,' he said. It was a stupid thing to say, really not much more than a sigh. He stared at her and went on staring for a very long time, not quite sure whether he was still breathing, listening to the thick silence in the house which spoke of the future.

'I'm so sorry, Mick,' she said, and she looked honestly at him, possibly for the first time. 'Henry is sending for someone to bring my luggage downstairs and to take me to the train. There isn't much luggage. I seem to have nothing to take with me somehow.'

He spent time trying to understand. It felt like a long time, but in fact he knew it wasn't. Time had become unreal long since.

'Henry wanted to take Connie, but I knew you would never stand for that and would fight us for her and I'm too exhausted for such things so I'm leaving her here with you. She's a lovely child, but she always preferred you to me. I think she's very like you, which is strange in the circumstances.'

'Where are you going?'

She was at the bottom of the stairs now. 'I have no idea. I don't really care. Henry has a great deal of money since you bought him out and he has promised me the world. His wife will go to London and live near her children and I think that Henry and I will go to Italy.

'Perhaps when we are settled, in Florence or in Rome, you will allow Connie to come and visit. I understand there are wonderful places to see and she will like to see a little more of the world, and I'm sure you wouldn't stop her. Do tell her the truth – I hate people who tell their children myths. I'm so very sorry and after all you have done.' She shook her head.

'Don't feel like that about it,' he said, suddenly under-standing.

She looked at him in surprise. 'I don't know what you mean.'

'You and I have tried so hard to make this work, but it hasn't for a very long time. We shouldn't have married.'

'I wanted to marry you.'

He stared at her. 'But because of Henry.'

'No.' She smiled suddenly at him. 'Because I thought it stood a chance, I knew I couldn't have Henry, he was so very married, and you, you were different, perhaps the future.'

'But Connie—'

'I thought she was yours, truly I did, and I even hoped because if she was then you and I could have had half a dozen children and I think then I would have been more content.'

Mick couldn't think of anything to say. The conversation reached to the very heart of him, or wherever it was that men knew their worth in life, and he didn't seem to have any, not that way. He couldn't father a child; he hadn't admitted it to himself before.

She walked past him.

'Isabel.'

She was about to open the door, but she turned back to him when he spoke.

'I hope you and Henry have a future together. I hope that you get what you want.'

She smiled at him and then she came back to him and

when she kissed him on the mouth it was a warmer kiss than he had felt from her in years, and then she touched his chin with her fingers and was gone.

24

Dr Blythe called on Mrs English. The rain had been falling day after day and it seemed to make her condition worse. It was the middle of the evening and she was at the academy, so Emma got to see him briefly. She would have merely nodded her goodbyes except that Dr Blythe stood in her kitchen after he had seen Mrs English in the little back room and said, with slight humour, 'My wife has ordered me to tell you that we would like our eldest child, Adrian, to come to your school next term.' He paused and shifted his feet a little.

Emma smiled at him. 'She ordered you?'

'She did,' he said gravely. 'Would you consider taking him?'

'I would be delighted.'

'I have to tell you though that shortly, much to the relief of us both since I work for the most part from home, the other two will be following with your leave and yes, I will be happy to be your school doctor. My wife considers that since we have three children we will also be obliged to pay for all of them and I will be your school doctor because these children are my patients and I am glad that you are here to help educate them in a way that my wife approves of. My wife has said, as well, that she would like to come and take tea with you in the morning on Wednesday, if that suits you, and that she would like to look round the academy.'

Emma could not help feeling completely triumphant when Sam Blythe left. If the doctor, who held such respect in the village, sent his children to her school she felt certain that other people would follow, but also that she might make a friend of his wife. Not many men would have gone about it in that way and when Mrs Blythe did come and see the academy with the dubious joy of watching her children run around the rooms, shouting with glee at being let out, she said to Emma, 'I wondered if you and the children would come to chapel with me on Sunday. My husband is Church of England and even though we were married at the chapel he makes that an excuse not to go, unless he can't get out of it. I don't know what you feel about these things, but I do know that the Ogilvies are kind people and would be happy to have you there and I would enjoy the company.'

Emma said she would be pleased though when Mr Higgins came for Sunday dinner he did look hard at her as she explained that the meal would be a little late as she had been drinking tea and socializing at the Methodist church.

She found people likely to accept her when she went there and was grateful to Marjorie Blythe for this but also Mr and Mrs Ogilvie greeted her like an old friend and introduced her to Mrs Barron, the wife of the hardware shopkeeper. Emma already knew Mr Boldon because they owned the draper's shop in the high street and she had bought clothes there for the children and Mrs Boldon said she had heard that Miss Appleby's school had many merits.

Emma had no idea who she had heard this from, but since Mrs Boldon had two small children Emma was inclined to smile and be pleased. Mr and Mrs Barron also had children and Mr Barron told all who might listen that Miss Appleby was a fearsome businesswoman and that she had taken on Jack Allen, whose mother was well respected in the place, and that Jack was going to be a fully-fledged teacher in time.

Mick came to the school on the Friday to pick up Connie for the weekend and Connie ran to him as she always did, chattering about what had happened so that he would be caught up with the doings at the school. For once he did not seem happy to see her, and since several other children were around and they were involved in some game he told her that she could have a few minutes more. He asked Emma if he could see her in her study and, somewhat reluctantly, she agreed.

Once inside he seemed to have nothing to say and wandered about as if he were waiting for a late train.

'I have the feeling you don't know that Isabel has left me,' he said, swinging round suddenly as though if he didn't tell her his breath would cease.

It seemed like an age to Emma before she heard what

he said, and before she understood. Her heart beat hard.

'I thought she was ill.'

'She's gone to Italy with Henry Atkinson,' he said evenly, 'and I have to tell Connie. I bought Henry Atkinson out, you see. I thought it might give us a chance to be a family if he wasn't there.' Mick shook his head.

'But – but that's extraordinary,' Emma said. 'What about his wife and children?'

'Isabel says that his wife doesn't care and she has gone to London to be with his children and since they have plenty of money now they can do as they like.'

'You own Henry Atkinson's business?'

He pulled a face against his own situation.

'The bank owns it and me.'

'Oh, Mick.'

'I know. So. I thought maybe I could tell Connie while I'm here and perhaps if she doesn't want to come home you would keep her for the weekend.'

'Would you like me to tell her?'

'I'll do it myself. Could I have the room for a few minutes and would you send her in?'

Connie came into the room as though she would be bitten when she got there.

'Something's the matter, isn't it?' she said, peering round the door. Mick got her to come inside and shut it. She was ashen-faced. 'Is Mammy ill again?'

'No.'

'Are you going to die?'

That made him want to laugh, but his child's face, white and drawn, was nothing to laugh at.

'Do you want me to go to boarding school? Have you changed your mind about it? Because I really do like it here, I don't want to go.'

'You aren't going anywhere.'

Connie looked slightly relieved at this.

'Your mother has left me. She's gone away with another man.'

Connie was astounded, he could see. In her world people didn't do things like that; in a pit village people couldn't afford to go anywhere, never mind change their marital relationships and do what they wanted. It was unheard of. It wouldn't be soon though, the whole place would talk of it.

Mick knew that he would be blamed in some quarters and she in others, and nobody would know the real truth, at least he didn't think so. He didn't care: he didn't have any pride left. For his marriage to be officially over was only the extended version of what had happened. He had not really had a marriage at all, and this child looked so like her real father that he wanted to shudder at the idea though he could not have loved her any more than he did.

'She wanted me to be different,' Connie said. 'I did try when I was little, but you can't be something you aren't and I never was going to be able to play the piano. Even Miss Appleby agrees with that, she says she never met anybody who knew less about music than me and I should because it's a source of joy to everybody, but I'm very good at other things, you know.'

He let her get all this out and then he said slowly, so that they might both get used to the idea, 'Your mother didn't intend to leave you. She would have taken you with her, and indeed if you want to go you may. They're going to live in Italy and it's very beautiful so I'm told, and you would learn a great deal about the Romans.' He tried to make a joke of it, tried to imagine what life would be like without her. How would he bear it?

Connie considered this. 'Will you get married again and have other children? Do you want me out of the way?'

The relief was like a tidal wave over his heart. 'I won't get married again—'

'But you never know. Women go around marrying even old men like you.'

He acknowledged the truth of this. Then he said, 'I would much prefer that you should stay here with me and keep on at Miss Appleby's school, but I won't hold you back if you want to go with your mother and if later you wanted to go I wouldn't stop you.'

'But I don't want to go anywhere,' Connie said, beginning to cry. 'I don't want to leave you.'

'I don't want you to go either. I love you very much and I want you here with me.'

He took her into his arms and held her close while she cried and cried, and when it was over and he disentangled her hot little self from him he wished he had the sense to carry a handkerchief and he said, 'Do you want to stay here for the weekend with Miss Appleby and George and the others or would you like to come home to me?

'Will you be at the house, you won't be working?'

'I'll be with you.'

'I want to come home,' she said, and gave an enormous sniff.

He took Connie home, and it was different from how it had been. The house and garden were still neat, as Mrs Dexter's nephew was now doing the outside jobs and Mick had already gone to Mrs Dexter and Mrs Hobson and got them to come back so that when Connie did come home it would be a place worthy of her – a real home if not a particularly conventional one. There was the smell of polish and also of baking.

He could not quite rid himself of the idea that he would find Isabel in the sitting room with the reek of alcohol all around her, but when he got in there a fire had been lit against the closing afternoon and everything was as it should have been.

Mrs Dexter brought tea in and smiled at Connie. She asked her how she was getting on at school and Connie told her all about it, which took some time, and Mrs Dexter, who had children herself, although grown up, stood there as though she were riveted and took it in and asked all the right questions. Mick was so grateful that he wanted to kiss her.

He could not remember there having been such peace before. In the evening they sat by the fire with Ulysses and Connie read to them, though Ulysses did go to sleep in the middle of it. Upstairs the night loomed as it always had. He had not got used to being up there alone without Isabel. Perhaps he never would, but he would have to endure it. There was nothing he could do about the circumstances, he would just have to be grateful for his child and work very hard to pay off all the debts.

Emma had not imagined anything could be worse than not being able to see Mick Castle, but after his wife ran away it was impossible to go into the village without hearing the gossip. There were those who blamed him; there were rumours that he had beaten her and kept her short of money because the poor woman was never seen out of the house, chained to the kitchen sink by that man. No wonder she had turned to drink, anybody would.

Others said that she had always been flighty and that he should never have married her: he was too ordinary, too common for a lady like Isabel Hanlon. That would teach people who wanted to go up in the world. And now he had taken on a huge amount of debt and would probably lose everything and end up beggared.

Emma found that sometimes people stopped talking when she walked into places, but she kept on with her work and gradually she understood that they had stopped associating her with him in any way. She had found her place here, she was respected in her own right. It meant a good deal to her.

She saw Mick only when he came to bring Connie to school on Mondays and to collect her on Fridays, and in some kind of unacknowledged agreement he did not stay a second longer than he needed to. They were never alone; he did not even drink a cup of tea in the kitchen with the children around, and very often Mr and Mrs English. She did ask him the first couple of times merely from politeness, but he thanked her and left.

She thought now of what luxury it was when he had been able to sit there and talk; it was so little, yet she yearned even for that. She tried not to think about him in other ways. She continued going to chapel with Marjorie Blythe.

They were on first-name terms by now, and sometimes she and Marjorie went out together to visit other people and she was introduced to more folk who sent their children to school, though all were day pupils it did bring in money. If she had any more boarders she would have had to move from the building and she did not want to do that. The house was all she seemed to have left of Mick. It was a proper school now with more than a dozen pupils and new children coming every week.

Connie was happy. She did not seem to miss her mother. She liked spending the weekends with her father, and sometimes, if he was going somewhere interesting, he took her out of school for a day. If he was away on business, which he often was now, Connie was content to be at school.

Emma was getting to the stage where she needed another teacher, or somebody just to look after the children if she could not be there, but she had no one she could trust completely. Jack was not old enough and Mrs English was not well enough and Mr English had enough to do, so she coped alone.

In time, as she got to know people, she thought she would find another teacher; if not she must advertise in the local newspapers, but she was not comfortable with this. She didn't want anybody she didn't know well to be left in charge of her school. She was proud to think of it this way, and she had a new sign erected, and this time nobody disfigured it.

Laurence continued to walk daily to Nell's grave. Emma didn't always go with him, she had too much else to do and they had both got used to the routine. His grief was part of his life and he gained comfort from being there. In the dark afternoons she found herself at Nell's grave before the light faded because she had nobody to talk to any more.

She didn't want to tell Marjorie Blythe her closest secrets, she didn't feel that she should say anything, but she knew that if Nell had been there she could have told her what it was like not to see the man you loved and to wish for him every day. It was frustrating, she told Nell's headstone, because his wife was gone but he was not free, and no matter how long Isabel Castle lived in Italy with Henry Atkinson he never would be free.

Not that he seemed aware of any of this. He called in more and more briefly over the few weeks which followed, and then he stopped coming altogether; he would instruct

Jack to collect Connie from the academy because he was busy. Emma had no doubt that he was. His work was the only thing holding him together, she guessed – that and his child being happy.

Connie talked a lot about what she did with her father at weekends. He had time for his child, it seemed, but for no one else. Emma understood. In such a small town the fragile social position she had reached would not survive the slightest scandal.

He took Connie away to Harrogate, the watering town in Yorkshire, where they stayed at a fine hotel, and to Newcastle where she went to the museums and walked along the river. They had three days in Edinburgh, and Connie talked so much about it that Emma sensed a restlessness in George. The next time they went away Mick wrote a carefully worded note, asking if George could possibly go too because Carlisle was a fine old town and he might enjoy the change.

Emma was grateful. There was no way she could take George to such places by herself and she understood that change was good, but being left with her school and all its benefits, she fretted and then was impatient with herself. This was what she had wanted, she was free, she was doing the thing she loved best. Was nothing ever enough?

George came back, and his conversation for days was about Mr Castle. Emma escaped to Nell's grave and complained about her lot and then felt guilty. Nell had never had an easy life, it was much harder than hers, and now she was dead. Emma started to cry and she concluded that it was for both of them.

One evening when Emma was visiting Nell's grave, she heard the gate at the entrance. Usually she wouldn't have taken any notice, many people did as she and went there to talk to people they had loved and tried to keep them alive in this way, but she turned around. A woman was walking in her direction.

Emma didn't recognize her at first in the rapidly failing light, and then she did, and thought herself stupid. She began to feel very strange because the woman was Nell: the same height, the same build, with Nell's pale looks. Emma had never been convinced of ghosts but these feelings were altering quickly now; she didn't know whether what she had wanted had come true or if she was losing her mind.

The woman came all the way to her and by then Emma was shaking.

'You must be Miss Appleby,' the woman said, and it was Nell's tones exactly. 'I'm Margaret, Nell's sister.'

She looked intently beyond Emma and Emma stood aside so that she could see the grave.

'An old friend wrote to me and said our Nell had died.'

Emma didn't like to say anything. She couldn't get used to the idea that this was not Nell and she feasted her eyes upon the woman's familiar face. After what seemed like several lifetimes Margaret seemed to be able to drag her gaze away from the stone and she said, 'I've been gone from here more than fifteen years. I hated it, I hated how our Laurence was and the way that Nell would look after everything. I couldn't manage it and me mam dying like that and – Mrs Inman wrote after I heard summat about what had happened and I asked her.'

Emma couldn't help thinking that Mrs Inman would, it was just the kind of thing she would delight in doing. She was an interfering busybody.

'I wasn't going to come back here ever and then I thought about our Nell's bairns. I haven't got any, I never married.'

'You've never seen the children then.'

'Nay, I know nowt about them.'

She didn't look rich, Emma thought, but neither did she look poor. She looked respectable, and Emma had the impression that she did not usually speak broad Durham, she was in a way assuring herself that she was home.

'Come back with me,' she said, 'and if you like you can stay.'

Margaret looked suspiciously at her. 'I don't know whether I want to stay. I just wanted to come and see our Nell's grave. We were close when we were bairns, and then she was the favourite and her and our Laurence got on and him and me never did so I packed my bags and went. Sometimes I think about this place and I think about my childhood and my family and I just wanted to come back.'

'Would you like to come and see the children?'

Emma waited. Margaret went back to watching the grave and Emma walked around the graveyard. It was quite dark now, but she was no longer afraid. Eventually Margaret came to her and they walked slowly back to the academy. Emma had no idea how she would tell the children about their aunt and decided there was no way round it so she ushered her guest into the kitchen where the two girls were sitting at the big table and introduced them.

Jack was there with them and looked as if he were fretting because he had said he would go to the Black Diamond since Mr Higgins was on his own, Mr Castle being away with George and Connie.

They sat down and had something to eat and then it was time for the girls to go to bed. She came back downstairs and Margaret was by the sitting-room fire, Hector stretched out on the rug before her.

'They're grand bairns,' she said as Emma came in.

'They miss her very much, but they can stay with me. Laurence will be in later, but there again he has a home here, so whatever you are doing or want to do with your life you don't have to get involved.'

They sat until Laurence came in. He didn't know her at first and then he thought she was Nell when he saw her by the lamplight, and then he realized she wasn't. There were several things about her which gave it away. She was older for one thing, she had been the first child, her hair was almost white and she was pale, perhaps she had lived in a city where the sunshine did not fall readily on the streets.

Laurence sat gazing at her and Margaret altered herself,

maybe deliberately, Emma thought, and became the person she really was. She held herself differently, she began to speak in a soft southern voice about what she had done and where she had been. She had travelled through Europe as a governess; she had been luckier than most women, she said, because of the family who took her on: the husband was a diplomat and there were three children.

She had been with them for twelve years. She had lived in Greece and in the Far East, she was good at languages, she said, and Emma could not help thinking that this woman, with all her knowledge and experience, would be a perfect teacher for the school. Emma waited, as she did not want to discompose her guest, who was now showing herself as she really was: interesting and learned.

25

Mick Castle was taking George and Connie to Carlisle.

'I don't ever want to go much further than that,' Connie announced when they were waiting for her dad to come for them.

George said nothing. He hadn't thought much about it before. He looked away toward the dale. He ignored the fact that she was looking at him. He knew the anxious way she did so since her mother had gone away. She seemed to want to grab people to her, not actually, but it seemed to him that when she went to see her dad for a day or two she almost fell in the front door of the academy, desperate to get back to his Aunt Emma.

It had surprised him that he felt the same and when he and Mr Castle were together he would move closer, hoping that in a way somebody might think that Mr Castle was his dad. He needed a dad and Mr Castle was not so old that he couldn't have been. He was much younger, George realized now, than his and Emma's father had been. That was comforting.

They stood in Carlisle cathedral. Connie was always restless and wanted to see everything immediately but

George stood there silently with Mick and hoped that passers-by saw them as family and thought, 'What a nice lad'. He was proud to be there with Mick.

Aunt Emma said that he must always call 'Mick' 'Mr Castle' but in George's mind Mick was closer to him than that.

Mick didn't go after Connie now, had learned not to, George thought, sure that she would come back or that they would catch up with her. George liked Mick's pace but he also liked that Mick took them to a lovely hotel right in the middle of the town where George was given a room of his own. He had never thought such a thing might happen.

Mick stood tall and in perfect command of himself. They stood there for so long that in the end Mick put a hand on his shoulder and smiled into his eyes and said, 'Shall we go back and have tea?'

George nodded, hoping he didn't look as enthusiastic as he felt.

'And dinner later.'

'Can we do other things?' George couldn't help the words and when they were out and Mick's gaze searched his face George pretended he hadn't said anything and looked away but Mick prompted him.

'Like what?'

'Nothing.'

'Howay man, George. Do you want supper too?'

George shook his head and smiled at the attempted humour.

'Nothing, it's just that . . .' and he blurted out what he had not known he was going to say but what he realized had been on his mind as a request for some time.

'I couldn't maybe come to work with you some time, could I?'

Mick looked surprised.

'It isn't all like the Black Diamond,' he said.

'I didn't mean like that. I want to see what you do.'

Mick looked even more surprised and then the look became pleased and the smile lit his gaze.

'In the spring, when the weather gets better, you could come round the hotels with me, but you know your education is the most important thing.'

'Aunt Emma says that education is not what happens inside the classroom, everything is part of it.'

'Aunt Emma has a habit of being right,' Mick said, and then, as though he was rather pleased at the idea, 'Are you sure you want to, George?'

'I think I'd like to start helping you, 'George said.

'You could,' Mick said and they went back to the hotel.

Through the sunshine in the cathedral the stained-glass windows showed blue, red and yellow upon the floor. Mick liked being there with the children. They stayed in a good hotel. Connie was getting used to these, but George had never stayed in such a place so Mick had the joy of watching him dress neatly to have dinner in the dining room and order what he liked from the menu; though few children stayed up to have dinner Mick

367

insisted, and the staff would not deny him since he spent money.

He showed them the castle and told them about the history of the place, making it sound exciting and bloody, it having been a border stronghold through many conflicts. George discomposed him slightly by saying that Mr English had told them all about this, but Mick was able to tell them more and could not help being quite proud of this.

He told them about the Lake District and promised that when they had more time they could climb the mountains and walk around the lakes and over the high fells where the Herdwick sheep, coffee-and-cream-coloured, grazed, and see the wild ponies. He wished he had had longer: he wanted to take them to all kinds of other places and he wondered if there would come a time when he could get away for a week.

He was sorry to have to take them back to the academy. He had soon grown to hate the circumstances of his life. He was obliged to see Emma while he could not even justify a private conversation with her. It was easier for him not to meet her eyes, not to hold conversation, and he thought she felt the same because she dismissed him with relief each time he went from her.

He comforted himself that the children had enjoyed their weekend and he had liked being with them. If that were to be the future then there were worse things. He found his work troublesome as he had far too much to do. Every time he left his office he felt guilty.

He didn't like being in the house alone. For him it was

a place where he could remember being happy. All that was gone now. It was as though a kind of cold perfection had taken its place; everything was cleaner than it had ever been. Mrs Hobson left food for him, which very often he did not eat; he usually ate at the small hotels which he had bought. It was a good way of checking their efficiency.

He often stayed in Durham. Remembering how he had hated city life so much when he was young he now took pleasure in the places he had been to with his parents. He could not believe how much he missed them now that he had nobody but a child to himself.

He took some pleasure from working in front of the fire in whatever room was available to him, and in Durham there was always the river in the background. He could not regret Emma, but he did regret that theirs was an impossible love and he tried to accept that it was likely he would never be able to spend any time with her.

It was the biggest loss of all, to have her so near and not be able to touch her. He hated going to the academy now: it was a particularly cruel form of torture. Neither did he think about Isabel because he had fallen in love with her at a dance in Durham and in his mind it was always now a tawdry thing. He felt like a fool.

His work became so important that he wished he did not have to go back to the country so often, and he determined to find somebody to take charge of the pubs there. At weekends he would take Connie and sometimes George into the city, and the sounds of it, the river and the street cries and the cathedral bells, were easier to bear than the low noise of the wind through the bare gorse and scrub which had always been home.

Christmas was somehow more difficult than ever. He tried to bribe Connie with ideas about going away, but she looked appalled and said that she wanted to be here with George and her friends and the two Miss Applebys and Uncle Laurence who did party tricks (she had heard), and that Jack and his mother had also been asked to the academy for Christmas, and Mr and Mrs English.

'What on earth would you want to leave your friends for at Christmas?' she said.

He was obliged therefore to face Emma on Christmas Day. He had been dreading it. He made it easier for himself by buying presents, something he had never done before. He had not had enough money to buy special things when he was first married and since Isabel would never go to see people at Christmas he had watched other people making merry, dressing up for parties and wishing one another all the best.

On Christmas morning he saw his child open her presents and for the first time fall in love with a dress. It was the same blue as her eyes and had a big white sash, but he had made sure to buy her many books, about the Romans in Britain (which she insisted on taking to show Mr English), novels which he thought she might enjoy and travel books about Italy so that she could imagine where her mother was.

She wore the new dress and was much admired by

everyone at the schoolhouse, so she even did a twirl and then she distributed the gifts which she and her father had bought between them: a lovely red sledge for George, which she insisted they would both fit onto; dolls dressed in velvet for the two girls; and a thick shawl for Mrs English because she felt the draughts around her shoulders. Mick had bought Mr English a bottle of single malt whisky.

Mick had not thought to make a friend of the schoolmaster, but he found that Mr English was rather like his father, gentle and learned. He bought chocolates for Emma, handmade from the city. They had made up a food hamper for Jack and his mother. Ulysses and Hector had a special dinner and romped in the garden.

That morning a lot of people came to the schoolhouse. He was delighted to see Sam and Marjorie, Mr and Mrs Ogilvie, drinking ginger cordial, friends Emma had made from the Methodist church and several of the business people, including Mr and Mrs Barron and other shopkeepers who had been kind to her. Mick had never thought to see the place so full of people eating, drinking and making lots of noise.

In the afternoon they played games. It snowed a little and the children went outside and threw snowballs at one another, and before it got dark a snowman appeared with coal eyes, a carrot nose and a red scarf which Emma had hunted everywhere for.

In the quiet of the evening the snow stopped and the stars came out, and his child held his hand and told him that it had been the best Christmas ever.

New Year was a series of drunken revellers causing problems both in the city and in the country, and after it he felt nothing but relief that it was over.

The Three Tuns had become his retreat during the week. Tired of Mrs Dexter's polishing and Mrs Hobson's dreadful food he kept a room there for himself and enjoyed being waited upon and even having various business meetings in what had been Henry Atkinson's office.

It was here on a cold February Friday, when he had decided that trying to get back to the country for the weekend was a waste of time, the ice and snow were bitter even here in Durham, that he had a visitor.

It was early afternoon and almost dark, the fire blazed bravely in the grate and the woman he had taken on to deal with the intricacies of his deskwork, Miss Calland, came in and told him in her flat, expressionless voice that Mr Atkinson was there.

He looked up from his papers in surprise. The last thing he wanted was to see this man. Henry Atkinson would no doubt tell him that he had been back to London for Christmas, that he and Isabel had made a home in some wonderful place in Italy, perhaps even that she was here in Durham, at the County, just across the street.

It made his heart beat hard and uncomfortably; he did not want to be reminded of the past and of the bearing it seemed to have on the future. He just wanted to be left alone with the enormous amount of work and the knowledge that he had done his best for his child.

Most of all there was a huge hole and in it a gaping mouth of fear, all fangs and red blood, which told him that Atkinson had come back for his child, that they were going to take her away from him and that no law in the land would be on his side when she was not biologically his child, when her mother and real father could make a home for her in another land so that he might never see her again. It was the one thing that he knew he could not bear.

To lose Connie now after what had happened made him want to run away, hide in a cupboard, not face this man who had from the beginning thought nothing of him; this man had taken almost everything, and here, it seemed to Mick now, he was coming to take the last thing of all, the most important.

He listened to Henry Atkinson's footsteps on the stairs and couldn't breathe. He didn't know whether to get up or whether to sit where he was. The fire had gone down and the room was cool. Outside people walked through the icy day and went about their business. He wished he was one of them and not about to meet once again the man who had seemed to steal away from him any happiness.

Mick didn't look up as the door opened. He didn't want to meet the man's eyes. It was cowardly he knew, but he was shaking, cold, despairing. All Mick said was, 'Come in,' and when Henry, did so, Mick was surprised and horrified by what he saw.

Henry Atkinson seemed to have become an old man. He had not looked that way a few months earlier, but his face was now grave and grey and his hair almost gone. He was as neatly dressed as ever in sombre clothes, but his body was shrunken as though it had caved in under impossible pressure. His clothes were much too big, his skinny white wrists protruded from his sleeves, his eyes were bloodshot and his cheeks yellow. The smile was something he deliberately held on his face as though he had grown used to putting it there.

He gazed around him. Mick followed his look. The office was neat. It surprised him too. Not a paper was out of place, and through the mirror on the other side of the room he could see himself: expensively dressed, clean-shaven, glossy hair, bright eyes (if he had been a dog, he thought, he would have been said to have been in peak condition). Hector would have been proud of him. He thought of Hector and Ulysses with some dismay. He moved around so much that Ulysses had gone to live with Emma too. It seemed cruel and incongruous that he could not do the same.

Henry Atkinson was stooped, skinny, his face had gone into lines so deep that one sagged over another. Mick got up to shake his hand instinctively, but Henry Atkinson waved him away with a cane Mick had not noticed until then.

'How is the business?' Henry asked as they sat down.

It gave Mick some satisfaction to be able to say, 'Thriving.' He had been to see the bank manager that very morning and all was well. He was on his way to being successful. It made him want to laugh. Was that business? Was how successful you were determined by your misery? If so, then no wonder the hotels and pubs were making money.

'I've never seen this office so tidy.'

Mick could have told him that he had one of the tidiest existences in the world. Everything was neat, slotted into place, he ran things to the minute, even to the second sometimes. It was driving him mad.

Henry sat back as though tired to his very bones, and then he looked Mick in the face for the first time.

'I thought you were in Italy,' Mick said.

Henry shook his head. 'Isabel took ill as soon as she left here. I thought we would get away, I thought we would have what we wanted. I thought she wouldn't drink when she was with me. One of my children was taken ill and I went to London. That was a mistake. Isabel could not bear my attention to be away from her even for a few hours.

'We were staying at a hotel there, just for a day or two, but as soon as I was gone she started to drink and by the time I got back she had forgotten how to stop. I saw then what you had gone through. She thought and I thought that I was some talisman, but it wasn't true.

'She told me that she loved me, but not nearly as much as she loved the taste of brandy. I found it impossible to stop her. I did think that if we had married when we had met this would not have happened, but I cannot be sure of it now. I did everything I could, I got doctors to see her, I tried taking it from her, exactly as you tried to do. She blamed you for it and that was not true either. I can see how hard you fought for her and I'm sorry.

'Within days she had gone to nothing. By the time that she died she didn't want to live any more, she hated herself so much. Why have they no cure for such a thing? People should not have to live and die like that. I held her in my arms, but she didn't want me, she didn't want anybody. I hadn't known how much she despised the very self that she was and how she did not really believe that she was worthy of love, even of life, that she thought she did not deserve to be here.'

His voice broke. He was a man heavy with grieving. He was alone in the world with his loss, left in the most solitary place of all with nothing to save him.

Mick was glad he was sitting down and that they were in the privacy of his office. He couldn't have done with anybody seeing his countenance at that time and the awful thing was that he and Henry thought exactly the same. Why was it that with so much perfection in the world people were fatally flawed? Even a pine cone was perfect in its symmetry, but people were condemned to miseries which the Church would say were of their own making.

He didn't think this was of Isabel's making. She had been disappointed. It seemed such a small word, but disappointment had started it. It was as though she had been born into the wrong place at the wrong time and had not been able to get out. This had led to boredom and boredom had led to depression and depression had led to despair. In a way, he thought, Isabel had destroyed herself because she could not bear her life.

Had it been that the dream of her time with Henry Atkinson had been spoiled because it was not perfect and she had realized? Perhaps, he thought, we are not meant to have those things we dream of, they are best left in the air, longed for but not gained.

Mick did not go to Emma to tell her that his wife had died. At first she wished he had, and then not. She had the news from a whey-faced Jack who had been to the Black Diamond when Mick finally arrived home, two days later than he had planned. She had been anxious and then told herself it was just that he was working so hard.

Jack had not even greeted the children, he had come straight through into her study and without asking. For the first time he had closed the door. She had not realized that Jack understood the relationship between herself and Mick Castle, but she saw then that he did.

The lad said, 'I wish I didn't have to tell you this, Miss, but Mrs Castle – the one that ran off – she's dead. That Mr Atkinson, he came special to Durham to tell Mr Castle. She died of drink and now it's all over the village, and Mr Castle he has a lot to do and he said to me would you keep Connie over the weekend and then he would come to the academy and tell her about her mam.'

Emma didn't remember what she said, just that she felt faint, possibly for the first time in her life, and had to sit down: Jack had to steady her and he went off to get Margaret, who made her a cup of tea and sat by the fire with her and said nothing though she looked hard. Emma couldn't tell her about it; it was not her story to tell. She felt guilt, she felt dismay, she felt sorry for Isabel Castle and for the life that was so wasted, just like Nell's life. Were women never to have a decent place on this earth?

Margaret was a discerning woman. She took the children and left Emma to drink her tea; it was the only thing she could do. Emma kept her tears for when she was alone that night and there she cried long and hard into her pillow. The final sting was that Isabel was dead and she felt responsible. She knew it was nonsense, that she had not ruined Mick's marriage. She remembered first meeting him: he had looked like a scarecrow, the Black Diamond had been such a mess and Connie had been lost amidst the wreckage of her parents' marriage.

Mick came to the academy. It took all Emma's fortitude to greet him formally in front of other people and then she gave him the study to tell Connie about her mother.

Emma made sure she was not within earshot. They were in there for a long time and in the end she walked the dogs around the garden in a freezing wind and then suddenly the golden-haired child burst from the door, screaming her name. She hurtled through the bitter day and flung herself into Emma's arms, and Emma had never been as glad to comfort a child since she had first found George.

After that Mick no longer came to the academy. It was just as well, Emma's sensible voice told her. She became glad of the day-to-day things: of the work which she had taken on, of her friends and family. Laurence had taken to Margaret as if she were Nell, and was happy to leave her and go to the Black Diamond on cold winter afternoons and drink by the fire and come back and find her there waiting for him.

It was the longest winter of Emma's life. The snow and the ice meant that on many days they could not go far. She would read by the fire if she had any leisure time and she was glad of Margaret's company. She did not think she could have stood it without her sister's help.

One bitterly cold day she sat down at her desk in the study and composed what she knew would be her final letter to Laurence and Verity. Through her new pupils paying in advance for their education she now had the money which she hoped was sufficient to pay for the pearls. She no longer wanted to say bitter things to her brother. In her honest moments she knew that her half-brother meant more to her than her true brother had ever meant. He had worked his way into her heart with his neediness, but also in the way that he was good with the children. He played games and listened to them reading, and though Emma knew that sometimes he did not fully understand what they were doing or saying he could always join in because he himself was in some way still a child and she loved him for it.

So the negative feelings had gone and she could tell Laurence and Verity that she was happy here as she had not been in her earlier life, that she had found family and friends and that her school was beginning to do well.

During March the snow was worse than ever, making everyday life difficult, and she longed for the spring. It seemed forever before the thaw arrived – it was almost Easter by then and she had seen nothing of Mick.

When Connie went home for the weekends Jack took her and she did not talk of what she did at home, nor say that she missed her father. It seemed to Emma that every time Connie came back to her there was nothing but relief and gladness in her eyes, that at the academy she had found the home that she had lacked, and Emma could not help being glad of that and of thinking that it was something she had managed to achieve.

In the spring finally Emma had a good reason to ask Mick Castle whether he would call. She sent a note to him and he replied saying that he could not get away for several days but he would call the following Tuesday.

It should not have mattered, she told herself, but every day until Tuesday was a fortnight. On the day chosen she watched for at least an hour before he was due and finally, half an hour late, when she was beside herself with tension, she watched him stride in at the gate.

He was like somebody from another world, not the man she had fallen in love with. He moved briskly, cleanly somehow, as though he could not wait to get on to the next thing, whatever it might be.

She went into the study. You could not call it hiding, she told herself. Margaret was there to receive him and she heard their voices at the door and then the scuffle of feet and Margaret brought him into the little study and went straight back out again and closed the door.

Neither of them said anything, and neither looked at

the other. Emma wasn't even sure they had greeted each another as the study seemed completely silent, but then Mick said impatiently, 'Is there something wrong?'

'Not exactly.'

He waited until she sat down before he did so. She glanced at him, sitting on the edge of his chair as though he couldn't rest.

'It's about Connie,' she said.

Now they looked at one another. She had his attention. He frowned.

'I thought she was happy and doing well.'

'She needs to move on.'

There was a moment before he sighed and then he relaxed and let his gaze roam the ceiling in frustration.

'She needs to go away to school,' Emma said. 'She is extraordinarily clever and we have taught her all we can. She needs the best possible education so that she can go to university—'

'How likely is that?'

'Things are changing,' Emma said. 'Universities allow women to attend lectures, not to take degrees yet, but perhaps they will soon, and I believe Connie has a great future. Don't deny her it because she's a girl.'

That made him smile. 'As if I would dare, sitting here,' he said. 'She's very young to go away.'

'She's beginning to get bored, and you know what happens then. She needs to be with people of her own age and ability, so that she isn't the only bright spark in the class. She could do so much. It would be wrong not to send her. Mr English has some ideas about this. I thought that perhaps he could come to the house and you could talk about it when you are free.'

'I can't think of anything I'd rather do,' he said bitterly. 'Do tell him to come at his convenience.'

At that moment the door burst open and Hector bounded in, followed almost immediately by Ulysses, and having not seen their idol in weeks they both threw themselves at him so that Mick was immediately covered in black Labrador. Instead of getting up and being more bitter, as Emma thought he would, he tried to hug both of them together and she heard an indistinct voice from black fur, saying, 'My boys, my boys.'

The door being open Connie and George also came in, Connie demanding, 'Where on earth have you been? You never come and see us,' and George saying, 'You promised we could go to Edinburgh as soon as the weather got better and the weather's been better for three weeks and you haven't said anything.'

'I'm busy,' Mick protested, trying to disengage himself from the dogs.

'You always say that,' Connie said.

'And the weather is awful.'

'Nothing but excuses,' Connie said. Emma could hear her voice in the child's, that was one of her expressions.

Connie had sometimes been very detached since her mother had died – one of the reasons why Emma thought she should go away to school. She wasn't altogether convinced that the child was happy.

George went back out with the dogs, but Connie remained, looking from one to another and finally declaring, 'I am not going anywhere.' She looked hard at Emma. 'I heard you talking to Miss Margaret last night and I am not leaving my dad. I don't care if I never learn another thing. My mother is dead and he has that awful Mrs Hobson making him eat fish in parsley sauce all the time which is why he stays in Durham.'

'Connie—' he said.

She fixed her burning gaze on him, her eyes glazed with tears and her mouth wobbling dangerously. 'You don't understand. I want you to be happy and if I go away is that going to make you happy?'

She would make a fine lawyer, Emma thought, if it were possible, and it would be.

'It's your happiness that matters to me,' he said, and that wouldn't get him anywhere either, Emma thought.

'And you think I'm going to be happy in some awful place like Jane Eyre went to?'

'It isn't like that.'

'I don't think it would be much better. Cold rooms and having to wear the same knickers for days on end. Miss Margaret has been to such places and she told me.'

'Connie!' Emma reproved her lightly.

'Well. What is the point in having children if you're going to send them away from you? I won't go, I won't ever go. It's totally ridiculous.'

Another of her own sayings, Emma thought. Connie was acknowledging in the silence which followed, Emma knew, that she had scored points here.

Connie said what was next on her mind. 'Miss Margaret has made mince and dumplings for dinner with carrots, so you don't have to go home to tepid fish,' and she left the room.

'Do by all means stay,' Emma's manners prompted her.

'I have to get back to work.'

They got up and went into the kitchen. Everybody was sitting around the big table and steam was rising and two seats were vacant.

'Miss Appleby sits at the top, but you can come and sit by me,' Connie told him.

So he did. He didn't speak all the way through the meal. It might have been because it was better than what he was used to, but Emma didn't think so. She thought that most of the time he was not around at all, he had retreated to the city and hotel food.

Emma had been torturing herself recently that he wined and dined other women at tables which looked out over the river and that one of these days, probably in the summer – men never lingered long over their dead wives – he would turn up there with a woman young enough to be his daughter, and Connie would fall in love with her too and transfer her love that up to now had been Emma's to somebody beautiful, somebody to take Isabel's place, and all she would be left with would be the fast-fading memory of a single night.

In her polite moods she wished him well, but all the time her heart did horrible somersaults in her chest. She remembered John Elstree and his family, watching them and their happiness. She didn't know whether she could manage again, but she didn't think she had any choice. This adventure had taken all the courage and spirit she had. She did not want to have to go away and start afresh.

After the midday meal it began to snow. Emma had promised the children and the dogs a walk in the afternoon, and as Mick made his excuses and tried to leave the dogs paraded round, turning into Dalmatians as the white hit the black. They danced in small circles in their joy and leaped up at Mick because they thought he was going to go with them. This was not going to happen, as he was wearing a good suit and city shoes.

Connie, never a child to be quiet when she could say something, tried to insist.

'I will come back tomorrow, suitably attired,' he said.

'You always say that,' she protested, and went back into the house in a huff. George followed her. The dogs were not so easily put off and ran about the garden, making long tracks in the snow.

'It's getting very bad,' Emma said, and it was true: she could hardly see through the snow any longer. 'You can't walk back to the house in this.'

She couldn't even offer him better footwear as Laurence had none and Jack came and went to his mother's house. The snow became a blizzard within minutes. They went back inside.

Very soon it was a white-out, what in the north is known as a hap-up, and there was nothing to do but stay inside and watch from the windows for a while. The snow went on and on even into the darkness. They had tea and sat over the fire. Laurence did not come back and they concluded that he was stuck at the Black Diamond for the night. It was no problem, Mick could have Laurence's room, Emma assured him, they could put clean sheets on the bed. In fact, the last thing she wanted was to have him stay there. She would never sleep, knowing he was in the house and not with her, a stupid and unbearable situation.

In the late evening, when the children had gone to bed and Margaret had retreated upstairs and everyone was tired, Mick stood by the window with Emma. The snow had finally stopped and a moon had risen, full and silver, above the black sky. And there were stars.

'So,' he said, and she thought he was going to announce he was going to bed. He paused and then he went on, 'I want to take Connie and George to Edinburgh soon, when the weather clears. I wondered if you—' and then he stopped, said, 'I wondered whether you—' and then stopped again. 'I wondered whether you might like to come with us.'

'Oh,' was all Emma could think to say.

'I'm sure your sister and Jack would look after the other children if we went away for three or four days. I'm gradually finding people to see to the business, though it takes a lot of doing, but I shouldn't be there all the time.'

Emma mumbled agreement at this, only glad he wasn't looking at her burning face.

'I have friends in the hotel business now,' he said in the same level tone. 'You could have a room to yourself. It isn't expensive.'

Emma said nothing at this; she couldn't think of a single thing.

'Do you think you might?' he ventured, and then looked at her.

'Perhaps.'

'What does perhaps mean?'

Emma got up, she couldn't think.

'Wouldn't people talk, even if it's – like that?'

'Do you want to or not?'

'Of course I do.'

'Do you?' His voice had taken on an insistent note.

Emma wanted to run out of the room, but she felt as if he were barring the door, even though he hadn't moved.

'Do you really want to?'

She glared at him. He was smiling just a little.

'Do you really want to, Emma?'

She felt irritated, frustrated, angry.

'Oh stop it,' she said. 'You know very well how I feel about you and this isn't fair.'

'I don't know anything of the kind. Tell me.'

'I will not. It's not respectable. Your wife has just died and—'

'And?'

Emma burst into tears. She hadn't cried in so long that now it had started she seemed to have no way of doing anything about it. She tried to stop and it was awful, all soggy and snotty and disgusting, and the breathy sobs fell over one another and she could no longer contain them. He got up as though to help and she attempted to get away, but he got hold of her.

'I want you to marry me. Will you consider that?'

Emma shook her head vehemently. 'Certainly not,' she said, and that was when the sobs eased and her whole body shuddered with relief. She found a handkerchief inside the cuff of her sleeve and blew her nose.

She went to open the door as though somehow she could get out of the situation, and the dogs woke up immediately – perhaps they thought she might let them go outside again. They skidded across the hall, dancing about in intricate dog fashion for the joy of being alive.

'Your dogs are the very bane of my life,' Emma said.

He went through and opened the outside door once again and they leapt outside. Since the snow was now very deep they pushed their faces into it as though they might make tunnels. Round and round they tore, weaving back and forth through the tracks they had made earlier which were already beginning to disappear.

'It isn't fair, you know,' Mick said. 'You have my house, my child and my dogs. You have to have me too. Please, Emma.'

'Oh, very well then,' Emma said, and they stood there together watching the two black Labradors playing in the garden in the snow on a winter's night.

If you enjoyed *Miss Appleby's Academy*,
please try Elizabeth's other novels in ebook:

THE SINGING WINDS

FAR FROM FATHER'S HOUSE

UNDER A CLOUD-SOFT SKY

THE ROAD TO BERRY EDGE

SNOW ANGELS

SHELTER FROM THE STORM